Ethan poked his head around the corner of the alley; his gaze instantly darted to the diner across the street again. Light pooled from the streetlights, it spilled across the road and sidewalk, illuminating the cars parked along the road. Light from the diner blazed out of its big, plate glass windows. The woman that had captured his attention was sitting in one of the booths, her blond head bent over the table as she read through something. She looked oddly familiar. Biting on his lower lip, his brows knit together as he studied her more carefully. He knew he'd seen her somewhere before, that he knew her somehow, he just couldn't remember where or how.

He pulled his head back and leaned against the cool stone wall. He closed his eyes, searching his memory for any hint of who she might be. He had been doing the same thing for the last five minutes, and it was proving to be a useless endeavor.

"What are you doing?"

He jumped in surprise, his eyes flew open as Mike and Jack stepped out of the shadows of the ally. "Don't do that!" he snapped.

They grinned as they exchanged amused glances. They knew he hated it when they cloaked their presence from him and popped out of nowhere to try and scare him. It often worked. The thing that aggravated him the most was that he couldn't do it to them; that he couldn't control his powers as well as they could, and they knew it. "So, what are you doing?" Mike asked again, his blond eyebrows drawn questioningly together.

Ethan scowled at them as he glanced around the corner again. "I was looking at that woman in the diner."

Their eyes widened as they stared at him in shock. "Ah hell," Jack finally groaned. "Don't tell us you're going to turn into your mother and father!"

"Hardly!" Ethan snorted, the thought alone made his stomach turn. "She looks familiar, but I can't place who she is."

Mike and Jack exchanged a glance before Mike poked his head out of the alley to look. "Where?" Ethan leaned around him and pointed to the small, pudgy woman in the diner window. Mike frowned thoughtfully, then his eyes widened in surprise, and his mouth dropped. "It's Kathleen!"

"What?" Jack demanded, shoving his way past them. "Wow! It is! Crap is that what we'd look like now?"

"She seems to have aged pretty well," Mike said thoughtfully. "She's got to be what, forty seven?"

"How old are you dumb ass?" Jack retorted sarcastically.

Mike scowled at him before turning his attention back to the diner. "Forty seven," he muttered.

Jack smiled triumphantly at him before turning his attention back to the diner. "There you go. Well, I guess she doesn't look that bad. I'm just glad we don't look like that. Wrinkles," he said with a shudder.

"Shut up Jack. Ethan, go over there and talk to her," Mike commanded.

"What?" Ethan demanded as he rounded on him in surprise.

Mike nodded toward the diner; his short blond hair was tussled as it fell around his face. "Go over there."

Ethan stared at him incredulously. "*You* go over there," he retorted.

Mike and Jack looked at him like he was an idiot. "We knew Kathleen in college, if she saw the way we look now, she'd probably have a heart attack," Jack explained slowly, as if Ethan were dumb.

Ethan was jolted as he suddenly remembered exactly who she was. Kathleen had been his mother's best friend in college, but he hadn't seen her in over fifteen years. He glanced back at the diner in disbelief. "What am *I* going to say to her?"

"Just go over there and see how she's doing. I'm sure your mom would like to know. Now, go on," Mike encouraged.

Ethan scowled at him. "I'm a little too old for you to be ordering around."

"You're not that big yet, now go."

He would have stayed and argued with them, but he knew that it was pointless. They always won, and besides he was more than a little curious to see how she was doing. He left the alley and jogged across the rain washed street to the diner. The bell above the door rang as he entered and the smell of human food instantly assaulted him. Wrinkling his nose at the smell, he glanced down the line of booths to the middle-aged blond sitting in one of them. Her short blond hair had been pulled into a ponytail, and strands of it had fallen free to curl around her small, heart shaped face.

For a moment he was unable to move as he stared at her. She was not the woman that he remembered. This woman had lines around her mouth and eyes, her forehead was creased, and her skin had begun to sag around her neck and chin. There were strands of gray streaked throughout her hair. This is what his mother should look like, he realized with a start. The thought was incredibly sad, and more than a little frightening. For the first time he truly began to realize his immortality.

"Can I help you?"

Ethan blinked in surprise as he was pulled out of his reverie. A pretty waitress stood before him, an admiring gleam in her dark brown eyes as she openly surveyed him. He returned her smile without thinking. She moved a little closer, the menus in her hand brushed against his chest. "Would you like to sit?" she asked softly.

"Oh, ah no," he replied, casting a glance at Kathleen as he recalled why he was here. "I just came to see someone."

Her mouth pouted prettily as she took a step back. Ethan brushed past her, instantly forgetting her existence as he made his way toward Kathleen. He hadn't seen her since he was ten years old, he highly doubted that she would remember him, but he might as well try and talk to her. Besides, Mike and Jack would be pissed if he went back with nothing, and he didn't feel like dealing with the two of them.

"Hi, Kathleen right?"

She looked up from the newspaper she had been engrossed in. Her large blue eyes blinked in surprise as her mouth gaped open. "Liam?" she gasped.

Ethan smiled as he slid into the booth across from her. "No, Liam's my father. I'm Ethan."

Her eyes widened even more as a bright smile spread over her pretty face. "I'm sorry, it's just... you look just like your father!"

Ethan slid an arm over the back of the booth. "So I've been told."

Kathleen's wide eyes rapidly scanned his face and posture as she shook her head in disbelief. "I can see some of your mother in you though. How is she?" she asked eagerly, leaning across the table as her blue eyes twinkled eagerly.

Although she had gained some weight, and her face was more lined, she was much like the Kathleen that he recalled. She was bright and energetic, with an easy smile, and an amazing amount of warmth pouring from her. For a moment he felt a stab of pain for his parents, and their friends. They had been forced to let Kathleen go, forced to push her out of their lives in order to protect Kathleen, and themselves. He knew how much it had hurt his mother, and from the haunted look in Kathleen's eyes, he could tell that it had hurt her too.

"She's doing well."

"Are they still living in Oregon?"

Ethan nodded. "Yes."

"Does she have the big family that she always wanted?" she asked eagerly.

Ethan snorted as he grinned brightly. *Big* was not the way that he would describe the mob that was his family. "Yeah, there are ten of us."

Kathleen's eyes widened in surprise, she chuckled softly. "Your father must be going insane with that many kids."

"Nah, he likes it. Mike and David swear that they're going to keep going until they have a thousand kids. Fortunately, they've decided to take a break for awhile." He bit on his bottom lip, stopping himself before he told her that they planned to have more later on. He wasn't at all accustomed to speaking with humans, and he knew that his comment would have only confused her.

"Honey, that's not a break, its menopause. Trust me I know."

Ethan's eyes widened as he chuckled softly. He'd forgotten how blunt, and open, Kathleen was. "I guess so."

"Mike and David are still around?" she asked in surprise.

He nodded as he thought of the giant pain in the asses hiding in the alley across the street. "Yeah, so are Jack and Doug."

"I can't believe it. I don't know how I lost touch with everyone, but I guess as the years go by..." she broke off as she shrugged and glanced down at the paper before her. "Ah well, such is life. So how about yourself? What have you been up to?"

Ethan chewed thoughtfully on his bottom lip. How was he supposed to tell this woman that he hadn't been doing anything but living with Mike, Jack, Doug, and David in the house that they had built behind his parents home? He didn't have to be up to anything. He didn't have to do anything but lounge around, enjoy his life, and help keep his unruly brood of brothers and sisters under control. He could do other things, he simply didn't want to.

"Ah, not much," he hedged.

She grinned as she pointed at him. "That's your mother."

"Huh?" he asked in surprise, his eyebrows drawing together in confusion.

"She always used to bite her lip when she felt uncomfortable, or nervous, or when she was deep in thought," she explained with a soft smile, her eyes wistful and distant.

"Yeah, she does."

Kathleen sighed and her eyes snapped back to his. "Well, you have to be up to something. College?"

"I graduated," he lied. He hadn't felt like being bothered to go away to school. His father, mother, and his friends had told him that he would enjoy the experience, even if he didn't need the education, but he hadn't wanted to go. "I do odd jobs here and there." This was at least true.

Kathleen nodded and took a sip of her water. "I'm sure you'll find your own way someday."

"Yeah."

Ethan glanced out the window. Mike and Jack were still hidden within the shadows of the alleyway, but he could see them clearly in the darkness. "What about you?" he asked, returning his attention to her. "The last I knew you were going to France, to ah, take pictures," he fumbled as he struggled to recall the details.

Kathleen smiled softly as she leaned back in the booth. "That was my ex-husband, he was the photographer. My daughter's and I went with him."

Ethan barely remembered her daughters, and he couldn't recall their names. He knew that one was two years younger than he was, and had been closer to his sister,

Isabelle. The other had been very young the last time he'd seen her. "I'm actually between jobs right now."

Her voice grew distant and thoughtful as her forehead furrowed with worry. Ethan realized that the paper she was reading was opened to the classified section. He frowned thoughtfully as he wondered what it must be like to have to work, or to worry about how to pay bills, and survive. He was extremely grateful that he would never have to know.

"What about your mom and dad?" she asked, pulling him out of his wandering thoughts. "What are they doing now?"

He forced himself not to bite his lip as he met her steady gaze. "Dad's a lawyer," he lied.

"Never thought I'd see that," she said with a rueful smile. "I never thought your dad was the type to settle down, at least not until he met your mom."

He shrugged as his gaze darted longingly toward the window. He was growing more uncomfortable by the second; he just wanted to be back outside, where he was free. And where Jack and Mike were waiting to bombard him with questions, he realized with an inward sigh.

"Well, I thought that I would say hi, and see how you were doing. I have to get going now," he said softly.

He was very adept at lying. He should be, he had been doing it his whole life and he thought nothing of letting them roll off his tongue now. "Oh yeah," she said quickly. "Of course. Tell everyone that I say hi, and tell your mom..." her voice trailed off as her eyes became distant again. "Tell your mom that I miss her."

Again, Ethan felt that pain. It was his mother that had given up her friends, more so than his father. He suddenly understood the wistful look that crossed her face when his father, David, Doug, Jack, and Mike recalled stories of their younger days in high school and college. Without thinking, Ethan reached out and gently squeezed Kathleen's hand. She seemed as surprised by the gesture as he was. He'd never touched a human being in order to offer them comfort, but this woman looked so sad that he'd needed to offer her some kind of solace.

"I will," he promised.

She patted his hand gently and released it. "Are they still living at the same place?"

"Yes."

She nodded her eyes still sad and distant. "Maybe I'll give her a call."

"I'm sure that she would like that."

He turned to leave. "Ethan."

"Yeah?" He paused to look back at her.

"Are they still as in love as they used to be?" Her voice was soft, and her eyes gleamed with a fierce wistfulness that tugged at his heart.

"Even more so," he said honestly.

She beamed at him as tears filled her large eyes. "That's wonderful," she said in a choked voice.

Ethan left before she started to cry. He didn't deal well with humans under normal conditions; he sure as hell didn't know how to deal with an emotional one. Not that his sisters didn't get erratically emotional sometimes, but they were stronger and tougher than any human could ever be. He darted across the street and was almost pounced upon by Mike and Jack.

"Let's get to the car first," he said briskly. "I'm ready to go home."

They exchanged glances, but shrugged as they followed him back to the car. Ethan filled them in on the conversation as they left California behind, and headed into Oregon.

CHAPTER 1

"For God's sake Ethan, get up!" Isabelle cried impatiently as she tugged at his arm.

Her brother groaned as he stubbornly refused to look at her. "Isabelle I'm telling you right now, if you don't get out of my room, I'll..."

"You'll what?" she demanded. "Nothing, that's what. Now get up!"

Planting her hands on her hips she scowled at him as he opened one emerald eye to peep up at her. "What the hell are you doing here anyway? Go back to your own house," he grumbled as he rolled over and buried himself beneath his sheet.

She reached down and ripped the sheet off. "Hey!" he yelled as he tried to pull the sheet back. She refused to relent it as they got caught in a tug of war that she was determined to win.

"Ethan Joseph, get out of this bed right now!"

His eyes snapped to hers as he scowled fiercely. She didn't back down as she met his look with one just as fierce, and even more determined. "What do you want?" he snapped.

"Kyle and Cassidy climbed up a tree, they refuse to come down."

"Get Ian," he growled, finally managing to wrench his sheet back.

She instantly seized it again. "Ian is with Mike, David, Doug, Jack, dad, and Aiden, so forget about Aiden too. They got out of bed this morning, unlike *some* people, and went to town to get more wood for the new house."

Ethan groaned as he threw his arm over his eyes. "They're immortal, tell them to jump."

"Ethan!" she cried in exasperation. "They can still break bones, and what if they accidentally stake themselves on the way down?"

She knew that he was trying to stifle a laugh at the image that conjured. The only thing that held him back from doing so was the fact that he knew his brother and sister as well as she did. The possibility of them accidentally staking themselves was very good. With a loud groan he threw the sheet aside and swung his legs out of bed. Isabelle smiled smugly as she took a step back.

He didn't bother to look at her as he tugged on his jeans and a T-shirt. "How the hell do they manage to get themselves into these messes?" he muttered.

"The same way we did."

He groaned as he shook back his tussled hair. "Who dared them to go up the tree?" he grumbled.

"Julian."

He snorted in disgust. "Of course."

Isabelle waited for him to slip his sneakers on before heading outdoors. She led the way down the path through the woods before veering off on another path that led further into the forest. They had spent many hours playing in these woods as children, and Isabelle knew the trails like the back of her hand.

"Does mom know?" Ethan demanded.

"Like I was going to tell her, she's got enough on her mind right now."

"Huh?" Ethan asked tiredly.

Isabelle shook her hair back as she cast a scowl over her shoulder at him. "Never mind," she muttered.

Ethan stuck his tongue out at her. Isabelle forced herself not to laugh as she made a face at him. They may be adults now, but he was the one person that could always bring out her childish side. She loved that the most about him. She turned down the path that led to the tree house. The distinct chant of, "Jump! Jump!" suddenly reached them.

"Ah hell!" Ethan muttered as he broke into a run. Isabelle was right on his heels as they burst into a small clearing. Willow and Julian were standing at the base of a huge sycamore, looking up into its high, leaf filled branches as they continued to shout at their younger siblings. Cassidy was scooting down a branch, trying to adjust her hold as she started to slide to the side. Kyle, the less daring of the twins, had a death grip on his branch. "Don't you dare jump!" Ethan bellowed, causing even Isabelle to jump in surprise.

Willow and Julian spun around; their eyes were wide as they gazed guiltily at them. Cassidy let out a yelp as she jerked in surprise. With horrifying clarity, Isabelle realized that Cassidy wasn't going to be able to retain her hold on the branch as she slid perilously to the side. Ethan rushed forward, catching her just before she hit the ground. He grunted under the weight of her tiny body, his knees hit the ground from the force of the impact.

Isabelle rushed up to them, slightly breathless as her heart hammered with fear. Cassidy lay for a moment, her tiny face scrunched tight. Then, one bright blue eye popped open and she looked warily up at Ethan. She twisted her head, her long sandy blond hair covering her face as she looked at the ground just inches beneath her. She turned back around and burst into a brilliant grin as she hopped easily out of his arms. "Thanks!" she cried.

"Don't mention it," Ethan grumbled, shaking his head as he rose slowly.

"Nice catch," Julian said in awe.

Ethan wiped the dirt off the knees of his jeans. "Show off," Isabelle teased. He scowled at her for a moment before smiling softly. She lifted her head to peer through the thick branches at Kyle. "How are you going to get the other one?"

"Think they could both fall out alive?" he asked hopefully

"Do you think a snowball could survive in hell?" she retorted.

"Yeah, that's what I thought too," he mumbled unhappily.

She slapped him lightly on the back. "When was the last time you climbed a tree?"

His face twisted thoughtfully as he shrugged. "Ten years, maybe."

Kyle was clinging tightly to his branch; his face was white as a ghost. "Jump Kyle, it's fun!" Cassidy urged her twin.

"Don't you dare jump!" Isabelle yelled at her brother, shooting Cassidy a silencing look.

Cassidy smiled happily back as she hopped from foot to foot, not in the least bit ashamed. "Well, it was!" she protested.

"And if I hadn't caught you?" Ethan demanded.

She shrugged, refusing to be intimidated by either of her older siblings. "It would have hurt, but I heal fast!"

Isabelle shook her head, trying hard not to laugh as she met Ethan's aggravated gaze. "How do you argue with that?" she inquired.

"Easily," he said softly before turning back to Cassidy. "Mom and dad would have found out what you did."

Cassidy's mouth dropped as she looked worriedly over at Willow and Julian. "We only climbed a tree! There's nothing wrong with that!" she protested.

"After those two dared you!" he snapped, shooting a censuring look at Willow and Julian. They didn't look remotely ashamed as they stared unabashedly back at him.

"Forget it Ethan, you're fighting a losing battle," Isabelle told him. "Kyle, scoot to the branch below you! It's a pretty clear drop from there," she mumbled to Ethan.

"I'm scared!" Kyle wailed. "I don't want to let go."

"What kind of immortal is scared to fall from a tree?" Julian taunted.

"The smart kind!" Ethan snapped.

"I think you're going to have to go get him," she told Ethan.

"I'm too old for this crap," he muttered as he angrily tugged on his shaggy black hair.

Isabelle grinned at him, not at all deterred by his sour expression. "You're only twenty five; just think how you're going to feel in a hundred years."

He turned away from her and grabbed hold of one of the thick lower branches. Isabelle shaded her eyes against the sun as he climbed higher, finally reaching their brother. Kyle slid his small arms around Ethan's neck and climbed onto his back, he clung to him for dear life. Isabelle stifled a laugh as Ethan's choking noise reached her. She knew he would be angry if he heard her laughing at him, but it took all she had not to. A lot of curses, scratches, and mumbled threats later, he slid safely back to the ground. The minute he hit the ground, Kyle hopped off his back and raced over to join his siblings.

"Not so fast!" Isabelle yelled as they turned to bolt down the path. "There will be no more climbing trees! And if I find out that the two of you dare them to do something stupid again, I'm going to tell mom and dad, and you'll be grounded for a month! Understand?"

"Yeah, yeah," Willow and Julian mumbled.

"Don't you yeah, yeah me, or I'll go and tell them right now."

"No don't!" they both yelled. "We'll be good."

"Good, and you two," she continued as she turned to her younger siblings. "I want your promise that if they do dare you to do something, you will *not* do it."

"We promise," Kyle and Cassidy vowed in unison.

Isabelle closed her eyes and sighed. It was a useless promise; it would only be a matter of time before they were back into some mischief or another. "Go," she said wearily.

They turned and bolted down the path, disappearing easily into the woods. "How long do you think it will be before they're in trouble again?" Ethan asked as he absently pulling a twig from his shirt.

"Before they hit the end of the path," Isabelle answered with a small smile.

"Most likely. So, what's going on with mom?"

Isabelle started back down the path. "Nothing really, she's just been awfully quiet since you told her that you ran into her friend Karen last month."

"Kathleen," Ethan corrected.

"Whatever," she replied absently. "Plus, with Aiden going to college this fall, she's a little upset."

"Starting to get empty nest syndrome?"

Isabelle laughed as she pushed lightly against his shoulder. "I don't think this nest will ever be empty."

Ethan grinned back at her, his bright eyes twinkled merrily. "Not with the two of us here. She was that upset about Kathleen?"

"Yeah, she was," Isabelle replied sadly. "She's been talking about her a lot since then, reminiscing and stuff."

Ethan frowned thoughtfully. "I know Kathleen really seemed to miss her."

"Mom feels the same way. Every time she mentions her name she gets this pained, distant look in her eyes. It's sad."

"Well, there's nothing that we can do about it."

"I know," Isabelle whispered.

"Hey don't get all glum on me now!"

Isabelle grinned at him as she shoved his arm. He smiled as he pushed her playfully back. Out of all of her siblings, Ethan was the most like her, and the one that she was closest to. Neither of them had much use for the human race, other than food, and Isabelle didn't even bother with them for that. The idea of actually going out in the world, and living amongst people, had never appealed to either of them. Unlike the two of them though, Ian was already attending the University of Oregon, and he loved it. Aiden was thrilled about going away to school in the fall, and although Victoria and Abigail were only fifteen, they were already flipping through college brochures.

However, she and Ethan were content to stay here. Isabelle rarely went out into the world, rarely even left her yard. Ethan went out more than she did, but not nearly as often as the stooges (as they had come to refer to Mike, Doug, Jack, and David), or Ian, Aiden, Vicky, and Abby. Isabelle wasn't particularly fond of humans as it was, and the idea of actually living amongst them wasn't something that appealed to her.

She liked her life here, the peace of it, and the security that it offered her. She supposed it was cowardly of her to stay hidden away when there was a huge world that she could easily explore. However, she harbored a secret fear, and the possibility of her fear actually coming true was enough to make her want to never leave.

She glanced over at Ethan to find him smiling softly, his hands in his pockets, and his black head bowed. "What are you thinking about?" she asked lightly.

Ethan instantly wiped the grin from his face. "Nothing."

She cocked an elegant eyebrow as she smiled slyly at him. "Girls?"

He snorted in disgust. "Hardly."

She laughed happily as she tossed back her hair. "Don't lie Ethan, I know you."

He scowled at her as they stepped out of the woods. "And what about you?" he demanded.

She frowned as she looked at him. "What about me?" she retorted.

He grinned at her as he slung his arm around her shoulders. "Boys?" he taunted.

Isabelle laughed as she leaned against his side. "I wouldn't waste my time, or my energy."

"Speaking of time and energy," Ethan groaned as a pickup laden with wood pulled into the driveway. Another followed up the hill and parked next to it. Isabelle started to laugh as she slipped free of his arm.

"It's for *our* house," she reminded him.

"Does that mean you're going to help?" he inquired with a quirked eyebrow.

"Yeah, right," she replied laughingly.

She was still laughing as she skipped away with Ethan muttering miserably behind her.

CHAPTER 2

Isabelle handed out bottles of water to Ethan, Aiden, Ian, and Jack. They eagerly accepted them, twisting the tops off as they tossed their tools aside. She looked quickly around the large frame structure they had been working on. The house was going to be two stories, with four bedrooms, a finished basement, dining room, living room, kitchen, three full baths and one half bath, but for now it was just an empty skeleton. When completed, it would be mostly hers and Ethan's, but when Aiden and Ian came home from school they would also be staying here.

"It's coming along nicely," she said softly.

"If you would help it would come along even faster," Ethan said.

"She'd have us cleaning up the sawdust as we went," Jack retorted.

Isabelle made a face at him as she surveyed the mess surrounding her. Power tools, sawhorses, and pieces of wood littered the ground. Extension cords ran in a hundred different directions, tarps had been laid out everywhere and slabs of concrete were scattered about. She was standing in what would be the dining room, but at the moment it was completely unrecognizable. The basement was the only thing that was done, but she knew it wouldn't take them long to finish everything else.

A little bubble of happiness rose inside her. She couldn't wait until it was done and they could move in. For the first time in her life, she would be able to have some semblance of privacy. Plus, her mother had already helped her pick out most of the counters, flooring, rugs, tiles, and paint that would go into it and she couldn't wait to start decorating.

"Where are David, Mike, and Doug?" she asked, holding up the three water bottles that hadn't been claimed.

"They got smart and took off early to get a shower," Ethan muttered, taking another bottle from her. He dumped most of it over his head before squirting the rest into his mouth to wet his throat. Shaking out his wet hair he sent droplets of water cascading over all of them.

"Gross," Isabelle protested.

He grinned at her and tossed the bottle into the trashcan nearby. "That's the closest I'm going to get to a shower for at least an hour, so leave me be."

She smiled back as Ian and Jack grabbed the remaining bottles. "I guess I get left out again," Aiden mumbled as he rubbed his arm across his dirt and sawdust streaked face. He looked amazingly like her father, and Ethan, with his dark hair, and bright green eyes, but Aiden was taller and leaner, his nose slightly larger, and his hair curly instead of straight.

"Move faster next time," Ian retorted, smiling happily. His golden hair was caked with sawdust, sweat, and dirt. Grime smeared his elegant face, and the goggles covering his blue eyes made them look even bigger. He was the tallest of them all at six four, and the most solidly built.

"Where did your dad go?" Jack asked.

"Mom," they all answered in unison.

Jack shook his head, throwing water everywhere. "I can't wait to get this done," he mumbled.

"Neither can I," Ethan agreed.

"Bathrooms," Aiden said longingly.

"Well, are you guys coming in, or are you going to stay out here all night?" she asked impatiently.

"I'll come with you guys, maybe a shower's open," Jack said hopefully.

"Doubtful," Ethan muttered.

They moved swiftly across the open field, and up the back steps of the porch. Willow was standing on the porch, silently watching them until they reached the top. "What are you doing out here?" Isabelle inquired.

"Vicky and Abby are driving me crazy," she muttered. "And if you're hoping for a shower, forget it. They've been in the bathroom for over an hour bickering over who has better hair."

"They're identical!" Jack muttered.

"No, really?" Willow replied sarcastically.

Jack folded his arms over his chest as he gave her a stern look. "No need to be a wiseass."

"I learned from the best," she retorted. Jack reached out and tugged on her hair as he strode past, struggling to hide his smile from her.

Ethan slid the glass doors open and stepped into the kitchen. Everyone filed in behind him. Willow darted into the adjoining room, and slid the wooden doors shut behind her. Almost immediately Isabelle could hear her squabbling with Julian. The TV in the basement was blaring, over the noise she could hear Kyle and Cassidy fighting over what they wanted to watch. Above it all, she could hear Vicky and Abby arguing over the hairdryer.

"There are *two* hairdryers!"

Isabelle grinned as his father's voice boomed through the house. She leaned against the counter, folding her arms over her chest as Aiden, Ian, and Jack slid tiredly into the kitchen chairs. Ethan leaned against the counter beside her, he crossed his long legs before him as her mother and father strolled into the room.

"Hi guys," her mom greeted happily. "You're a mess."

"And it doesn't look like we're getting a shower here either," Jack grumbled.

"I'll get them out of there," her father told him.

He turned and strode back down the hall, yelling for Vicky and Abby to get out of the bathroom. He came back into the kitchen to the accompaniment of pounding footsteps. "Dad!" they yelled as they burst into the kitchen. "We're not done!"

"Get ready in your bedroom then," he told them, not at all deterred by their pouting.

"But..."

"No buts," he said firmly.

They both stared at him with pleading green eyes as they lifted damp, light blond hair and held it out. "The light isn't as good," Vicky protested.

"Victoria, there are other people that need the bathroom. Go ahead Jack," Isabelle's mother said.

"Hey shouldn't your kids go first!" Ian protested instantly. "We're filthy too!"

Jack was gone in a blur of motion before Ian even could finish his sentence. "Damn I have to learn how to do that," Aiden said in awe. Isabelle flashed past him, pulling his hair as she moved. "Ow! You witch! That wasn't fair!"

Isabelle laughed happily as she returned to her spot on the counter. She had finally managed to master that particular power last year, when she had reached maturity. It aggravated the hell out of her brother's that she could do it, and they couldn't. She loved to use it on them. "What about us?" Abby demanded.

Her mother took a deep breath as she bit into her lip and closed her eyes. Her father wrapped his arms around her and pulled her against his chest. "Use the bathroom in the basement," he told them. The twins sighed angrily before turning and stomping down the stairs. "You really want more?"

Her mother laughed as she shook her head. "Not for a long time."

"Good," her father sighed.

Isabelle watched as her parents grew quiet, and then her mother burst out laughing and hit her father playfully. She had long ago adjusted to the silent conversations they had with each other. Sometimes, when she watched them, she wondered what it would be like to meet someone that would make her that happy, but more often than not the idea frightened the hell out of her.

She couldn't imagine needing someone so much that she would die without them; it terrified her to even think about it. It was the main reason that she kept herself locked away. That was the last thing she ever wanted to have happen to her.

She would gladly stay here for the rest of her existence before she gave up her heart, her soul, and her freedom to someone else. Her parents couldn't stand to be apart for long periods of time, and when they were apart, they were in constant communication with each other's minds. She knew that their love was rare, and precious, and something wonderful, but to never be able to part with someone was something that she didn't even want to contemplate, let alone experience.

"So how are things going with the house?" her mom asked.

"They're going," Ethan answered tiredly.

A knock on the front door snapped all of their heads around. "Who could that be?" Aiden pondered.

"Probably some of the material I ordered for the new house, it was supposed to come today," her mom answered. She untangled herself from her father, headed swiftly past the fridge, and down the stairs to the front door.

"I'll go help her," Isabelle said.

She couldn't wait to get her hands on the new material. It had to be the paint that they had ordered, or maybe the kitchen cabinets. She was beginning to really smile with anticipation when her father suddenly stiffened. His eyes flashed a vibrant red, before he was gone. They stood gaping at each other for a moment, before turning and running toward the front door.

CHAPTER 3

By the time they reached the front door, her mother and father were outside, kneeling over a woman. Isabelle skidded to a halt, her eyes widened at the sight of the middle aged woman on the ground between them. "Kathleen!" Ethan gasped.

Isabelle's mouth dropped open as she gaped in surprise. "What happened?" Aiden demanded.

Her mother looked up at him, unshed tears in her wide violet blue eyes. "She fainted," she whispered.

"Mom! Mom!" It was then that Isabelle noticed the young girl kneeling over Kathleen, lightly tapping her face in an attempt to wake her.

"Who is that?" Aiden insisted.

"Kathleen," Isabelle answered.

"Who?" Ian asked in confusion.

She sighed impatiently as she rolled her eyes at them. If it didn't have to do with a girl, or blood, they paid no attention to anything. "Mom's friend from college!" she snapped impatiently.

"Oh," he said dully. "Oh shit!" He exclaimed more loudly when the full realization sank in.

"Liam, get her up, we'll take her inside," her mother ordered briskly

Her father bent and scooped Kathleen easily up. "Put her down!" the girl screamed as she pulled at her father's arms. "Put her down now!"

"What the hell is going on?" Jack bellowed from the back of the pack still crammed in the doorway. "Is that... oh shit this can't be good."

"Get out of the way Jack!" her father snapped as he carried Kathleen quickly inside.

Her mother followed eagerly behind, her beautiful face pinched with worry. "Ethan, please take care of ah... Kathleen's daughter."

They all turned to look at the young girl as she stared fearfully back at them with wide blue eyes. Tears were streaming down her pretty face as she tried to shove her way past them. Ethan seized hold of her shoulders, pulling her back from the doorway. "Just calm down," he said gently.

The girl's bright, sky blue eyes flashed to him, they boiled with anger and fear as she shoved at him again. He seized hold of her slender arms and pinned them to her sides. "Your mother is fine; she just went inside to catch up with her good friends." The girl's eyes began to glaze over as his power started to wrap its way into her mind. "You decided to stay out here with us while they catch up. Okay?"

She nodded slowly as he released his hold on her. Isabelle nudged him out of the way and seized hold of the girls limp hands. "What's your name?" she asked gently.

"Delia," she replied numbly.

"Delia, that's a nice name. How old are you Delia?"

The girl continued to stare dazedly at her. "Sixteen."

"What brings you here?" Isabelle prodded as she tried to break the girl from her trance.

Delia blinked in confusion, and then her eyes focused fully on Isabelle. "My mom wanted to see yours."

Isabelle let out a small sigh of relief as the girl began to regain full consciousness. "I'm sure that they'll have a good time."

"Yes, they will. Who are you?" the girl asked quietly.

"I'm Isabelle and these are my brother's Ethan, Aiden, and Ian. The ugly guy with the wet hair is Jack, one of the stooges."

"Hey!" Jack protested angrily at the same time Delia asked. "The stooges?"

Isabelle grinned at Jack as he scowled disapprovingly back at her. "Yeah, that's what we call our parent's friends Jack, David, Mike, and Doug."

Delia frowned, her forehead puckered as her light eyebrows drew tightly together. "There were only three stooges."

"You're forgetting Shemp," Ethan interjected. "Everyone forgets Shemp. Trust me, once you get to know these four they are just like the stooges."

"Hey!" Jack protested again as he frowned angrily at all of them. "We helped to raise your ungrateful asses!"

"Yes, and that's why we are the way we are," Aiden retorted happily, pushing Jack's shoulder lightly.

Delia smiled as she looked over Isabelle's shoulder toward the group gathered on the porch. She was a pretty girl with high and delicate cheekbones, and a full mouth full. She was taller than Kathleen, and leaner, but she had her mother's curvaceous figure.

Another set of headlights flashed into the driveway. "Who the hell is that?" Jack's kidding air vanished in an instant as they all stiffened in preparation for what was to come.

"That's my sister Jess; she rode up with her boyfriend. You probably remember Jess." She turned back toward Isabelle, her face eager as she looked hopefully at her. "She remembers you."

Isabelle vaguely remembered Jess. The last time she'd seen her, she'd been eight years old. Jess had been a pudgy blond, with bright blue eyes, and a zeal for mischief. They'd been fast friends then, as Jess had been the only girl that Isabelle had to play with at the time, Abby and Vicky having just been born. To her surprise, Isabelle suddenly found herself looking forward to seeing her again. Jess had been so much fun when they were younger, and it would be nice to have someone other than her sisters to speak with.

"Oh wonderful," Jack muttered. "I'm going to get the others."

"I think you should," Ethan said softly.

They all turned as car doors opened and slammed shut. Isabelle's brow furrowed as the night air suddenly shifted and stirred. She glanced worriedly at her brothers, their casual postures were gone. They now stood stiffly as they scanned the night. Ethan's nostrils flared as he scented the air for the source of the sudden disturbance. Isabelle turned her attention back to the car. There were two people standing in front of it, hidden within the shadows of the night.

"Do you feel that?" she whispered.

"Yes," Ethan's eyes narrowed sharply. Aiden and Ian stepped forward, their bodies tense, and their eyes locked intently upon the shadows.

"What *is* that?" Ian hissed.

Isabelle didn't know, but it radiated through the inside of her, shaking her to the core. Something was off, something wasn't right. It was not a scary feeling, not one that rocked her with fear, but it upset her nonetheless. There was something in those shadows that she'd never felt before, something that she didn't understand.

"What are you guys talking about?" Delia demanded.

"Isabelle go inside," Ethan commanded sharply.

Isabelle shot him a nasty look as her jaw clenched and her hands fisted at her sides. She wasn't going anywhere if it meant leaving them alone with whatever the strange presence was. "No."

"Come on." A girl's voice, Jess's, cut through the air. Isabelle could tell that she was pulling on the man's hand beside her, but he wasn't moving.

"Stop." The deep, husky voice was a solid command that stopped Jess's movements instantly. It also caused a bolt of surprise, and something else, something that she didn't recognize, to jolt through Isabelle.

"Stefan," Jess said impatiently.

Isabelle strained to see through the shadows. Her night vision was exceptional and she was able to make out a small, thin girl, with light blond hair before the car. Her hand was on the arm of the man next to her. Isabelle's gaze sharpened on him. His shoulders were broad, his build large and muscular, and his hair was as dark as the night surrounding him. The disturbance in the air was coming from him. It radiated off of him, pulsing through the night.

"It's him," Ethan whispered.

"Yes," Aiden agreed his voice barely audible.

"Huh?" Delia asked in surprise.

They all ignored her as they focused their attention on the strange man hidden within the shadows. Isabelle could barely make out the hard planes of his face and the firm set of his jaw. He looked as cold as concrete, and he was as still as stone. His eyes were dark, and narrowed upon them.

"Come on Stefan!" Jess pulled on his arm again.

He shrugged off her grasp as he stood stiffly; the shadows enfolded him within their embrace. Isabelle's heart leapt into her throat. She suddenly knew what it was that was off, what he was. "Like knows like!" she gasped.

"What?" Delia asked in confusion, as she took a quick step away from Isabelle and her siblings.

"Shit," Ethan's stance became even more rigid as his hands fisted at his sides. Her brothers stiffened around him and grouped tighter together.

"You people are strange," Delia said as her eyes darted fearfully over them. "I want to see my mom."

"What do we do?" Aiden whispered.

There was a shifting among the shadows, a small bristling as the man moved ever so slightly. "I wouldn't do anything," he informed them coldly.

Jess had called him Stefan, Isabelle remembered as she took an instinctive step closer to her brothers. There was something about his voice, something strange, but not unpleasant as it enveloped her like a warm cloak. It did something to the inside of her, caused something to stir and shift in a way that she had never experienced before. "Ethan," she whispered fearfully.

He took a step forward, shielding her even more. The man, Stefan, laughed softly as he finally started to move forward. "I'm not going to hurt you."

Another shiver wracked through Isabelle at the sound of his voice. The shadows parted around him as he moved swiftly into the light. Isabelle's breath froze in her lungs; the world seemed to rock on its axis as her eyes locked upon him. He was perfect, broad, tall; magnificent. The hard planes of his perfectly sculpted bones were highlighted by the light now playing off of his strong face.

His gaze traveled swiftly over her brothers before settling on her. His eyes were as black as onyx, and just as cold. They penetrated through her, racking her bones as they seemed to steal straight into her soul. For a moment, he was the only thing that she could see, the only thing she could feel.

Everything else disappeared.

Then, his gaze moved from hers, breaking the brief connection. Isabelle felt an amazing sense of loss as the breath rushed out of her, and the world slammed into place. With a startled cry, she turned and shoved her way past Aiden and Ian as she fled into the sanctuary of her house.

***

Stefan couldn't move as his gaze locked on a pair of pure violet eyes. The young woman stared at him with a deer in the headlights look of pure panic. Her hair was dark, with soft gold streaks running through its shimmering depths. It curled around her beautiful, delicate face, before spilling down her back in thick waves. Her nose was small, and narrow, her tiny nostrils flared as she gaped at him.

She was tall and slender, with the elegant grace that was innate to all of their kind, but with her, he knew that it would have been present even if she were a human. She was beautiful, perfect, unlike anything he'd ever seen before, or had ever thought to see. He was surprised by the bolt of lust that ripped through him as the delicate tip of her tongue came out to nervously wet her full, luscious lips.

For a moment, she was all he could see, all he could sense. Then, the man next to her moved. Stefan's eyes darted to him as his instincts kicked into high gear. He knew what they all were, and he knew that they were going to defend their home, and each other. He had sensed them miles down the road, but he hadn't known that he was heading straight into their lair. He still couldn't believe it. Never had he seen so many of his kind in one place, and he knew that there were still more of them in the house, and he could sense even more somewhere else.

He also knew that they were not killers, but he didn't know if they were going to attack him. He had come into their territory after all, and he knew full well just how territorial his kind could be. A strangled cry snapped his gaze back to the woman as she turned and fled. Startled looks came over the faces of the two that she shoved past, but they didn't make a move to stop her. The other one took a step forward, his body rigid as his hands clenched into fists at his side.

"I don't think you should be here," the man said coldly.

Stefan didn't think he should be here either, but he wasn't going to tell him that. He was stronger than most of his kind, but with so many of them here he knew that he would be in for a hard battle. A battle he would not walk away from unscathed, especially if he had to protect Jess and Delia from them.

"You are the creepiest people I have ever met!" Delia cried angrily. "I want to see my mother!"

"Delia shut up!" Stefan hissed. His gaze darted to the young girl by the porch, Delia was easily within their reach, and if they wanted to hurt her they could have her in seconds. The last thing he needed was for her to draw even more attention to herself. He needed all of his senses at the moment, and Delia's yelling was not helping.

"Stefan!" Jess cried at the same time that Delia started shouting angrily.

He purposely shut them out as he tuned his senses to the air around him. Detecting the approach of others, he turned so that his body was halfway between the porch and the shadows at the edge of the house. He knew immediately that there were four of them.

They ran around the corner and skidded to a halt as their eyes landed upon him. He half crouched prepared to fight to the death as a soft hiss escaped him. Their eyes widened in surprise, and then narrowed dangerously. The three on the porch took a step toward him, hostility radiated from every inch of them. Stefan's muscles bunched in anticipation of a fight.

Jess and Delia took a frightened step back. Delia began to scream hysterically, causing Stefan to wince at the harsh sound of her grating voice.

"Stefan!" Surprise snapped through him as one of the newcomers called his name and took a step forward. The animosity that had surrounded the man moments before vanished instantly. Stefan remained rigid as he straightened slowly. His eyes were intent upon the tall, blond man that had spoken his name. For a moment he couldn't recall who he was, then recognition sprang forth, and a small laugh escaped him.

"David?" Stefan asked in disbelief.

"Yeah, what the hell are you doing here?" David grinned at him as he strode forward and extended his hand. Stefan accepted it and shook it briskly.

"What the hell is going on?" Jess planted her hands on her hips as she glared at them.

"That's what we'd like to know," one of the other newcomers muttered.

David peered over his shoulder, his eyes widened as he finally noticed the two humans gathered behind Stefan. "Who the hell are you?" he demanded.

"Kathleen's kids," the tall man at the front of the porch answered.

David's eyes widened as he spun toward him. "What?" he gasped.

"Yeah, don't ask. Who is that?" he asked nodding toward Stefan.

David blinked in surprise, shaking his head slightly as he glanced quickly between Stefan and the group gathered on the porch. "This is Stefan. I met him when I went to college in Pennsylvania. He's the one that told me about what was going on with Liam and Sera."

Stefan's eyes widened as his mouth dropped. "Are these *their* kids?" he blurted.

"Some of them. That's Ethan, Aiden, and Ian," David nodded to the group still gathered on the porch. "Those are my friends Mike, Doug, and Jack. I told you about them before."

"Yeah, I remember," Stefan replied dully. He'd heard of vampire children, had been told that they were normal looking, but he'd never actually *seen* one. It was completely amazing. "Who was the girl?" he inquired.

"The *girl* was our sister, Isabelle," Ethan, or at least he thought it was Ethan, replied coldly.

Stefan's eyebrows rose at the fierce tone in the boy's voice, but he refrained from saying anything. "What is going on?" Delia asked shrilly.

"Someone's going to have to take care of them," Stefan said, waving a hand dismissively at the humans behind him.

"Not me," Jack announced. "I had enough of doing that with Kathleen years ago."

"What did you do to my mother?" Jess nearly shrieked.

"What are going to do to us?" Delia cried as she backed away from the porch.

"That's all you guys, it's a perfect training session for honing your powers of persuasion," David said to the men on the porch. "Why don't we go somewhere a little less chaotic and catch up?" he asked Stefan.

"That sounds like a very good idea," he replied.

CHAPTER 4

Isabelle woke with a groan to the endless pounding of a hammer, and the annoying buzz of a saw ringing in her ears. Moaning miserably, she grabbed her pillow and pulled it over her head. She had barely slept last night, and this was not the way that she wanted to be awakened. Why the hell were they working on the new house so early in the morning? She wondered angrily.

Then she realized that she was being ridiculous. If they had started later, she would have been dragging them out of bed in order to get them moving. She was just angry because she hadn't fallen asleep until the sun had started to peak its head over the horizon. She groaned again as she clearly recalled the reason why she'd had so much difficulty falling asleep.

Him.

Moaning again she pulled the pillow tighter over her head. The gesture was useless, it dimmed the pounding, but it did nothing to shut out the image of him that had been seared into her brain. She clearly recalled the story her mother had told about the first time she'd seen her father, and how the world had seemed to disappear for a moment. Nausea twisted in Isabelle's stomach. She didn't want to be her mother and father. She wanted a quiet, peaceful life, where she needed no one but herself to survive.

With another loud moan, she finally conceded defeat to the fact that she wasn't going to get anymore sleep. Sighing angrily she threw the pillow aside and tossed off her sheet. She was getting ahead of herself where he was concerned. Just because the world had seemed to disappear when she saw him didn't mean that she had met her soul mate. All it meant was that she had finally encountered her first vampire, outside of her close knit family and friends, and it had shocked her. That was all. That was the *only* reason that things had been so strange last night.

However, no matter what she told herself she couldn't shake the image of him from her mind, or the strange feelings that he had invoked in her.

Thankfully, he would be gone today. Hopefully he already was. She had thought that notion would be pleasing; she was disgusted to realize it wasn't.

"Isabelle!"

Her door burst open with a loud bang as it slammed forcefully against the wall. She jumped in surprise and sighed as her sisters burst into the room like a tsunami. She didn't bother to turn and face Abby and Vicky as she swung her legs out of bed. She had never known privacy; she didn't bother to try and have any now. She quickly gathered her clothes together as she moved toward her small half bath.

"What's up?" she asked tiredly.

All she wanted was to wash her face, it would help her feel better, and wake her up. "What's up?" they demanded as the followed her to the doorway.

"Don't you know?" Abby charged.

No, she didn't know what their new melodrama was, and at the moment she didn't care. Isabelle shut the door on Abby and leaned against it. "Hurry up!" Vicky yelled.

Sighing, she moved away from the door. She turned the cold water on and liberally began to splash her face. Feeling much better, she dressed quickly, pulled her thick hair into a ponytail, and opened the door to face her sisters. They were sitting on her bed, their hands clasped before them as they stared eagerly at her. Whatever they had to tell her had them nearly bursting at the seams.

She knew she was going to regret asking, Vicky and Abby could go on endlessly when something had them excited. Isabelle usually ended up with a headache from trying to follow their inane chatter by the time they were done, but ask she did. "Know what?"

"They're staying *here!*" Vicky exclaimed. "We can't get in the bathroom now! Let alone with two more people in the house!"

Isabelle blinked in confusion as she dropped her nightgown into the hamper. "Who is staying here?"

"Kathleen and her kids!" they cried in miserable unison.

Isabelle swung toward them as her mouth dropped open. She had completely forgotten about Kathleen, Delia, and Jess in her own confusion, and self pity, last night. "What?" she nearly yelled.

"Yeah," Abby said, nodding her golden head enthusiastically. "Kathleen starts a new job in two weeks, she thought it would be nice to stop by and surprise mom. They invited them to stay for the *entire* time!"

Isabelle felt as if someone had dumped a bucket of ice water over her head as her entire body went completely numb. "What about Jess's boyfriend?" she croaked.

"He is *so* hot!" Vicky batted her eyes dreamily as she folded her hands under her chin. "Do you know he's the one that told David what was going on with mom and dad? He's over two hundred years old!"

Isabelle didn't care about any of that. There was only one thing she did care about. "Is he staying here?" she managed to choke out.

"Yeah, he's helping out with the new house right now!"

Isabelle's eyes widened as her throat went dry and her heart jumped into her throat. There was no room in either house now, where would everyone stay? A cold chill of apprehension began to trickle through her as she gazed wildly around her room. There was more room at the other house. There was an extra bathroom, and if someone bunked up... Isabelle shut the thought down as panic began to constrict her chest.

"He's going to be staying at the other house with Jess. She doesn't go back to college for a few weeks. Maybe they're soul mates like mom and dad! That's so romantic!" Abby cried.

Isabelle felt as if she had been slammed in the gut with a fist as she struggled to catch her breath, and absorb everything that they were saying. He was staying *here*? With Jess? For two weeks? Her thoughts were a scattered mess, none of which were in the least bit romantic.

"I don't think they are," Vicky contradicted Abby. "They sure don't act like mom and dad. I mean he didn't even see Jess after he left with the stooges last night."

"That's true," Abby said as she bit thoughtfully on her bottom lip.

"Isabelle what's wrong? You look like you've seen a ghost?" Vicky demanded.

Blinking herself out of her horrifying thoughts, she forced herself to focus on the identical faces before her. "Ah, nothing. How are they going to stay here? I mean, Kathleen is mom's friend from school; she fainted when she saw her last night! They can't possibly stay here! How can any of them possibly explain that none of them have aged in the past twenty five years?"

"Stefan took care of that. His powers are really strong since he's so old!" Abby breathed reverently. "He's made it so that whenever Kathleen, Jess, and Delia look at mom, dad, and the stooges they see people that look like they're in their forties."

Isabelle gaped at them in surprise and horror. She could forge people's memories, but only a moment or two of them, and it always left her tired and drained. She couldn't begin to imagine the amount of power it would take in order to accomplish such a feat. "He can do that?" she breathed.

"Yeah, isn't that awesome!? Can you imagine what else he must be able to do?"

No, she couldn't, and she didn't want to. She shuddered involuntarily as her sisters continued to prattle on about Jess's boyfriend. "Isabelle."

She jumped in surprise as her mom's head appeared in the doorway. "Yeah?" she asked shakily.

Her mother frowned as she stepped fully into the doorway. "You okay?"

"Yes," she lied.

Her mother's gaze searched her face, but Isabelle forced herself to remain outwardly serene, even though she was a seething mass of turmoil. "I see you've heard the news."

"Yes."

"It will only be for a little while, and Jess goes back to school in two weeks. Plus, the new house will be finished soon."

Isabelle nodded numbly. "It's okay mom."

"Well, until the house is ready, I was wondering if um..." Isabelle's cold chill became a frozen iceberg as her terror from earlier blazed back to fierce life. If somebody shared a room, there would be more beds open at the other house, and Aiden was leaving soon for football practice. Please no, she begged silently. Please. "If you wouldn't mind staying at the other house with the guys, and Jess?"

Isabelle's shoulders slumped as her silent pleas went unanswered. "I know it's a lot to ask, but Aiden leaves for college on Monday, and Ian leaves in a week and a half. In no time at all you'll actually have more privacy over there." At any other point in time Isabelle would have jumped at the opportunity, but now the thought made her stomach cramp painfully. "It will also give you a chance to catch up with Jess. You two were close as children," her mom continued.

"Do you think they're soul mates mom?" Abby asked excitedly.

Her mother smiled kindly as she shook her head. "I don't know honey, maybe."

"That would be so awesome!" Abby gushed, ever the romantic at heart.

"So Isabelle, what do you say?" her mom asked, her violet blue eyes intent as she studied Isabelle hopefully.

Isabelle wanted to say no, she wanted to *scream* no, but she couldn't bring herself to do it. Her mother had been so sad after Ethan had told her he'd run into Kathleen. The nostalgia in her mother's voice when she'd spoken of her old friend had torn at Isabelle's heart. This was her mother's chance to catch up with Kathleen, to spend some time with her friend, and to regain some of the time she had been forced to give up. Her mother would do anything for her; Isabelle couldn't refuse her this simple favor, no matter how unhappy it made her. It would only be for a couple of weeks, she could handle a couple of weeks. Nothing bad was going to come of it. She hoped.

"Sure mom, no problem." She had to choke out the words past the painful lump in her throat.

Her mother beamed at her. "Thanks Isabelle, I owe you one." More than one, Isabelle thought silently. "Why don't you guys take some drinks down to the building site," her mom suggested to the twins. They bounced eagerly off the bed and fled down the hall, bickering over which one of them would get to serve Stefan. "I think they have a crush on him."

"Yeah," Isabelle muttered absently. Her mind was already focused on how she was going to get through the next weeks.

"Are you sure you're okay?"

"Yeah mom, I'm fine."

"Do you need a hand moving your stuff?"

***

Two hours later Isabelle was greatly regretting the fact that she had turned down her mother's offer of help, opting to recruit Abby and Vicky instead. They had done nothing but talk her ear off about Stefan, and how wonderful and amazing he was. She had a pounding headache, and she swore that if she heard his name one more time she was going to scream.

Not to mention, they were almost no help at all. She had only packed three bags, and two suitcases to take with her. She had already packed most of the things in her room in preparation for the move to her new home, so she had very little left to take with her.

Ethan opened the screen door for her when they stepped onto the porch. He took one of the suitcases from her as he glanced back at the twins with an amused quirk of his eyebrow. They were each carrying one small backpack, while she had both of her suitcases, and a bag. "Taking a break?" she asked irritably.

He flashed a grin at her as he walked back into the house. "Damn right. It's hot as hell out there. I can see you have a lot of help."

Isabelle sighed wearily as she looked at the kitchen tile they had stepped onto. It was so covered with dirt and footprints that it was hard to tell that the tile was actually a light blue instead of dingy gray. The kitchen was pretty much clean but that was only because they didn't use it often.

"Yeah," she mumbled.

"Doug's going to bunk with David, so you'll have the basement to yourself. There's a half bath down there."

"I know," she mumbled.

He flashed another grin as they headed into the living room. She kept down her moan of disgust; it was painfully obvious that a bunch of bachelors lived here. There were two forest green couches that centered around the big screen TV on the far wall. Two green reclining chairs were set at an angle at the end of the couches; their worn footrests were still in the air. The coffee table in the center of the oval was made of dark wood, but the tarnish was faded and scratched, and there were at least a dozen water rings marring it. A screen in the corner had once been a bright white, but dust and time had yellowed it and the picture of a deer in a wild, color filled meadow, had faded.

The room was painted a light cream, but the walls were marred by dirt and fingers marks, and in desperate need of repainting. Dust coated the TV and the light green curtains. The windows were as smudged as the walls. The bookshelf, in between the two windows on the left hand wall, was cluttered with old paperbacks that had been tossed haphazardly onto it.

Wrinkling her nose, Isabelle studied the room with mild distaste, wondering how long it would take to clean everything. "We're only going to be here for a few weeks," Ethan said.

"I know."

He glanced at her over his shoulder as he strolled across the room. More footprints marred the old, dark green carpet. It was tattered and worn with age, and torn straight to the floor in some places. "So don't plan on redoing everything, and don't go too crazy with the cleaning."

Sometimes it was nice to have someone who knew her as well as Ethan did, at other times, he was a pain in her ass. "I wasn't," she muttered as she followed him down the stairs to the basement.

"Liar."

"You're going to have so much fun over here Issy!" Abby cried enthusiastically.

Isabelle rolled her eyes as she stepped into the basement that had been divided by a simple plywood wall. They were standing in the laundry and weight room, both of which she knew were rarely used. Ethan led the way to the door in the simply assembled wall and threw it open. Isabelle stepped in and groaned silently.

The room was large, and plain. The bed was queen size, with a small wood headboard, and no footboard. It was stripped completely bare to reveal the old, indented mattress. A TV sat on an aged, rickety looking metal stand, both of which were gray with dust. A small window was set in the far right wall, a shabby black curtain hung over it to block out the sun. The door to the half bath was ajar; Isabelle didn't even want to know what it looked like. The entire room was cool and damp, and reeked of mildew.

"I am definitely cleaning this," Isabelle said, dropping her suitcase on the dirty, dark cream carpet.

"I wouldn't doubt it," Ethan muttered.

"Ugh, it smells in here." Vicky wrinkled her tiny nose.

Isabelle crossed to the small set of stairs on the left hand side and shoved the storm doors open. She inhaled the fresh summer air gratefully. "Could you open that window for me!" she called over her shoulder.

Abby quickly threw the curtain back and pulled the tiny window down. She stuck her nose into it and inhaled deeply. "Just don't get any ideas about the rest of the house," Ethan told her. "You're going to have a brand new one to decorate, and scrub, soon."

"Yeah, yeah," Isabelle replied distractedly. Her mind was already trying to figure out where she was going to start.

Ethan groaned as he moved across the room. "Just don't have the whole place reeking of flowers, or some other girly scent. We're manly men here." Isabelle was trying hard not to grin as he shook his head and turned away. "Ah crap, we're screwed. I'll see you later."

He fled swiftly up the storm doors, still muttering to himself as he disappeared from sight. "Do you want us to help?" Vicky asked.

Isabelle groaned inwardly as she nodded. She may not *want* it, but she was going to *need* all the help that she could get.

***

Hours later, she had the walls scrubbed nearly white again, the rug vacuumed and washed, everything dusted, the bed neatly made, and the room smelling wonderfully of fresh air, and apple. She was a filthy mess, her hair hung in straggly wet strands around her face, and her clothes were dirty and sweaty as they clung to her. Vicky and Abby looked just as bad, fortunately they weren't complaining any more, or rattling on about Stefan. Now, they just sat silently on the bed, too tired to move.

"I'm going to take a shower."

They nodded as Isabelle gathered her clothes and headed out of the basement, and up the stairs. Making her way through the living room she went upstairs to the full bath, which was also in desperate need of a good cleaning. She forced herself not to groan as she took in the absolute mess. Toothpaste and toothbrushes were scattered haphazardly around the sink, and the soft yellow of the sink was nearly white from the toothpaste and shaving cream. The floor was filthy, she didn't even want to look at the toilet, and the shower was mildewed.

She forced herself not to think about any of it as she took a quick shower, dressed, and left the room before she started to clean it now. It would be her first project tomorrow. She wondered if she could recruit Vicky and Abby again, but she doubted it. They had only helped her today in the hope of seeing Stefan, but he had stayed at the building site with everyone else. She wondered if Jess would be willing to help. She was definitely going to need it.

She entered her new room again and threw her dirty clothes into the hamper. She would also gather everyone's dirty laundry tomorrow and do that. While she was here, she was going to make sure that everyone had plenty of clean clothes, and a clean house. She turned her attention back to Vicky and Abby, who looked as if they hadn't moved an inch.

"Would you guys want to help me tomorrow?"

They exchanged quick glances. "Well, we were going to ah..."

"Don't worry about it," she interrupted with a soft smile.

"Maybe we'll stop by later in the day," Vicky offered.

"That's okay," Isabelle assured them.

"Isabelle!"

She nearly jumped out of her skin as Willow's head appeared in the doorway of the storm cellar. She didn't even have to ask, the look on Willow's face said it all. "Ah hell, what did you do now?" she mumbled as she leapt up the stairwell.

Willow turned and started to run before Isabelle even reached the top. She followed her around the back of the house and toward the woods. Willow darted gracefully down a trail, easily dodging the tree branches that slapped at Isabelle. Cursing and muttering angrily, she wasn't paying any attention to where they were going. Willow pulled up abruptly in a small clearing, if she hadn't reached out and grabbed Isabelle, she would have plummeted right over the edge of the pit in the middle of the clearing.

Skidding to a halt, her eyes widened as they landed upon the gaping hole that was about ten feet in diameter. It looked grotesquely out of place in the middle of the small clearing. "What the..."

"Isabelle!"

Surprise ripped through her as the small voice came from the hole. She stepped carefully to the edge of the pit and looked down. Her heart leapt into her throat, and her blood ran cold as she spotted Julian about four feet down, clinging to a tree root with his feet dangling in the air. Beneath him were at least a hundred old, deadly looking wooden stakes. It took her only a moment to realize that he had fallen into a bear trap that had been long forgotten.

Isabelle dropped to her knees and scooted to the edge of the whole. Julian stared at her with wide, pleading blue eyes; his black hair was matted to his forehead with sweat and dirt. "Isabelle help me," he begged.

"Hold on Julian, don't you dare let go of that root."

"Tell me something I don't know," he replied miserably.

"No need to be sarcastic," she muttered as she dropped to her belly and scuttled closer to the edge. She leaned into the hole, reaching for him, but he was even further down than she had thought. "Damn," she muttered, wiggling further over the edge. "Willow, grab my ankles!" she yelled.

When her ankles were grasped tightly she wiggled a little further out so that she was half in, and half out of the hole. "Julian grab my hands!" she gasped, barely able to breathe from the pressure on her stomach. He hesitated for a moment and then reached up and seized hold of one of her arms. She grasped his tiny forearm tightly. "Now the other one."

He bit into his bottom lip as his face paled visibly. He released his hold on the root and seized hold of her other arm. "Isabelle!" Willow gasped. "You're too heavy!"

Dismay ripped through her as she struggled to breathe. "Don't you dare let go!" she yelled.

"If you let go I will haunt you for the rest of my afterlife!" Julian shouted.

Isabelle cocked an eyebrow as she stared down at him. "That's a threat," she mumbled. "She already has to deal with you for eternity; she might take her chances on you not being able to bother her in the afterlife."

His eyes widened even more, and she hadn't thought that it was possible, but he became even paler. "That's not funny!"

"Willow, pull us up!" Isabelle commanded.

"I'm trying!" Willow cried.

Isabelle closed her eyes and ground her teeth as she tried to wiggle backward. Her arms were beginning to ache painfully, and it was becoming increasingly difficult to breathe. Willow tugged at her ankles, pulling them back inch by excruciatingly slow, inch. The three of them cried out as Willow lost her footing and slid to the ground. Isabelle slid back over the edge, this time to her hips, before she was jerked to a halt. Julian looked about ready to burst into tears as he was jerked to a halt. Her arms screamed in agony as her shoulders were nearly ripped from their sockets by the force of his weight.

"I'm sorry," Willow panted. "I can't do this."

Isabelle closed her eyes and groaned. What the hell was she going to do? Where the hell were Vicky and Abby? "Isabelle," Julian panted.

"It's okay, just hold on. Willow, you have to do this!"

"I can't," she cried, her voice choked with tears.

"Then go get help!" she snapped, her patience at an end. She was scared senseless, holding her brother over certain death, and damn close to her own death. She didn't have time to deal with Willow's tears.

"But..."

"Go!" she and Julian yelled at the same time.

Her ankles were released and she slid a few inches forward. Fear slammed her heart into her throat as she struggled to dig her feet into the ground. The slow slide stopped as she managed to plant her toes into the soft dirt. Fear and adrenaline shook her as she stared down at Julian; his eyes were even wider in his small face.

"I swear if we get out of this I am going to kill you!" she grated through her teeth.

Julian managed a wan smile as he cast a worried glance behind him. "Please don't let go."

"I'll never let go," she assured him. She'd go plummeting over with him before she ever let go. Julian's hands dug painfully into her skin as he lifted his head to look at her again. His eyes were bright with unshed tears as his lower lip began to quiver. "How do you manage to get yourself into these messes?"

"We were only walking," he whispered plaintively.

Isabelle closed her eyes and dropped her head. The cool dirt filled her nostrils as she inhaled deeply and tried to ignore the tortuous pain in her arms and shoulders. Her legs were beginning to ache, and her feet were beginning to cramp from digging into the ground. She didn't know how much longer she was going to be able to keep them both up. She grit her teeth, determined to hold on for as long as it took.

"Your hair is tickling me," Julian said softly.

"Sorry," she mumbled as she lifted her head.

Hands suddenly seized hold of her waist. She cried out as she was lifted easily off the ground, Julian along with her. Stumbling back, her trembling legs barely supported her as she was set on the ground. A strong hand in the small of her back quickly righted her. A small jolt of something ripped through her, but it was forgotten as Julian fell against her. His arms encircled her waist as he buried his head in her chest. She dropped her head to his as she absorbed the shudders wracking his body.

"It's ok," she soothed, gently stroking back his hair as the hand fell away from her back.

He lifted his head, tears slid through the grime on his cheeks, leaving clean tracks in their wake. Isabelle's eyes widened in surprise, she hadn't seen Julian cry since he was four years old, and that was over eight years ago. He always tried so hard to emulate his older brothers, and be as tough as he thought they were.

"Hey, it's okay now." She wiped the tears and dirt from his cheeks as he buried his head against her again.

"Are you still going to kill me?" he muttered.

She laughed softly as she hugged him. "No, but I will next time."

"It's a deal," he promised fervently.

He pulled away from her, wiping the tears from his face as his gaze traveled behind her. His eyes widened in surprise as his face turned thirteen shades of red. Isabelle frowned as she turned to see which one of her brothers had pulled them from the hole. By the look on Julian's face, it had to be Ethan; he was the one that Julian most admired.

Her breath froze in her chest as her eyes locked on a pair of perturbed onyx ones. Stefan stood stiffly, his jaw locked, dirt, sawdust, and sweat coated his strong boned, handsome face. His shirt was off to reveal his broad chest and wide shoulders. Muscle and sinew rippled beneath the layers of dirt, and sweat, coating him. His stomach was ridged with even more muscle, and Isabelle suddenly understood the term washboard abs as her mouth went dry.

She swallowed nervously as her gaze slowly traveled over his narrow waist before moving further down. The filthy jeans he wore clung to his hard, well muscled thighs and the obvious bulge between his legs. Her heart leapt into her throat as her eyes traveled back up. Thick dark hair curled over his chest, circling his nipples before traveling down in a V that would have drawn her attention lower again if she hadn't adamantly refused to look. She couldn't look back down there again, it did odd things to her body that she didn't understand, or appreciate.

Her gaze slowly traveled back to his face. It was magnificent. His jaw was square and hard, with dark bristles just beginning to show along the firm line of it. His cheekbones were high and sharp, his nose narrow, and finely chiseled. His lips were full and hard, and compressed into a tight line. Isabelle shuddered as the sudden desire to kiss those lips tore through her. It took all she had to stop her knees from shaking.

He was dangerous looking and he radiated an aura of power that shook her. She wished that Julian was still in her grasp so she could use him as a barrier against Stefan. Use him as a barrier against the racing of her heart, her suddenly dry throat, and the fierce urge to touch him that was wracking her.

"You ok?" he asked in a deep voice that sent small shivers of delight through her.

Isabelle nodded slowly, not trusting herself to speak. She had thought, hoped, prayed, that the reaction she'd had to him last night had been some kind of fluke. She was dismayed to realize that it wasn't. She wanted to flee into the woods and hide until he was long gone.

She didn't want to be anywhere near him, and she fervently wished that he would stop staring at her like he wanted to devour her. Stop staring at her like he could see straight into her soul. It was a look she had often seen on her father's face when he looked at her mother, and she didn't want it directed at her. Anger and resolve stiffened her spine.

"Thank you," she said coldly.

Humor flickered through his eyes as his gaze traveled slowly over her. Isabelle stiffened even more as he seemed to undress her with his eyes. She scowled at him as he finally met her gaze again. "No problem."

Isabelle forcefully turned away from him and draped her arm around Julian's shoulder. "Let's get you cleaned up."

Julian shrugged her arm off and straightened his shoulders. "I'm good."

Isabelle grit her teeth in exasperation. When he had needed her help, she'd been there for him, but now, when she desperately needed his, he was abandoning her. "Fine," she grated.

"Thank you," Julian said to Stefan as he strode proudly by, showing absolutely no sign of the immediate death he had just faced.

Willow burst out of the woods, slamming into him, and knocking them both to the ground. "Hey!" Julian yelled angrily.

"Oh, sorry!" she cried as she jumped to her feet.

Isabelle sighed as she ran a hand tiredly through her still wet hair. If any of her younger siblings survived to maturity, she would be truly amazed. Vicky and Abby suddenly appeared behind them, their eyes wide as they caught sight of everyone. Isabelle glowered at them as they came forward, openly admiring Stefan, before stepping to the edge of the hole. "And where were you two?" she demanded.

"We were tired!" they both cried in unison.

"How were we supposed to know that they were in trouble again?" Abby demanded.

"Yeah!" Vicky yelled.

Isabelle took a deep breath as she attempted to control her anger and frustration. It wasn't only them that she was annoyed with, but also herself, and Stefan, and the whole damn world for playing this cruel joke on her. "By Willow's tone," she retorted.

They both gave her identical looks of disbelief as they propped their hands on their hips. "Willow always panics when they do something wrong! We just thought that they had dared the twins to do something stupid again!" Abby protested her green eyes flashing angrily as she gazed rapidly between Isabelle and Stefan.

"I do not!" Willow protested vehemently.

"Wow that is deadly!" Vicky breathed as she gazed into the hole.

"No kidding!" Isabelle snapped.

Vicky looked at her in surprise, not used to catching Isabelle in a bad mood, or even having Isabelle yell at them. "What's got you in such a mood?"

Isabelle's jaw clenched as she bit hard on her bottom lip to keep from exploding. "He could have been killed."

"So could you."

Isabelle's eyes snapped to Stefan. He was standing in the same spot, his arms folded causally over his chest. There was an amused gleam in his eyes that set her teeth on edge.

It was as if he knew that he was really the reason she was perturbed and he was thoroughly enjoying it. As if he knew exactly what had been on her mind when she looked at him.

She realized with a jolt that he had. Just as she had known exactly what that hungry gleam in his eyes had meant. He was a very handsome man after all; of course he knew what he did to a woman. Pride and anger stiffened her spine as she tilted her chin defiantly. It didn't matter what he knew, she had every intention of staying as far away from him as possible.

A small smile curved his full, hard mouth as his hungry gaze traveled leisurely back over her. A small tremor began to wrack through her as his gaze burned into her, causing her skin to warm everywhere that it touched upon. When it lingered upon her heaving chest, Isabelle was horrified at the prickling sensation that caused her nipples to tingle and harden. She forced herself to shove the new sensations he awoke aside as she glowered at him. She didn't know what he found so amusing about this situation, but she didn't find anything at all funny about it.

"Yeah Issy!" Vicky cried grabbing hold of her arm. "You are so lucky that Stefan was coming back to the house!"

Yeah, she was the luckiest person alive, Isabelle thought in annoyance as Stefan smirked smugly. She turned away from him, taking a deep breath as she forced herself to remain calm. She had to get away from him, all of them. All of her fear for Julian, and herself was gone, but there was a new fear gnawing at the pit of her stomach. One that was threatening to strangle her.

She hurried back to the path, ignoring Vicky and Abby's chatter as she mumbled a quick thanks to Stefan. It took all she had to hold her head high and keep on walking as she felt his gaze burning into her back with every step she took.

CHAPTER 5

Stefan wiped the sweat from his brow as he grabbed a bottle of water and dumped it over his head. His gaze settled on Delia, Jess, Vicky, and Abby. They had set up lounge chairs and donned their bathing suits in order to absorb the sun. Suntan lotion, magazines, and a radio were scattered around them and soft music drifted through the air.

They looked extremely relaxed as they flipped through the pages of magazines. He couldn't hear what they were saying, nor did he particularly care. He knew for a fact that Jess's ability to communicate about anything other than fashion, or hair, was severely limited. He didn't know how someone who went to college could know so little of the world, but somehow, she had managed to do it.

He shook his head as he grimaced slightly. Raising an eyebrow his gaze ran back over them as he wondered why Isabelle wasn't with them. From what he had gathered, Isabelle was usually with one relative or another, so he'd assumed she would be with her sisters and the other girls.

Popping the top off his bottle, he drank a long swallow of water to wet his parched throat. Ethan appeared beside him, his gaze settled on the quartet spread across the lawn. "I wish I could work on my tan," he grumbled as he grabbed a water bottle.

Stefan nodded his agreement as he took another swig of water. "Why isn't Isabelle with them?"

Ethan laughed. "Isabelle, work on her tan? That's a joke."

Stefan looked at him in surprise. "Why is that?"

"Isabelle is one of those people that are always on the move. Plus she's a bit of a tomboy, lounging around in the sun is about as appealing to her as eating a box of ants," Jack answered as he appeared beside Ethan.

Stefan's eyebrows rose in surprise. The last thing he would have pegged Isabelle as was a bit of a tomboy. She was too much of a tempting, desirable woman to ever be pegged as anything else. He had pictured her spending hours brushing her hair to get it to shine like it did, painting her nails, and flipping through fashion magazines in order to keep up on the latest styles. The picture they painted of her though didn't fit in with his image at all.

"Plus, she's cleaning the house," Ethan added.

"What?" Jack roared.

Ethan's grin grew as he turned to face an irate looking Jack. "I told her not to bother, but apparently, and I quote, 'We're all filthy slobs'."

"I like being a slob!" Doug declared as he dropped his hammer and stormed over to Ethan. "Go over there right now and tell her to stop!"

Ethan laughed as he shook his head. "While I'm at it why don't I jump in front of a charging bull, wave my red flag, and hope that he stops," he retorted. Doug's eyes narrowed as Jack folded his arms firmly over his chest. "Besides, what harm can it do?"

Their scowls deepened. "She'll have us smelling like women!" Jack snapped.

Stefan stifled a laugh as he turned away from them. "How much do you expect her to get done in one day?" Ethan retorted.

"Knowing Isabelle that house is already repainted, with scented candles, and potpourri everywhere!" Doug yelled.

"Why is she all by herself?" Stefan interrupted.

They looked at him in surprise before shrugging absently. "Vicky and Abby had enough of work yesterday," Ethan answered.

Apparently they were all used to Isabelle being on her own, and not having any help. He didn't know why, but for some reason the thought of that didn't sit well with him. "And Jess?"

They all looked at him as if he were crazy. "I don't think she wanted to help," Jack answered.

Stefan nodded, but didn't say anything. Of course Jess wouldn't want to help; the idea of getting her hands dirty was enough to make her squirm her way out of anything. He groaned inwardly, wondering for the thousandth time why he was still with the girl in the first place. He had his answer almost immediately, she was good in bed. She was also whiny, clingy, and truly beginning to grate on his last nerve. The sex was becoming not worth the trouble.

A flash of wide violet eyes unwittingly blazed through his mind, and to his amazement, he found himself hardening instantly. He could clearly recall how Isabelle had felt when he had seized hold of her tiny waist, a waist so narrow that his hands had nearly encircled it. Her skin had been warm, silky smooth, and utterly tempting.

For a moment, the touch of her had blazed through him and aroused him instantly. She smelled of apples, and fresh dirt, and her underlying natural scent had assaulted him instantly, and aroused his baser instincts. He hadn't wanted to release her, and since he'd touched her he hadn't been able to get her out of his head. Or his cock, he thought ruefully.

He shifted uncomfortably as the force of his erection became almost unbearable. "Go stop her Ethan," Jack ordered briskly.

Ethan sighed as he ran a hand through his tangled hair. "Leave her be Jack. It's not going to hurt us to have a clean house, and clothes. Besides Jess is staying there too, and Isabelle is the one that realized that if there's no human food in the house she'll think it's odd. You know that none of us would have thought about it. She sent David and dad shopping for groceries."

"That's fine and dandy, but...."

"Jack," Ian interrupted as he approached them. "Leave her be. You know how Isabelle is when she's upset about something; this is just her way of working things out."

Jack's scowl faded as he nodded slowly. "What is she upset about?" Doug demanded. "Oh, Julian."

"Yeah," Ethan said tiredly. "I had a long talk with the four of them last night."

"Did you tell your parents?" Doug demanded.

"I wouldn't have, but..."

"They could have both been killed," Ian finished for his brother.

Stefan glanced back at the four people stretched out in the sun, his aggravation mounting. He was half tempted to walk over there, drag Jess up, and force her to go help Isabelle. The house was obviously a bachelor's place, and even he'd been a little amazed by the amount of dust and filth in it. Jess had complained endlessly about it yesterday, the least she could do was help clean it today.

"Yeah, so if this makes her happy than let her be," Ethan said firmly.

"Anything for Isabelle," Jack muttered, but there was a soft smile on his face.

Stefan raised an eyebrow as he turned back to them. "What, are you scared of her?" He was trying to sound light, but there was a tension in him that he'd never quite experienced before.

"Of Isabelle? Hardly!" Doug snorted. "She growls like a grizzly, but inside she's as mushy as a teddy bear. We just hate seeing her unhappy."

"Isabelle's our favorite," Jack said jokingly.

"Hey!" Ethan and Ian objected.

Jack laughed at them as Doug eagerly nodded his agreement. "Well she is," he told them, biting on his lip as he attempted to keep from laughing at them.

"That's good to know," Ethan mumbled.

"Oh, she's your favorite too, and you know it!"

Ethan grinned as he ran a hand through his hair again. "What is this, break time?" Mike demanded as he strolled over to them. "Someone could have told me."

"Trust me, this isn't a break that you want to be involved in," Jack muttered.

"Why is that?" Mike inquired.

"We were talking about Isabelle cleaning the house."

Mike grimaced as he shrugged his shoulders. "It needs a good cleaning; we've been over here so much that it's filthy, even by our standards. Leave her be, she's upset about Julian. They both could have been killed."

"Both?" Stefan asked in surprise. "It was Julian that was hanging inside the pit."

They turned to look at him, their faces hard, and their eyes dark. "She never would have let go of him," Ethan said with a shudder. "She'd have followed him into that pit first."

Stefan opened his mouth to protest that statement; no one would follow someone else to their death, no matter how much they cared for the person. Then he thought about Isabelle hanging over the side, holding on to her brother for dear life. She wouldn't have let go, he realized with a start. A shiver of fear raced up his spine as he recalled the dangerous spikes at the bottom of that pit.

Suddenly he understood why the people gathered around him were so determined to make sure that she was happy, why they capitulated to her wishes. He didn't know anyone else that would have gone over that edge. They would have tried to save Julian, yes, but fear for their own life would have caused them to release him before they went over too. It was a shock to realize that he actually respected and admired her for it. He couldn't recall a woman he had ever felt that way about.

"It's a good thing you were there," Ethan said.

Stefan nodded briskly. They had already thanked him more than enough for his liking. "Yeah," he replied absently. He didn't know why he'd gone back to the house yesterday, but he'd suddenly felt a compelling urge to make sure that everything was all right. He'd run into Willow along the way.

"So, how serious is it with you and Jess?" Ian asked with a sly grin.

"Not at all, why?"

He shrugged as his gaze wandered out to the field. "She's pretty hot, but I thought because you guys were dating that it was serious. I know I don't stick around with one woman."

Stefan laughed softly as he ran a hand through his hair. "Neither did I, but when you get to be my age one night stands become tiring. It becomes a little more convenient to just stay with one woman for a little while."

Ian grinned. "Tiring? I think not."

"Oh, trust me, they do." He knew how Ian felt; he had felt that way in the beginning, for over two hundred years actually. Then, things had changed, and not for the better. Stefan forced his mind away from the past, it was better forgotten anyway. He forced himself to focus his full attention on the disbelieving faces surrounding him.

"Never!" they all declared loudly.

They couldn't even put a dent in the amount of women that he'd had, so there was no point in trying to tell them that they were wrong. They would learn it eventually. "Well if you want a turn at Jess..."

Ian's eyes widened as he smiled slyly. "Thanks, but no. She's sticking around here a little too long for my liking."

"There's the queen of clean now," Jack muttered.

Stefan's gaze darted toward the house. Isabelle had come outside and was making her way toward the group gathered on the lawn. The gold highlights in her dark hair flashed in the bright light. Her long, bare legs were delicately curved, and gleaming in the sun as she swiftly covered the ground toward the quartet on the lawn.

To his amazement, he found himself growing even harder as he admired the gentle sway of her hips, the soft bounce of her full breasts. She stopped by her sisters, and one of the twins dropped their legs down for her to sit at the end of the chair. She bent forward, revealing the soft curve of her back, and a patch of creamy skin that caused his mouth to water.

Isabelle closed her eyes and took a deep breath as she allowed some of the tension in her shoulders to ease. She was stiff, tired, achy, and absolutely filthy from attacking the house with a vengeance. The bathrooms were done, the kitchen cleaned, the living room dusted and vacuumed. She only had the mound of laundry left to get through, and the dusting in the dining room. She desperately needed a break though, and some fresh smelling air.

"You look beat Issy," Abby said gently.

She nodded tiredly and shifted her weight as the plastic of the chair bit into her upper thigh. Giving up on being able to get comfortable, she slid off the chair to sit on the cool, refreshing ground. Her fingers instinctively curled into the prickly grass. Inhaling deeply, she savored the fresh scent as the sun beat warmly down on her. She tilted her head back to get the full extent of its soothing rays, a soft smile played over her mouth.

"Do you want help Issy?" Vicky asked.

"No that's all right, I'm almost done. What are you guys up to?"

"Working on our tans," Jess replied, her tone clearly stating that she thought Isabelle was an idiot for asking the question.

Isabelle stiffened slightly as a flash of anger washed through her. Most of her tension came flooding back as she opened her eyes and turned to look at Jess. She was leaning back in the chair, her long legs stretched out before her as she tilted her head to stare at Isabelle disdainfully. Her anger notched a level higher as she met Jess's clear blue eyes. She remembered Jess as being fun, energetic, and mischievous. She didn't know what had happened to the little girl, but she was beginning to greatly dislike the woman.

When she had asked Jess if she would help her clean the house, Jess had sniffed contemptuously and informed Isabelle that she didn't clean her own house, she sure as hell wasn't going to clean someone else's. Isabelle had managed to keep her temper then, mostly because cleaning the house was the only hope she had to keep her mind focused on something other than Stefan. However, her mission had failed, and her anger had mounted with every passing moment that she had scrubbed, cleaned, dusted, and vacuumed with him consistently filling her thoughts. Jess's attitude, on top of her own misery, was pushing her very close to a snapping point.

"We were talking about how Jess and Stefan met," Vicky said quickly, obviously detecting Isabelle's mounting ire.

"Go on Jess," Abby urged eagerly.

"We met at a bar, by my school," Jess said, yawning as she stretched her arms before her.

"How long have you been together for?" Vicky inquired.

"Three months."

"So it's serious then?" Abby's eyes took on a dreamy look.

Isabelle felt her tension growing again as she grit her teeth and tried to remain relaxed. She had been determined to try and forget about him, she didn't want to hear about him now. "I guess so," Jess replied absently. "I mean he did come up here with us."

"He is so hot!" Vicky gushed.

Isabelle shifted uncomfortably as a flash of black, piercing eyes swept through her mind, bringing with them a wave of heat that far exceeded the warmth of the day. "He's even hotter in bed," Jess replied slyly.

Isabelle's eyes flew open as her mouth went dry and her heart leapt into her throat. A fierce wave of something like jealousy swept through her. Never before had she felt jealous of anything, but she was fairly certain that was the emotion that was clutching at her chest right now. It scared the hell out of her, at the same time that it made her want to rip her hair out in aggravation and disgust. What the hell was the matter with her? She wanted nothing to do with him; she had nothing to be jealous of.

Delia laughed softly as Abby and Vicky stared at Jess in disbelief. Their eyes darted to Isabelle as their mouths gaped open. They weren't used to hearing such blunt statements, and by the blushes creeping up their cheeks they weren't comfortable with them either. "Uh yeah," Vicky muttered shyly.

Jess and Delia laughed. Isabelle's eyes narrowed at the obvious enjoyment they took in her sister's discomfort. Isabelle opened her mouth to let loose with her anger, but Abby seized hold of her shoulder. Gritting her teeth she turned to look at Abby, who shook her head slightly. It took all she had to remain silent, but in the face of Abby's obvious pleading, she managed to do so. They were Kathleen's daughters, and her mother wouldn't be at all happy if she started a war with them.

Even though she didn't say a word, her moment of relaxation had been completely ruined. "The laundry should be done," she mumbled.

"Did I make you uncomfortable Isabelle?" Jess asked with false sweetness.

Isabelle's temper flash boiled as her gaze locked fiercely on Jess's. A soft, mocking smile curled Jess's mouth as she stared down at Isabelle with malicious amusement in her eyes. She was about to let her temper fly, to hell with the consequences, when a shadow fell over her. Isabelle's mouth instantly went dry as fear seized hold of her.

Instinctively she knew who it was, knew that he was there without even having to look at him.

"Stefan!" Jess greeted. "We were just talking about you."

"I heard," he replied coldly.

Isabelle's face flooded with color at the thought of what he had just overheard. She realized then that the sounds of the saws, and hammering, had stopped. Her face grew even redder as she wondered if everyone at the building site had heard too. Swallowing heavily, she forced herself to look up at him.

His shoulders were so broad that they blocked out the sun behind him, throwing him into sharp relief against its bright rays. His hair was damp, and tussled as it fell boyishly across his dirt streaked forehead. For a moment Isabelle couldn't breathe from the force of his enticing dishevel, and the hungry gleam in his onyx eyes.

"Good thing it was nothing bad," Jess said laughingly.

Stefan forced his gaze away from Isabelle's wide violet eyes, and beautifully blushing face. He folded his arms over his chest as he turned his attention to Jess. She smiled slyly at him, a seductive twinkle in her bright blue eyes. The small blue bikini she wore revealed almost every inch of her long, slender, tanned body. She was sleek with sweat, and suntan lotion, a condition that would have turned him on at any other point in time, but did nothing for him at the moment.

He had been on his way over here when he'd overheard the conversation. For some reason, instead of laughing at it like he normally would have, it had angered him. The discomfort he had felt radiating from Vicky and Abby, and the joy that had poured out of Jess and Delia, had not helped the anger.

If he were truly honest with himself though, he'd admit he didn't want Jess talking to Isabelle about their relationship, and what went on between them. Which was absolutely ridiculous, considering the fact that they were staying in the same room, and everyone knew what went on between them.

His gaze returned to Isabelle as she climbed swiftly to her feet. Her hair was wet with sweat; it was a tangled mass in its loose ponytail as it clung to her shoulders and face. Dirt streaked her delicate nose, and high cheekbones, emphasizing her tomboyish nature. The clothes she wore were filthy as they clung damply to her, emphasizing her full breasts, slender waist, and gently flaring hips. Even though she was a mess, she was still exquisitely beautiful, and the most tempting thing he had ever laid eyes on. The erection that he'd managed to rid himself of suddenly reared back to full, excruciating life.

Isabelle stared silently back at him, her heart hammering as she struggled to breathe normally. She was acutely aware of how awful she looked, especially compared to Jess, and for some strange reason that fact bothered her. She didn't want him to see her looking like this. Silently, she cursed herself for behaving like an idiot. She didn't care what he thought of her, or how she looked, she wanted absolutely nothing to do with him, or his bitch of a girlfriend.

There was a gleam in his eyes though, a gleam that left her breathless and trembling. A gleam that told her that he didn't think she looked as awful as she felt. In fact, he looked as if she was the most desirable woman in the world, as if he wanted to devour her. A fierce shiver made its way down her spine, it caused her to tighten, and harden, in places that she had never felt sensitive in before. Part of her desperately wanted to be devoured by him, while the saner part wanted to run screaming for help and never look back.

"You look tired Stefan, why don't you take a break?" Jess's voice dripped with so much ice that it was able to tear Isabelle's gaze away from Stefan.

Apprehension filled her as she turned slowly to look at Jess. She was focused on Stefan, but her amusement was gone as Jess stared at him with narrowed eyes and a locked jaw. Then she glanced at Isabelle, Jess's eyes flashed with malice before she turned back to him. Isabelle bit into her lip as she took a step to the side, eager to get away from all of them.

"I have to get the laundry," she said quickly, desperate to escape.

"Why don't you wait, I'm sure that Jess will help you," Stefan said coldly.

"I offered, but Isabelle said that she didn't need my help," Jess replied sweetly.

Isabelle's mouth gaped open in disbelief as she spun back around. Jess was smiling sweetly up at Stefan, batting her lashes as if she were the most innocent thing in the world. Exasperation blazed to life in Isabelle as her eyes narrowed and her hands fisted at her sides. "The hell I did!" she snapped, unable to keep her temper under control for a moment longer. It usually took a lot to truly annoy her, but when she did blow, she could put Mount Vesuvius to shame with the force of her explosion. Jess's lie, on top of everything else that was going on, was the final straw.

Stefan's eyebrow lifted in surprise as he tried to suppress a smile of amusement. It was quite obvious to him that the teddy bear Doug had described was gone, and the grizzly bear had leapt forward. He'd seen her sister subtly tell her to keep her mouth shut before, and had felt Isabelle trying to control her anger at Jess, but it seemed as if her control had snapped. The fire in her eyes, and her rigid stance, were both fetching and interesting.

"Of course I did," Jess lied easily.

Stefan found his amusement fading as she persisted in the lie. Vicky and Abby leapt to their feet. "Come on Issy, we'll help you," Vicky said as she pulled at her arm.

Isabelle shrugged them angrily off, determined to bring Jess's lie to the forefront, and wipe that smirk off of her face. "Mom," Abby whispered so softly that Stefan barely heard her.

Isabelle closed her eyes and took a deep breath as she struggled for control. She longed to lash out at Jess, to put her in her place, but she couldn't. She just couldn't do anything to hurt her mother. Jess wasn't worth it. She turned quickly on her heel, determined to put as much distance between herself, and Jess, as possible.

"See that proves that I'm right," Jess said victoriously.

Stefan's anger continued to mount as he turned back to her. She smiled seductively up at him as she leaned victoriously back in the chair, stretching her arms behind her head in a gesture meant to make her breasts more alluring. She failed miserably. "We both know that you're lying."

Her eyes narrowed as she leaned forward in the chair, her blatant attempt at seduction forgotten. "You would believe her over me?" she demanded haughtily.

He smiled coldly as he nodded. "Yes." He didn't wait for her reply as he turned and headed back to the house, her anger beat against his back as he moved swiftly across the ground.

CHAPTER 6

Stefan leaned back in his chair as he surveyed the group of people surrounding him. The dining room was exceptionally large, but it seemed minuscule with everyone crammed into it. Ethan, Ian, Aiden, and Doug were sitting on the left side of the mahogany table, casually sprawled in their chairs. Mike sat across from him at the head of the table while David, Jack, and Jess took up the right side.

Jess's hand rested lightly on his thigh as she teasingly drifted it toward his crotch and then back down again. Her earlier ire at him seemed to have been forgotten. He seized hold of her hand, and for the fifth time, dropped it back down. Even if she wasn't still mad, he was, and he was also more than a little disgusted with her. She shot him an angry look, but he turned his attention away from her as he listened to Ethan argue with Aiden and Ian over the best way to finish off the last bathroom in the new house.

"You're not going to be living there!" Ethan announced.

"We will when we come home for vacations!" Aiden snapped.

"Why are you guys even arguing about this? You know that Isabelle is going to be the one that decides what color tile you use," Mike interrupted.

The two sides scowled at each other, but they quit squabbling over blue verses green. "Where is Isabelle?" Doug asked.

Stefan had been wondering the same exact thing. "Finishing the laundry," Ethan answered absently.

"We really are going to smell like a girl," Jack muttered miserably.

"This room looks pretty good, and it smells like lemons instead of flowers" David defended. "Did you know that those curtains were blue?"

"I'd forgotten," Doug replied with a laugh.

"It is nice to have the place clean again, but if my laundry comes back smelling like flowers, or perfume, I am not going to be happy," Jack said.

"Trust me Jack, perfume won't help you."

Stefan's gaze darted to the doorway as Isabelle swept in. A red bandanna was wrapped around her thick hair but strands of it had straggled free to curl around her exquisite face. Her high cheekbones, delicate chin, and small nose were now free of dirt to reveal the creamy perfection of her porcelain skin.

A barrage of sexual images flashed through his mind, images of what he would like to do to that lithe body, and what he would like it to do to him. Jess's stroking hand had been doing nothing to arouse him, but now blood rushed to his groin and caused him to harden painfully. He shifted uncomfortably and grit his teeth against the lust that filled him.

"There are times when I wish I hadn't had a hand in raising you," Jack mumbled unhappily.

"Trust me Jack, so do I," she replied with a laugh.

She smiled at him as she ruffled his dark hair. Jack scowled at her as he fixed his hair and smiled softly. Isabelle grabbed the chair from the corner and shooed Jack over to wedge it between him and Mike. She purposely kept her gaze away from Stefan and Jess. Try as she might to ignore him, she was still acutely aware of his presence, and the aura of power that he radiated.

"The tile in the bathroom is going to be a light rose, and the counters are going to be emerald green," she told them as she settled into her seat.

"Oh Isabelle!" Ian moaned.

"Don't oh Isabelle me, mom and I already ordered them," she retorted as she fiercely returned the dark scowls her brothers gave her.

"It's so girly!" Aiden complained.

"You'll be at school most of the year!" she shot back.

"Yeah, but I don't want to get sick every time I come home."

Isabelle rolled her eyes as she folded her arms fiercely over her chest. "Just make sure that you clean up after yourself when you do."

Ian slapped Ethan forcefully on the back. "Sure you don't want to change your mind and come to college with us?"

Ethan just shook his head. "At least I can decide my room and bathroom," he mumbled.

"Well actually..." Isabelle started.

"Don't even think about it!" Ethan interrupted fiercely.

Isabelle smiled sweetly at him. "Who's going out tonight?"

"We are!" Ian and Aiden responded eagerly.

"Jack and I are going too," David said. "What do you need?"

Her eyes involuntarily flicked toward Stefan as she turned toward them. He held her gaze for a charged moment. She was certain that the air sizzled with electricity before she tore her gaze away. "I just need some cleaning supplies, and other stuff." She was amazed that her voice sounded completely normal.

David nodded and leaned back in his chair. "No problem, make a list."

"Thanks." She stood abruptly and had to fight the urge to flee from the room. "The last load should be done. You guys will be glad to know you won't have to buy new clothes this week, you'll actually have clean ones."

"I like buying new clothes!" Jack yelled at her quickly retreating back.

"You'd better fold them nicely!" Ian taunted.

"Go to hell Ian!" she shouted from the hall.

"I'm going to be living there on school breaks!" he shot back.

"You keep it up and you'll be living there a lot sooner!"

"You keep it up and you're going to wake up to a bed full of snakes," Ethan told him with a smile.

Ian shuddered and leaned back in his seat. "Snakes?" Jess asked in surprise.

"Yeah," Ethan shivered as he made a face.

"What are you talking about?" Jess demanded.

They exchanged amused glances that caused Stefan's curiosity to be peaked. "Ian, Ethan, and Isabelle got into a fight when she was what?" Mike asked.

"Fifteen," Ethan answered.

"Ian was thirteen, and Ethan was seventeen. I don't remember what it all started over."

"Ethan dared me to take all her clothes and throw them out the window," Ian recalled, a small smile on his face as his eyes took on a distant gleam.

"So I did," Ethan said with a bright grin. "She threw a fit. To get even with us she put rubbing alcohol in my aftershave bottle, and threw all of Ian's clothes into the lake."

Stefan leaned forward; a smile curved his mouth as he listened to the story. They all wore amused grins and their eyes twinkled mischievously. They picked up the story where one left off with the easy rhythm that only people who know each other so well could create. "So, of course we put pink hair dye in her leave in conditioner. You know, the one that women leave in for over an hour or so," Ian said happily.

"You should have seen her!" Jack cried laughingly. "Her hair was this muddled pink color, but her scalp was hot pink!"

"That was a good one!" Mike cried. "They took pictures of her the minute that she walked out of the bathroom. The look on her face was priceless. We all had a good laugh that night."

"Yeah, after you grounded us," Ethan muttered.

They exchanged knowing grins as Ian leaned forward. "So then it was all out war. She put super glue in my shampoo. I had to cut it all off in order to get my hands free, and then it took another week to get all the hair off the palms of my hands. She crept into our room the next night and used Nair on Ethan's eyebrows."

Stefan had to stifle a laugh as he found his amusement growing by the second. He had a clear mental image of a teenage Isabelle creeping silently into her brother's room with the intent of burning his eyebrows off. "That's awful!" Jess cried.

The looks on all their faces told Stefan that they thought it was anything but awful. They thought it was downright hilarious, and he agreed. "It took over a month for them to grow back, and my skin was burnt for two of those weeks," Ethan said happily.

"We have some good pictures of that too," Doug said happily. "Of both of them actually."

"Needless to say, for about a week, no one slept, and we had to buy new bottles of shampoo every day just to make sure that they were sealed tight. Finally, Ian and I cornered her, held her down, and chopped her hair off. It had been down to her waist, we cut it to just beneath her ears."

"I kind of regretted that one," Ian said sadly. "She cried for a week."

"Yeah, that one wasn't as funny," Ethan said ruefully. "But she declared a truce."

"Our mistake was that we actually believed her. We should have known that wasn't going to be the end of it. Two weeks later, when we were certain she really wasn't going to do anything else, she got us. She went out and hunted up dozens of snakes," Ian continued.

"It took her the entire two weeks to get them all. She went out every night, and caught a few more. She waited till we were sleeping, tied our hands to the headboards, and put them in our beds."

"That's awful!" Jess gasped.

They were all smiling now, and Stefan actually found himself chuckling. He couldn't remember the last time he had laughed, but the picture in his mind was vastly amusing. He could only imagine the victorious gleam in her eyes when they had awoken. "It was horrendous," Ethan said with a shudder. "We *hate* snakes! I woke up to them slithering all over me. I've never screamed so loud in my life!"

"Isabelle got good pictures of that too," Jack said. "It was hilarious!"

"Mom freaked out," Ian continued. "No one would come close enough to untie us, and Isabelle refused to. It took a whole lot of threats from our father before she finally relented and took the snakes away. For months afterward we wouldn't go to sleep without making sure that there weren't any still in our room."

"*We* called the truce after that. The only one in our family that can stand snakes is Isabelle, and there isn't anything worse than the thought of waking up to them again," Ethan said.

"Needless to say, we declared Isabelle the winner of the wars and didn't ever do anything to her again," Ian said.

"Yeah, they focused their torment on me instead," Aiden said. "Unfortunately, I hate snakes too."

Stefan started to really laugh. He could picture how awful, and wonderful, it must have been to grow up in such a large household. "That is the most horrendous thing I have ever heard!" Jess cried indignantly. "That is disgusting and cruel!"

Suddenly they were all laughing. "What's so funny?"

He looked up to find Isabelle standing in the doorway, her brow furrowed questioningly as she balanced a laundry basket against her hip. "We were telling Stefan and Jess about the snake war," Mike answered happily.

Isabelle smiled brightly; her vivid eyes twinkled merrily as she glanced at him. For the first time since he had met her, she was actually smiling at him, and he found it amazing. The smile slipped from his face as he was rocked by a fierce wave of desire that hardened him painfully. Her smile quickly vanished as she ducked her head.

Stefan felt an odd sense of loss as the intimate contact was broken. The breath rushed back into his lungs as he inhaled sharply. He shifted again as his erection suddenly became unbearable. "You named it the snake war?" Jess's eyes were narrowed angrily on Isabelle.

All his humor vanished as a fresh wave of anger washed through him. Isabelle met Jess's gaze, before she turned her attention back to her family. Jess reached out to touch his leg again; he instantly batted her hand away. She glared angrily at him for a moment before plastering a fake smile to her face and turning away.

"We have had a few wars," Ethan answered. "We started to name them when I was about twelve."

"That way we could keep track," Ian explained happily.

"What were some of the other ones?" Jess inquired sweetly. She looked exceedingly innocent, but Stefan could feel the resentment seething within her.

"Well, let's see." Mike leaned back in his seat as he thoughtfully tapped his chin. "There was the ice war, the water war, the fire war...."

"The paint war," Ian chimed in. "Mom almost killed us over that one! I've never seen her as mad as she was that day!"

"What did you do?" Stefan inquired as he tried to divert his attention from Isabelle, and the aching pain in his dick.

"Our mom left out a bunch of paint that she didn't want," Ian explained.

"Red paint," Ethan elaborated. "We found it and decided to paint each other with it. I was eleven at the time, Isabelle was nine, Ian was seven, and Aiden was four."

"I never stood a chance," Aiden declared. "These guys corrupted me!"

"Hey!" the other three protested. Stefan found himself grinning again in response to Isabelle's exquisite smile, and gleaming violet eyes. When she smiled, she was the most beautiful woman he'd ever seen. He found himself oddly captivated by her, and the realization was more than a little unnerving.

"I think we were playing cowboys and Indians," Ethan elaborated. "And we wanted to paint the Indians, or at least that's the way it started. By the time we were done, we were completely covered with it."

"It was in my hair for a week," Isabelle said brightly.

"At least your hair was already darker by then; I looked like Opie for a month!" Ian cried.

They all laughed loudly as their faces, and eyes, took on fond looks of remembrance. Stefan found himself becoming enchanted with the entire group. He couldn't imagine what it must have been like to grow up in such a warm, loving environment. Especially since his own childhood had been a cruel time that he'd spent his entire existence trying to right.

"There was also the dare war. Whoever did the dumbest thing, and survived, won. Ethan won it by throwing himself off of a forty foot cliff," Aiden continued.

"We quit after that move," Isabelle laughed.

"You're lucky you weren't killed!" Jess gasped in horror.

They all exchanged secret smiles as Ethan shrugged. "Broke a few ribs, but I heal quick," he added with a wink that caused all of them to chuckle.

"There was the fish war, the parakeet war..."

"That was the least funny," Isabelle interrupted Ian. "Vicky and Abby cried for a week."

They all looked pointedly at Aiden who threw his hands up defensively. "Hey, it's not my fault! They thought that they were old enough to get involved! Besides, they started it by putting itching powder in my bed."

"He retaliated by turning their ten parakeets lose in December. We found five of them frozen in the front yard, the others disappeared," Mike shook his head disapprovingly.

"Vicky and Abby never got involved in anything after that," Aiden said.

"Yeah, and we've gotten too old to continuously torture each other," Ian said. "But Willow, Julian, Kyle, and Cassidy have taken up where we left off with a vengeance."

"Except they're more likely to get themselves killed," Isabelle muttered. "I think they're crazier than we were."

"You're forgetting about the time that you climbed to the top of that same sycamore tree, and threw yourself out of it in the hope that I would catch you," Ethan reminded her.

"Which you did," she said with a grin.

"You broke my damn ankle!"

"Stop complaining, mom babied you for a week, and I got stuck on diaper duty with Kyle and Cassidy. I definitely got the raw end of that deal."

"Yeah," Ethan smiled fondly. "That was a good week."

Isabelle grinned at him. Stefan watched the exchange with a small amount of awe. It was becoming increasingly clear that Ethan and Isabelle were exceptionally close as they smiled at each other. A small bolt of jealousy ripped through him and he stiffened in surprise. His eyebrows drew together as he forced himself to relax. He was acting like an idiot. He didn't even know the girl, yet he was fully aroused by her, and suddenly jealous of the fact that she had a close relationship with her brother.

He shoved the thought forcefully aside as he forced his gaze away from her. David stood up and leaned his hands on the table. "I think we'd better get going."

Aiden, Ian, and Jack climbed swiftly to their feet. "You got that list?" David asked.

"Oh, yeah." Isabelle chewed on her lip as she shifted the laundry basket, pulled a piece of paper from her pocket, and handed it to him.

David glanced at it and nodded. "No problem."

"Thanks." Isabelle left the room and the other four others filed out behind her.

Stefan sat for awhile as he contemplated his strange thoughts, and behavior. The room was oddly quiet without the laughter that had filled it. Without Isabelle. That realization did nothing to ease his darkening mood. He folded his hands behind his head and pretended to listen as Ethan, Mike, Doug, and Jess exchanged pleasant conversation, and more stories. He didn't hear a word they said, and he found his gaze drawn to the door every few moments. It wasn't until the fiftieth time he looked that he realized he was hoping for Isabelle to reappear.

When she didn't, and Jess placed her hand on his thigh again, he decided that it was time to go to bed.

CHAPTER 7

It was some time later that Stefan left his room. Jess was wide awake, still yelling at him when he slammed the door in her face. He was edgy, restless, and aggravated as hell. He sure as shit wasn't going to waste his time, or energy, fighting with her. She wasn't worth the bother. The thing that bothered him was what had started the fight. For the first time, in his exceptionally long life, he had been unable to keep an erection.

It was only when he'd had a flash of violet eyes that he'd responded in any way to Jess's attempts at seduction. It hadn't lasted long. When Jess had crawled on top of him, a feeling of disgust had instantly flooded him. He had shoved her off, unable to stomach the feel of her any longer.

Now he felt like a caged animal, desperate to escape, as he made his way quickly downstairs. He didn't know what the hell was the matter with him, but he didn't like the feeling at all.

The light in the dining room was still on. He was drawn there by soft laughter, and voices. He walked into the room, pausing as his eyes landed on Isabelle. Her eyes widened in surprise as they met his. For a moment he simply held her gaze as his cock instantly pulsed and throbbed to life with the fierce sexual urge that ripped through him. Fear darted quickly through her bright eyes as she looked quickly away. Stefan remained where he was, stunned by the sheer force of the physical reaction that rocked him.

"Hey, I thought you'd gone to sleep," Ethan greeted.

Stefan shrugged negligently as he walked carefully over to the chair he had abandoned earlier. His physical condition made it difficult for him to walk. "Couldn't sleep."

"Hmm. Got a two?"

"What?" Isabelle asked distractedly.

"A two?" Ethan inquired again.

She glanced at the cards in her hand, barely seeing the numbers on them. Stefan's hungry, dark gaze had made her feel extremely uncomfortable, and edgy. Her blood seemed to be burning in her veins, and that odd tingling sensation was back between her thighs, and in her breasts. She shifted uncomfortably as a fierce yearning, that she didn't understand, began to make its way through her. Silently she cursed herself for stupidly thinking that Stefan wouldn't be coming back down tonight. She should have stayed in her room, buried under a pile of books like she had planned.

"Go fish," she mumbled.

Of course, it didn't help that he looked unbelievably sexy in his lose jeans, and tight, dark blue shirt. His hair was tussled, giving him a boyish appeal that was almost irresistible. Almost, but not entirely. She planned to resist it, and she planned to stay far away from him for now on.

"Isabelle," Ethan said sharply.

"What?" she demanded, aggravated by the strange feelings coursing rapidly through her.

His eyes narrowed as he studied her, his brow puckered. "Are you going to go?"

She blinked at her cards as she tried to force her attention back to them. "Do you have a four?" He tossed a card across the table at her. She scooped it up and dropped her cards onto the table. "Ten?"

"Go fish."

Isabelle reached across and grabbed a card from the deck. "Jess sleeping?" Ethan inquired.

"No," Stefan replied.

Isabelle stiffened as she recognized the scent that was clinging to him. She had smelled it often enough on her brothers, parents, and the stooges, and she knew exactly what it was. Disgust coiled within her stomach at the smell of sex, along with another emotion, one that she was beginning to become uncomfortably familiar with, jealousy. She bit her lip, wanting to bolt from the room, but unable to humiliate herself by doing so.

She lifted her head to find Ethan grinning knowingly as he stared at his cards. "Pig," she muttered.

He glanced up at her, a mischievous twinkle in his eyes. "What?" he inquired innocently.

Isabelle glared at him as she lowered her gaze to her cards again. "When will they be getting back?" Stefan asked.

Isabelle glanced at the clock in the corner, it was after twelve already. "Whenever they feel like it," Ethan answered.

"Hopefully soon," Isabelle added. She had been a little hungry earlier, but her distress over seeing him again made it burn into fierce, brutal life.

"They bring people back for you?" Stefan asked.

"No!" Isabelle cried, her eyes flying to his in horror. Stefan's eyes widened in surprise, he was startled by the amount of alarm in her gaze, and the revulsion in her voice.

Ethan sighed and leaned back in his chair as he dropped his cards to the table. The game was officially over, and Isabelle was more than a little grateful. She couldn't concentrate, and she just wanted out of the suddenly small, stuffy room. "Isabelle doesn't feed off of humans."

"Ethan!" she hissed her intent to leave flying out the window in the face of her brother's casual statement. If she could have reached him she would have firmly kicked him under the table. There were some things that were private and personal, certain things that she didn't want everyone to know. Especially not the frustrating stranger sitting across from her.

"What?" Stefan asked in surprise.

Isabelle scowled fiercely at her brother as he folded his arms over his chest, a brow cocked questioningly as he grinned at her. "It's true!" he protested.

She took a deep breath as she tried to calm her growing anger and resentment. "So how do you feed?" Stefan asked.

Isabelle sighed and dropped her cards. She leaned back in her chair and defiantly met his gaze. "There is such a thing as blood banks. It's what our parents did for us when we were little. I choose to keep doing it."

"Don't want to hurt the humans?"

Isabelle ground her teeth. "That's right," she said coldly, although it was a lie. She didn't like being around them, but she was more afraid that she would accidentally stumble across one that would turn out to be what her mother was to her father. Other than high school, she had tried to keep herself away from as many humans as she could. Now she was afraid that what she had been avoiding her whole life had stumbled into her sanctuary.

"Isabelle and I are the outsiders, the outcasts," Ethan said with an amused grin. "We're not social, especially not with humans. Although, I will at least feed off of them and go out once in awhile. Isabelle stays close to home."

"And why is that?" Stefan was a little surprised by what they were telling him.

Ethan shrugged as Isabelle shifted uncomfortably. She knew that Ethan feared the same thing that she did, but she didn't know if he was going to tell Stefan that. She sure as hell wasn't going to. "We're content here," he replied nonchalantly. "What about you, how old are you exactly?"

Stefan lifted a brow as he looked questioningly at the two of them. Isabelle was sitting silently, her dark head bent as she refused to meet his gaze. He knew that there was something more to Ethan's simple explanation, but it was obvious that neither of them was going to elaborate further.

"Two hundred and sixty seven," he answered as he leaned back and folded his hands behind his head.

Isabelle's head shot up, her eyes were wide as they landed on him. He stiffened as that gaze shot a bolt of lust straight through him. "What exactly can you do?" Ethan asked.

He shrugged but his gaze remained locked on Isabelle's. Biting nervously on her bottom lip she turned away from him. Her long lashes fluttered down to cast shadows over her delicate cheeks. He had to fight against the overwhelming urge to touch her cheek, to see if it was actually as soft as it looked. He scowled as he tore his attention away from her, and back to Ethan's curious gaze. He was beginning to act like a boy in the throes of his first love he realized. And he didn't like it one bit.

"Lots of things," he replied absently.

"Such as?"

"Such as I can move faster than you ever dreamed, my strength is ten times yours, my hearing, eye sight, and other senses are ten times yours. My powers of persuasion, memory erasing, and cloaking my presence could make you look like a new born baby." He knew he sounded arrogant and hostile, but the growing tension in his jeans was becoming almost unbearable, and making him edgy. "I can make humans, and you, see something that isn't really there," he continued in a lighter tone. "That's what I've done to Kathleen, Delia, and Jess."

"Why didn't you cloak your presence from us that first day?" Ethan asked.

"I didn't expect to step out of the car, and into a nest of vampires."

"If your powers are so strong, then how come you didn't sense us before you got here?" Ethan demanded, obviously a little annoyed by Stefan's arrogance. Stefan tried to lighten his tone, and stance, even more. He liked Ethan, and he didn't want Ethan angry because he sounded like a condescending ass.

"Because I wasn't searching for it, and I was busy arguing with Jess over the fucking radio. I knew you were here a few miles down the road, I just didn't expect that this was the place we were heading to. Even if we hadn't come here, I would have come on my own."

They both looked at him in surprise. "Why?"

Stefan shrugged casually as he folded his hands before him. "Because our kind usually doesn't group together like you have. In fact, the most I've ever come across is five together. Usually, we're too territorial to be grouped so tightly together. We prefer to be alone. I was curious about the amount of presence's I sensed here. I would have come here simply to investigate, and discover why there were so many in one place."

Isabelle frowned at him; her eyes darkened as she hesitantly met his gaze. He smiled back at her as he unfolded his hands and leaned forward. "We're happy here," she whispered. "It's why we all stay."

"I can see that, all I said was that it was unusual. I'm surprised that everyone has stayed for as long as they have."

"Where else would they go?" Isabelle asked, her face reflecting her innocence and confusion. "David, Jack, Mike, Doug, and my dad have been friends since childhood. They were all changed around the same time, and by the same vampire. They've always been together, helping each other out. They all helped to raise us; they're like our older brothers. They're our family."

"What about your other siblings, are they all going to stay?"

"Aiden and Ian are going to college, and Abby and Vicky practically have their bags packed, even though they still have three years to go."

Stefan's brow furrowed. "Do they go to school now?"

"We all went to high school," Ethan answered. "Willow will start school in the fall. By the time we're thirteen we're able to control our ability to change. Before that age it can be a little iffy and hard to control, especially when we get mad, or upset. Most of our wars were conducted as full on vampire if we were mad enough."

Stefan studied the amused smiles on both their faces as they exchanged glances. "And none of you ever had a problem at school?" he asked softly.

"I did once," Isabelle admitted reluctantly. "I got really mad at this guy Ralph. He was always making rude, nasty comments to me, and we ended up getting into a fight. I changed right in front of him. Thankfully Ethan was there to help me change his memories afterward; otherwise, I don't know what would have happened. No one else has had any problems though."

Stefan knew exactly what would have happened if Ethan hadn't been there, but it wasn't a pleasant thought, and obviously not one that Isabelle wanted to contemplate. He leaned back in his chair and folded his hands behind his head again. He found himself fascinated by their existence, and how they had survived, and he wanted to learn more. Actually, if he was honest with himself, he wanted to learn more about *her*. "Didn't you have friends that wanted to come over, or school plays, or sports competitions that your parents wanted to go to?"

"Ethan and I didn't join anything. Aiden was on the football and basketball teams, and Ian was on the swim team. Abby and Vicky are cheerleaders. Our parents go to some of the events, but they look like any other spectator when they're there, and unfortunately can't present themselves as their parents. Mike, Doug, David, and Jack go too."

"Why didn't you guys join anything?"

"Like I said, we're the unsociable ones," Ethan replied with a grin.

Stefan truly wanted to know why they were the unsociable ones, but he didn't ask. "What about friends coming over?"

"Aiden, Ian, Vicky, and Abby have brought their friends over, not in large groups, but a couple here or there. We just alter their memories a little when they leave and make them think that our parents are older."

Stefan frowned as he unfolded his hands and leaned forward. "What are you going to do in another ten years, when people begin to question why *you're* not aging?"

"We don't go into town very often. Most people think that we have already moved off, and now live separate lives. The few times that we do go into town, it's always at night, and we alter the memories of the few people we meet. We usually go to Portland where no one notices anything, or California."

Stefan sat silently, slowly digesting everything they were saying. "So, you have no fear of people becoming curious about you?"

"It's very rural here," Isabelle answered. "My graduating class was forty two kids. All of whom went to college, and all of whom no longer live in the area. Our closest neighbor is five miles away, and not once, in the past twenty five years, have they stopped by. Hell, the football team has to travel forty five minutes to get to their closest game. Most people stick to themselves around here, and no one has bothered us yet. I don't see why that would change."

He was stunned by the fact that neither of them had any intention of leaving. "And you just stay here all the time?" he asked.

"We leave sometimes," Isabelle replied softly. "We go to the city too, not as often as the others, but we do. Ethan and I go to California mostly. I love Napa Valley."

He frowned at her as she hesitantly met his gaze. They had led very sheltered lives, where their younger siblings wanted to get out and explore the world, these two were content to stay hidden away. Isabelle was young, vibrant, and the most beautiful woman that he had ever laid eyes on. He couldn't help but feel that she was wasting her extremely long life away. He felt the sudden urge to tell her about all that she was missing, to *show* her all that she was missing.

He ground his teeth in self disgust and anger. He really was turning into an idiot around this girl. She was content in her life, he had no business questioning her motives, or wanting to change her. "What about your parents?" he asked to distract himself from his thoughts. "Do you find it odd to consider them your parents, when they look as young as you?"

Ethan and Isabelle exchanged a quick look; confusion was evident on both of their faces. "No," Ethan answered slowly. "Maybe it seems odd to you, because you were human at one time, but we were raised like this. It's all we've ever known. Trust me; our parents can still scare the crap out of us, no matter how young they look."

Stefan supposed that it wouldn't be odd to him if he was them, but he remembered his parents, and their aging. He couldn't imagine having them with him now; then again, he had lost them when he was too young to even think about what it would be like to have them with him now. They had been dead before he had been changed, dead long before he had reached adulthood. Stefan turned his attention away from the past, determined not to relive it.

"What age did you stop maturing at?" he inquired.

"I just stopped this year," Ethan answered.

"I stopped last year," Isabelle said proudly as she grinned smugly back at her brother. Apparently it was a bit of a sore subject with Ethan that his younger sister had reached maturity before him.

"You stopped at different times?" he asked in surprise.

"Yeah, we don't know exactly how it works, or what makes our bodies decide to stop aging, but Isabelle did before me."

"How did you know you were done?" Stefan asked.

She met his gaze hesitantly. "I just knew. There's no other way to explain it, except that I just *knew*."

"Yeah," Ethan answered. "I woke up six months ago, and knew. At first I'd thought that Isabelle was lying to me about it, to torment me." They exchanged quick smiles. "But that is the way it works. There is no way to know when we'll stop, only when we do. Our powers develop more quickly afterward."

"You don't have any powers until you mature?" he asked in disbelief.

"We have some, we can alter memories a little, but it's extremely draining. If I hadn't been there to help Isabelle with Ralph, she never would have been able to do it herself. We were faster and stronger than humans, but not by much. It isn't until we fully mature that our speed increases, our power of memory erasure becomes stronger, and we can really see and hear a lot better."

"Amazing," he muttered.

"How old were you when you became a vampire?" Isabelle asked softly. She hadn't meant to ask the question, she didn't want to know anymore about him, but she found herself oddly curious about him.

He looked over at her, pleased that she was showing an interest in him, and his life. A little too pleased, he realized with an inward grimace. The girl asked one question about his life and he instantly began to wonder if he could get her into his bed tonight. Then, with an inward groan, he remembered Jess, and his hope evaporated. Maybe he could get into *her* bed. The direction of his thoughts startled him, as well as aroused him to a very uncomfortable state. For crying out loud, she had only asked one stupid question and he immediately leapt to the thought that he could take her to bed. He was acting like a damn idiot.

It was then that he realized they were both looking at him expectantly. He pulled himself out of his lustful thoughts and forced his attention back to the conversation. "Twenty eight," he answered.

She nodded as she slid back in her chair, her gaze darted to the clock in the corner. She was tired, and hungry, and she really needed to get away from Stefan before she found herself even more curious, and attracted to him. Before she lost all resolve to stay away from him completely. "I'm going to go to bed."

She stood suddenly; her chair skidded back with the force of her abrupt movement. "You don't want to wait for them?" Ethan asked in surprise.

"No, I'm tired."

"Good night," Stefan said his voice deep and husky.

Isabelle couldn't suppress the shiver that raced down her spine as his voice seemed to caress, and envelop her. "Good night," she replied as she quickly made her way out the door.

When she left, Stefan was surprised by the odd sense of loss that filled him. If Ethan hadn't been sitting beside him, he knew that he would have gone after her, that he would have stopped her. However he didn't think that Ethan would take kindly to the idea of Stefan hauling his sister downstairs to ravish her. There would be other nights, and better times, to ease his lust.

CHAPTER 8

Stefan was still sitting in the dark dining room two hours later. He couldn't seem to find the energy, or the drive, to go back upstairs and crawl into bed next to Jess. The thought alone caused a cold knot of disgust to form in his stomach. It was past time to end it with her. He'd grown tired of the relationship a couple of weeks ago, but today had been the final straw. Especially now that he had another option set firmly in his head, and he was intent on pursuing it.

Besides being tired of her, he could sense the fanciful thoughts of marriage and children that were beginning to run through Jess's head. He thought that he might like to have that kind of life one day, but definitely not with Jess. She had been fun and easy when they'd first met, but she had long since become a bore.

He found it nicer to have a woman constantly around, and had started adopting girlfriends for short periods of time, instead of one night stands. He had kept Jess around a little longer than most of the others, but it was time to cut the strings. Hell, the only reason he had come up here was to drop her off with her mom, and leave. He'd been thinking about heading up to Canada to explore the wilderness. It had only been the fact that he had run into his own kind, and Isabelle, that had made him stay. He could stay now, and get rid of Jess.

He was not looking forward to the scene that was sure to follow, or the angry environment that it would cause. Maybe it would be better if he waited until Jess went back to school. Then, he thought better of it. He couldn't stand being around her now, let alone another two weeks. It was better to get it over and done with as soon as possible.

He leaned back in his chair as he stared into the dark room. To him, it was as well lit as it had been when all of the lights were on, and he could easily make out every detail. He liked this home, and to his surprise, he actually liked the whole atmosphere of the warm, family environment. He'd never stayed with his own kind for long periods of time, except for Brian, but Brian was part of his past, and he had no intention of seeing him again. The thought brought back memories that he preferred to forget, memories of what he had been, and would never be again.

It was easier to forget about it when he was here. He had never settled down anywhere before, but when he saw how close and secure everyone was, he almost longed to have a place like it for himself. He enjoyed the laughter, the warm familiarity, and the stories. There were bonds of love woven throughout the entire place that would never be broken. Bonds he found himself a little jealous of.

He understood why David, Doug, Jack, and Mike stayed here, even though they were freer than the others to leave. He didn't understand why Ethan and Isabelle seemed determined to stay so far away from the outside world though. They would always have a place to come home to, even if they did go out and see the world.

Then again, he had seen everything that there was to see, and been everywhere. Yet, he had never felt as at peace, and as comfortable, as he felt here. He was glad that he'd found it. One day he might even set up a home of his own somewhere, and settle down for a little while. Although, it would probably be lonely with just him, and he'd probably be bored within a month, but at least he would have a home base to go back to when his wanderlust dimmed again.

Then again, his wanderlust had been dimmed for the last fifty years or so. Ever since he had killed Brenda, he'd felt oddly detached, without a purpose, and tired of traveling the world. His entire existence had revolved around destroying her, and once she was gone, there had been no reason for him to continue on. At first he had at least had

Brian, but when Brian had changed he'd lost Brian's friendship too.

He had only been going through the motions of surviving for awhile now. He just hadn't wanted to admit it to himself. Now, he had a place where he could stay, a place that he actually liked, a place that he felt a little alive in again. David had asked him to stay for as long as he wanted, and Sera and Liam had insisted upon it. At first he had refused their offer, but after tonight, he'd changed his mind. For the first time in awhile he didn't feel as oddly detached, or lonely.

It would be fun to stay here, listening to stories, helping with the house, and getting to know Isabelle better. A *lot* better. He would enjoy taking the time to figure her out, and he would truly enjoy bedding her. There was no doubt in his mind that he would get her into his bed, he hadn't met a woman yet that had refused him, he just didn't know how long it would take. She was very hesitant around him, and for some reason she truly seemed to fear him. Once he got past those two obstacles, he would be home free. He didn't even consider Jess as a possible obstacle, as far as he was concerned, she was already gone.

A small thud in the kitchen drew his attention. Instantly he knew who it was, and his pulse accelerated with the small thrill that traveled through him. Planting his chair back on the ground, he climbed swiftly to his feet. Moving silently through the darkened dining room, and hallway, he stepped into the doorway of the large kitchen.

Isabelle was standing in front of the refrigerator, silhouetted against its dim light. The light blue nightgown she wore ended at mid thigh. His mouth went dry and his dick ached painfully as he savored the sight of her long, shapely legs. The way she was bent allowed him a tempting view of a pair of black, lace panties. He shifted uncomfortably as his hardened cock jumped eagerly in his pants. She was the most tempting thing he had ever seen.

He was certain that even the Goddess Venus could not compare to the lovely vision before him.

She stiffened suddenly and slammed the door shut as her back became ramrod straight. "Don't you sleep?" she asked coldly.

Stefan forced himself to take a deep breath before answering her. "I could ask the same of you."

She turned toward him, her violet eyes bright in the dark. The gold streaks in her hair shimmered and danced in the moonlight, while the dark of it blended into the shadows. It caused a startling effect that highlighted her enchanting beauty. "I was hoping that they had returned."

"Hungry?"

Her eyes flashed dangerously as she tilted her delicate chin. "Not all of us have a ready supply available," she retorted fiercely.

"By all means, enjoy Jess." He nearly snarled the comment, but he couldn't help it. She had him as hard as a rock, and her haughty demeanor was infuriating the hell out of him.

Her exquisite mouth parted as she gaped at him in surprise. "What an awful thing to say! Don't you have any respect?"

Stefan shifted uncomfortably as he leaned his hip against the large counter dividing the kitchen from the tiled entry way. "I wouldn't want to see you go hungry when there's a ready supply available."

It took her a moment to realize that he was mocking her. When she did, her eyes snapped with fury and her hands fisted at her sides. "Are you always such an ass?" she demanded fiercely.

He grinned cockily at her, his white teeth flashed in the dark, his onyx eyes gleamed with the hunger that she was becoming uncomfortably familiar with. A hunger that evoked the strange tingling sensation in her no matter how hard she tried to fight against it. "Most women find me charming."

"I find you infuriating."

"So I've noticed, and trust me, the feeling is mutual."

She blinked at him in surprise. Was it possible that she affected him in the same odd way that he affected her? She quickly shook the thought off. He looked too unperturbed by her presence to be feeling any amount of the desire that was burning through her. Even standing a good ten feet away from him, she could feel the heat of his presence, the force of his power. It burned through her, made her heart hammer, and caused her legs to tremble no matter how hard she tried to fight it. She didn't want this; she didn't want *any* of this.

Her eyes darted toward the narrow opening. All she wanted was to run from the kitchen, and back to the safety of her room. However, she would be within inches of him if she left, and she didn't want to be that close to him, ever. She'd been so certain that he would be in his bed by now, with Jess, and that it would be safe to come out again. She was firmly kicking herself in the ass for her stupidity. After earlier she should have realized that there was never a safe time to come out of her room.

"So, what is it that you don't like about me Isabelle?"

His husky voice sent shivers down her spine. Suddenly she was seized by the insane urge to cry. She had locked herself away to avoid this, and he had walked right into her yard, right into her home! And the absolute worst part of it was that he didn't feel anything like she felt. She had seen the hunger in his eyes a few times, but he didn't seem at all upset by her presence at the moment, not like she was by his.

Maybe she was wrong, she thought hopefully. Maybe he wasn't her soul mate. If he was, than surely he would feel something too. Her parents couldn't keep their hands off of each other, and both of them had told her that there had been an instant connection, even if they hadn't realized it at first. If Stefan wasn't feeling anything, then maybe he was simply just the first man that she had ever been attracted too, and she was wrong about everything else.

Surely she could be attracted to a man, and not have to give her life over to him. Her sisters were forever falling in and out of love. Just because she'd never felt anything for anyone before didn't mean that she couldn't feel it now. That made perfect sense, she decided. He was good looking, amazingly built, and the first vampire she had met outside of her family. Of course she would be attracted to him, but it didn't mean anything, it was only a simple attraction.

"I don't dislike you," she finally answered, and she didn't, he just scared the hell out of her.

"Could have fooled me," he retorted, his voice chillingly cold.

"I um, I need to go to sleep. I'm tired," she managed to stammer out.

"Spent all of your energy cleaning?" The taunting tone of his voice raised her hackles, and her temper. "You should have let Jess help you."

He hadn't meant to goad her, but her obvious need to escape from him as quickly as possible aggravated the hell out of him. Her eyes turned a deeper shade of violet as anger flared through her. At least when she was angry she wasn't looking at him as if he were the wolf, and she was the rabbit that was about to be devoured. Instead she looked as if she wanted to kill him, and he found that he preferred it.

Isabelle clenched her jaw, fully infuriated by the arrogant jerk before her. He completely deserved Jess; they were perfect for each other. "I didn't want to interrupt her important tanning, I'm sure that you wouldn't want her to have any unseemly lines!" she snapped, fully aware of the jealousy that colored her words. She only hoped that he didn't notice it.

Anger flared through him. He had baited her, he had brought out her ire, but he hadn't expected her to turn it back on him. He had expected her to tell him the truth; that Jess had refused to help her, not to have her go along with the lie, and not to have her blatantly remind him of his relationship with Jess. It took all he had not to reply in kind, not to grab her and shake some sense into her. Not to grab her and kiss the fury from her.

Instead, he decided to change tactics. "Why are you scared of me?"

The question had the effect that he wanted as her eyes widened, and her luscious mouth parted in surprise. The anger radiating from her diminished, shock blazed forth. "I'm not scared of anyone!" she cried.

He found that very easy to believe, but something about him truly upset her. While something about her was causing him to damn near burst out of his jeans. He shifted uncomfortably again and moved to the back of the counter in an attempt to try and ease the fierce pressure. He forced himself to keep his gaze focused on her face, and not the thin nightgown that emphasized her delicate curves, and bared her creamy thighs. Thighs he was very tempted to touch, to feel, to taste, to have wrapped around him as he buried himself deeply within her.

He groaned inwardly as he became unbearably hard. He hadn't thought it was possible, he sure as hell hadn't seen it yet, but she looked aroused. Her lips were parted slightly, her breathing had become quicker and shallower, and her eyes had grown darker as they warily met his. He smiled softly as he finally deduced the source of her fear. She was as attracted to him as he was to her, but for some reason she didn't like the feeling, and it frightened her. For some reason, instead of giving into her urges like any sane woman would, she was determined to fight him every step of the way.

Isabelle stood, trembling slightly as the force of his lingering gaze slammed through her body. Everywhere his eyes had touched her was on fire, especially between her thighs. The tightening in her loins, the throbbing that his gaze had aroused was unfamiliar, more than a little frightening, and yet oddly pleasurable. That realization sent a bolt of dismay through her so strong that she almost stumbled backward. She needed to get out of here. She needed to get away from him. He had moved away from the doorway, she would still have to go near him, but at least she wouldn't have to go so close.

"I have to go." Taking a deep breath for strength, she hurried across the kitchen, refusing to look at him as she stepped through the doorway. He reached out and grabbed hold of her arm the second that she stepped out of the kitchen. She cried out in startled surprise as he halted her. His touch seared into her skin and blazed through her entire body as she turned wild eyes on him. "Let go!"

His eyes were dark and dangerous as they met hers. There was a predatory gleam in them that caused her breath to catch in her throat. "Is that what you really want Isabelle?"

The way he said her name sent shudders down her spine, and caused her legs to tremble with longing. "Yes!" she cried, while her entire body screamed no.

"I don't think so."

Before she knew what was happening, he pulled her roughly forward. She gasped in surprise as she was brought up against his massive chest. She didn't even have time to register the heat beneath her hand before he pulled her head back and seized hold of her lips. The world seemed to drop away as his mouth, hard and hot, claimed hers. He moved over her, caressing and stroking her with a ferocity that shook her.

His tongue ran lightly along her lips, tasting her as he nipped softly on her bottom lip. He took advantage of the startled cry that escaped her to invade her mouth with deep, penetrating thrusts as he tasted and teased. Isabelle whimpered in response to the searing waves of heat that burned through her veins as he stroked the roof of her mouth, her teeth, and her tongue.

"Kiss me back Isabelle," he whispered hoarsely as he pulled slightly away from her.

His hand tightened in her hair as his steel arm encircled her waste. His eyes burned into hers with a hunger so fierce that it took her breath away, and she was unable to tell him that she didn't know what he meant. Before she could catch her breath, his mouth recaptured hers. Her heart hammered painfully as a coiling desire wrapped through her stomach, and the tingling in her loins grew fiercer.

This time, when his tongue touched her lips, she parted her mouth willingly to his invasion. His tongue was hot and heavy as he thrust into her, and she hesitantly met it. A shudder rocked through him, causing his arms to tighten around her as he pulled her more forcefully against his chest. The fact that he seemed to be as effected by her kiss, as she was by his, served to make her bolder, and more sure of herself. She eagerly began to mimic his movements, meeting him thrust for thrust as their tongues entwined in a mating ritual as old as time.

She allowed herself to be swept away by the taste of him, and the delicious feelings he arouse in her. The hand that had been pressing against his chest, involuntarily curled into his shirt. The warmth of his chest, the thick muscles that bunched and flexed beneath her palm burned into her hand. The strength and power of him enveloped, and overwhelmed, her senses. All she could feel, all she could taste, was him.

He turned her swiftly, pressing her against the counter. His hard leg braced between her quivering thighs as the hand at her waist began to stroke the small of her back, causing chills to race up her spine. Unable to stop, she pressed herself more firmly against him. The feel of his hard chest against her nipples aroused delicious sensations unlike anything she had ever felt before, or had ever imagined feeling.

She relished in the feel of his body against hers, so strong and different. He was hard, where she was soft, broad where she was small. The rough bristles along his jaw rubbed against her skin, and beneath her hand she could feel the crisp hairs of his chest as he held her within his steel embrace. Leisurely, the hand in the small of her back slid over her hip bones, along her stomach, and left a burning trail across her skin as he stroked and caressed her.

Tremors shook her, her heart hammered in her chest as he clasped her breast through the thin material of her nightgown. Isabelle gasped in surprise as pleasure, and desire, tore through her. Instinctively she arched against him; her hands released his shirt to wrap around his neck. She clung to him as liquid heat spread through her. He rubbed and kneaded her, teasing her hardened nipple with his thumb as she pressed tighter into the exquisite heat of his palm.

He released her mouth to travel down her neck, leaving a trail of burning heat as he nibbled and licked lightly at her skin. Gasping with pleasure, her knees gave out as she was swamped with a passion so fierce that she could hardly breathe through it. His hard thigh served to keep her upright as her entire world became filled with him.

The feel of his thigh between her legs brought something new and unexpected forth. She rubbed herself experimentally against him. A soft gasp escaped from her as a new bolt of pleasure caused her legs to tremble, and her entire body to go weak. He groaned, his hands tightened on her as she rocked against him again.

"Isabelle," he grated hoarsely in her ear.

He seized hold of her waist; his mouth reclaimed hers with a wild frenzy that startled and overwhelmed her. Then, the fear vanished as she found herself consumed by his obvious need. Lifting her easily off of him, he settled her onto the counter. He grasped hold of her calves, his hands burned into her skin as he wrapped her legs around his waist.

Everything was going too fast, the world was spinning as she turned into a quivering mass of nerve endings that tingled everywhere. She knew that she should stop him, stop all of this. This was the last thing that she had wanted, the one thing that she had been denying, but it felt so right, and so unbelievably good. He seized hold of the collar of her nightgown, pulling it roughly down to free her breast. His hard hand instantly seized upon it.

Any protest she might have made died instantly as she writhed beneath his searing touch. The feel of his rough, callused palm on her breast was the most exquisite thing she had ever experienced, and there was no way that she could stop him. His arm wrapped around her waist, dragging her across the counter top, and pressing her tightly against his pelvis. A cry of surprise escaped her as she felt the hard proof of his fierce arousal, pressing against his jeans, and rubbing deliciously against the sensitive area between her quivering thighs.

Stefan couldn't seem to get enough, he felt as if he was drowning in the sweet taste of her, in the intense way that she reacted to him. Her skin was as soft and smooth as silk as he ran his hands lightly along her thighs. She smelled of fresh air, soap, and apples, but beneath it all he could smell her delicious, natural womanly scent that pulsed through her blood and body. A scent that enveloped him and burned into him as it heightened sharply, a scent he knew that he would never forget.

She was so wild, so free and uninhibited. She responded to everything he did with small gasps of surprise, and beautiful whimpers that made him even harder, and more frantic to have her. It took all the control he had not to rip the nightgown off of her and take her upon the counter. If it wasn't for the fact that he believed her to be a virgin, he would have done so already, but he didn't want to hurt her anymore than he would when he did enter her.

He needed to slow things down, to get her downstairs, but the feel of her, the taste of her was driving him beyond all reasonable thought of control, and sanity. He wanted her with an urgency he had never experienced before, with a longing that was coming close to making him snap. Beneath his palm, her hardened nipple burned into his skin as he rubbed and kneaded her with a growing sense of urgency. He lifted his mouth to drop soft kisses along her sensitive ear and neck; he traveled down her breast plate, before seizing upon her nipple.

She moaned; her body bucked wildly against his as her fingers wrapped tightly into his hair. He licked and nipped, savoring her as he drew her into his mouth. He suckled upon her until she was squirming with passion, and grinding herself against him with a wild abandon that made him nearly breathless.

"Stefan!" she gasped, unable to stand the tight anticipation building inside of her. She didn't know what was happening to her, but she knew that he could ease her torment, and she desperately wanted him to. Unable to help herself, she opened her eyes and looked down at him. Her breath caught in her throat at the sight of his dark head bent over her breast, her nipple drawn into his mouth as his tongue teasingly circled it. It was the most erotic thing she'd ever seen. Unable to bear the tightening in her body, the passion that enveloped her, she dropped her head to his shoulder.

That was when she smelled it.

She stiffened instantly; her legs fell away from him. All of her pleasure vanished immediately as anger and disgust threatened to choke her. They instantly replaced all of the pleasure that she had been experiencing. "Stop! Get off!" she cried, shoving angrily at his chest and shoulders as she squiggled to break free of his iron grasp.

For a moment, he didn't move. She shoved angrily at him again, but it was like shoving at a brick wall. Tears of frustration and anger welled up in her as she fought back rolling waves of nausea. Finally, he lifted his head from her breast to gaze down at her. She stopped shoving at him to quickly pull her nightgown back into place; embarrassment rose up to mix with the fierce tangle of her emotions.

Clinging to the neckline of her nightgown, she forced herself to lift her chin and stare defiantly up at him. She moved to get off the counter, but he planted his hands on either side of her. His arms shook slightly as his dark, smoldering eyes met hers. There was a mixture of anger and regret in his gaze as he kept her from escaping.

"Isabelle..."

"No! Get away from me!" Releasing her nightgown, she went to shove at his chest again but thought better of it. She didn't want to touch him again, didn't want to feel the heat of his body again. She was afraid she would lose her will if she did. "You just left her bed and now... now..." She broke off, unable to speak through the anger and humiliation. She was appalled at herself, infuriated with him, and all she wanted to do was run to her room, bury herself under her blankets, and forget that this awful experience had ever happened.

His eyes narrowed as they gleamed dangerously in the dark. Isabelle inhaled sharply as his gaze traveled slowly over her. "You didn't mind a minute ago," he replied with a sneer.

The breath rushed out of her as all of her composure snapped and rage sprang forth. Without thinking, she swung her hand up with every intention of hitting him. He caught it easily, holding it tightly within his large, powerful hand. For a moment she was truly frightened as his face became as hard as granite, and his eyes became cold chips of brutal black ice. He looked unbelievably deadly, and she knew that no matter how strong she was, he could snap her in half if he chose to.

"Don't," he growled in warning.

Her eyes blazed with fury, the fear left her gaze, and she glared hatefully at him. Stefan stood for a moment longer, shaking with anger and unfulfilled lust as he met her furious stare. Then, he dropped her arm and stepped away from her before he found himself unable to let her go. Her eyes flickered uncertainly over his face before she slid warily off the counter. He made no move toward her as she tilted her chin, cast him a scathing look, and stormed away.

Sighing angrily, Stefan leaned against the counter and admired the sway of her hips as she hurried away. He closed his eyes against the fierce pressure in his throbbing dick, and the overwhelming disappointment that seized him. Damn, he thought silently. He hadn't meant to say what he had to her, hadn't meant to be so cruel. It was himself that he was mad at, not her. But he had been so aroused, and so irritated when she'd told him to stop, that he hadn't been able to stop himself from getting nasty with her.

And the kick in the ass of it all was that it was *his* fault. He knew that she had been willing, that he could have had her before she even knew what was happening, but he had completely forgotten about Jess. Of course she would smell Jess on him, in him. She was one of his kind after all.

"Shit," he muttered as he slammed his hand on the counter in frustration.

Shoving himself away from it, he stormed over to the door and flung it open. He was desperate to escape from the suddenly stifling confines of the house. A nice dip in the lake was just what he needed to douse his arousal as he attempted to sort out the mess that he had gotten himself into.

CHAPTER 9

Isabelle was in the worst mood of her life when she woke the next day. Not only had she gotten almost no sleep, but that miserable jerk had ruined what little sleep she did get by invading her dreams. Dreams that had left her tingling, and aching, and longing for something that she didn't understand. Dreams that started where last night had ended, and that she didn't want to recall, but couldn't forget.

She dressed quickly in a pair of cut off shorts, and a lose tank top before pulling her hair into a ponytail. Glancing at the basement window she was surprised to note that the sun was just starting to rise. She scowled angrily, she was never up this early, and that was his damn fault too. So was the fact that she was extremely hungry.

Closing her eyes, she took a deep breath in an attempt to calm the fire racing through her veins. She tried to recall the last time she had fed, but she couldn't remember. It had been before Stefan came, four, no five days ago. Hunger suddenly raged through her, hot and burning with its intensity. She had never let herself go this long before, but she'd been so obsessed with him, and trying to stay away from him, that she had completely forgotten about it. Her body was now painfully reminding her.

Hurrying out of the basement, she practically ran up the stairs in her eagerness to ease the pain in her body. She froze in the doorway of the living room when Jess came out of the downstairs bathroom and headed for the kitchen. She looked exceptionally pretty with her light blond hair flowing down her shoulders and back. She was dressed in a pair of formfitting jeans, and a tight tank top that emphasized her full chest, and curvy figure.

Isabelle was suddenly rocked by a fierce bolt of jealousy that shook her to the core and left her breathless. Determined to smother the emotion, she grit her teeth fiercely against it and took a deep breath. She didn't give a shit what the arrogant ass did, or who he did it with. After last night, she knew that she had been right; she had not stumbled across her soul mate, but just the first man that she had ever been attracted to. The man was too infuriating, too arrogant, and way too cruel to ever be someone that she was meant to spend the rest of her life with.

The attraction she had felt for him was officially over, she would not allow herself to be charmed by him ever again. No matter how he made her feel, no matter how much she wanted to respond to him. A fierce flush started to creep up her cheeks as she recalled exactly how wantonly she *had* responded to him. She'd never thought, never imagined, that she could be so easily swept away by passion. She wanted to blame that on him too, but it was the one thing that she was willing to take part of the blame for. She had reveled in his kisses, in his caresses, and if she hadn't smelled Jess...

Isabelle closed the thought off as her face grew even hotter. She didn't want to think about what could have happened, what she would have *allowed* to happen if Jess's scent on him, and *in* him, hadn't assaulted her. It didn't matter anyway; it was never going to happen again. Isabelle closed her eyes and took a deep breath to steady her nerves. It was too damn early in the morning to have to deal with Jess on top of everything else.

"Hi," Jess greeted coldly.

She opened her eyes to find Jess staring at her in anger as she stood with her hand on the handle of the fridge. For a horrifying moment, Isabelle feared that she still reeked of Stefan. It took her a minute to recall that Jess was human, and wouldn't be able to smell him on her. Sagging with relief, she sighed softly as her fear vanished. Jess's hostility had nothing to do with last night. For some reason, she simply didn't like Isabelle, and Isabelle didn't particularly care why.

"Hey," she forced herself to mumble in return.

Jess's blue eyes narrowed slightly as Isabelle moved toward her. "Have you seen Stefan?"

Isabelle looked at her in surprise, a fierce wave of guilt rushed through her. Not only had she acted like a wanton whore last night, but she had done it with Jess's boyfriend. She may not particularly like Jess, and Stefan may not care about Jess's feelings, but Isabelle did. Never had she thought of herself as a careless, hurtful person, but her behavior last night proved that she was. And that was his damn fault too!

"No," she managed to say. "Why?"

Jess's eyes narrowed on her for a moment and it took every ounce of control she had to keep her face as impassive as possible. Inside, she was a seething mass of guilt and horror. Jess finally shrugged and turned away from her. "He wasn't in bed when I got up this morning. He usually doesn't get up until late."

"Hmm," Isabelle grunted in reply. Now she could add lazy to his ever growing list of faults.

The scent of Jess's blood suddenly assaulted her, causing the fierce burning in her veins to become almost unbearable. She closed her eyes, willing the beast to go away as she leaned against the long counter, trying to get her breathing under control. She never should have gone this long without feeding, and she never would have if she hadn't been so preoccupied with trying to avoid the idiot living with them.

In the past three days he had managed to turn her world entirely upside down. She fed the flames of her anger and resentment, determined to use them as weapons against him if he ever tried to come near her again.

Jess's startled cry caused her to jump in surprise, and her eyes to fly open. "What is it?" Isabelle demanded.

Jess spun away from the fridge, her mouth gaping, and her eyes wide as she held up a bag of blood. Isabelle had only a moment to blink in surprise before Jess started making awful, strangled cries, and flung the bag across the room. Isabelle moved quickly, snatching it out of the air as Jess's cries echoed loudly in her ears. "Jess, calm down! Just calm down!" she urged.

"What is *that* doing in the fridge?" she yelled hysterically.

The smell of the blood suddenly wafted up to fill Isabelle's nostrils. A wave of dizziness, so fierce it nearly knocked her off her feet, slammed painfully into her. She stumbled back as her veins seemed to burst into flames, and her body was consumed by a raging inferno of hunger and pain. Her stomach cramped agonizingly. She gasped as she doubled over, her arm wrapped around her stomach as the beast within burst forth. Panting with pain, her vision blurred as she spun to get as quickly out of the room as she could.

She slammed right into a massive chest and stumbled back from the impact of it. Hands seized hold of her arms, quickly righting her and dragging her against the massive wall of flesh. Soft mewls of pain issued from her as the strong hands wrapped around her head and pressed her face firmly against the solid mass of warmth and comfort.

"Jess, it's all right, everything is fine. There is no problem. You saw nothing this morning, not me, or Isabelle. Now, make some pancakes for breakfast."

Shudders wracked Isabelle as Stefan's voice washed over her and his hands gently soothed her hair. The amount of power that flowed from him, and into her, eased the fire burning through her veins as the demon slowly receded. The amount of powers they possessed truly couldn't compare to his. They had to touch people in order to change their memories, but Jess was on the other side of the kitchen, and Isabelle could already hear her opening and closing cabinets as if nothing had happened.

Holding her firmly against his side, Stefan hurried her from the room. He could feel the weakness in her body, the tremors that shook her as he led her swiftly down the basement stairs. Gritting his teeth, he fought back the anger, and worry, that were growing in him as he crossed through the weight room to the door in the wall. He thrust the door open and was immediately enveloped with Isabelle's fresh scent. He inhaled deeply, savoring in the wonderful smell as he closed the door behind him and led her over to the bed. She slumped gratefully onto it, the pathetic bag of blood clutched in her trembling hands.

"Eat," he commanded.

She looked up at him, her eyes flashing rapidly between violet and red. "Could you please go away?" she asked tremulously.

Scowling down at her, he planted his hands on his hips and refused to move. She looked absolutely miserable as she gazed back at him. For a moment he was almost swayed by the pleading look in her eyes, but he was determined to show her that he was the dominate one, and he wasn't about to back down. It was the only thing he had managed to sort out through the long, aggravating night. He would have her, and the sooner she realized that, the happier they would both be.

"Now is not the time to fight," he told her coldly.

"I'm not fighting!" she snapped. "I don't want you to watch me!"

"I'm not going anywhere!" he hissed.

His eyes widened in surprise as tears suddenly filled hers. She blinked them angrily back as her eyes flashed a violent red. "If you don't leave, then I won't feed!" she spat. "I don't do it in front of anyone!"

"Not even your family?" he retorted sardonically.

"*Especially* not my family!" she cried.

For a moment he was about to argue with her, but the distress and agony in her eyes was enough to sway him from his stand. Arguing with her was pointless, especially when she was wildly unstable, and in desperate need of sustenance. He couldn't say what he had to say to her when she was obviously in pain, and determined not to ease it as long he was standing there. "Fine," he grated reluctantly.

He turned and walked back out the door. Standing impatiently on the other side, he angrily tapped his foot as he waited for a few minutes. When he was sure that enough time had passed, he walked back into the room. She was still sitting on her bed, her head in her hands so that her long hair cascaded forward to shield her face. "I knew it was too much to hope that you had left," she muttered bitterly.

"Yes, it was. When was the last time you fed?"

She lifted her head to glare at him through dark violet eyes. "Why the hell do you care?"

Stefan took a deep breath as he struggled to control his temper. "I care because there is a human living in this house. I don't need you losing control, and killing her," he replied coldly, deliberately being just as nasty to her as she was with him.

The color drained from her face as she gaped at him. "Get out of my room!" she hissed.

"I am not leaving until you tell me."

Fury radiated from every inch of her body as she leapt to her feet. "I've never fed off of a human, so you can trust me not to lose control and kill your precious girlfriend!"

She was nearly screeching like a banshee by the time she was finished speaking, but he was so damn infuriating, so damn arrogant and condescending that she couldn't take it anymore. The fact that he would even remotely think that she would hurt someone was more than she could stand.

Stefan's jaw clenched as he stared back at her, a muscle twitched rapidly in his cheek from the force of his locked jaw. This conversation was not going at all the way that he had planned. He never should have baited her, never should have been deliberately cruel to her, but she brought it so easily out of him with her maddening attitude. She pricked his temper just as easily as she brought out his arousal, and earlier in the kitchen, a fierce surge of protection. He had needed to get her to safety, needed to make sure that she was shielded from Jess's horror, and her own pain.

He took a deep breath to calm himself before he spoke again. "That was not what I asked you."

Isabelle folded her arms over her chest as she inhaled a shuddery breath. "And I told you that it was none of your concern," she replied more calmly.

She never even saw him move, never even saw the blur that her father, mother, Ethan, the stooges, and herself made. She never even had time to blink before he had hold of her arms. She gasped sharply as his onyx eyes filled her vision with black fury. "And I told you that it was!"

Isabelle gaped at him before she snapped her mouth closed, tilted her chin up, and stared defiantly back at him. "Let me go."

He didn't release her as he stood, towering above her, dark and dangerous. His hands burned into her flesh, and his chest brushed lightly against hers, warming her from the inside out. She wanted to shudder from the force of the heat that wracked through her. The new feelings that he had managed to awaken in her flared to the forefront, melting away some of her anger. She forced herself to remain still, and not to let him know how he affected her.

"When was the last time that you fed?" he grated.

Despite the fierce set of his jaw, the anger burning in his eyes, the strength of his body, and the sheer power that radiated from him, she was amazed to discover that she wasn't afraid of him. That she wasn't the least bit scared of him. For some reason, she was certain that he wouldn't hurt her. Try to intimidate her yes, but he wouldn't harm her. She knew it with every ounce of her being, and the realization shook her more than the feelings he had awakened in her ever could have. Some of her defenses melted as for the first time she began to see him as a man, and not just her enemy. It was a scary comprehension that dissolved some of her resistance.

Stefan was very close to shaking some damn sense into her. She was absolutely the most aggravating, annoying woman that he had ever encountered. He didn't understand why she wouldn't just answer his question. Why she couldn't be like every other woman he had ever met that had tripped all over themselves to get near him. Instead, it seemed that she purposely went out of her way to avoid him, or exacerbate the hell out of him. He forced himself to take a deep breath, and not to rattle some sense into her thick skull.

"I told you that I wouldn't hurt her," she replied softly.

That was it. He had officially had it! He pulled her up so that her face was a mere breath away from his, and only the tips of her toes touched the ground. To his surprise, and admiration, she didn't flinch. Hell, she didn't even stop glaring at him as her eyes spit violet fury. "I didn't ask that. I don't care about her. I care about *you*, and I don't want to see you like that again!"

He was shaking with anger by the time he was done yelling. Her eyes widened in surprise and her mouth parted slightly. For a moment, he simply stared at her as his words echoed loudly in the room. Shock registered quickly, and his eyes widened in surprise as the truth of his words slammed home with sickening horror.

He didn't even remotely want to think about what he had just said. Nor did he want to think about the fact that it might even be true. All he wanted to do was show her, once and for all, that he was the one in control. He seized hold of her mouth with a fierce, punishing savagery.

She whimpered softly from the shear brutality of his kiss as she began to squirm in his arms. He didn't ease his hold on her, didn't lessen his bruising onslaught. He wanted to punish her, to show her that he was stronger, that he was the one in control. When she whimpered again, and her hands fluttered up to push at his chest, he finally eased the force of his mouth against hers.

His hands loosened on her arms as he lowered her to the ground, refusing to relinquish her mouth. Her hands pushed against his chest, but he wrapped his arm around her waist and pulled her tightly against him. He ran his tongue lightly along her lips, but she refused to open to him, refused to yield.

He moved slowly over her, licking and tasting, determined that she would give into him. She gasped slightly as he nibbled at her bottom lip and he used that opportunity to slip his tongue into her mouth. For a moment she remained stiff in his grasp, then her hands stopped shoving against his chest to curl into his shirt and her tongue hesitantly came out to meet his.

He groaned softly as a bolt of desire shot through him, hardening him instantly. She tasted so good and felt unbelievably right as she melded against him. Her full breasts pressed against his chest as her tongue entwined with his in a thrusting, mating dance. He was certain that no woman had ever felt as wonderful, never been so soft, or sweet. She moaned softly, the erotic sound causing his hard shaft to jump in anticipation.

He released her waist to lightly stroke the exposed skin of her flat stomach. She trembled slightly as he moved steadily higher, tracing his fingers over her delicate ribcage before skimming across the lacy edge of her bra. Her trembling grew stronger as he molded his hand over her firm breast and gently began to massage it. Her nipple hardened beneath his touch as her shaking increased. He wanted to smile with triumph, but he was too far gone with her to do so.

He released her hair and seized hold of her waist again, holding her up as he moved his hand to her other breast. He rubbed his dick against her as he pressed his pelvis against hers. She moaned with pleasure and instinctively arched into him. Releasing her mouth he began to kiss his way across her long, delicate neck. He grew even more aroused by the scent of her blood, so pure and sweet as it pulsed wildly through her veins.

He groaned as he rubbed against her, felt her, tasted her; was consumed by her. Never in his life had he felt so lost with a woman, so totally out of control with lust and desire. He couldn't get enough touching her, couldn't get enough of the way she felt and moved. He wanted, needed, to feel every inch of her, to posses her.

Isabelle jerked in surprise as his mouth descended on her nipple, lightly biting and sucking on it. Even through the thin material of her tank top, his mouth seared into her, turning her into liquid heat. Never had she imagined that something could feel as wonderful as he made her feel, that something could be this consuming. Her fingers wrapped into his hair as he nipped at her, causing her body to buck in surprise as a gasp escaped. Causing her to melt everywhere at the same time that she caught on fire.

"Stefan!" she gasped.

The sound of his name on her lips in that erotic, husky tone, damn near drove him over the edge. He hungrily reclaimed her mouth as his hand slid down to the edge of her shorts.

"Isabelle!" She jerked in surprise, pulling her mouth away from Stefan's as her carnal haze was broken by Ethan's loud pounding on the door. "Isabelle, are you in there?"

"Ye... Yes!" she stammered out in a shaky voice.

"Is Stefan in there with you?"

Her eyes jumped to his, wide, and uncertain. His eyes were impossibly black now, the pupils not even noticeable in the cloud of desire that smoldered within them. "No! Why?"

"Because Jess is up there making a thousand pancakes and we can't get her to stop! Do you know what's going on?"

At the mention of Jess's name she wrenched free of his grasp and cast him a scathing look. She closed her eyes and took a deep breath to ease the remaining passion in her body. "I'll be right out!"

"Well hurry up! She's like a damn robot that we can't turn off, and she's freaking me out!"

Isabelle would have snorted with laughter at the distress in his voice, if she hadn't been so angry. She berated herself for letting Stefan touch her, arouse her, when she had resolved to never let it happen again. But whenever he touched her, all of her will, and anger, melted. She was beginning to hate herself for the obvious weakness that she possessed. A weakness she never would have known existed if he hadn't walked into her life, into her sanctuary. She hated him for it, hated herself for it, and vowed fervently that it would never happen again. He would never touch her again.

She waited for Ethan's retreating footsteps to fade away before turning back to Stefan. Her body still burned from his touch, but she was determined to stand her ground. She could do it; she could refuse him anything, as long as he didn't touch her again. It was only when he touched her that she lost all control. She'd never thought that lust could be stronger than reason, but she knew now that it was.

"You had better go stop her," she said coldly.

He raised a dark eyebrow as he surveyed the incensed, distant woman before him. She was back to being angry at him again. Well, by the time that he was done with her, she would be too tired to even think about anger. Hell, she wouldn't even be able to think. "And why is that?"

Her eyes narrowed as she glared at him. "Because she's your girlfriend!" she spat.

"Jealous?"

Isabelle nearly screamed with fury. He was the most aggravating, infuriating man to walk the face of the earth. He was also the most sensuous, desirable, and irresistible one too. She firmly shut those thoughts out. She didn't even know where they had come from. She fisted her hands at her sides as she glowered at him. "Hardly!" she snorted.

To him, it was completely obvious that she was jealous, and the realization greatly pleased him. Smiling smugly he folded his arms over his chest as he eyed her with obvious pleasure. "Could have fooled me."

He thought she was going to start spitting with rage as her eyes flashed a dangerous shade of red. "Get out!" she hissed. "And stay the hell away from me!"

"That, Isabelle, is not going to happen, so get used to that fact right now," he growled in warning.

"How dare you!" she snapped.

He took a step closer to her, but she backed up quickly, shaking her head as she held up her hands to ward him off. "I'm not going anywhere until you tell me how long it has been since you last fed."

Isabelle was shaking with frustration and anger. She couldn't take much more of this. Her emotions were swinging wildly back and forth, and she felt as if she were being torn in ten million directions at once. "I told you I wouldn't hurt her," she whispered.

Stefan grit his jaw as a wave of fury swept through him. "And I told you that I don't care about her!" he snapped. "Now answer me!"

Isabelle was rapidly batting back tears. She hadn't cried since Ethan and Ian had cut off her hair, and she refused to cry now, especially in front of him. She didn't want to give him the satisfaction of answering him, but she needed to get away from him. She needed some space and distance, and if her answer would make him leave, than she would give it to him.

"Four or five days."

His breath hissed out of him as he clenched his jaw. "Which is it, four or five?" he demanded fiercely.

Isabelle wrapped her arms around herself in an attempt to ease the chill that was wracking her. "Five," she muttered miserably.

His hands seized hold of her arms. She jumped in surprise; her gaze flew wildly to his as he glared down at her. "You will not do that again," he commanded.

Isabelle's eyes widened at the commanding, hostile tone of his voice, and her ire immediately surged to the forefront. "I told you that I wouldn't hurt her!" she yelled, unable to stop the jealousy tearing through her.

His eyes narrowed dangerously as he brought her to within an inch of his face. "And I told you that I don't care about her. If you had lost control and hurt Jess, you never would have forgiven yourself, would you?"

Isabelle swallowed the tight lump in her throat. "No," she whispered.

He put her back down, unable to touch her anymore without wanting to take it all, to taste it all. "Now," he grated through his teeth. "We are going to get a few things straight between us. Jess means nothing to me. If you want her gone I'll toss her out right now..."

"No!" she cried as guilt and self loathing flowed through her.

Stefan's eyes narrowed, but he forced himself not to argue with her. He was going to set the rules right now, and she was going to start obeying them. "Fine, she can stay if you want, but I think it will be a little awkward because I plan on having you."

Fury surged through her veins as she took a quick step back to make sure that she was out of his reach. Not like it would do her much good, he moved faster than anything she had ever seen. He could easily grab her again if he wanted to. "You arrogant bastard! If you even remotely think that just because you say you're going to have me, you will, than you are dead wrong!" she spat.

"No Isabelle, I am very right. You can fight it all you want, but it is the simple truth. You want me, I want you, and I *will* have you."

She sputtered in disbelief, unable to believe the full extent of his arrogance. "Get out!" she nearly screamed. "Get out now!"

He grabbed hold of her arms, dragging her against him as she struggled wildly within his grasp. He held her for a moment as he waited for her to settle down. Her eyes flashed red with rage as she ceased her useless struggles and stood trembling within his grasp. She looked so amazingly beautiful, and tempting, that it took all the restraint he had not to kiss her again. He knew that if he did he wouldn't be satisfied with just one kiss, and he wanted Jess effectively out of his life before he took Isabelle. He knew she would feel guilty afterward if Jess wasn't gone, and he didn't want that.

He realized with a start, that for the first time in his existence, he was actually putting someone else's feelings ahead of his own. He didn't know how she had managed to get to him so much, nor did he particularly care. Right now, he just wanted to get his point across.

"You're going to stop fighting me Isabelle, and yourself. It will be good between us, you'll see."

She should have been infuriated at his highhanded attitude, but suddenly all of her anger vanished and she couldn't seem to regain it. She knew that it would be good between them, but she was so very afraid of just how good it would be. Of what it would mean. She didn't want to think about it now, couldn't think about it now. All she wanted was to be free of him for just a few moments.

"Go out through the storm doors," she said softly.

"Are you going to stop fighting me?"

All of her frustration and anguish reached a boiling point. "Yes!" she cried in exasperation. "Now please go! If you don't stop her, Ethan will have a nervous breakdown, he hates robots."

Satisfaction gleamed in his black eyes as he smiled smugly. He dropped a quick kiss on her nose and set her on her feet. Isabelle instantly jumped back to put more distance between them. She had promised to stop fighting with him, she hadn't promised to stay anywhere near him though. She kept her own smug satisfaction hidden from him as she met his gaze with an angry glare.

"Did you ever torture him with one of those?" he asked lightly.

"Go!" she yelled.

He grinned at her as he strolled by and tugged on a piece of her hair. She jumped further back, her eyes wild with anger as she glared at him. He turned away from her, smiling happily as he ascended the stairs and opened the door. "Oh, Isabelle!" he called back.

"What?" she snapped.

"Change your shirt before you come up."

He laughed softly as her curses followed him out the door.

Somehow, even though she'd had to change her shirt (his mouth had left a wet mark right over her nipple), she still beat him up the stairs and into the kitchen. She shoved her way through Ethan and Aiden to the counter, and froze. Jess was walking back and forth in the kitchen, pouring batter into frying pans, and flipping them over. Isabelle's eyes widened at the sight of the stack of pancakes filling the plates, overflowing the counters, and spilling onto the floor. In the short time that they had been gone, Jess had managed to make at least fifty or so pancakes.

"Wow," she breathed as Jess flipped another pancake onto an already overflowing plate.

"What the hell happened?" Ethan demanded.

Isabelle snapped her mouth shut as she turned to look at him. He was the only one that wasn't highly amused; everyone else was wearing grins as they watched the endless pancake assembly line. "I uh... well... I, oh I'll explain later," she finished lamely.

The front door banged open and Stefan came striding in. Although she still felt flustered from their encounter and more than a little embarrassed and angry, he looked cool, poised, and anything but ruffled by it. Isabelle scowled as she turned her gaze forcefully away from his. His arm brushed against her back as he passed her, causing her to nearly jump out of her skin as a bolt of desire pierced through her.

"What did you do to her?" Jack asked with a bright smile.

"I told her to make breakfast."

Jack started to laugh. "For an army?"

Stefan cast him a grin as he moved around the counter toward where Jess was pouring more batter into a pan. "She probably thinks you're growing boys."

"She'd have us be exploding boys," Ian replied.

Everyone but Isabelle and Ethan found this to be extremely hilarious. Stefan grabbed hold of Jess's arms and turned her toward him. Jealousy suddenly exploded through her, causing bright lights of anger to burst before her eyes. She turned quickly away so she couldn't see anymore. Heading out the door, she hurried to her parent's house.

CHAPTER 10

Isabelle somehow managed to avoid him for the next two days. She spent all of her time at her parent's house, helping her mother plan Aiden's going away party. She was irritable, snippy, tired, and achy from sleeping on the couch. Her mother questioned her bad mood, and why she was crashing on the couch, but Isabelle simply told her that she was too tired to go back at night. She knew her mother didn't believe her for a second, but she let it slide and didn't push Isabelle.

There were a few times that Isabelle almost poured her heart out about all of her frustrations about the infuriating man. But, she bit her tongue, and somehow managed not too. She was too frightened that her mother would confirm her worst fear, and that was the last thing that she wanted to have happen. So, she stayed silent, and miserable.

It didn't help that she found herself constantly thinking about him throughout the day. Found her mind wandering to him, and what he was doing, and with *whom*. Although, she knew what he was doing, and who he was doing it with. The thought always caused a surge of envy, and anger to spurt through her, which made her dislike him even more.

He had done this to her. If he had just stayed away she wouldn't be unhappy, she wouldn't be sleeping on a couch, and she sure as hell wouldn't be having the awful dreams that she had every night. Well, the dreams weren't awful, they were actually kind of pleasant, but they caused her to wake up feeling edgy, and out of sorts, unfulfilled, and even madder at him, and the world for upsetting her life this way.

She simply didn't know what to do anymore. She longed for the day that he left, and at the same time the idea of him leaving caused her to feel even more miserable, and irritable. It opened a pit of loss in her chest. A loss that she

was sure would go away just as soon as he got out of her
home, and out of her life. It was simple attraction; that was
all. She would have felt it with other men, if she had only
spent more time around them. Hell, there were probably
even a few humans that she would feel attracted to if she
gave them a chance.

She hadn't liked anyone in high school because they had
all been immature idiots. If she actually went out, and spent
time with men, she was certain that she would find a few
that she liked. Her brothers, and the stooges, were attracted
to human women all the time, and it never meant anything.
Vicky and Abby had an endless parade of admirers that
they were always going out with. What she was feeling for
Stefan meant nothing; she could find someone else she felt
the same way about. At least that's what she told herself
during the day, over and over again, but at night her mind,
and her body, betrayed her. She hated both of them for it.

"Isabelle, will you bring out the lemonade?"

She glanced up as her mother tore her from her morose
thoughts. She glanced down at the spoon in her hand, and
the big jug of lemonade she had been stirring for... ah hell,
she didn't know how long she had been stirring it for. She
tossed the spoon angrily aside.

"Yeah," she muttered.

Her mother glanced up at her, her violet blue eyes dark as
she studied her. "Are you ready to tell me what's wrong?"

"Nothing is wrong."

Her mother raised a delicate eyebrow, but refrained from
saying anything more. Her eyes took on the distant look
they got whenever she was communicating with her father.
Isabelle almost sighed in disgust. What she used to find
wonderful, and reassuring, now made her feel even edgier
and out of sorts.

"Well, come on," her mom said as she lifted a plate of
hamburger patties.

Isabelle grabbed the lemonade and followed her mother into the bright sunlight. She blinked rapidly against its rays, waiting until her eyes adjusted before moving down the stairs, and out to the large back yard. A volleyball net had been set up, horse shoes were already clanking loudly, and the smell of human food hung heavy in the air. Aiden had invited some of his friends from school, who had brought their girlfriends. There were now eleven humans in their midst's, including Kathleen, Jess, and Delia. There were more here now than there had ever been before, but Stefan had assured her mother that he could handle them all.

That only aggravated Isabelle even more. Her mother and father truly liked him, Aiden was ecstatic because of it, and everyone else was happy that they weren't going to have to go out to feed. They had made him into the hero of the day. Isabelle scowled as she slid the pitcher of lemonade onto one of the long tables that had been set out. Potato chips, Doritos, cheesy puffs, hamburgers, buns, hot dogs, chicken, soda's, alcohol bottles, plates, and cups covered them. Isabelle's stomach turned at the sight of all the food. *Human* food.

She turned quickly away from the table. She honestly didn't know what the matter with her was. Human food had never bothered her before, now it suddenly made her nauseous. She decided that was his fault too. If she wasn't feeling so awful, and grouchy, and if she could just get one decent night of sleep it wouldn't be bothering her at all.

Her eyes quickly scanned the people gathered around. Kathleen, Delia, Jess, Abby, and Vicky were sitting in lawn chairs with sunglasses on as they absorbed the sun, and watched the people around them. Aiden and his friends were tossing horse shoes, laughing happily. Ethan, Ian, Stefan, her father, and the stooges were standing by the keg. Her gaze lingered on Stefan, her pulse instantly picked up at the sight of him.

He was wearing a tight black T-shirt that showed off his amazing biceps and forearms, and clung to the muscles of his broad chest. His jeans were snug, emphasizing the narrowness of his waist, while clinging to his hard, muscular thighs. To her utter horror, and dismay, she felt the familiar tense anticipation she had been experiencing in her dreams, seize hold of her.

"He is good looking," her mother said softly.

Isabelle groaned inwardly, she had been staring at him, and of course her mother would notice. She turned her gaze away from him as she scowled. "He's an ass."

"He seems very nice to me. Just look at what he's done for Aiden today."

"You don't know him very well. He is an arrogant, insensitive *ass*!"

Her mother's eyes twinkled merrily as she looked at the group by the keg. "Maybe, but so are your brothers, your father, and the stooges."

"No one is as bad as him," she grated.

"So, you like him then?"

Isabelle grit her jaw as her frustration simmered to a boiling point. "I can't stand him!" she hissed.

Her mother smiled softly as she patted her arm lightly. Isabelle stood seething, feeling like a child. She hated it. She turned away from her mother, scowling angrily, as she moved swiftly over to the empty chair near Vicky and Abby. She didn't want to be near Jess, but she didn't know where else to go. She couldn't hide in the house all day. It would only draw more questions that she couldn't answer. She didn't want to let him know how much he had gotten to her. However, she was sure that he already knew, and that he was reveling in the fact, secretly laughing at her.

The thought brought a fresh surge of anger forward as she propped her feet up and laid back. "Hey Issy," Abby greeted.

"Hmm," she mumbled by way of greeting.

"Aiden's friends are really cute," Vicky gushed. "I especially like the redhead; do you think I should go talk to him?"

Isabelle looked at the redhead playing horse shoes. His girlfriend, a small, petite brunette was hanging on his arm. "I don't think his girlfriend would like that."

"Oh, who cares about her?"

Isabelle ground her teeth as she closed her eyes. Why couldn't she be more like her sisters? They liked every boy that crossed their paths. They flirted outrageously with them, kissed them, and threw themselves at them. Isabelle had never even been kissed before the ass had walked into her life, nor had she ever wanted to be.

"We haven't seen much of you lately."

Isabelle chose to ignore the hostility in Jess's tone. In fact, she chose to ignore her completely. "Isabelle's been helping mom," Abby answered for her.

Isabelle didn't speak at all for a long time. The day passed slowly in a torrent of games that Isabelle steadfastly avoided. It wasn't until late afternoon, when her mother and father reappeared, that her father announced the one thing that she had been dreading all day. "Time for football."

Abby and Vicky groaned; Jess paused in the middle of applying her suntan lotion, while Delia frowned thoughtfully. Her mom was smiling happily as she slid into the chair next to Kathleen. "You two are unbelievable," Kathleen said to her. "It's like you're still in college."

"Yep," her mom said brightly.

"Isabelle, come on!" Ethan yelled.

Isabelle closed her eyes, she didn't want to play, she didn't want to go anywhere near that game, and Stefan. "Come on Isabelle."

She opened her eyes to look up at Aiden. He was grinning down at her, his hand stretched out. "I don't want to."

He blinked at her in surprise; shock momentarily crossed his face before he grinned brightly at her again. "You have to play, it's my last game."

Isabelle frowned at him as she shook her head. "You'll be back."

"But it won't be the same, come on Isabelle you love playing, and I want you to."

She couldn't refuse the pleading look in his eyes, and the fake pout on his face. She sighed wearily and slipped her hand into his. He hauled her to her feet. She followed him slowly out to where everyone had gathered in the middle of the backyard. Mike and David were always the team captains, and the assigned teams they usually played with had already taken their positions. Jack, Ethan, and Julian stood by Mike, and she walked over to join them. David, her father, Ian, Aiden, and Doug stood opposite them, smiling smugly as David picked Stefan for his side. Mike immediately picked Kyle, who was being allowed to play for the first time. The remaining four humans were divided between them.

She walked to her side of the field, feeling stiff, and wooden. Their football games could get rough and rowdy, her brother's had no problem with slamming her into the ground, and neither did the stooges. That's why she loved to play, but now...

Isabelle was chewing nervously on her bottom lip as she glanced quickly over at Stefan. Would he tackle her? Would he *touch* her? She found herself shuddering with dread, and anticipation, at the thought. She listened half heartedly while Mike outlined their first play. The ball was coming to her, which she wasn't at all surprised by. Mike was hoping that Aiden's friends wouldn't want to tackle her.

They lined up, and her eyes instantly darted to Stefan. He was standing next to her father, and across from Ethan. She sighed in relief as she realized that he wouldn't be anywhere near her. She turned her attention back to Aiden, who was grinning as he walked over to stand before her. Isabelle forced herself to smile back.

"My friends refuse to tackle you," he said happily.

"Your friends wouldn't be able to catch me," she retorted.

"Hey!" one of them protested.

Isabelle glanced quickly at his friend before turning her attention back to Aiden. His eyes darkened with worry as he stared at her. All of their special abilities were called off for their games because the stooges, and her father, were stronger than her brothers, and her. Even without them though, Isabelle was the fastest. She didn't have the physical strength of the others, but if she broke away, none of them could catch her. Her team loved her for it, while David's team hated it. They usually flipped a coin to decide who would have to cover her. Aiden had obviously lost, and he didn't look happy about it.

Mike called hike, and they all broke. Isabelle darted to the right, laughing as Aiden scrambled to keep up with her. She caught the ball easily, tucked it against her chest, and dashed down the field. She crossed the spray painted line on the ground, and turned to hold the ball laughingly out as Aiden panted to a halt beside her.

He shot her a disgruntled look as he took the ball from her hands. "Slow poke," she teased.

"Hmm," he grunted.

The game went by quickly in a blur of laughter, and lighthearted banter. After a half an hour of play, Isabelle began to truly relax. She had been nowhere near Stefan, and he seemed content to stay away from her. In truth, it somewhat aggravated her, but it was what she wanted after all, wasn't it?

She shook the thought, and the confusion away as half time was called. She gratefully trotted over to the cold water on the sidelines, drinking it eagerly down to ease the dryness in her throat. She stood between Ethan and Ian, feeling secure between their tall, solid bodies. She poked her head around them, her eyes instantly landing on Stefan as he talked with David. Seeming to sense her gaze, he turned slowly toward her.

His eyes sparkled mischievously as a soft smile curved his full mouth. Her eyes widened as she realized that she had been caught looking at him, and a dull heat began to stain her cheeks. She was never shy, and very rarely got embarrassed, but one look from him caused heat to suffuse her body, and her throat to close up. For a moment she felt like a child who had been caught with her hand in the cookie jar.

She quickly turned her gaze to less threatening things. Her mother and Kathleen still sat on the sidelines; her father was now by her mother's side. Isabelle rolled her eyes as she looked away from them. She wasn't going to be like them, she wasn't going to let that happen to her. She refused to. She turned her gaze angrily toward Jess and Delia. She was momentarily startled by the fierce hostility that radiated from the both of them as they met her gaze. An uneasy feeling settled into the pit of her stomach. She had never been hated by anyone before, but she was certain that they both did hate her.

"I'll be right back," she said around the lump in her throat.

Ethan glanced quickly down at her. "Where are you going?"

"Inside for a minute."

"Hurry up, the games going to restart soon," he replied impatiently.

Isabelle hurried away from them and up the steps of the porch. She just needed some time to get her thoughts back together, and to shake off the lingering dread from Jess and Delia's look. They truly hated her. The thought brought a tight knot to her stomach, and the hot sting of tears to her eyes. She batted them angrily back as she slipped into the cool comfort of the kitchen.

This was his fault too, she decided. Jess wasn't stupid; she had to have noticed that something odd was happening.

Isabelle locked herself in the bathroom and leaned against the door as she tried to steady her nerves. Sighing heavily, she walked over, turned on the cold water, and liberally doused her face with it. By the time she was done, her anger had grown. She was an idiot to get upset over what Jess thought about her. What did she care what the girl thought, she didn't even like her? Stefan was her boyfriend, and if she chose to be mad at Isabelle because he was a horny bastard, than that was her own damn fault, not Isabelle's.

She turned the water off, determined not to let Jess bother her anymore. Stefan was an entirely different matter. No matter what she did, he bothered her. She avoided him physically, he invaded her dreams. She tried not to think about him, but he was constantly on her mind. One look at him caused her to tremble and heat. She didn't know what to do about him, but she knew that she couldn't stay hidden in the bathroom forever. Ethan and Aiden would come in and drag her out by her hair if she didn't get back to the game soon.

She cast a quick glance at her reflection, and froze. She looked like hell. Her face was flushed from the game, her hair was in wild disarray, and there were dark smudges under her eyes from not sleeping. She didn't want to think about the reason why she wanted to look better, she knew why; she just didn't want to admit it. Hurriedly, she pulled her hair into a neater ponytail. It didn't do much for the overall effect, but at least it was a little improvement.

Feeling a little better, and a little more in control, she straightened her shoulders and flung the door open. Stefan was standing before her with an eyebrow raised questioningly, and a bright gleam in his eyes as he surveyed her. Isabelle's heart leapt into her throat as all of her new found composure vanished and fire flashed through her body. His eyes came slowly back to hers; the gleam in them was gone as they darkened with a ravenous hunger. For a moment, her breath froze in her lungs, and the world around her vanished as his gaze burned into her soul. With heart stopping certainty, she knew that he was ready to devour her, and she found herself welcoming it.

"I was sent to get you." His voice was deep and husky with desire.

Isabelle forced herself not to shiver. "Okay," she managed to say. She took a step forward, but he put an arm out, effectively blocking her exit. She looked back at him, determined not to let her fear, or her fierce longing for him, show. "I thought you were sent to get me?"

A predatory smile curved his full mouth as he took a step toward her. She took a step back, but he planted his other arm behind her, blocking her escape. Isabelle's eyes widened in surprise as her mouth parted in anticipation. She turned to face him, her back pressed firmly against the doorway as he leaned closer.

"I was," he said hoarsely. Isabelle swallowed nervously. Her whole body was aching and trembling. She just wanted to touch him, to feel him. She needed to with a desperate longing that shook her from head to toe. "You've been avoiding me."

She wanted to lie, to deny it, but it would be pointless. She had been avoiding him; he knew it as well as she did. "I've been helping my mom," she hedged.

"Ah, I see." His finger brushed against her cheek, causing her to jump as a bolt of electricity, and need, sizzled through her. Isabelle couldn't stop herself from turning her head into his gentle touch. He took a step closer as his hand wrapped around the back of her head. "You said you were going to stop fighting me Isabelle."

She licked her lips nervously, instantly regretting the action as his eyes latched onto her mouth. The look of a starving man, who had just found food, came over his face. A small gasp of anticipation escaped as she realized his intent. His head bowed as he gently brushed a kiss against her quivering lips. He lightly nibbled and teased as her body began to tremble in response. His hand tightened upon her hair as the kiss deepened. His tongue thrust in to take possession of her mouth. She grasped hold of his shirt, clinging to him as her knees grew weak, and all of her senses were flooded with the taste and feel of him.

Stefan reluctantly broke the kiss. He shouldn't have come here, he knew that, but he had been so aggravated at her for avoiding him. He'd needed to confront her on it, but the minute that he'd seen her, he'd had to touch her, to feel her. To remind her of the passion that so easily bloomed between them so that she would stop ignoring him, and driving him crazy. He'd made the mistake of thinking that he would be able to control his own desires. He'd been wrong. She was driving him damn near insane.

"You are going to stop avoiding me!" he ordered in a much harsher tone than he'd intended.

The passion faded from her clouded eyes as anger sparked forth. Her jaw clenched and her hands fisted in his shirt as she tilted her chin to glare at him. "Why don't you just leave me alone and go molest your girlfriend, you arrogant, unfaithful, horny bastard!" she spat.

Stefan almost laughed, would have laughed, if he hadn't been so hard. He almost told her that Jess wasn't his girlfriend anymore, that he had ended it with her and was now sleeping on the couch, but he bit his tongue. He didn't want Isabelle to know that she had any power over him but something inside of him had changed, and he knew that it had everything to do with the woman standing across from him. He couldn't seem to get her out of his head. Even when he slept, she haunted his dreams. The things that he did, that *she* did in those dreams were enough to drive him insane.

He had never been so sexually frustrated in his life, and yet he couldn't seem to do anything to ease it. She wouldn't get out of his dreams, wouldn't get out of his head, and the idea of Jess disgusted him so much that he'd had to end it with her.

Jess hadn't taken it well at all, and she insisted upon staying in the house in the hope that they could work things out. He hadn't spoken a word to her since then, and the tension in the house was almost palpable. However there was no way the little hellion before him could know that because she had gone out of her way to avoid him, and the house. If she insisted upon being a stubborn, infuriating witch, than he wasn't going to tell her about Jess. He didn't owe her any explanations, he didn't owe her anything. She was the one that should be offering explanations, not the other way around. The sooner she learned who was in charge, the happier they would both be. He had every intention of teaching her that very soon.

"And soon you will be calling me your lover."

He thought that she was going to explode with fury. Her eyes turned violently red as her whole face suffused with color. He didn't wait to hear what she was going to start yelling at him. He jerked her head forward and took fierce possession of her mouth. She shoved angrily at his chest, her mouth clamped shut as she squirmed to get free. He kept a firm hold on her as he licked and nibbled at her full bottom lip. She *would* yield to him, and when she did, she would realize that it was useless to keep fighting what their bodies desperately wanted.

Isabelle was so angry, so irate, that she almost wanted to kill the egotistical, overbearing idiot. Almost, but not quite. She was fighting desperately to keep hold of her anger, but his mouth and his tongue were slowly melting her resolve. Slowly melting away all of the fury that was shaking her.

She couldn't yield to him; she wouldn't give him that satisfaction. But even as she thought it, her traitorous body was responding to him. Starting to give him exactly what he wanted.

Her hands involuntarily dug into his shirt as she stopped shoving at his chest. Her breath escaped in a gasp that allowed him to invade her mouth. His tongue stroked over hers in a slow, passionate dance that left her weak and trembling, and in desperate need for more. What had started as a ferocious kiss on his part, turned into something slow, and sweet, and enticing as she leisurely matched him stroke for stroke.

Stefan wrapped his arm slowly around her waist; all satisfaction at making her bend vanished as he lost himself to her sweetness, and uninhibited response. He had started out to make her concede defeat, but he was beginning to realize that she could just as easily make him lose control of himself. And at the moment, he didn't care.

"Isabelle! Issy! Where are you!?"

Isabelle groaned as Vicky and Abby's voices penetrated through her very pleasant haze. Stefan pulled slowly away, his eyes dark and confused as he lightly stroked her cheek. She tried to recall her anger at him, but she couldn't find the resolve to do it. Instead, she simply stared at him in dazed amazement. It wasn't just desire, or hunger for him, she realized with a start, but she was truly beginning to like the man.

The realization caused a flurry of emotions to rip through her, all of them jumbled and confused. For a moment, she actually wanted to sit down and cry out her frustration and anguish, but she couldn't do it. She refused to cry. He was already proving to her that she was weaker than she had ever known herself to be, she would not be even weaker by crying.

"Issy!" Abby shouted angrily.

"You had better go," she whispered, licking her swollen lips nervously. His eyes instantly latched onto her mouth and the fierce hunger in his gaze was enough to make her tremble all over again. "Go," she whispered.

He nodded slowly, but the look of reluctance was obvious on his face, and in his eyes. "Till later," he whispered, dropping a quick kiss on her mouth.

Isabelle stared dazedly after him as he slipped out the door and made a left toward the downstairs entry. She slumped against the door, trembling. Vicky and Abby popped up, identical looks of consternation on their pretty faces. "Here you are! Why didn't you answer us?" Vicky demanded.

Isabelle stared at them for a moment as she tried to gather her scattered thoughts, and warring emotions. "I was washing my face," she answered dully.

"Did Stefan find you?"

"No, I haven't seen him," she lied easily.

"That's just as well," Abby said.

Isabelle's eyes narrowed as she focused her full attention on her sisters. "Why is that?" she demanded sharply.

Their eyes widened at the hostility in her voice, but they chose to ignore it. "Issy, we need to talk to you," Vicky said urgently.

Isabelle recognized her melodramatic look instantly, and couldn't help but wonder what new "tragedy" had occurred. "Can't it wait till later, I'm sure the game is about to start again."

"It is, but they can wait two more minutes, we *have* to talk to you!" Abby gushed.

Isabelle shoved herself away from the wall and headed out of the bathroom. "Talk while we walk," she said over her shoulder.

They scurried to catch up with her on the back porch. "Jess thinks you're trying to steal Stefan!" Abby blurted.

Isabelle grit her teeth, forcing herself not to let her step falter as she swiftly descended the steps. She wasn't after Stefan, it was the other way around, but if she was honest with herself, she didn't really put up much of a fight when he was near. In fact, she turned into a quivering mass of Jell-O that he could bend and mold however he liked. She was more than a little disgusted with herself for not being able to put up a stronger fight against him, but he was so irresistible, and the way that he made her feel...

Isabelle shut the thought off before her knees gave out on her. "That's ridiculous," she told them as she reached the ground.

They exchanged a quick look that infuriated her. "Is it?" Vicky asked softly.

"Yes!" Isabelle nearly shouted in exasperation.

"Isabelle, come on!" Ethan yelled across the yard.

She glanced over to find everyone gathered together, including Stefan. Her gaze darted involuntarily to Jess, who was glowering at her with a look of absolute hatred. Her eyes widened slightly, and to her amazement, she looked back at Stefan, instinctively searching him out for some sort of protection, or help. The realization of what she had just done rocked her so hard that she stopped moving. He was looking at Jess, his face cold and hard, his eyes narrowed and hostile. Isabelle's breath froze as his gaze swung toward her, his features softened as he cast a small smile at her.

"Is it really?" Abby asked triumphantly.

The identical, knowing grins on their faces were enough to make her want to scream. She clenched her jaw, fisted her hands, and stormed over to join the group in the middle of the field. "It's about time!" Ethan snapped.

She shot him a withering look as she stepped into the huddle, barely listening to Mike's plan. "You get it again Isabelle."

"Fine," she mumbled angrily.

She had scored two of the five touchdowns they had, but she really wasn't in the mood to play anymore. However, the game was tied, and her team needed this win. They kept track of all the games they played, and at the moment they were one down from David's team. She would be letting everyone down if she didn't keep playing, and they would probably kill her.

"Let's go."

Isabelle moved back to the line. She froze as her eyes landed on Stefan. He stood casually across from her, smiling softly as his black eyes twinkled mischievously. For a moment she was unable to move, unable to breathe. Then she drew in a deep breath and forced herself to calm down. She would appear as completely unaffected by their brief encounter as he seemed to be.

"Lose the coin toss?" she asked haughtily.

He grinned at her. "Volunteered, someone has to catch you."

"And you think that you can?" she retorted.

His eyes darkened as they leisurely traveled over her. Her body quickened in response, but she refused to let it show. "I know I can, and I will."

Excitement coursed through her at the promise in his words. She smiled back at him as she lifted an eyebrow. The hell he would! She decided fiercely. She had been taking it easy on Aiden because she had seen no need to stress herself. Now, she would. Mike yelled hike, and she took off, darting easily through the crowd of bodies. She knew where the ball was going and she headed straight for it. She snagged it easily out of the air and ran as if the devil himself was on her heels, which he was.

She could hear him behind her. He was close, so very close. Determination and adrenaline burst through her as she tucked her head down and pushed herself to run faster. A gasp of relief rushed out of her as she triumphantly crossed the goal line. She turned, grinning brightly as she tossed him the ball. "I would rethink what you can, and cannot do," she said brightly.

He smiled in amusement as he took her in. She was sweating, and panting, some of her glorious hair had escaped from her ponytail to cling wetly to her exquisite face. He had to admit that she was the most determined, stubborn, beautiful woman he'd ever seen. They were traits that he would have respected greatly, if they weren't serving to undermine his control, and his goal of having her.

"I see that you were taking it easy on Aiden."

"Of course," she replied with a flashing grin.

"Good, because I was taking it easy on you."

Her eyes narrowed as she planted her hands on her hips. He flashed a smug smile before turning and walking away. Isabelle's temper was quickly reaching its boiling point, and he was going to be on the receiving end of it when she blew.

Four plays later Mike wanted to give her the ball again. She almost refused, not wanting to take the chance that Stefan just might be able to catch her, but she quickly changed her mind. There was no way that he would be able to get her, and this was the perfect opportunity to show him that he was completely wrong. No one was going to break her, least of all him!

She flashed him a cocky grin as she waited for Mike's command. She bolted off the line, caught the ball, and put every ounce of energy she had into running. Her legs were burning, and her lungs were aching painfully as she neared the goal line. She was only ten feet from it when she felt his arms wrap around her waist. Despair washed over her. She hugged the ball tighter against her chest as the ground rushed up to meet her.

Grunting from the force of the impact, she lay still for a moment, unable to believe that he had actually caught her! Then, his hands were upon her shoulders, and he was turning her hurriedly over. The anger that had rushed to the forefront of her mind disappeared as his troubled eyes scanned her face worriedly. "Are you okay?" he demanded harshly.

Isabelle was surprised to discover that he was truly concerned about her, truly afraid that he might have hurt her. "Of course, you tackle like a girl," she couldn't help but tease.

Stefan searched her face again to see if she was lying to him. He knew that her pride would keep her from admitting any kind of pain to him. Her violet eyes were twinkling happily though as she grinned at him. That grin caused something to shift inside of him. Something melted in him as he realized that he had been truly afraid he'd hurt her in his overzealous attempt to prove that he could catch her. That she couldn't avoid him. He had never been worried about anyone in his life before.

"Well, you would know," he retorted before he could begin to think about what that worry might mean.

Isabelle laughed softly as he grinned down at her. His black hair was matted to his forehead with sweat, and his skin was glistening with it. The shirt he wore clung to every hard muscle of his chest, and upper arms. Suddenly, she became aware of the heat of his arms, of the way that they felt around her. Their encounter in the bathroom flashed through her mind as her body tensed with anticipation.

He must have seen something in her face for his smile suddenly vanished, and his eyes darkened with desire. Isabelle's breath froze in her lungs as she felt him harden and lengthen against her thigh. Desire ripped through her and she shuddered in response to the fierce hunger that radiated from him.

"You caught her!" Aiden was grinning as he effectively shattered the moment.

Stefan sighed angrily as he cast a lingering look down at her passion clouded eyes. He was truly getting sick of all the interruptions that her family caused, and he was beginning to think that he would never have a moment alone with her. Isabelle shifted beneath him and he had to stifle a groan against the bolt of fire that caused his hardened shaft to jump. He ground his teeth as he forced himself to his feet and pulled her up with him.

"I can't believe you caught her! No one's caught her since she was thirteen! This is great!"

Aiden's team rushed up to gloat as her team walked over to stand behind her in silent misery. Isabelle risked a glance at Stefan, expecting to see smug satisfaction in his eyes, but his jaw was locked firmly and his eyes were troubled and distant.

CHAPTER 11

That night, Isabelle gave into common sense and returned to the other house. She could no longer stand her mother and father's questioning looks. Nor could she stand her own cowardice. She couldn't avoid Stefan forever, and hiding from him was proving to be a useless endeavor. He would find her; she just had to make up her mind as to what she would do when he did. She was becoming more eager to just give into temptation, and cast all reason out the window. However, her lingering fear about the consequences that might follow kept holding her back.

She could no longer deny the fact that the attraction she felt for him was more than a simple, passing fancy, but something more. It was the possibility of what that something more might be that scared the hell out of her. She would just have to take her chances and see how the chips fell. There was still the hope that he wasn't her soul mate, that maybe she was wrong, but every day that hope became smaller and smaller. She wasn't even entirely sure that she wanted to hold on to it anymore.

In the short time that he had been here, he had managed to totally disrupt her life. She wasn't quite ready to concede defeat, but she knew that her determination was wavering. She just needed time to think, and to sort through everything.

She had stayed to help her parents clean up, but her mother had shooed her away when only a few dishes were left so the house was dark by the time she returned. She was grateful for that fact. She was completely exhausted, and she didn't want to deal with anyone tonight. Her body ached from the football game, a game that they had managed to win by the skin of their teeth, and she longed for a comfortable bed instead of an uncomfortable couch at her parents.

She pulled her shoes off and moaned in pleasure as she wiggled her cramped toes. Opening the screen door quietly, she picked up her shoes, and crept into the silent house. She tiptoed through the entryway and into the living room. "You came back."

Isabelle almost shrieked as she jumped in surprise. Her shoes slipped from her numb fingers. She spun quickly, her eyes wide, her heart hammering, and her breath coming in rapid pants. "Didn't mean to scare you."

Isabelle inhaled sharply as the adrenaline jolt she had just received slowly dissipated. "Crap," she whispered her hand flying to her badly abused heart. "Don't do that!"

Stefan chuckled in amusement. "Sorry, I figured you would have sensed me."

Now that she wasn't shaking with terror, and her heart was beginning to return to normal, she was able to think again. "I wasn't paying attention."

"So I noticed."

His dark eyes gleamed predatorily in the moonlight streaming through the windows. He was sprawled out on the couch, his hands propped behind his head on one of the couch pillows. His long legs were crossed, his lower calves, and feet, dangled over the edge of the armrest. He looked relaxed, but she could sense a tension in him that belied his demeanor. He also looked absolutely delicious, she decided.

"What are you doing down here?" she whispered breathlessly.

"Resting."

"You have a bed."

"I know." It was just being occupied at the moment by someone that he didn't want in it. In fact, the one he wanted in it had finally returned, and was staring at him as if she couldn't decide if he were a monster, or if she wanted to devour him. He was going to make the choice very easy for her. "Finally decide to stop avoiding me?"

She shifted uncomfortably as she bent to pick up her shoes. He looked dark and dangerous sprawled out on the couch. For a brief moment she wondered what he would do if she walked over to him and laid down beside him. Actually, she knew exactly what he would do, and what she would let him do to her. Her body was beginning to tighten just from the thought of what would happen, of what she *wanted* to happen. She was desperate to learn what it was that her body was seeking, and what he could teach her.

She swallowed heavily and took a deep breath as she tried to get herself back under control. All of her resolve was slipping away, and she couldn't let that happen. She just couldn't. She needed a few moments to breathe, to relax. The thoughts she was having were wrong. She was supposed to be staying away from him, not fantasizing about joining him on that couch.

She took a deep breath, strengthened her resolve to treat him as casually as he treated her, and seized hold of her shoes. Standing back up, she crossed her arms at her waist, holding her shoes as if they could be used to ward him off.

"I was tired of the couch," she said softly.

"I know the feeling."

Isabelle frowned as she studied him. "What?"

He chuckled at the bafflement in her voice. Swinging his legs down, he sat up, his gaze never leaving hers. "They do get uncomfortable."

"Then go to bed," she replied crisply.

"Is that an invitation?"

Isabelle's mouth gaped open as her heart rate accelerated. She took a small step back, shaking her head in denial, while her entire body was tense with want, and need. He stood slowly, tall and dangerous in the moonlight as his broad shoulders blocked out the window. "Don't," she whispered, holding her shoes out to ward him off.

"Then go to bed Isabelle."

She found herself unable to move, unable to blink as a hard lump formed in her throat. She wanted this, wanted him, but she couldn't, she *shouldn't*. He took a step toward her, and all reason, and logic, flew out the window. Her shoes fell numbly to the floor as she began to tremble with anticipation. All she wanted was to feel him again, to touch him, to have his hands and mouth on her. His eyes gleamed ferociously as she took a step toward him, not caring about the consequences of what she wanted.

"Stefan?" The soft voice jerked both of their heads around. Reality slammed down on her as she took a step into the shadows. "Stefan, are you down here?"

His eyes flashed dangerously as they remained locked on Isabelle's. For a moment she was more shocked by the loss of control that his red eyes revealed than she was by Jess's interruption. Then, the full reality of Jess's interruption slammed down on her, and anger blazed forth. She slipped further into the shadows, hiding herself behind the screen in the corner as the kitchen lights flicked on.

"Why do you insist upon sleeping down here?" Jess demanded.

Isabelle's blood was boiling as she swung her leg silently over the banister, desperate to escape from this awful situation. Her gaze landed upon her discarded sneakers, and she froze. The last thing she needed was for Jess to see those sneakers. Gritting her teeth, she tried to decide if she could grab them without drawing any attention to herself.

"You know why Jess!" he snapped.

Stefan studied Jess as she stood in the doorway of the kitchen, her arms folded over her chest as she glared at him, but his entire body was focused upon Isabelle behind the screen. He knew she had to be angry, and as soon as he got rid of Jess he was going to have to deal with that anger, and explain what was going on. As much as he hated to admit it, he supposed that he would have to tell her the truth. "You've slept down here for the past three nights."

Isabelle forgot about her sneakers as she turned her head in surprise. She could see his shadow through the screen, he hadn't moved an inch. Her forehead furrowed as she puzzled over Jess's words. He had been sleeping on the couch for the past three nights? She swallowed down the lump of hope that suddenly formed in her throat. Why would he do that?

"Jess, go back to sleep," he said impatiently.

"I'll stay down here with you." Isabelle's breath froze as Jess's shadow appeared before the screen. Her hips swung seductively as she approached him. "I've missed you."

She threw her arms around his neck and pressed herself against him. Isabelle's temper flash boiled as her eyes narrowed. A bolt of jealousy, so fierce that it took her breath away, ripped through her. For an emotion that she had never experienced before she met him, she was becoming all too familiar with its clawing effects.

"I haven't missed you, now go upstairs," Stefan grated.

Isabelle didn't care if he was getting rid of Jess, didn't care if he had slept on the couch for the past three nights. All she cared about was what he had managed to turn her into. A whore. He was dallying with her on the side, while keeping a girlfriend dangling on the side. She had never thought of herself as immoral, but she realized now that was exactly what he had made her, and she hated it. She hated herself for allowing him to keep on doing this to her over and over again.

She had been blaming him for this mess, for the way that he made her feel, but it was *her* fault. She was the one that continuously allowed it to keep happening. She was an absolute idiot. A fool. She had been about to give herself to a man that had his girlfriend in the same house as her! What the hell had she been thinking? What the hell was the matter with her? Self loathing and disgust crashed through her in waves that left her nauseous and drained. She needed to get out of here, now.

"Stefan, come on," Jess whined.

He winced as her voice grated over his nerves. She ground suggestively against him causing the erection he had experienced with Isabelle to vanish instantly. He grabbed hold of her arms and lifted her away from him. "Go upstairs Jess," he grated. "I told you that it is over."

Her eyes narrowed with anger as she planted her hands on her hips. "It's Isabelle, isn't it? She's why you don't want to be with me anymore! You just want to add another conquest to your list by screwing her!" Stefan winced inwardly as his eyes darted toward the screen. Isabelle had to be truly seething by now, but at least he wouldn't have to tell her that it was over between him and Jess. This conversation was ample proof of that.

"Jess..."

"Don't you Jess me!" she yelled. "I can't believe that you would screw that slut!"

The anger that seized him was swift and violent; it caused him to react before thinking as he seized hold of her arms. "Don't talk about her like that!" he hissed, drawing her up so that her eyes were even with his. Jess's eyes widened in fear as she stared at him, Stefan clenched his jaw and forced himself to release her. "Be out of this house tomorrow."

Jess's eyes filled with tears as she spun on her heel and raced out of the room. "Fine!" she shouted over her shoulder as she pounded up the stairs.

Stefan stood silently as his eyes rested on the screen. He suddenly didn't want to go anywhere near her. Shit, what had she done to him? The anger that had just seized him was so unexpected, so out of character, that he was absolutely stunned. For a moment he had been ready to rip Jess's throat out just because of what she had said.

He took a deep breath to steady himself before striding over to the screen and ripping it back. She was gone. For a moment he contemplated going after her, finding her, talking to her, and much, much more. Then, he changed his mind. He needed time to think, time to sort through his jumbled mess of emotions. He was beginning to realize that it was more than a desire to have her in his bed, but something more, something that he wasn't sure he wanted. He was actually beginning to care about the infuriating witch.

It was the first time he had allowed himself to care about anyone since he'd been a child. He had vowed never to let it happen again, but somehow she had managed to wedge her way under his defenses. Maybe she had the right of it; maybe they should just stay away from each other. His entire existence had been nothing but death and destruction. An existence that Isabelle could not even begin to fathom, that didn't even come close to the happy peacefulness of her life. His had been an existence that he had every intention of never letting her know about. Growing closer to her may just be the biggest mistake he ever made, but something about her kept drawing him to her, something about her made him determined to posses her.

The best thing for her, probably for both of them, would be for him to leave but he couldn't bring himself to do it. Not yet anyway. He just wanted to be near her for a little longer. He frowned as he thrust the screen back into place. For the first time he began to realize that when Isabelle was near, the darkness that had been haunting him, the loneliness that he had experienced since destroying Brenda didn't tear at him anymore. For the first time since he had been thrust into this dark existence, there was actually a little bit of peace in his soul.

And it was because of *her*.

Confused, angry, and extremely disgruntled, he returned to the couch. He lay awake for a long time before sleep finally claimed him. And then, the dreams started again.

CHAPTER 12

Isabelle managed to avoid him, and everyone else, for most of the next day. She was scared that Ethan would sense her humiliation, and discomfort. That the stooges would make some comment about her staying at her parent's house, and she was petrified that she would run into Jess. Her self-hatred was bad enough, without having to see Jess's hatred on top of it.

She got up before the sun rose, knowing that Aiden would be leaving early in the morning. She wanted to say goodbye to him before everyone else got up. She managed to corner him by the bathroom as soon as he rose. She had ended up in tears by the time they had broken apart. The tears had shocked them both, and it fully made her realize just what an emotional mess she had become.

He'd promised that he would be back soon to visit, and had pleaded with her to stop crying. Although he was too much of a man to cry, he had been as reluctant to release her as she was to release him. When she'd finally managed to let him go, she had turned and fled from the house. She knew that her absence from his departure would be remarked upon later, but she didn't care.

It had been years since she had gone to the tree house, but that was where she sought her sanctuary. She sat in the tree for hours, watching the sun move across the sky as she tried to sort through the mess of her jumbled emotions. As the sun began to set, she realized that she hadn't even come close to figuring out how she felt. She wasn't sure that she ever would.

She refused to cry again, no matter how much she wanted to. Crying was not going to solve her problem, and she was already disgusted with herself for being weak. With a resigned sigh, she climbed out of the tree house, tired, and emotionally drained. She reached the ground and wrapped her arms around herself to help ward off the cold chill that permeated her entire being. She made her way slowly down the path, and back to the house.

She couldn't avoid him forever; she couldn't avoid all of them forever. She was just going to have to deal with it, and take everything as it came. She couldn't keep living like this. He would be leaving soon, Jess would be leaving soon, and then it would all be over. That thought didn't give her the reassurance that it used to, but she refused to linger over the reason why. She couldn't allow herself to be alone with him anymore.

Isabelle sighed tiredly as she climbed the steps and opened the screen door. Everyone had come back from working on the new house, and they were now watching a movie in the living room. They all turned to look at her when she entered. "Where have you been all day?" Ethan inquired.

Isabelle shrugged absently. "Around."

"You missed Aiden."

"I said goodbye to him this morning."

She moved forward to lean against the doorframe. She stared blankly at the action movie that they all turned back to watch. She found her gaze traveling involuntarily toward Stefan. He was sitting in one of the recliners; his feet propped up, and his gaze intent upon her. It took all she had to turn away.

"Where's Jess?" she asked as she moved toward the fridge.

"She moved out!" Ian called to her.

Isabelle froze with her hand on the handle. "What?" she asked in surprise, her heart leaping painfully as a bubble of hope bloomed forth. She quickly shoved it aside. "Why?"

She stepped back to peer into the living room again. All heads were turned toward Stefan. He looked at her, his face hard, and his eyes distant. "We broke up."

Isabelle's eyes widened in surprise as his gaze burned into her. She swallowed heavily as her emotions swung like a pendulum. For a moment she feared she would be sick. She closed her eyes, took a deep breath, and swung the fridge open. She was hungry, and in desperate need of a shower to ease the chill in her. She grabbed a bag of blood and headed for the stairs.

"I'm going to take a shower so don't even think about flushing the toilets!" she yelled over her shoulder.

"Would we do that?" Jack called innocently. Isabelle ignored their laughter as she made her way up the stairs.

"Why does she do that?" Stefan asked the minute Isabelle was out of earshot.

"Boss us around? Because it makes her feel better," Ian answered absently.

"It makes *us* feel better," Ethan added with chuckle. "It keeps her happy, which in turn keeps the rest of us happy."

"Yeah, Isabelle can make your life a living hell if she's mad at you," Mike supplied.

Stefan quirked an eyebrow as he stifled a laugh. He knew firsthand just how miserable she could make someone's life when she wanted to, but all of that was going to change tonight. Jess was gone, out of the house, and Isabelle no longer had any reason to fight him, or herself. He began to harden as he thought about all of the wonderful things that he was going to teach her, and do to her.

"I already figured that out," he said softly. They all shot him questioning looks that he chose to ignore. "I meant why doesn't she feed in front of you?"

Ian and Ethan exchanged a quick smile. "Because we used to tease her about it when we were younger. We told her that she was ugly when she did it, that she looked like a freak, and all kinds of other stuff. She hasn't fed in front of anyone since she was eight," Ethan explained.

Stefan was surprised to find himself highly irritated with them. All he could picture was a small Isabelle, in pigtails, crying over her brothers taunting. It was something that had obviously affected her. His jaw clenched tightly as his hands curled involuntarily into the arms of the chair. It didn't matter that they had all been children, or that they had all taunted and teased each other, all he could think about was the pain that they had inflicted upon her. He wanted to tell them that it wasn't funny, but he bit his tongue, they didn't need to suspect any of his intentions toward her.

He'd never felt so protective, or defensive, of someone. He really was growing to care for the girl, he realized with a mixed feeling of awe and dismay. No matter how much he had never wanted it to happen, it was actually a pleasant realization he decided. It was a thought that helped to ease the torment of his dark soul, a soul that he had no intention of ever letting her glimpse.

He would have her, she *would* be his, but she would never know anything about his past. It was the only conclusion that he had come to in the long, discomforting night. She helped to ease his torment, because of that he wanted her more than any other woman he had ever met, but he had also vowed that she would never know the darker side of the world, or himself.

He closed his eyes and took a deep breath, a small smile crossed his face as he thought about what tonight would bring. He just had to get the little witch to concede to his will, but he was certain that it wouldn't be hard. He was beginning to understand why she had been staying away from him. For all of Isabelle's bluff and bluster, inside she was scared, and frightened of being hurt. He could, and would, ease that fear.

The screen door swung open again. He opened his eyes, tensing as Jess came into the house. He had spoken to her a little this morning as he'd helped her carry her stuff out, but he hadn't expected to see her again, and he didn't want to see her now. Their eyes widened in surprise as they all took her in.

"I forgot my toothbrush." Before Stefan could stop her, she was heading up the steps.

Isabelle was coming out of the bathroom, dressed in one of Ethan's old T-shirts, with her clothes tucked under her arm when Jess stepped into the hallway. For a moment Isabelle couldn't breathe from the force of the hostility that radiated from the girl.

"I hope you're happy now!" Jess hissed.

Isabelle blinked at her in surprise, taken aback by the waves of hatred beating against her. She had never thought it possible for someone to hate her as much as Jess had grown to. "Jess, I didn't want this," she whispered.

Jess snorted angrily. "I seriously doubt that."

"I really didn't!" she protested. She wanted to tell her that nothing was going on, but she wasn't going to lie to her. There was something going on, she just wasn't sure what it was yet.

"Don't for a moment think that you're special, you're just like all the other sluts he's been with. He'll use you and toss you aside too, you're..."

"If I were you, I would get your toothbrush, and get out."

Isabelle's eyes flew to Stefan as he stepped off the stairs. The cold hostility in his voice sent shivers of fear down her spine as Jess turned to face him. Isabelle wanted to tell her to run for her life, but her throat clogged with fear. Isabelle had never seen him look so deadly, so dangerous. Even when he had been angry at her, even when he had grabbed her, she hadn't been as afraid of him as she was now. For a moment she truly feared, truly *believed*, that he would hurt Jess.

Jess hung her head and darted quickly past Isabelle into the bathroom. Light pooled into the hall, illuminating Stefan as he glided forward and stopped a foot away from the bathroom door. His posture was casual as he leaned against the wall, but the hostility that radiated from him was almost tangible. She could feel the fury that caused his jaw to clench, and a muscle to twitch in his cheek. Isabelle wanted to shudder in fear, she knew that his anger wasn't directed at her, but it still frightened her.

Jess came quickly back out, flicking the light off, and casting them into the dark. She stood uncertainly in the hall, her toothbrush clutched in her hand as she stared warily at Stefan. Stefan waved his hand elegantly for her to pass, his eyes narrowed dangerously. Jess bowed her head as she bolted quickly past them.

"Are you ok?"

Isabelle swallowed heavily, no she wasn't ok. She was terrified of him, of everything that was happening to her. Jess's words echoed loudly in her head, and the truth of them had caused a gaping pit to open in her stomach. She bit into her lip as she lifted her gaze to his, and forced herself to nod. Strands of wet hair fell into her face and she instantly pushed them away. He stood silently as his gaze bored into her soul. She didn't know what to say, what to do. All reasonable thought fled under his intense scrutiny.

"I uh... I'm sorry about you and Jess," she managed to stutter out.

"Why? I'm not. It's been over for three days now; I just finally got her to leave the house."

Isabelle knew that he was trying to tell her something with that statement; she chose to ignore it. Just like she'd chosen to ignore the fact that he'd slept on the couch for the last three nights. She didn't have all of her feelings sorted out as it was; she needed more time to be able to assimilate this bit of information on top of everything else.

"If it had anything to do with me I'll explain that there's nothing going on between us," she said hesitantly.

"Isn't there?" he asked quietly, dangerously.

"No!" she cried.

His eyes were feral in the dark as a small smile curved his full, hard lips. "If we hadn't been interrupted last night..."

"I would have come to my senses!" Isabelle cried as a dull heat suffused her body at the reminder.

"And tonight?"

Her eyes widened as her heart began to trip hammer painfully in her chest and her mouth went suddenly dry. "What about tonight?" she managed to choke out.

"What will you do when I come to your room tonight, and there is no one to interrupt us?"

Isabelle's body tightened in anticipation as she stared breathlessly at him. She wanted to tell him that she would welcome him with open arms, but it stuck in her throat. It got stuck on her pride. She wouldn't give into him that easily. She couldn't. "I'll tell you to get out."

The shadows caressed his body as he moved closer to her. She tilted her chin defiantly, but she felt anything but defiant. She felt like a quivering mass of raw nerve endings, all of which were screaming for his touch. His hand gently stroked her cheek. Isabelle jumped in surprise as everything in her reacted to his touch. Her heart hammered so rapidly that she was certain it was going to explode.

"Will you really?"

It took her a moment to recall what they had been talking about. His hand had begun to stroke her neck, sending chills down her spine. "Yes," she managed to choke out.

He took a step closer so that his chest brushed against hers. Isabelle tilted her head back to meet his smoky gaze as he bent his head. His lips brushed against hers in a butterfly touch that caused her knees to tremble. The soft flicker of his tongue against her lips caused the room to tilt, the floor to fall away, and the entire world to become centered on him, and only him.

Her mouth opened beneath the soft flickering of his tongue. He tasted her slowly, stroking over the roof of her mouth, skimming across her teeth. His hand tightened upon her neck as she moaned softly. He had only meant to taste her, to tease her, to show her there was something between them, but she tasted so good, and she was so responsive that he found himself losing track of his intent, and wanting to devour her.

He broke away before he couldn't. She blinked dazedly up at him, her eyes dark and smoky as shivers ran through her body. "We'll find out tonight."

The bewildered look in her eyes vanished almost instantly as anger sparked through their deep purple depths. "You wouldn't dare!" she gasped.

"Maybe, maybe not."

He turned quickly away from her and descended the stairs before he drug her into his room and took her now. The thought of the others downstairs was the only thing that stopped him. He had every intention of seeing her later, but he didn't want them to know about it. Her room would be much more private, and secure, for what he intended. There would be no stopping him tonight.

Isabelle slumped against the wall, fear and anticipation warring through her so fiercely that she could hardly breathe. She wanted to run for her life, at the same time that she wanted to curl up in bed and wait for him to come to her. She had no doubt that he would show up in her room tonight. She just had to decide if she would be there, or not.

***

As it turned out, the decision was taken from her hands. The minute she returned to the living room Ian asked if she wanted to go into the city. Normally she would have said no, but tonight she jumped at the opportunity. She ignored everyone's surprise as she eagerly accepted, and darted down to her room. This would be her chance to prove that she could be attracted to other men, that Stefan wasn't the only one that affected her.

She threw on her favorite black dress. Her mother had given it to her for Christmas two years ago, she'd never worn it out, but she'd tried it on often, loving the way that it felt, and fit. It was lose and flowing, yet it emphasized the gentle swell of her breasts, her small waist, and flaring hips before ending at mid thigh. She knew that Ian went to clubs when he went out, and she was certain the dress would fit in perfectly. Quickly brushing out her wet hair, she grabbed her black high heels, and bolted out of the room.

Everyone's eyes widened as soon as she stepped back into the living room. "Shit Issy, I don't remember the last time I saw you in a dress!" Mike cried.

"What?" Jack demanded as he poked his head around the doorway. His eyes widened in surprise as his mouth dropped open. "You're not wearing that!"

"Shut up Jack!" she snapped.

"I'm with Jack." Ethan folded his arms firmly over his chest and stared at her in disapproval.

She cast him an angry glare. "No one asked you."

"Isabelle..." Jack started.

"You go to clubs, right?" she interrupted angrily.

"Well uh, yeah, but..."

"I can't walk in there wearing jeans."

"But..." he stammered.

"For crying out loud Jack I'm twenty three years old! I think I should be able to wear whatever the hell I want!" she snapped, tired of being babied and coddled.

His hazel eyes gleamed angrily, but he nodded briskly and ducked out of the doorway. A minute later the screen door opened and banged shut. "You'd better hurry up, he might leave you behind," David warned.

"I'll kill him!"

She hurried toward the door, slipping her shoes on as she went. "Isabelle, you look nice!"

"Thanks Doug." At least she could count on someone not to act like a total ass all the time.

She hurried out the door and toward Jack's idling car. Throwing open the back door she slid in, eager to escape the house and Stefan. Ian gaped at her in the dim light, his eyes wide in shock. "Not one word," she growled in warning.

"What the hell are you wearing?" he demanded, completely ignoring her.

Isabelle rolled her eyes and turned to slam the door shut. A pair of gleaming onyx eyes stopped her in her tracks. Her heart and breath froze as Stefan stared at her from the front seat. There was anger in his gaze, but also a fierce hunger that caused her toes to curl in her shoes. It was only then that she realized he hadn't been in the living room.

"Shut the door!" Jack snapped apparently still angry at her for the confrontation in the house.

Isabelle glanced longingly out the door. She could jump out now, say that she had changed her mind and run back into the house. Surely he wouldn't follow her. Although, she was certain that he would. She was good and trapped. If she got out now, he would be in her room. If she stayed, she would be able to get away from him at the club, and she *would* find another man that she desired. With a resigned sigh, Isabelle slammed the door and the light turned off.

Stefan turned around in his seat, his jaw clenching tightly. He couldn't believe that she had thought to evade him by taking off with her brother, and Jack. He also couldn't believe what she was wearing. A muscle began to twitch in his cheek from the fierce clenching of his jaw. Every man there was going to be after her. The thought infuriated him beyond belief. His hands clenched into fists as he turned to look out the window.

If this was the way that she wanted to play that was just fine. He was going to give as well as he got. There would be lots of women there. Lots of women, who would be more than eager to warm his bed, not run away from him.

"I cannot believe that you're wearing that," Ian muttered in disgust.

Stefan had to hide a grin as he realized that her brother was almost as upset about the provocative dress as he was. Although, her brother was worried about it because of men like *him*, who wanted nothing more than to rip it off of her, reveal her splendid body, and take her. He was worried that he might just rip it off of her before the night was over.

"It's a perfectly fine dress," she retorted.

"For a hooker," Jack mumbled.

Isabelle's face reddened in anger. "You would know!" she snapped.

"Hey! I have *never* paid for it! And we're only looking out for your safety!" Jack protested hotly.

Isabelle was seething as she clenched her hands in her lap. She really didn't need this, especially not in front of Stefan. "And how is that?"

Ian and Jack both sighed wearily. "You're such an innocent Isabelle," Jack muttered. "Abby and Vicky have more common sense than you do."

She stared at them in disbelief. "Are you telling me that you would rather see Vicky or Abby in this dress, than me?" she demanded.

"Yes!" they both cried.

Isabelle sat in stunned silence, unable to believe what she was hearing. "Why?" she inquired softly.

"Because Vicky and Abby at least have some idea about men, you don't," Ian retorted. Isabelle's face flamed red. She despised the fact that they were talking about her like this right now. In front of *him*! "They can handle a man, you can't."

She was fighting the fierce urge to punch them both in the face. "That's ridiculous!"

Stefan didn't think it was at all ridiculous. She really didn't have any idea about her effect on a man, or what a man was capable of doing. "*Do* you have any concept of men?" Jack demanded.

"Maybe if I had ever met one I would!" she snapped furiously.

Stefan bit on his bottom lip to keep from laughing. To think he had been feeling sorry for her because her brothers had teased her about feeding. He now realized that Isabelle gave as good as she got, and was more than capable of handling them. "We're going to have to beat the guys off of you!" Ian yelled.

"Then there will be less of them for you to worry about while you're looking to get laid," she retorted hotly. "Besides, I can handle myself perfectly fine, thank you."

"Isabelle..." Jack started.

"Look, I am a grown woman; I don't need anyone to raise me anymore. I can handle myself, and anything that happens. Besides I'm stronger than any human male, so I think I can protect myself around them. Now just back off!"

"Never could talk reason into that thick skull of yours so forget it," Jack muttered.

"Isn't that what I said when I got in the car?" she demanded.

Isabelle turned to the window, her face flushed with anger, and embarrassment. There were times she greatly wished that she had no family at all, and this was definitely one of them. It didn't help that she could sense Stefan's humor. They were yelling at her about the men in the club, yet the one they should be worried about they had invited to come with them! Well, she'd show them all. She was a grown woman, and she could definitely handle herself, especially with a human. It was the man sitting in front of her that she couldn't handle herself around.

CHAPTER 13

Isabelle immediately began to wish that she wasn't such a coward. She could have stood up to him in her room, she could have told him to leave. She could have *made* him leave. Instead, she had run like a deer straight into the lion's den. The club was packed; the flashing lights, pounding music, and overwhelming smell of sweat, alcohol, and blood were enough to make her head pound the minute that they walked in.

Isabelle stopped in the doorway, as she struggled to take everything in through the mass of bodies, and the pulsating lights that were nearly blinding. The dance floor was beneath them, down a narrow set of metal stairs. There was no room on it as men and women ground against each other.

She was wearing more clothes than most of the women here. Her anger from earlier returned with a vengeance as she scowled at Jack and Ian, who wisely chose to ignore her. Hell, she was dressed like a nun compared to most of the women there!

Lights of all different colors flashed on and off all over the floor. The music was so loud that it shook the metal balcony beneath her feet. Isabelle had to fight the urge to cover her ears and close her eyes in order to block everything out.

"Come on Issy!" Ian yelled in her ear.

She really didn't want to go, but he already had a firm hold on her elbow and was propelling her down the stairs. She halted at the bottom, uncertain of where to go. Ian released her elbow and began to make his way through the crowd, somehow finding a path that she never would have known existed. A young girl reached out and grabbed his arm. He was instantly swallowed up, and so was the path.

She found herself momentarily engulfed by the thick mass of bodies, completely uncertain of where to go.

Stefan grabbed hold of her elbow and pulled her along as he easily parted the crowd. Isabelle followed silently behind, to afraid of getting lost in the mob to protest his high handed treatment of her. They reached the end of the floor. She breathed a sigh of relief as the crowd parted, and a group of tables were revealed, most of them empty. Stefan led her over to one and she slumped gratefully into a chair.

"Do you want a drink?"

A drink was exactly what she needed to help her relax. "Yes, a Coors light!"

He nodded and turned to push his way back through the crowd. Isabelle saw the bar then. It was on the right hand side of the floor, a horseshoe shape that curved out to the edge of the mahogany floor. It was flashing with blue and green neon lights that pulsed throughout the glass bottom. There was a huge crowd surrounding it, all of them leaning over to yell their orders at the scurrying bartenders.

Isabelle watched in amazement as Stefan made his way through the yelling crowd. It was obvious that he was used to being in such places, and wasn't in the least bit intimidated by the huge crowd. Jealousy flashed through her as she wondered how many women he had taken out of clubs similar to this one. She knew what the stooges and her brothers were like, and Stefan was much older than they were. That added up to a lot of women, a lot of women that she didn't even want to think about. She tried to shove her jealousy aside, but it had become a hard lump in her stomach that wasn't going away. How could she ever compete with *that* many women?

The thought jolted her, nearly causing her to fall out of her chair in surprise. She didn't want to compete with any other women, as far as she was concerned they could all have him. Even as she thought it, she knew that she was lying to herself, which was something that she had never done before, and she refused to do now. She *did* want him, it was beyond time that she admitted that, but now she had the worry of how inexperienced she was to add to her growing list of worries.

For a moment, she wanted to cry. Life was so very unfair. She had hidden away, determined not to meet someone that made her feel the way he did. Then he had shown up at her house, invaded her life, and turned everything upside down. But even worse than that, he was arrogant, conceited, harsh, unbending, and a complete womanizer. Why couldn't she have found a nice, simple, human that wouldn't be able to affect her the way that he did?

"Would you like to dance?"

Isabelle blinked in surprise at the young man before her. He was tall and lean; his hair was dyed a platinum blond that stood up in short spikes. His face was narrow and pointy, his eyes a dark blue. He was smiling at her as he extended a long, fine boned hand. She opened her mouth to say no, and then recalled the entire reason that she had decided to come here. Being a wallflower was not going to help in her mission to find someone else that she desired.

She may want Stefan, but she was still determined to try and find someone that could make her feel even a little bit of what he did. That would at least be proof that he wasn't her soul mate. That she wasn't going to have to spend eternity with him.

She smiled sweetly at the man as she accepted his hand. He pulled her to her feet and led her onto the packed dance floor. She had a moment of panic when she realized that she hadn't danced since her senior prom, and she had no idea what kind of dancing these people were doing. Then she realized that there seemed to be no rhyme, or reason, to anyone's movements. They all seemed to be flowing to the beat of the music.

It took her a few minutes to relax, but when she did, she was surprised to actually find herself having fun. "My name's Frank!" he yelled above the pounding music.

"Isabelle!"

He smiled at her as he wrapped a hand around her waist. For a moment she tensed, her whole body going tight with a feeling of wrongness, of not belonging. Her mind instantly flashed to Stefan, and she ground her teeth. She was going to prove to him, and to herself, that she could, and *would*, be attracted to other people. She forced herself to smile back at him as she found the rhythm of the music.

So what if she didn't want Frank, there were lots of other men here. The music changed and Isabelle found herself swept into someone else's arms. She forced herself to keep smiling through the shudder of revulsion that swept her when the tall brunette wrapped his arm around her waist. At least she was having fun dancing, and if she kept on going, she would find someone who made her feel like Stefan did. She was sure of it.

Stefan stood stiffly on the sidelines watching as Isabelle was passed from one man to another. A fierce anger was slowly working its way through him as one man after another touched her, held her. He had to set their drinks down before he crushed them both. He saw the looks in the men's eyes, the way that they stared at her, and it took everything he had not to march across the floor, rip her out of their arms, and destroy them. Gritting his teeth, he closed his eyes for a moment and took a deep breath in order to steady himself.

He opened his eyes slowly, immediately fastening on her as lust tore through him. She looked absolutely stunning as she danced and smiled; the lights played off the golden highlights in her hair and emphasized the startling violet of her eyes. The simple black dress she wore was more enticing to him than any lingerie could have been. All he wanted was to slip it off and reveal the treasure beneath.

He tore his eyes away as lust, and rage, threatened to consume him. He glanced quickly over the dance floor, noting the admiring looks he received. He slowly began to rethink the way that he had been going about getting Isabelle. He had been chasing after her, trying to force her to bend to his will. The more he got to know her, the more he realized that trying to force her to do something wasn't going to work.

He would eventually wear down her defenses, but it would take longer than he was willing to wait. However, if she began to realize on her own that she truly did want him, she might not fight as hard. If she felt an ounce of the jealousy that he did she would come to him. Besides, if it didn't work, he could at least find someone here that could ease his need.

Stefan smiled as he made his way out to the dance floor, making sure that he stayed near Isabelle so that she could see him, and so that he could kill anyone that tried anything with her. He grabbed the first girl he saw and swept her into his arms. She grinned brightly at him as he pulled her against him.

Her hips ground against his as her chest pressed provocatively against his. He clenched his jaw tightly as a wave of revulsion swept through him. Damn, what was the matter with him? The girl was pretty enough, and more than willing, but he found himself disgusted by her overt movements, and obvious desire.

He wanted Isabelle, even cared for her, but he would be damned if he didn't want other women too. No one had ever been able to have that kind of power over him, and he was determined that she wasn't going to have it now. His new plan with Isabelle was completely forgotten as he became resolved to get her out of his mind, and to find someone else that could arouse him as she did. Maybe she had the right idea after all; they should just avoid each other. So what if he never had her, he'd had many disappointments in his long life. This wouldn't be the first, and it sure as hell wouldn't be the last. It was probably better for the both of them if he left her alone.

Involuntarily, his gaze darted to Isabelle as she laughed with the tall, dark haired man she was dancing with. A bolt of sizzling jealousy, and rage, swept through him. His hands clenched upon the tiny girl in his arms. She seemed to take it as an invite as she pressed tighter against him. It took everything he had not to shove her away in disgust, storm across the dance floor, and pull Isabelle out.

He would not do it; he would *not* let her get to him that way. He refused to. He realized then that he had to leave, that he had to get as far away from her as he could. It wasn't just a desire to bed her anymore, it was becoming an obsession. One that he needed to be free of. She was beginning to ruin his control, and his damn life! Tonight he would go back to the house, get his stuff, and leave.

Yet, even as he thought it, he found himself feeling a strange sense of loss. He didn't want to leave her, wasn't even sure he could leave her. He ground his jaw harder. Yes, he could leave her, and he *would*. She was just a woman for crying out loud, a woman like the thousands of others he'd met. The song ended and he released the girl that he had been dancing with. Isabelle was quickly claimed by someone else. The small girl before him moved back toward his arms, but he turned away from her, searching for someone else, *any*one else that could spark some kind of lust within him.

Isabelle danced for well over an hour. She was passed between many men, none of whom aroused her in anyway. With each new one, she became more and more determined to feel something, to experience any kind of desire, any kind of urge. Dancing was becoming less fun as her aggravation mounted with the pain in her feet.

She had seen Ian and Jack dancing happily. And she had seen *him*. The jealousy that had threatened to strangle her at

the sight of him dancing with another woman, only served
to fuel her determination. She flirted more outrageously,
and danced more suggestively with them, but nothing
happened. The only thing she felt was a growing sense of
revulsion, and a growing urge to move into his arms, to
touch him, to have him touch her. She refused to do it
though. He seemed quite content without her, and she
would be damned if she was the one that went to him.

Instead, she just wanted to get off of the floor, find a
place to curl up, and give into the tears of frustration that
were threatening to choke her. It was all so unfair, all of it,
and she resented every single second of it.

When the next song ended, Isabelle stepped away from
her dance partner, determined to escape. She made it two
feet before arms swept around her. She knew instantly who
held her by the fierce jolt that rocked her body. Her urge to
flee vanished as she turned toward him. His dark hair was
damp with sweat, and clung to his forehead with a tussled
boyishness that melted her heart and caused a fluttering in
her stomach. Without thinking she reached up and gently
brushed it back, startled by the wave of tenderness that
washed through her. The amount of caring that swamped
her.

She hesitantly met his gaze as he stared down at her with
dark, turbulent eyes. His jaw was clenched so tightly that a
muscle began to twitch in his cheek. The anger, and self
loathing, in his gaze caused her eyes to widen in surprise.
There was an air of hostility surrounding him that shocked
her as she tried to figure out what could have caused it.

Then, the look vanished as the fierce hunger she had
become accustomed to replaced it. For a moment, her
breath left her as that look sizzled through her. Then, he
was pulling her tightly against him. Her body melded to his
as if he was the missing jigsaw piece that she had been
searching for. The world disappeared as he rested his
forehead against hers. His dark eyes filled her vision and

pierced her soul. What she had been trying so hard to find with everyone else blazed to life. She pressed against him, her heart thumping wildly in her chest as a feeling of contentment, of coming home, stole through her.

She wrapped her arms around his neck and turned her head to rest it against his shoulder. It didn't matter that the music pulsing around them was fast and hard. Nothing mattered as she moved slowly with him, relishing in the feel of his hard arms around her, in the warmth of his body enveloping her. She welcomed the feeling of strength, security, and desire that rushed over her.

Stefan closed his eyes and rested his cheek on top of her silky head. The fresh apple scent of her hair enveloped him. Beneath that, he could smell the sweetness of her blood, and her delicious natural fragrance. He found himself growing hard as desire was finally awakened in him, desire and something more, something shocking. Something that shoved all of his earlier resolutions away.

He felt as if he had come home, as if he had finally found the place where he belonged. A fierce urge to protect her, to keep her safe, and to cherish her rocked through him. With horrifying clarity he began to realize how much he truly did care for her. He wanted so much more than just her body, he wanted all of her.

Fear lanced through him as his hands tightened upon her. He didn't need this; he didn't want to feel like this. It made him vulnerable in a way that he hadn't been since he was a child, and he didn't like the feeling one bit.

He wanted to get away from her as fast as he could, but he couldn't bring himself to release her, couldn't bring himself to step away. The music ended, and it was Isabelle that pulled away. Her eyes were dark and cloudy; tears brimmed in their vivid depths. The sight of those tears rocked him. He instantly wanted to get rid of them, to shield her from whatever was hurting her. Then, he realized that it was him that was causing her hurt, *him* that was tearing her apart.

He released her instantly, to shaken up to do anything else. She stared at him for a moment longer before turning and bolting off the floor. He watched her go, his own fear keeping him rooted in place as she hurried through the crowd. A sense of loss began to enfold him, but he refused to go after her, refused to stop her.

He needed to figure out his own emotions, needed to get rid of the horrible vulnerability that was filling him before he could be near her again. He needed to get the hell away from her before he began to care for her even more than he already did. He knew what happened when he cared about people, and he was not about to let it happen again.

Isabelle pushed her way through the crowd, determined to put some distance between her and Stefan. It seemed useless. His scent clung to her; her skin still burned everywhere that he had touched. The door at the back of the club beckoned to her like a homing beacon. She slammed into the bar, shoving roughly against it, and nearly falling in her eagerness to be free.

Fresh air assailed her and she inhaled gratefully. She was still shivering from the aftereffects of his touch, and the burning desire that coursed through her. She couldn't do this anymore, she simply couldn't do it. She wrapped her arms around herself and fell against the cement wall as she desperately fought back the tears that wanted to fall. She hated him for doing this to her, for making her feel like this, for disrupting her perfectly nice life. She hated him for the fact that, even now she wanted to feel his arms around her again. Wanted him to hold her. Wanted to know every inch of him.

In his arms she had felt whole, complete. Now, without him, she felt vulnerable, and open, and wounded. She didn't even like him, how the hell could he make her feel like this, when she didn't even like him? And yet, she had to admit to herself, she did like him. She liked his lazy smile; the way that he looked at her, the fact that he had been willing to help out with the house, and to help her mother with Kathleen. She liked that he had made it possible for Aiden to have a large party, the way he had saved her and Julian, the way that he had protected her from Jess. And she was truly beginning to like the way that he made her feel like a desirable, precious woman. The way he made her feel like she was something that he couldn't part with.

She was even beginning to like the way that he made her body feel.

A tear slid free as she began to realize that everything she had been fighting so hard against was happening anyway. He had managed to work his way through all of her defenses, and he had managed to work his way into her body. Into her soul. She wanted to hate him for it, but she found herself unable to summon up the strength for that emotion, or the desire for it. She couldn't hate him, she could never hate him. She knew that now.

Isabelle bent her head as she shuddered. It was time to concede defeat. There was no use fighting against the inevitable. She wanted him, and God help her, she was beginning to need him. She was beginning to feel empty, and alone, whenever he wasn't near. Why fight something, if it was meant to be? Why keep putting herself, and him, through this torture?

She sighed wearily as she straightened away from the wall. All she wanted to do now was go home. She was completely drained. She was reaching for the handle when a thick, large hand seized hold of her arm and spun her around. Isabelle cried out in surprise as she was shoved into the wall.

"Look at this!" a man cried.

Isabelle blinked in surprise at the four men in front of her; one was tall and blond, another short with red hair, and the other two of average height, with brown hair. All of their eyes narrowed as they slowly, leeringly, scanned her body. She stiffened angrily and stepped away from the wall. "What the hell do you think you're doing?" she demanded.

Then, the smell of them hit her. She instantly recognized what they were as their eyes came back to hers. "Well, I'll be," the redhead said, his eyes slowly surveying her again.

Isabelle's hands clenched, but she didn't make a move. They were her kind, but unlike the feeling she had experienced on first meeting Stefan, fear was beginning to coil tightly within her belly. She forced herself not to show it, forced her face to remain impassive as they surveyed her. They smelled awful, they smelled *wrong*.

They smelled like death, and she knew instantly that these were the ones of her kind that took pleasure in killing humans, thrived off the feeling of power that it gave them. She had never encountered anything like them before, but she had heard about them, and she knew that they existed. She'd just never thought that she would meet them.

"Excuse me," Isabelle said coldly.

"No need to get so haughty," the blond said. "We've just never run across a female of our kind that was so lovely before. We're a little curious."

"Well, now that your curiosity has been satisfied, I need to get back inside."

She moved to go around them, but the blond grabbed hold of her arm and shoved her back. Isabelle's eyes flashed with rage. "Oh, she's a feisty one," he leered.

"I like it," one of the brunette's chimed in.

"Let me by," she hissed.

"Just calm down gorgeous," the redhead said. "We just want to talk to you."

"Let me by!"

"I don't like her attitude."

"Neither do I," the blond agreed.

"And I don't like yours!" she snapped.

"I think she needs a lesson in manners."

"So do I," the other brunette said.

Fury and fear were waging a fierce war inside of her as she tilted her chin defiantly. "Trust me, you won't be the one to give it to me," she snarled.

They all exchanged quick, smug looks. "I always wondered what our kind tastes like. She smells sweet."

Fear caused the demon inside of her to burst free. She lashed out, tearing across the blonde's chest and spilling his tainted blood. He jumped back in surprise as his face twisted in a grimace of pain. She darted quickly to the side, determined to get back inside while he was off guard. A hand seized hold of her hair, ripping her back, and slamming her into a massive, solid chest. The blond quickly recovered, his eyes blazed red with fury as he came at her again. The other two came forward, their teeth gleaming brightly in the dim lights of the alley, their eyes a vivid, malevolent red.

Full fledged panic tore through her as she clawed at the hands holding her hair. A moment of satisfaction spurted through her as she tore into his skin. A fierce hiss echoed in her ear, but the grip didn't lessen as her head was jerked back with a sharp crack that sent pain blazing down her neck. The redhead, and one of the brunette's, seized hold of her arms, pinning them to her sides as the blond stopped before her. She kicked out at him, but he deftly avoided her as he came to her side.

Panting heavily, and trembling with fury and fear, Isabelle's panic was starting to become all consuming. For some reason, a picture of Stefan formed in her mind. She silently screamed his name as the blondes teeth sank into her neck. She lost all thought as agonizing pain tore through her body, blurred her vision, and knocked all of the fight out of her.

Never had she felt anything so hurtful, never had she imagined such pain could exist. Her entire body felt as if it were engulfed in flames that licked over every inch of her skin, and seared the marrow from her bones. She wanted to struggle, wanted to break free, but she found herself unable to move through the agonizing torture that was tearing her body to shreds.

A loud roar echoed in her ears, moments before the teeth were ripped from her neck ripped across her skin. She stumbled back, slamming into the wall, as her hand reached up to cling to the jagged wounds in her neck. "Isabelle!" She blinked dazedly at Stefan as he grabbed hold of her shoulders. "Isabelle are you all right?"

She focused on him for a moment, saw the worry, and the fury that twisted his face as his eyes blazed a violent blood red. She opened her mouth to tell him that she was all right, but a wave of blackness washed over her, and all thought was lost as it pulled her under.

Stefan swung her easily up, cradling her head against his chest as his hands wrapped into her silken hair. A fierce wave of protection washed over him, pushing out some of his fury. Then, he thought about what could have happened to her and the fury blazed forth again. He anxiously scanned the alley, searching for any sign that they might still be around. Hoping they were so he could rip them to shreds. But they were all gone, including Jack and Ian.

Stefan pulled back her hair, the fury in him nearly exploded as he saw the jagged lacerations that ripped through her delicate skin. His hands were shaking as he lightly touched the marks. She whimpered softly, but didn't awaken. He instantly dropped his hand back to his side; a snarl curled his lips as he cradled her tighter. The constricting pain in his chest was almost unbearable as he realized that he could have lost her, that they could have taken her from him.

He bit back a roar of fury, and anguish as he quickly scanned the alley again. He should have gone after them, should have destroyed them himself, but he had been unable to leave her side. He had been unable to go anywhere until he knew that she was ok, and that they hadn't destroyed her. Unable to be anywhere, but at her side.

Jack appeared beside him, panting slightly, his eyes wide with worry as he gazed at Isabelle. "Is she all right?" he asked anxiously.

"No. Where are they?" he snarled.

Jack's eyes sharpened on Stefan. "They're gone," he said slowly.

"They were old." Jack's brow furrowed, but he didn't question how Stefan knew that. "We need to get her out of here, now."

Jack nodded as Ian reappeared. "Get the car," Jack told him.

"Is she all right?" Ian demanded.

"Get the fucking car!" Stefan snapped.

Ian's eyes darkened with anger, but he didn't argue with him. Instead, he nodded sharply and took off around the building. Stefan shifted his hold on Isabelle as blood began to trickle onto his fingers. Fierce anger ripped through him again as he fully realized that someone else had touched her, that they had hurt her. He was trembling with his urge to kill, with the fierce need to destroy. He had mistakenly thought that he had managed to rid himself of such urges, managed to leave them in his past, but he knew now that he had been completely wrong. The killer in him was still very close to the surface, and it was Isabelle that brought it out in him.

He inhaled sharply as that realization sank in and rattled his thin thread of composure even more.

When her fear had slammed into him inside the club, he had been jolted by the amazing fact that she had been able to communicate it to him at all. Only vampires who had a bond with someone were able to communicate with them. That bond was usually forged through blood or sex.

Then, all of those thoughts had fled as he was seized by the overwhelming drive to get to her, to kill whoever was hurting her, and anyone that got in his way. He had been seized again by the bloodlust that had driven him for centuries, a bloodlust that he had been determined to rid himself of. He now knew that he had failed miserably in his attempt to do so.

He had also failed in his need to keep her safe. She had been hurt by a part of the world that he had never wanted her to know existed, and all because he'd been too stubborn to go after her when she'd left. It was his fault that she was hurt. If it hadn't been for him, she never would have come to the club tonight, she never would have been outside, and she sure as hell wouldn't have been hurt. At that moment, he hated himself completely.

"How much did they take from her?" Jack asked worriedly.

"I don't know," Stefan said coldly.

"We need to get her blood, now!"

Stefan searched her face. She was extremely pale, her lips nearly white, but her heart was beating soundly, and she was breathing regularly. He closed his eyes and used his power to push himself into her body, to feel out the amount of damage that they had inflicted upon her. It wasn't something he would be able to do if she was awake, and fought him. However, now that she was unconscious, and vulnerable, he was able to drift into her and sense how much they had taken. He sighed in relief as he realized that it hadn't been much, that they hadn't even gotten the same amount of blood as one of her bags. He pulled slowly out of her, lightly stroking her velvety cheek as he gazed at her unconscious form.

"They didn't take much," he said quietly.

"They must have! Look at her!"

"No, they didn't," Stefan grated.

"Then why is she out like a light!?" Jack shouted his fear evident in his slightly shrill voice.

Stefan grit his teeth and closed his eyes against the raging anger, fear for her, and self loathing that was tearing him to shreds. "Because of the pain."

"What?" Jack asked in confusion.

Stefan's eyes flew open. Jack's eyes widened in surprise, his mouth parted slightly, and he took a quick step back. "The pain!" he hissed. "When you're a human, and your blood is drained unwillingly, it hurts like hell. Trust me, I know. When you're a vampire and it happens, it feels as if the fires of hell are searing through your body. It's why she couldn't fight them off."

"Oh," Jack said softly, his eyes slowly scanning Stefan before returning to Isabelle. "Will she be all right?"

Jack took a step toward her, his hand reached out to touch her. Stefan immediately stepped back, anger flared through him as a soft hiss escaped. Shock over his reaction coursed through him, but his body remained tense, and rigid, with animosity. He didn't know why he had done it, he knew that Jack would never hurt Isabelle, but the idea of him touching her had instantly brought the demon out of him.

He knew he would lose control if Jack insisted upon touching her, the thought alone made him shake with fury. Jack's eyes came back to his, but to Stefan's surprise, he didn't argue with him, and he didn't try to get near her again. His eyes were filled with a sad acceptance as he took a wary step back and his hand dropped limply to his side.

Stefan's eyes narrowed on Jack as he clung tighter to her. She was so vulnerable, so frail and fragile that it was tearing at his insides. He eyed Jack warily, unable to understand why Jack, a man that had helped raise Isabelle, had just backed away from him without a protest. Stefan's emotions were becoming more tumultuous and disordered by the second. He was losing complete control of himself, because of her.

"Will she be okay?" Jack asked again.

"Yes. She just needs some rest, and some blood."

Headlights swung into the alley as Ian drove at them. He pulled up with a screech of brakes and hopped out of the car and raced toward them. "Jack, you drive! Give her to me!"

He stopped before Stefan and held his arms out to take Isabelle. Stefan's nostrils flared as his jaw clenched, and his rage began to build again. "No," he spat.

Ian blinked in surprise, and then anger flooded his face. "Give *my* sister to me!" he demanded.

He reached out to grab her. Stefan hissed angrily, turning so that his body was between Ian and Isabelle. Ian's eyes flashed fiercely as his nostrils flared and his jaw locked. Jack grabbed hold of Ian's arm and pulled him roughly back. "Get in the car Ian!" he ordered.

Ian rounded angrily on him, his hands clenched at his sides. "I will not! Not without..."

"Now! Get in the car now!" Jack bellowed at him.

Ian's eyes widened in surprise as Jack shoved him toward the passenger side of the car. "Jack..."

"Ian, if you want to live, you will get in this car!" Jack hissed.

Ian stared at him in shock as Jack flung the door open and shoved him inside. Stefan stood silently, his anger slowly ebbing as astonishment began to replace it. What the hell was going on with him, with Jack? "Let's go!" Jack yelled.

Stefan shook off his confusion, now was not the time for it. He slid into the backseat and closed the door. He cradled Isabelle on his lap, unable to let her go as Jack tore out of the alleyway.

CHAPTER 14

Stefan carried Isabelle swiftly into the house behind Jack. David, Doug, Mike, and Ethan looked up from the baseball game they were watching, shock registered on all of their faces seconds before they leapt to their feet. "What the hell happened?" Mike demanded.

"She was attacked," Jack answered. "Put her on the couch Stefan, I'll get some blood."

"Shit!"

They came rushing around the couches toward him. Stefan glowered at them and pulled her tighter against his chest. If he had to, he would kill everyone in this room to keep them from touching her. David, Doug, and Mike skidded to a halt behind the couch, while Ethan kept on coming. "Get away from her!" Stefan spat as Ethan stopped before him.

Ethan's eyes widened and then narrowed fiercely in anger. "I don't know who the hell you think you are, but that is *my* sister!"

"I'm telling you right now to get away from her!" he nearly roared.

Mike jumped forward to grab hold of Ethan's arm and rip him back. "Get your hands off of me!" Ethan snapped at him.

"Go get your parents, now!" Mike ordered.

"But..."

"Now!"

"I'm not going anywhere!" Ethan yelled. "Until I know what happened, and he gets his hands off of my sister!"

Ethan's eyes flashed red as he took a step forward. Stefan hissed and lunged forward. Seizing hold of Ethan's throat, he lifted him easily off of the ground. Ethan struggled in his grasp, his hands clutching wildly at Stefan as he dug into Ethan's throat. "Shit Stefan, no!" David moved swiftly forward to stand in front of him, but made no move to stop him. "Isabelle will *hate* you if you hurt him!"

Stefan was struggling wildly against losing complete control as bloodlust, and fury, raged through him. David's words slowly managed to penetrate the wild frenzy growing within him. Isabelle *would* hate him if he hurt Ethan. It was that thought alone that enabled him to shove the killing frenzy aside and release his hold on Ethan's neck. He hit the ground, stumbling back his eyes flashed with rage as his hand flew to his bruised throat. David grabbed hold of Ethan's arm, shoving him forcefully to the side as Mike grabbed hold of the other one.

"Get your parents," David hissed.

"Neither of us is going anywhere." Ian said forcefully.

"You need to get your parents, *now!*" Mike shoved them both toward the door.

"Mike..."

"Go!" David bellowed.

Stefan shot a warning look at Doug as he moved past him. Doug took a quick step back, his gaze focused worriedly on Isabelle as Stefan laid her gently on the couch. Jack rushed back into the room with a bag of blood hand. He skidded to a halt next to Doug, his gaze flickered quickly to Isabelle, and then apprehensively back to Stefan. Anger shot through him at the thought of Jack feeding her, but Jack made no move toward her as he held the bag out to Stefan.

Stefan stared at him for a moment before snatching the bag out of his hand and ripping it open with his teeth. Stefan lifted her head cautiously and opened her lips to place the bag against them. She moaned softly, her eyelids twitched as she opened her mouth to receive it.

Relief flooded through him as he gently stroked her hair and continued to slowly feed her. "Is she going to be ok?" Mike asked softly.

"Yes," he growled.

He was a little wary that they would attack him for what he had done to Ethan, but he knew that he could destroy them if they even attempted it. He was not going to leave Isabelle alone with them. It didn't matter to him that they were like her brothers, or that he had attacked first, he wasn't going to allow any of them near her until he knew that she was completely safe.

However, as they made no move to take her away from him his wariness quickly turned to confusion. Why weren't they attacking him? Surely they would, if they thought that he would harm Isabelle, or them. Instead, they seemed to accept the fact that he had assumed control over her, and that he had attacked one of them.

From everything he'd seen over the past week, any of them would willingly die for one of the others. He didn't understand their silent acceptance of the fact that he had come damn close to killing Ethan. It made absolutely no sense to him. What was the matter with them? Why were they taking this so well? And what the hell did they know that he didn't? His jaw clenched as a million questions raced through his head, but then Isabelle moaned softly and all thought fled as he focused his attention solely on her.

"What the hell happened?" David demanded.

Stefan lifted his head, his eyes flashed dangerously as his jaw clenched. Their eyes widened slightly as they stared at him, but none of them said anything, and the looks on their faces were ones of awe. "I'll tell you later," Jack said quickly.

Stefan searched their faces, but he didn't much care what they thought. His attention returned to Isabelle as the last of the blood slid slowly down her throat. He tossed the bag aside, lifted her head gently, and slid onto the couch. He laid her head in his lap and gently stroked her soft, pale face. She rolled over and her delicate hand curled tightly into his thigh.

A surge of protectiveness flowed through him as his hand curled into her hair. He wanted to get as close to her as possible, he needed to keep her safe from the world. From himself. He was even more dangerous than the men that had attacked her, even more deadly. He was especially dangerous now, when his emotions were in a rioting turmoil that felt as if they were going to explode.

The screen door banged open as Sera and Liam came rushing inside. "What happened!?" Sera raced toward him, terror etched onto her delicate face.

She cast David and Doug a scathing look as they moved to intercept her and darted around them. She fell on her knees before Isabelle. Tears spilled freely down her face as she stroked Isabelle's hair back. "Is she okay?" she sobbed.

"She will be," Stefan assured her.

Liam appeared behind her and reached out to grasp hold of Isabelle's hand. Stefan instinctively stiffened; a snarl curved his mouth, as he pulled Isabelle tighter against him. Liam's eyes flashed with fire, a growl escaped him as he ripped Sera backward. "What the hell are you doing?" she demanded angrily, as he shoved her behind him.

"Whoa!" Doug jumped in between them both with his hands held out. "Calm down! Both of you!"

Sera poked her head around Liam, her eyes widened in surprise before she began to laugh. "Liam, move," she said as she pushed at his back.

"No!" he snapped.

Sera drew glaring looks from both Stefan and Liam as she laughed harder. Suddenly, Doug began to chuckle softly, and from behind him, he could hear more muffled laughter. "I think that we should all go into the dining room," Sera managed to say. "Stefan will take care of Isabelle."

"I am *not* leaving my daughter alone with him," Liam grated.

"Yes, you are," Sera said firmly. Liam's eyes slowly changed back to green as he turned to look down at her, an eyebrow raised questioningly as they silently communicated with each other. She nodded briskly as she took hold of his arm, skirting wide of Stefan as she led him away.

"What about Isabelle?" Ethan demanded.

"She'll be fine," Doug said.

"But..."

"Ethan trust me, she'll be fine," Sera said softly. "Come on."

Stefan found himself alone with only the dark mass of his twisting emotions for company. For a moment, he had been willing to kill Isabelle's father simply because he'd wanted to touch his daughter. He had almost killed her bother for the same reason. He knew now that there was something seriously wrong with him, that she was causing him to lose all of his control. Hell, he felt like he was going insane.

She moaned softly, burying her head deeper into his lap as his hands tightened convulsively on her. A fierce surge of guardianship seared through him again, but he quickly shoved it aside. He needed to stay cool, and calm. He needed to think. He knew that he had to get away from her before he truly hurt someone, before he caused her even more pain. Before he brought the monster that he had once been down on them all.

He could easily destroy everyone in this house, and for some reason, Isabelle made the demon in him even fiercer, and wilder, than it had ever been before. If he didn't get away from her, he would become the one thing that he'd truly hated over the years. The one thing that he had fought so savagely against becoming. She deserved much better than anything he could ever give her, much better than the dark world of pain and torment that he lived in, and he meant to see that she was never again touched by it. He had been selfish in his lust for her, but he knew now that he had been wrong, and he was going to right it.

**

"I cannot believe that you're leaving her alone with him!" Ethan exploded. "He's obviously unstable! He was going to kill me! He could kill *her*!"

"No, he couldn't," Sera said softly.

"How do you know that?" Ian yelled.

"Calm down," Liam said. "He won't hurt her, he loves her."

"What!?" Ethan and Ian demanded.

Liam and Sera exchanged an amused look as they turned back to them. "They're meant to be together," she said softly. "They're soul mates."

Mike, David, Doug, and Jack grinned with amusement as Ethan and Ian started to sputter. "Trust me, we know the signs," Doug said with a small chuckle.

"What? Total insanity?" Ethan bellowed.

"Yep," they all said.

They exchanged confused glances. "I don't understand," Ethan said wearily.

"You wouldn't, you didn't see your father when he first met your mother. When soul mates meet each other they are totally unstable, especially the male, until they have completely branded their mate. Your mother was still human, a vampire cannot have that. They sense the mortality in their mate, and they need to change it. Your father was so volatile that if we even touched her, he wanted to rip our throats out. If your mother hadn't changed willingly, he would have forced it on her, no matter what," David explained.

"Until their relationship is solidified Stefan is going to be very unstable," Mike stated.

Ethan and Ian's eyes were questioning as they turned to Liam and Sera. "My guess is that neither one of them knows what's going on yet," Sera said softly. "And they're both fighting their feelings."

"Stefan is the one that told me about you two, he should know." David's brow was furrowed in confusion as he studied them.

"Sometimes it's easier to see something when it isn't right in front of you. Plus, I know Isabelle, if this isn't something that she wants than she is going to fight it every step of the way. For now, just stay away from Isabelle, and don't touch her when he's around," Sera said softly.

"But..."

"I know you don't like it Ethan," Liam said. "But you have to. Until they figure out what is going on, and everything stabilizes, you need to stay away from her. He will be volatile, and he won't mean to be. I know I would snap for no reason. I thought I was going insane. I had no idea what was wrong with me, what was going on, and I would have killed anyone."

"Threw me across a room," Doug mumbled.

Ethan and Ian gaped at him in astonishment before turning to look at their father. Liam shrugged as he reached out to pull Sera against him. "If it ever happens to you, trust me, you'll understand. Something inside of you changes. All rational thought, and all control vanishes, until you know that she is yours. Although, I'm not sure how it works between two vampires, but I suppose it's similar."

"They'll probably need to exchange blood, and..." Mike broke off; a dull flush stained his cheeks as his face twisted in chagrin.

"I don't want to think about that!" Liam yelled.

Sera bit into her bottom lip to keep from laughing. "Neither do I," Mike muttered.

"Well I hope they do, whatever it is that they have to do, soon," Jack said. "It was hard enough dealing with Liam, but if that guy snaps it is not going to be pretty. His powers are a lot stronger than ours. He lifted Ethan like he weighed no more than a twig."

Ethan smiled sheepishly as he rubbed his bruised neck. "Yeah he did."

"Should we tell him what's going on?" Ian asked.

"I'll talk to him," Sera said softly.

"You will not!" Liam hissed as his hands tightened on her.

"He's not going to hurt me Liam; I was the only one that he let near Isabelle. I don't think he knows what's going on, and once I tell him I think he'll be a lot calmer, and things will start to make more sense to him. Right now, he's just as confused as you were."

"I don't want you anywhere near him."

Sera sighed impatiently. "I'll stay on the other side of the room, and you can stand right by my side. Someone needs to tell him something, and I'm the least threatening of you all."

"Fine," Liam relented. "But you'll be staying in the kitchen, far away from him."

Sera smiled as she looked at everyone. "I can't believe that we have to go through this again," Doug muttered.

"I can't believe we're going to have to deal with another sickening couple," Jack snorted.

"Ugh!" they groaned.

CHAPTER 15

Isabelle knew that he was gone the minute she woke up. A crushing sense of loss descended on her as a dull ache bloomed in her chest. She scrunched her eyes tight as she tried to shove the hurt away. It was what she had wanted after all. What she had been longing for since he had arrived. She should be happy that he was gone; she was *going* to be happy that he was gone. She opened her eyes slowly and blinked against the bright light that filled the living room.

"You're awake." She turned to find her mother sitting on the other couch, her hands clasped before her as she worriedly scanned Isabelle's face. "How do you feel?"

"He's gone." It wasn't what she had meant to say, but the words had popped out anyway.

Her mother's eyes darkened as she nodded briskly. "He left after he brought you home."

Isabelle swallowed heavily and closed her eyes against the pain in her chest. She was going to be happy, she told herself fiercely. Tears filled her eyes, but she refused to shed them. "Why?" she whispered.

"I don't know. He left before any of us could talk to him."

"I hurt," she murmured, not sure if she was talking about her ache for Stefan or the lingering discomfort in her body.

"What hurts?" her mother asked gently.

'Everything!' she wanted to cry in anguish. "My body," she lied. "I'm sore."

"It will get better." Her mother moved over to kneel before her. Isabelle opened her eyes to meet her dark, violet blue gaze. "About Stefan..."

"I'm glad he's gone," she said forcefully. "Now my life will get back to normal."

Her mother's eyes searched her face as she lightly stroked back her hair. "Yes, I'm sure it will." Isabelle closed her eyes firmly, refusing to see the pain, and pity, in her mother's gaze. "Are you hungry?"

"Yes."

"I'll be right back."

Isabelle listened as her mother moved away, but she refused to open her eyes. The annoying tears were threatening to come again, and she refused to shed them. Not for him. He didn't deserve her tears. This was exactly what she wanted, and she was going to rejoice in the fact that he was gone. She was going to get her life back together, and she was going to forget that he had ever existed.

Even as she told herself this, the pain in her chest intensified, and a single tear slid free.

***

The next two days passed by in a blur of misery. Isabelle found herself disjointed, irritable, and exceptionally moody. She snapped at everyone, cried for no reason, and constantly ached in every part of her body. Her heart had become a constricted lump of muscle that blazed agony through her with every beat. There were times that she thought she was simply going to die from the pain that wracked her.

She saw the looks that everyone gave her, heard their whispered comments, but she couldn't bring herself to care about any of it. Her mind was a foggy mess that didn't want to function. She couldn't bring herself to eat, and sleep was the only solitude that she found. She would curl up in her bed, drag the comforters over her head, cry out her anguish, and when she was completely exhausted, sleep would finally claim her.

Then, she would dream of him, and in her dreams the pain eased, and everything was right again. When she woke, the pain instantly reclaimed her body, seizing hold of her, and shaking her until she broke out in a cold sweat, and tears of anguish were wrenched from her. She would curl into a ball and cry until she was too weak to cry anymore. Then, she would fall back asleep, and the whole process would start again.

On the third day, her hunger began to get to her. She made her way upstairs, every step an act of sheer will power. She felt horrible, she looked horrible, and it was *his* fault. It didn't matter that she had wanted him to leave, that she had gotten what she wanted, because she could no longer recall why she had wanted it. She only wanted him to come back, but he had abandoned her, and left her to feel like this. Left her here to suffer miserably while he went off gallivanting, doing whatever he wanted. That thought only made the pain worse, and she tried desperately not to allow herself to think about what he could possibly be doing, and with whom.

The pain didn't ease with every day like she had hoped, it only got worse. Much worse. She was beginning to fear that if it didn't ease, she would die from it. She had never imagined that anything could hurt like this. Not even when they had drained her blood had it hurt like this. She had a permanent black cloud of misery enfolding her, making it hard to breathe, hard to live. She felt as if she was missing a piece of herself, the piece that had made it possible for her to exist, and she didn't know how she was going to survive.

Ethan was in the kitchen when she made it upstairs. His eyes widened in surprise as they landed on her. He had always been her rock, her best friend, the one person that she had turned to in times of comfort and need, but she didn't even speak to him, *couldn't* speak to him. "Isabelle," he said gently.

She shook her head, unable to deal with him at the moment. He took hold of her arm and settled her onto one of the stools before grabbing a bag of blood and opening it for her. She accepted it and drank it quickly before tossing it aside. "That's the first time I've seen you feed since you were eight."

Isabelle looked into his warm, worried green eyes, and burst into tears. Ethan stood in stunned silence before wrapping his arms around her and pulling her tightly against him. He rocked her as she clung to his shirt and buried her head in his solid chest. The comfort she had always found in him was nowhere now. She hurt too much to find any comfort anywhere. She cried herself out, but still clung to him, unable to move for fear that she'd fall off the stool.

"It will be all right," he soothed.

"No it won't," she whispered. "I want to go to bed."

"You can't spend the rest of your life asleep Issy."

She started crying again, but she was so exhausted that only dry sobs wracked her. Ethan helped her climb to her feet, and led her into the living room. She curled up on the couch; drawing her knees to her chest, she wrapped her arms around them as she tried to ease the agony in her body. He sat nervously beside her, uncertain of what to do, of how to help her as he lightly stroked her hair until she fell back asleep.

He looked up as David, his mother, and Mike came through the door. "I thought you said that he couldn't hurt her!" he snapped.

"He'll be back," his mother said softly. "He has to come back."

"And if he doesn't?" Ethan demanded.

His mother's eyes filled with tears as her gaze met his. "They say that one can't live without the other," David said softly. "They go insane and have to be destroyed, or they kill themselves."

Ethan swallowed heavily as his hand convulsed in Isabelle's hair. He had never seen her look so bad. No matter how much sleep she got, there were still dark shadows under her eyes. She had become so pale that she was almost translucent, and he could clearly see the tiny blue veins in her temples, eyelids, and neck. Her hair was lackluster, its natural shine gone. Her face was pinched tight, even in her sleep, and she had lost a good five pounds.

"She'll die," he said softly.

"Maybe, maybe not. We don't really know how it all works. They may not have known each other long enough, they may not have been able to form a strong enough bond for it to end that way," Mike said hopefully.

"They formed a bond," Sera said softly. "Ian said it was Stefan that knew she was in trouble the other night, and he would have killed Ethan if David hadn't managed to get through to him. Their bond is strong already. Trust me, I know."

"Why would he leave then?" Ethan demanded.

"I don't know. Maybe he thought it would be for the best, but if Isabelle is going through this much pain, than so is he."

"And if he's not? If you're wrong about that, and he doesn't come back?"

"I don't know Ethan!" she cried, tears streaking down her cheeks. "I don't know!"

***

Isabelle rested her chin on top of her drawn up knees. She wrapped her arms around them as she stared at the moonlight spilling across the lake. It had taken every bit of strength and energy she had to get out here, but her mother had insisted upon a walk, and she had been too tired to put up an argument. Her mother sat silently beside her, gazing out at the lake as she slowly rocked the swing back and forth.

"I miss him," Isabelle mumbled.

"I know you do."

"I never wanted this," she whispered. "I never wanted to feel like this. I tried so hard to avoid it." Her voice broke on a sob; she had to pause to take a deep breath before she could go on. "I stayed away from everyone, stayed away from humans, just so this wouldn't happen."

Her mother looked at her questioningly. "So what wouldn't happen?" she asked gently.

"*This*! Look at me! I'm a mess!" she cried. "I hurt so bad that I can hardly breathe. I never wanted to be like you and dad. I didn't want it!" She was sobbing again, her body shaking as tears slid down her face. Her mother touched her arm gently as she continued to sob out her misery. "Before he came, I hadn't cried since Ethan and Ian cut off my hair, and now I can't stop. I feel like I'm dying! I *never* wanted to feel this vulnerable because of another person!"

"Isabelle, hiding away from the world wasn't going to stop anything. What is meant to be is meant to be. You two were meant to be together, no matter what you did, you weren't going to change that fact."

"No, we're not!" she yelled. "He wouldn't have left then! What is the matter with me?"

"Nothing," her mom assured her. "There is nothing wrong with you Isabelle."

Isabelle hugged her legs tighter as she fought against the fierce tremors that wracked her pain stricken body. "Yes, there is. Abby and Vicky like every guy they meet. I've never felt anything, for anyone, until I met him."

Her mom sighed softly, her hand curled gently around the back of Isabelle's head. "Because a part of you knew that he was out there, that he would come for you. Vicky and Abby may not have that person."

"Why couldn't that have been me? They want soul mates. I don't. I don't even know if he is, or not. I don't know anything anymore." She started shaking with the force of her sobs, and misery. She leaned against her mother as she hugged her tightly. "I never wanted my life, my existence, to hang on someone else's. I know that what you and dad have is special, but if he dies, than you die, and vice versa. I never wanted to be so vulnerable! Now... now..."

She broke off, unable to speak through her sobs. She buried her head in her mother's shoulder as she continued to gently stroke her hair. "It's a wonderful thing Isabelle," she whispered. "It's frightening, and it's scary, but it is truly wonderful. What you have discovered is something magical, something that most people never find. Something that your sisters, your brothers, and the stooges may never find."

Isabelle shuddered; agony tore through her as she felt Stefan's loss deep in her bones. "It doesn't matter, he's gone, and it hurts so much," she whispered.

Her mom sighed gently, her hand stilled on Isabelle's hair. "You could try and find him."

Isabelle shook her head. "He doesn't want me, otherwise he wouldn't have left."

"Do you love him?"

Isabelle closed her eyes as she thought over her mother's question. "I don't know. I didn't even like him, but he made me feel things I've never felt before, made me feel complete, and whole, and safe, and so many other things," she finished shyly.

Her mom chuckled softly. "I understand," she assured her.

Isabelle knew that she did, but it didn't help to ease the awful pain that twisted her entire being. "Do you think that he really is my soul mate?" she asked softly.

"Yes."

"Why?"

She sighed and gently pushed the swing back. "You didn't see him when you were hurt Isabelle. He wanted to attack everyone that came near you, including your father. He *did* attack Ethan." Isabelle shuddered at the thought of what could have happened to Ethan, if David hadn't intervened. It would have killed her if Ethan had been seriously hurt. "He was losing control of himself. I think that's why he went away. It's a very frightening thing. When your father went through it he was confused, and angry, and scared that he would hurt everyone, including me."

"Daddy would never hurt you."

"He wouldn't have meant to, but he would have if I had insisted on staying human. It is confusing Isabelle, and it is frightening, but it is worth it. I promise you that much."

"What do I do?" she whispered forlornly.

"I don't know sweetie."

Isabelle grew silent as she allowed herself to be somewhat comforted by her mother's warm embrace, but it wasn't enough. She had fought him so hard, and he had left because of it. Now all she wanted was to have him back. She wouldn't fight him now, if he would just come back. She wished that there was some way that she could bring him back, some way that she could reach him and tell him to come back. Tears slid silently down her cheeks as she closed her eyes.

The air was warm and still, not even a breeze stirred it, and yet, something did. Isabelle sat up quickly and her gaze darted toward the woods.

"Isabelle," her mom said softly.

Her legs dropped to the ground as she stood slowly. She saw him then, standing at the edge of the forest, his eyes as dark as the night enveloping him. Her heart leapt into her throat as happiness burst through her. For the first time in days, her body wasn't burning, wasn't dying, and she was able to breathe without difficulty. The moonlight spilled over the hard set of his jaw, and illuminated the fierce hunger in his gaze as he took a step forward. A small cry escaped as her paralysis broke. She raced across the small distance separating them and threw her arms around his neck as tears of joy spilled down her cheeks.

CHAPTER 16

A low growl of pleasure escaped him as he pulled her against him. All of the tense anger, and burning fire that had been searing through him for the last three days, evaporated the moment that he touched her. Everything was finally right again, everything finally made sense again. Sera stood, nodded to him, and slipped silently away.

He wrapped his hand tightly into Isabelle's hair, pulled her face out of his shoulder, and savagely seized hold of her mouth. She whimpered softly against the brutality of his kiss, but he couldn't stop himself, couldn't ease it. He needed her like a drowning man needed air. Needed her with a longing so fierce that it snapped the tenuous thread of control he had just barely managed to hold on to for the past three days.

Her mouth parted beneath his and he thrust his tongue inside to ferociously taste her, taking and demanding everything that she had. His control slowly began to come back to him as her sweetness washed over him, enveloped him. It caused the fierce wildness within him to diminish as she eased the torment that had been haunting his soul for centuries. She eased the darkness that had been clawing to break free, and had grown almost uncontrollable over the past three days.

Her hands wrapped tightly around his neck as she pressed herself firmly against him, returning his kiss with an urgency that matched his own. He released her hair and seized hold of her waist, lifting her easily up. She gasped in surprise as he settled her on his waist and her long legs instinctively wrapped tightly around him.

She gazed down at him as tears slid silently down her cheeks and her violet eyes smoldered with passion. She scanned his face reverently, looking at him as if she were afraid to believe that he was actually here. Something inside of him changed, something different began to come forth, something that he had never experienced before, or had ever thought to. He cared for her more than any other person he had ever met, he had missed her, and he had come to realize that he actually liked her infuriating ways. He liked her laughter, her smile, her independence, her strength, her determination, and her courage. He even liked the little vindictive streak she exhibited with her brothers.

The past few days had been nothing but hell for him. He had been unable to do anything but think about her. He had barely been able to function, had felt as if he was on fire as his veins had burned with her absence. The demon within him had constantly been at the forefront, and his sanity had been a tenuous thread that had come close to snapping completely. He hadn't slept in three days as he'd been unable to settle down long enough to let his body relax enough for sleep, and he hadn't fed.

He had nearly killed a man in a bar because the man had accidentally bumped into him. Fortunately, he had regained control of himself in time, but never had he lost it like that. Not even with Ethan.

He had picked up a woman, taken her back to her place, determined to try and ease the anger, and burning in his body. Disgust had filled him the moment that he had touched her, the moment that she had touched him. He had felt nothing for her, had experienced no sense of arousal. He had been so enraged, so shaken up, that he hadn't even fed off her because he knew that he would kill her if he did.

After that, he'd decided that he needed to come back here, needed to see her. He had to sort everything out, had to know if she hated him for what he had done to her brother, what he would have done to her father. He needed to know if she could forgive him for causing her to be hurt at the club. He had been determined to see her, to touch her, to ease his torment.

When she had run to him all of the misery of the past three days had vanished instantly. She didn't hate him, and he knew that she would no longer fight him, that she had been going through the same torture he had. He had felt her pain and anguish far down the road, had sensed her misery, and it had driven him faster, harder. He had become desperate to ease her suffering, desperate for her to never hurt again.

Seeing her, touching her, he knew that this was where he belonged. That she was the only thing that could ease the torment he had been experiencing. Ease the torment of his entire existence. He didn't know why, and at the moment he didn't care. He just needed her, now.

He seized hold of her mouth again, his hands tightened in her thick hair as he carried her swiftly out of the woods and across the field. She met his hunger with her own as her hands curled into his back and her tears dried. He was so hard that it hurt, and he was throbbing painfully. She wiggled against his erection, moaning softly as she pressed herself more firmly against him. He groaned in pleasurable agony as she lifted herself up and slid down again.

He almost spilled himself then as a fierce tremor racked his body. If she didn't stop, he was going to lay her down and take her in the middle of the field. He ripped her shirt up, his hand skimmed over her flat stomach, and delicate ribcage before seizing upon her breast. She moaned and ground harder against him as she bit into his lower lip. He grunted impatiently as he pulled her bra down, determined to feel her flesh against his. Her hardened nipple seared into the palm of his hand as he rubbed and kneaded her.

"Stefan!" she gasped as her head fell back.

The passion in her voice only served to urge him faster. He was in a near frenzy by the time he reached the storm doors. He bent, flung a door open, and slipped swiftly down the stairs. He paused only long enough to throw it closed before striding across the room to the bed. Laying her down, he fell on top of her, unable to part with her for even a moment. He seized hold of her lips again, driving his tongue into the sweet recesses of her mouth with deep, forceful thrusts that imitated what was to come as he savored the wonderful taste, and feel of her.

She tugged eagerly at his shirt, needing to feel his skin, needing to feel *him*. Her hands skimmed over his warm, hard flesh. A tremor of delight rippled through her as he pulled slightly back, allowing her to pull his shirt free, giving her access to what she desperately sought, desperately needed. Her breath froze in her lungs as she took in the broad magnificence of his hard chest. Black hair curled across it, encircling his small nipples, before narrowing down his hard stomach. Her mouth went dry as she lightly ran her hands across him and shuddered with desire, and anticipation.

He bent back to her, seizing hold of her mouth and ravishing her until she was breathless, and shaking. She moaned softly as her hands wrapped around his back and dug into his flesh. His muscles bunched and flexed beneath her touch as she clung to him. She was frantic to get closer to him, to feel more of him, all of him. Her body was burning with want, aching and trembling as she pressed herself as tightly to him as she could.

Stefan couldn't take anymore, couldn't slow down, no matter how much he wanted to. He had been away from her for too long, had been denying himself for too long. She had denied him for too long. He had to have her, now. He ripped her shorts off, heedless of the cry of surprise that she issued. He met her gaze for a moment, but there was no fear in her eyes like he had expected, only a fierce passion that seemed to match his own. He pulled her shirt quickly off. Unable to take the time to bother with her bra hooks, he tore it free, determined to expose her full breasts, and luscious body.

He took only a brief moment to savor the sight of her as she lay beneath him, panting slightly. Her delicious lips were swollen from his kisses. Her beautiful breasts, with their inviting strawberry buds, heaved as she trembled and quivered beneath him. A shudder tore through him as he bent his head and seized hold of her nipple. He licked and nipped at the hardened bud. He relished in the feel of her as she bucked and moaned beneath him, her hands dug into his hair as she pulled him tighter against her.

Her frenzied motions, and soft cries, only served to fuel his passion even more, only served to push his lust further out of control. He fumbled with the button on his jeans; his hands shook so fiercely with anticipation that he couldn't get them undone. Frustration seized hold of him as he tore them open, wrenching them off with a violent, jerking motion. He tore at her underwear, pulling it free as he settled himself between her long, inviting thighs.

His hand slid to the juncture of her thighs, groaning as he discovered her already wet, and hot, for him. He slid a finger into her, stroking and loving her as she gasped in surprise and arched wildly against him. Stefan knew that he should take more time, prepare her more, but the feel of her tight, hot sheath clenching his finger was more than he could stand.

He seized hold of her hips as his mouth reclaimed hers. Everything was happening to fast, a part of him knew that, and tried to stop it. But the other part, the bigger part, was beyond any sense of control, or reason. He needed her, he had to have her. He was on fire, burning with the intensity of his emotions, and the passion that seized him. He drove into her, tearing through the barrier of her virginity with a fierce cry of possession.

Isabelle cried out, her nails clawed into his back as pain tore through her. He was so large, so big that he filled her to the point of bursting, and for a moment she feared that he was going to rip her in two. A whimper of pain escaped as he went still inside her, and the muscles of his back tightened beneath her hands.

"I'm sorry Isabelle," he grated hoarsely in her ear, his body was hard and hot against hers.

An emotion so fierce welled up in her that she almost started to cry again. She clung to his hard, sweat slicked body as her muscles slowly began to loosen around him and she eased to his invasion. He kissed her neck softly, nibbling lightly on her ear as he slid out of her, and slowly back in. Isabelle eased even more around him as the pain began to fade, and the passion of moments before began to return. His mouth seized hers again and his tongue slid slowly into her, imitating the deliberate, undulating movement of his hips.

He kissed and touched her everywhere, unable to get enough of the feel of her silken body against his. He stroked her breasts, kneading and massaging her as he seized hold of one of her nipples with his mouth again. Her hands dug into his back as she arched against him, and delicious whimpers of pleasure escaped from her. Now that he was inside her, now that he had her, the fierce urgency had receded, and he was able to take the time to enjoy the sensations that she arose in him. He had never felt anything as wonderfully tight, and warm, and wet as she was. Never experienced such pleasure in his life.

"Wrap your legs around me," he grated against her lips.

Her eyes opened, clouded and dazed with passion as she wrapped her long legs around his waist. A soft cry of rapture escaped her as the movement caused him to slide even further into her. Stefan groaned; he clenched his teeth against the urge to spill as her legs tightened around him. He enjoyed the play of emotions that slid over her face, the desire that darkened her eyes to deep purple. Her lids started to close.

"No, watch me," he ordered.

Her eyes flew back open, wide and startled. Then, she smiled softly and wrapped her arms around his neck. Her hips began to rise and fall with him as she found, and matched, his rhythm. He watched her intently as his hands fondled and caressed her, watched the passion that parted her lips, caused her breath to quicken, and her body to quiver. He knew that she was nearing release by the flicker of fear and surprise that crossed her face.

He slid his hand between her thighs, stroking the quivering bud that begged for his attention. Her eyes grew wider as soft cries began to escape her, and she wildly met his fierce, pounding rhythm. "Now," he commanded. "Cum for me now Isabelle!"

He drove hard into her as he reached his snapping point. She cried out loudly, her body tightening around him as the force of her contractions ripped his orgasm from him. The fierceness of it tore a bellow of satisfaction, and delight, from him. Never had he experienced anything as wonderful, or as fulfilling. He hadn't thought that it could exist.

He nearly collapsed on top of her, but managed to catch himself in time. Instead, he wrapped his arms around her and rolled her to the side as small tremors continued to shake her body. He remained inside of her as her head settled onto his shoulder and her hands lightly stroked his chest. His breathing was still rough and ragged, and he was pleased to note that hers was too. Their bodies were coated with sweat as he pulled her tighter against him, a feeling of utter contentment stealing through him. This was where he belonged, he realized.

"You left me," she whispered softly.

His hands tightened on her as he gently nuzzled the top of her head. "I'm sorry."

"Don't do it again."

"I won't," he promised.

"Good."

She snuggled closer to him and was instantly asleep. Stefan smiled as he held her against him, savoring in the scent of their love making, and the feel of her delicious body against his. He knew that he should be afraid of how much he had come to care for her, knew that the darkness inside of him was not something that he should have ever exposed her to. However, for the first time in his long existence, he actually felt at peace. He was never going to let her know about his past, never going to look back again. He savored in the feel of her as he drifted slowly to sleep.

CHAPTER 17

Isabelle woke slowly the next morning and instinctively nestled closer to Stefan's warm body. His arm tightened around her as he drew her closer. "Good morning," he murmured in her ear.

She smiled softly as she rolled over to face him. His hair, tussled from sleep, fell across his forehead with a boyish appeal that warmed her heart. Her smile deepened as she gently brushed the hair off of his forehead. His arm tightened around her as a small smile played at the corners of his mouth. The impact of that smile was enough to make her melt.

"Did you miss me while I was gone?" he asked softly.

"I hardly even noticed," she lied.

His smile deepened as his hand began to lightly stroke her back, causing a small tremor to work its way through her. "Really?"

Isabelle bit her lip; her body tightened in anticipation as he caressed her hip, and came slowly back up to circle her breast. Her nipple hardened as his finger traced around it. "Maybe a little," she whispered breathlessly.

His smile was wicked as he bent and lightly licked her hardened nipple. Isabelle gasped as she arched into him. He pulled away from her. "Just a little?"

She bit into her bottom lip as she stared into his bright, gleaming eyes. "Did you miss me?" she demanded.

"Did I miss being avoided, run away from, tortured, tormented, and sexually frustrated?" Isabelle scowled angrily at him as he smiled happily down at her. "Yes, I did." She laughed as she wrapped her arms around his neck. "More than a little?" he growled as his hand tightened on her waist. A small thrill shot through her at the feel of his hard, hair roughened chest against her sensitive breasts as she pressed closer.

He slid his leg between hers and nudged her thighs apart. Isabelle's breath froze in her lungs as his hand slid down and he began to lightly stroke her. A small gasp escaped as his finger slid inside and her hips began to move slowly with the pace that he set. "More than a little?" he murmured against her lips as his other hand leisurely fondled her breast.

Isabelle could barely think through the pleasure that was beginning to consume her, let alone speak. His hand slid away from her. Isabelle groaned her protest as she wiggled closer to him. Chuckling softly, he nibbled lightly on her bottom lip. He grabbed hold of her hips, pulling her against him and rubbing the tip of his hardened shaft teasingly against her aching, wet center. Isabelle opened her legs to accept his invasion, but it didn't come.

"More than a little?" he demanded.

Her lips parted as he continued to rub against her. She couldn't take anymore of the sweet torture that he was putting her through, at the moment she would have conceded anything to him to have him ease her torment again. "Yes!" she cried.

He smiled victoriously as he slid slowly into her. Isabelle gasped in delight as she wrapped her arms tightly around his neck and drug his mouth down to hers. The world fell away as his body moved over her, enveloping her with his strength, security, and warmth. He caught each of her soft sighs and gasps with his mouth as he leisurely explored and tasted her, making love to her slowly. She touched him everywhere, relishing in the feel of the strong muscles that corded his back, his chest, his thighs, and buttocks as they grew slick with sweat.

Her hands dug into his back as he drove her closer to the brink of ecstasy that he had pushed her over last night. She gasped loudly as she clung to him; he was her only anchor in the sea of pleasure that she was engulfed in. He seized hold of her hands, dragging them above her head and pinning them down as he drove more fiercely into her. Isabelle's legs clenched around him as she eagerly met his increasingly fierce movements. He seized her wrists in one hand as he reached between their bodies to rub against her quivering, hardened nub. She screamed loudly as the world splintered around her and waves of ecstasy tore through her.

He drove fiercely into her, spilling everything into her as her body contracted fiercely around him. He collapsed; his breathing ragged as he pulled her against his chest, absorbing the tremors that shook her. He rolled her to the side as he tried to calm the fierce pounding of his heart, and catch his breath. It was only then that he thought about what he had just done, how roughly he had taken her, twice now. He should have taken it easier on her, been gentler; she had to be sore from last night still. He had hurt her then, and he had to have hurt her again now.

"Are you okay?" he grated.

"Uh huh," she replied contentedly as she nuzzled against his chest.

"Did I hurt you?" he demanded.

Isabelle frowned at the worry, and concern, in his voice. She lifted her head to look down at him. He was studying her with intense, dark eyes, the worry apparent in the pinched lines around his mouth and eyes. "No, why would you think that?"

He continued to search her face intently, obviously not believing what she had told him. "I know I hurt you last night."

"Only a little," she assured him.

"And today, it was too soon, I should have waited a day or two before taking you again."

She smiled sweetly down at him as she shook her head. "I would have taken you."

He laughed loudly as he pulled her down for a long, lingering kiss. "Would you now?" he murmured against her lips.

"Yes, I would," she said with a fierce nod and a soft smile.

"I wasn't too rough with you?"

"No," she assured him as her fingers lightly curled into the hair on his chest. To his utter amazement he felt himself growing hard again as she smiled seductively down at him.

"Next time, we'll go slowly and really make love."

Her forehead furrowed as she stared at him in confusion. "I thought we already did."

He laughed softly as he shook his head. "No, there is so much more to learn, and I am going to enjoy teaching you *all* of it."

Her eyes darkened as she bit into her bottom lip. "I see," she whispered.

Isabelle lowered her lashes before he could see the hurt that tore through her. She had managed to forget all of her fears about her inadequacy in her happiness to see him, to have him, but they all came flying rapidly back to her now. His words had made her realize just how little she did know, and how very much he *did*.

She wanted to crawl out of the bed and run away from him, but she didn't want him to know how hurt she was. It would help if he would at least say something to reassure her, tell her that she hadn't been a disappointment, or even worse, completely awful, but she would die before she ever asked him about it.

"Isabelle." She turned back to him, hopeful that he had somehow sensed her insecurity and was going to reassure her. "I told you you wouldn't kick me out of your room."

Her mouth dropped open as her eyes widened in shock. There was a teasing gleam in his eyes, but his words, coupled with her doubts, brought a surge of anger spurting forth. She rolled instantly away and climbed quickly out of the bed. "Hey, come back here!" he protested laughingly.

Isabelle's anger flashed boiled at the sound of his mocking, taunting laughter. "No!" she snapped as she made her way to the bathroom.

"What the hell is the matter with you?" he demanded.

She spun to face him, planting her hands on her hips as she glared angrily at him. "Why can't you ever just say something nice? Why do you always have to be such an arrogant ass!?" she nearly screeched.

Stefan's eyes widened in surprise, he would have been amused by her obvious ire, and especially her stance, if it wasn't for the hurt blazing fiercely from her eyes, a hurt that he didn't understand. He had only been teasing her, but it was apparent that she had taken it the wrong way. "Isabelle..."

"You know what, just get out! Get out now!"

Fury snapped through him as he thrust the tangled sheet away and sat up. Isabelle's eyes narrowed as she fiercely met his gaze. "I am not going anywhere," he growled.

"Yes, you are. I want you to leave."

Normally he wouldn't have gotten so incensed, but after the torment of the past three days hearing her telling him to get out was not something that he was willing to tolerate. Hell, he knew she had been just as miserable as he had, but she was more than willing to toss him out of her life again, and the last thing he wanted was to lose her. It was that knowledge that made his anger escalate to rapid, volatile proportions. He had no idea how he had allowed her to get so much control over him, when it was obvious that he had almost none over her and it absolutely infuriated him.

"I don't care what the hell you want!" he snapped. "I'm not going anywhere just because you can't take a joke!"

Her eye blazed with anger and unshed tears. "You're an insensitive, cruel, idiot! Get out, and don't come back!"

The tears nearly blinded her as she whirled quickly, darted into the bathroom, and slammed the door behind her. She was acting like an idiot, she knew that, but she couldn't seem to stop herself. The last thing she wanted was for him to leave again. She had just wanted him to reassure her, to ease all of her doubts and fears. Instead, he had managed to make her feel even weaker than she had already proven herself to be around him, and even more insecure. His words about teaching her how to make love, on top of his smug superiority about getting into her bed, were more than she could handle.

There was no way she could ever compete with the women of his past, and she didn't want to. All she had wanted was for him to tell her that she was special, that she was different, that she wasn't just another conquest. Not to remind her that she was just like every other woman that hadn't been able to refuse him. She slid onto the counter, drawing her legs up as she buried her head in her hands and tears slid freely down her face.

"Isabelle, come out of there," he ordered from the other side of the door.

"No."

Stefan forced himself to take a deep breath before he ripped the door off its hinges and drug her out. He knew that there was more behind her anger, and hurt, than what he had said. The tears in her eyes had proved that, but he couldn't think of what it could be, and he wasn't in the mood to puzzle it out. His anger was growing by the moment. He'd had enough of fighting with her, and he wasn't about to let her lead him around. It was beyond time she learned that he was the one in charge. He grabbed the handle and pushed the door open. She quickly shoved it shut again.

"Let me in that room, or I'm going to rip this door off its fucking hinges!" he bellowed, his patience snapping as he shoved the door back open.

Isabelle scrambled forward to kick the door quickly shut again. The breath froze in her lungs as he grew eerily quiet on the other side. For a moment she feared that he truly would rip the door off, but when seconds ticked by with no sound, and no further attempt to enter, her shoulders slumped in relief, and her head bowed.

The loud crashing snapped her head up. Her eyes widened in surprise, and a strangled cry escaped her as the door, and part of the wall, was torn away and flung easily aside. Wrath radiated from every inch of his body as he stepped into the room and towered over her. Unable to move, her breath froze in her lungs as his eyes blazed a violent red at her. Pure terror spurted through her veins, her heart jack hammered wildly in her chest, and a thick lump constricted her throat. She would have jumped up and fled the room, but he blocked her only chance to escape.

"Get up!" he hissed.

Isabelle knew that her legs wouldn't hold her. Instead, she shook her head numbly, unable to tear her gaze away from his thunderous expression. She hadn't thought it was possible, but his eyes blazed even brighter. The fury radiating from him beat against her in waves that threatened to drown her within their terrifying depths. She started to recoil, but he seized hold of her arms and lifted her easily.

Isabelle didn't even attempt to struggle for fear that he would truly kill her if she did, he certainly looked irate enough to do it. She was fairly certain that he would never hurt her, but she wasn't about to take her chances in the face of his hostility. Instead, she hung limply, waiting to see what he was going to do as fear hummed through every inch of her body. However, even though he was trembling with rage his hands upon her arms were not painful, or overly tight.

He threw her onto the bed and climbed on top of her so that his knees were on either side of her hips, and his hands clasped her arms at her sides. She stared breathlessly up at him, trembling slightly with dread as he glowered fiercely down at her. Power and strength radiated from him. She clearly recalled how he had ripped the door from the wall, and tossed it aside as if it weighed no more than a feather. She didn't even want to think about what he could do to her if he truly wanted to.

"Now, you are you going to listen to me!" he spat. "I am *not* going anywhere. So you had better get that realization through that thick skull of yours right now Isabelle, or so help me I will ram it in there! Do you understand me?" When she didn't answer fast enough for his liking, his hands tightened upon her arms, and he shook her slightly. "Do you understand me?" he bellowed.

Her lower lip trembled slightly as she managed a weak nod. "Yes," she whispered softly. Some of his anger melted away as he slowly unclenched his rigid jaw. Finally he was beginning to make some head way with her. "But you left before."

His head snapped up and his eyes narrowed fiercely as fury raced through him again. He should have known better than to think that she would concede so quickly. Just once he wished that she would make things easy for him, not constantly put him on the defensive. "I left because I thought that it was the best thing for you, for me," he grated through clenched teeth. "I got you hurt that night..."

"No you didn't!" she cried.

"Yes, I did," he growled. "You were trying to avoid me; that's the reason you even went to that club. I thought it would be better if I left, but like it or not Isabelle I came back, and I am not leaving again. Do you understand that?"

"Yes," she whispered.

The anger melted again, but he remained completely rigid on top of her, knowing better than to think she would acquiesce so easily. Not Isabelle. Never his Isabelle. "You are going to stop fighting me Isabelle, I mean it. There will be no more of this. You're mine, and the sooner you realize it, the happier we will both be."

She looked up at him as some of her fear, and doubt, melted away. His eyes had returned to their dark onyx color, but there was still a savage gleam in them. She was his, she knew that, but it wasn't enough. "Are you mine?" she demanded haughtily.

His jaw clenched again. He was hers, he knew that. He had learned it over the past couple of days, but to tell her that, to let her know exactly how much he had come to care for her, would be opening himself up to vulnerability that he wasn't sure he was ready for. Her eyes darkened with pain, and in that instant he knew he would have told her anything to make her happy. No matter how much he hated how weak, and exposed, it made him feel.

"Yes, I am."

The beautiful smile that spread over her face would have made him rip the moon out of the sky if she had asked for it. "And I am yours," she whispered.

The remaining dregs of his anger vanished as he lifted his hand to gently stroke her silky cheek. "Now, do you care to tell me what you were really so upset over? And don't even try to tell me it was over what I said, because you know as well as I, that there was more to it than that."

"No," she mumbled.

His jaw locked again as his hand stilled on her cheek. "You said you were going to stop fighting me," he growled.

"I'm not fighting you!" she cried. "I just... I..." Her face turned a bright shade of red as she lowered her long, inky black lashes.

Stefan stared down at her in confusion as she refused to look at him. He knew that it took a lot to embarrass her, but her entire body was becoming suffused with heat as she bit nervously into her lower lip. "Isabelle, tell me." She quickly shook her head. He sighed wearily and stroked her warm cheek. "Please."

That please tugged at her, making her want to pour her heart out to him. To tell him all of her insecurities, but what if he didn't reassure her, but only confirmed her worst fears. Sighing softly, she decided to just take the plunge and ask. He would just keep bothering her anyway, and try as she might, she couldn't come up with a plausible lie to keep him at bay. Besides, she was fairly certain that she couldn't lie to him, even if she could come up with one. Lifting her eyes back to his, the last of her hesitance melted away as he gazed at her with concern and tender warmth.

"Am I any good?" she whispered so softly that he had to strain to hear her.

When her words finally penetrated, he almost laughed, but managed to catch himself in time. He didn't want to think about what she would do if he burst into laughter. Instead, he continued to lightly stroke her cheek as he remembered clearly now that she had started to grow distant when he told her that he would teach her how to make love. Sometimes, he really was an insensitive idiot, he realized with an inward groan.

"I have never felt anything like what I feel when I'm with you. Trust me darling, you are much better than good, you're spectacular."

She looked back at him, a tender vulnerability in her eyes that tore at his heart. "Really?" she whispered hopefully.

He shifted slightly, nudging her thighs gently apart so that he could press the hard evidence of his arousal against her inner thigh. Her eyes widened in surprise as passion bloomed within their depths. "This is what you do to me," he grated hoarsely. "No one has ever affected me like this Isabelle, no one. I sure as hell have never put up with as much aggravation with anyone else as I have with you."

Her eyes twinkled with amusement as the fear slowly left them. "You're no barrel of laughs you know."

He cocked an eyebrow as he smiled playfully back at her. "And why is that?"

"Well, you're arrogant, inconsiderate, bossy, demanding and more than a little temperamental."

Stefan's eyebrows rose as he shifted slightly to press the hard tip of his head against her wet, inviting folds. Isabelle gasped as she bit into her bottom lip and she lifted her hips to him. "You flatter me, but you do realize that you have just described yourself."

"I am not inconsiderate!" she cried indignantly.

He slid his head slowly into her. She drew her legs up, bracing them against his hard, slick sides as she opened herself further to his invasion. "But you admit to being the other things?"

Her eyes twinkled merrily as she wrapped her arms around his neck to lightly play with the hair curling along his nape. He shuddered as he fought the urge to plunge into her, but he was enjoying teasing her and watching the variety of emotions that crossed her face. "Sometimes," she said softly. "But at least I don't rip doors out of the wall."

He laughed as he bent to nibble on her lip. "No, you just cause me to do it."

She grinned up at him. "That was your temper that caused you to do that."

"Trust me; no one can provoke my temper like you."

"I know the feeling," she gasped as he drove all the way into her.

CHAPTER 18

"Isabelle!" Isabelle groaned as she buried herself deeper into her pillows. "Isabelle!"

"Go away Willow!" she shouted.

"Isabelle get up!" She lifted her head slowly as she realized that Stefan was no longer in bed with her. Her brow furrowed as she wondered where he had gone, and when. "Isabelle!"

"What?" she snapped.

"I can't find Cassidy and Kyle!" Willow cried.

"Get Ethan!"

"Everybody went to get more supplies for the new house, and they've been missing for almost an hour!"

She groaned again as she thrust the tangled sheet off of her. An hour was a long time for the two of them to be gone. "Hold on!"

She dressed quickly, wondering if Stefan had gone with everyone for supplies, or if he was around here somewhere. Brushing out her hair she pulled it into a loose ponytail and opened the door. Willow's pretty face was stressed with worry as her dark violet eyes nervously scanned Isabelle. "I don't know where they went," she said anxiously.

"We'll find them," Isabelle assured her. Willow's dark blond hair bobbed up and down as she nodded vigorously. "Come on."

Willow followed her up the stairs, through the living room, and outside. Isabelle paused on the porch as her gaze darted to the new house. They had made a lot of progress on it in the past few days, progress that she hadn't even noticed until now. The outside walls had been assembled, the porch was built, the large oak door was in place, and most of the windows were in. A tingle of excitement raced through her as she realized that the house would be done soon.

"He went with the others," Vicky informed her.

Isabelle tore her gaze away from the house as Vicky and Abby stepped onto the porch. Willow sighed impatiently as Isabelle took a deep breath and hopped quickly down the steps. "Where was the last place you saw them?"

"I left them at the tree house," Willow answered.

Isabelle nodded as she moved toward the path to the tree house. "You must be happy that Stefan came back," Abby said.

Isabelle cast a glance over her shoulder to find the twins grinning knowingly at her. She couldn't stop herself from smiling back at them. "Jess is going to freak when she finds out that he came back," Abby said.

"She doesn't know yet?" For a moment her good mood darkened at the thought of Jess's reaction.

"No, she was still asleep when he went into town, and I don't think mom is going to tell her."

"I'd like to," Vicky chimed in. "Just to see her face."

"Be nice," Isabelle scolded softly.

"Why?" Vicky demanded her face scrunched in anger. "She's not nice to you."

"Do you blame her?"

"Yes!" they both cried.

Isabelle sighed softly as she shook her head at them. "If it was one of you guys, you wouldn't be saying that."

They both scowled at her. "Obviously the two of you are supposed to be together," Vicky said.

"She doesn't know that," Isabelle reminded them gently.

"Well, she will now!" Abby snapped.

Isabelle stopped as they reached the tree house. She glanced around the small clearing, but there was no sign of Cassidy or Kyle. A feeling of impending doom began to grow in the pit of her stomach. An hour was much too long for them to be missing. "You guys head to the lake, Willow and I will go toward the canyon."

Vicky and Abby nodded, the amusement on their faces was gone as they broke off to take the path to the lake. Willow followed behind Isabelle as she moved swiftly down the path, calling loudly for Kyle and Cassidy. Sun splashed through the thick leaves, casting a myriad of patterns across the pine needles and rotten leaves as they moved rapidly along. The forest seemed eerily quiet, too quiet. She broke into a brisk jog when the canyon was only a hundred feet away.

She was panting slightly as she skidded to a halt at the end of the canyon. It was about twenty feet long and forty feet down. It was the same one that Ethan had thrown himself off of when he was fifteen. She swallowed her fear and forced herself to look down. Isabelle scanned the bottom and the jagged rock walls quickly, but there was no sign of either Kyle or Cassidy.

"Maybe they went home," Willow said softly.

Isabelle wished that was true, but the awful feeling in her stomach had begun to spread to her chest. Glancing quickly at the woods she ignored the bird calls, and the animals that moved within its shadowed depths. She forced herself to concentrate on her brother and sister, hoping to get some glimmer of where they could be.

Then, a sinking possibility crashed around her. She broke into a sprint as she rushed down another path. She darted around tree branches and twigs, and ignored the thorns that tore at her clothing and skin. She forced herself to move faster, blurring as she rushed down the path. Please no, she pleaded silently. Please no.

She burst off the path and rushed through the clearing to the edge of the bear trap. Holding her breath, she peered into its shadowed depths. Cassidy was huddled against the wall, looking up at her with tears streaming down her dirt, and blood streaked cheeks. She held Kyle tightly in her arms, his head cradled gently in her lap. Blood had soaked through his clothing and onto Cassidy. His wheat blond hair was caked with blood and dirt, and his clothes had turned a fierce shade of red.

Isabelle's heart jumped into her throat as tears sprang instantly into her eyes. Willow let out a startled cry as she skidded to a halt beside her. "He fell," Cassidy whispered pitifully.

That heart breaking whisper snapped Isabelle out of her fear filled paralysis. "Get help!" she hissed to Willow.

Willow nodded quickly and took off into the woods. "Isabelle," Cassidy whispered.

"Hold on Cass, I'm coming."

She glanced worriedly at the stakes as she sat at the edge of the pit. Now that she wasn't hanging over the pit, she was able to get a better look at the jagged, deadly stakes. They were old, and some of them had rotted and broken off from time and weather, but even the blunted wood was lethal looking. She scooted closer to the edge as she tried to figure out the best way to get down. Finally deciding that there was no best way, she lowered herself over and slid down the side.

A cry of pain tore from her as one of the stakes pierced through her shoe and tore into the bottom of her foot. The sudden agony almost caused her to pitch backward onto all of them, but she managed to catch herself in time. Flinging herself forward, her fingers dug frantically into the dirt and tree roots of the wall as she steadied herself. Breathing heavily, she remained against the wall as she slowly pulled her foot free of the stake. She winced, gritting her teeth against the throbbing pain in her foot as the stake slid slowly free of her flesh, and shoe.

She took a deep breath before turning herself slowly around. Cassidy watched with wide eyes as she began to edge her way carefully around the stakes, trying to keep her weight off of her abused foot. It seemed like hours passed before she reached Kyle and Cassidy, but she knew that it was only a matter of seconds before she knelt at their side.

Kyle was still, his breathing labored as it rattled out of him. The sound of that rattle sent a bolt of fear through her so fierce she almost choked on it. He was so pale that even his lips had become white, and all of his veins were clearly noticeable through his nearly translucent skin.

It took everything Isabelle had to push through her fear, and nearly choking sorrow. With trembling hands she pulled his shirt gingerly up. There was a huge, gaping wound in his stomach that was slowly oozing bubbles of blood. Cassidy began to cry harder as Isabelle shoved his shirt the rest of the way up to find another large, jagged tear in the middle of his chest.

He was bleeding out so fast that he hadn't even begun to close the wounds on his own. "Oh no," she whispered.

Cassidy was shaking from the force of her tears. "Please help him Isabelle," she pleaded.

Isabelle ripped her tank top off and pressed it firmly against Kyle's chest. His eyelids flickered, but he made no other movement, no sound. "Hold this," she commanded Cassidy.

Cassidy pressed a trembling hand against the shirt that was quickly becoming saturated with blood. Isabelle fought back tears as she bit into her wrist and forced Kyle's mouth open. She needed to replace the blood that he was rapidly losing, needed to attempt to keep his strength up.

She lifted her head to quickly scan the edge of the pit. It was a good ten feet up; there was no way that she could get them out on her own. Fighting back tears of hopelessness and agony, she turned her attention back to her brother. Her blood wasn't even making a dent in the amount that he had lost, but she hoped it would be enough to keep him alive until help arrived.

*＊＊

Stefan threw the board into the back of the truck and turned to accept the next one from David. "This should be the last load," Mike said.

"Good." Jack wiped his arm across his sweaty forehead. "I can't wait to get this damn house finished."

"Wish I could have gone back to school sooner," Ian mumbled.

"Just think about how nice it will be when you come back," Ethan replied.

Ian grinned as he tossed a board into the back of the other truck. Stefan grabbed another board from David and threw it in. He was beginning to wish that he hadn't agreed to come with them. There was a clawing sensation in his chest that was growing more intense, and more uncomfortable with every passing minute.

He couldn't keep his mind on the conversation around him; he was becoming increasingly agitated, and irritable. All he wanted to do was go back to the house, curl up in bed with Isabelle, and forget about the rest of the world. However, he had needed to feed. It had been over three days since he last had, and when he awoke again this morning, the hunger burning through his body had been almost unbearable. Now, sated on two of the employees from the lumberyard, a new sensation had sprung forth to take the place of the fierce hunger.

He ground his teeth as he tossed another board into the truck. He just wanted to get this wood loaded as quickly as possible and get back to the house. He would see Isabelle before he returned to helping with the new house, which he wanted finished as soon as possible. It would be much nicer to stay there with Isabelle. Of course, Ethan would be there too, but at least it wasn't a house load of people.

Tossing another board onto the load he quickly wiped the sweat from his brow. He glanced over at Ethan as he bent to pick up another board. He had apologized to him about the other night, and Ethan seemed to have accepted it, but he could still sense wariness in him.

Stefan didn't blame him in the least; he was a little wary of himself. There was something that wasn't right with him still, but he didn't know what it was. He was beginning to feel like he had when he'd left, unstable and angry. Isabelle had helped to ease it when he'd seen her, but now that he wasn't near her, it was starting to come back with a vengeance.

He became even more aggravated when he thought about the fact that this might be the way he felt every time that he left her. That wasn't a possibility he wanted to think about. He'd always been free to come and go as he pleased, and although he had come back for her, he'd never thought about the possibility that he might not be able to leave her again. It wasn't that he wanted to leave her; it was the last thing he wanted to do, but the idea that it might never be able to happen was more than a little overwhelming.

He also couldn't rid himself of the feeling that something wasn't right, wasn't complete. That something was lacking, he just didn't know what it could be. He thought that if he could figure it out things would be better, but he couldn't think through the aggravating clawing in his chest, and stomach.

He sighed wearily as David handed him another board. The bolt of panic that hit him froze him instantly. The board slipped from his hand and hit the ground with a clattering thud that caused David to turn to him with his eyes wide in surprise. Stefan's heart seemed to stop beating as Isabelle's fear rolled over him, through him, and nearly swamped him with its intensity.

"Stefan are you ok?" David asked worriedly.

"Get back to the house," he hissed.

"What?"

Stefan didn't bother to answer him as he turned and disappeared. "Shit!" Jack gasped in surprise.

CHAPTER 19

Stefan froze as he looked into the hole, and a riot of emotions crashed through him at once. Fear surged forward as his eyes landed on Isabelle. She was covered in blood; her face, chest, and throat were streaked with it. It took him a moment to realize that it wasn't her blood, but Kyle's. When he did, anger surged through him as he realized the danger she had placed herself in. "Stefan."

All of his anger vanished as she looked at him with wide, pleading, tear filled eyes. The pain and hopelessness in her gaze tore at his heart. His eyes narrowed on Isabelle's wrist pressed to Kyle's mouth as anger tore through him again. Suddenly, he knew what was missing, what would get rid of the clawing sensation that he'd been struggling with since he'd left her side. He made himself take a deep breath and shove the anger aside. Now was not the time for it.

"He won't stop bleeding." Tears streaked her blood and dirt caked face.

Stefan dropped to his knees he reached into the hole. She lifted Kyle gently from Cassidy's lap and stood swiftly. Pain flashed across her face as she gasped softly and shifted her weight. He clenched his jaw against the anger, and fear that rocketed wildly through his body as he realized that she had hurt herself.

Isabelle lifted Kyle to him; her arms shook as a soft sob tore from her. Stefan clenched his teeth against the pain that she radiated, both physical and emotional, as he wrapped his hands around Kyle's arms and pulled him easily up. He laid him on the ground and quickly scanned the severe wounds in his chest and stomach before turning back around. He reached down as Isabelle handed Cassidy to him. She was sobbing so heavily that her tiny body shook from the force of it. Relief filled him the minute that Isabelle's hands enclosed his, and he pulled her free.

She released him instantly as she fell to her brother's side, a bloody shirt clutched tightly in her hands as she pressed it to his wounds again. Lifting his head to her lap, she pressed her wrist to his mouth. She was covered in dirt, and blood, her white bra was more red than white now.

Anger pierced through him again at the sight of her undressed state. He knew that he was acting like an idiot, that he had no reason to be angry. But the others would be coming soon, and the idea of them seeing her like this sent a bolt of fury and jealousy through him that he was unable to stop. Yanking his shirt briskly off, he walked over to crouch by her side.

She lifted her head to look at him, the anguish in her eyes almost more than he could bear. "Put this on." He handed her the shirt as he picked Kyle up. Blood instantly clung to his skin, matting against his stomach as it oozed through Kyle's shirt to cling to his fingers. Isabelle stood beside him, trembling as she twisted his shirt nervously in her hands. "Put it on!" he ordered, more sharply than he had intended.

She started in surprise as she glanced at the knotted shirt in her hands. Her hands trembled as she slipped it over her head. His anxiety lessened instantly as the shirt fell over her and dropped down to mid thigh. She looked childish, and vulnerable in the oversized shirt, and he found himself liking the fact that she wore it.

He tore his attention away from her and back to Kyle. Stefan shifted his hold as he bit deep into his wrist. He held it to Kyle's mouth and felt a moment of relief as the boy swallowed it down. Isabelle followed anxiously beside him, limping badly as he moved quickly down the path toward the house.

"Are you okay?" he demanded. Her eyes flew to his face, wide and anxious as she nodded. "Why are you limping?"

"A stake went through my shoe."

Fury seized his muscles and caused his arm to convulse around Kyle. Isabelle's eyes widened in surprise as her lower lip began to tremble. "You could have been killed!" he spat.

"I had to," she whispered.

"Is he going to be all right?" Cassidy asked anxiously.

Stefan clenched his jaw as he turned to look at the small girl hovering at Isabelle's side. Isabelle's arm was wrapped around her trembling shoulders as she held her tight. Her big blue eyes were wide and bright with tears as she looked anxiously at her twin brother. "I don't know," he answered honestly.

He broke free of the woods and strode across the yard toward Liam's house. Vicky and Abby broke into a run as they spotted them. "What happened?" Vicky cried. "Oh no, Kyle!"

Tears streamed down their faces as they peered anxiously over Stefan's shoulder at him. Stefan carried him swiftly upstairs as Isabelle hurried forward to slide the glass doors open. Willow rushed to the right and flung open the closed wooden doors of the living room. Stefan walked briskly in and laid Kyle down on the couch. He pulled Kyle's shirt over his head so that he could get a better look at the jagged wounds.

"Mom! Mom!" Vicky yelled as she took off up the stairs.

Isabelle hurried to the bathroom and ripped towels out of the cabinet. She ignored the burning pain in her foot as she rushed back to the living room. Her mother raced down the stairs, her eyes widened in horror as she took in Isabelle. Then she turned and her mouth dropped as she spotted Stefan and Kyle.

"Kyle!" She rushed into the living room and fell beside Stefan as she reached out to try and stop the blood flow with her hands. Isabelle hurried forward to hand her mother the towels that she had collected. Her mother's hands shook as tears slid down her cheeks. "Come on baby," she whispered as she used the wet towels to wipe the blood away.

The wounds appeared to be healing now, slowly. Isabelle's hands trembled as she handed her mother another towel. Isabelle's gaze went to Stefan as she instinctively sought him out for reassurance, or some sort of help. His eyes were dark and turbulent, his face, chest, and abdomen were streaked with her brother's blood as he reached for her. She clasped his hand tightly, immediately comforted by his touch as the heat of his hand burned into her. She choked back a sob as she slumped against the back of the couch.

He squeezed her hand tightly, and released her. The sob tore free of her at the loss of contact. An overwhelming feeling of despair washed through her as her gaze returned to Kyle. Stefan's wrist was pressed tightly against his mouth, his other hand cradled beneath Kyle's head as he held him firmly against his arm. Another emotion began to come forth, an emotion that was just as strong, and just as overwhelming as her fear and despair as she watched how gentle and kind he was being with her brother.

It took her a moment to pinpoint it, a moment to understand what it was, and when she did, it slammed into her gut with the force of a fist. She gasped loudly as she fought back the extreme wave of panic that tore through her. Stefan's eyes were dark and stormy as they shot back to her. Her gaze rapidly searched his blood streaked face.

She loved him, she truly did love him. Isabelle forced herself to take a deep breath before she fainted, or threw up. She didn't know how or when it had happened, but it had. It scared the hell out of her. She started to tremble with fear, and the overwhelming emotion of love that was tearing through her. She hadn't wanted this, had never wanted to be this vulnerable to anyone. She knew in that moment that she would die for him, and that she would surely die without him. She needed him as much as she needed blood, as much as she needed her family. The need was stunning in its ferocity.

"Isabelle," he said gently.

She forced herself to push the emotion aside as she focused on her brother again. The wounds seemed to be getting better by the second as her mother took away a towel that was only splotched with blood, not saturated. She could see sinew starting to rebuild, closing the wound that had gone straight through before. Relief flowed through her, leaving her weak and trembling as she placed a hand against the back of the couch and leaned against it for support.

"What happened?"

Isabelle turned as Kathleen, Delia, and Jess appeared in the doorway. Jess's eyes locked on Isabelle, hatred blazed through them as they quickly took in the fact that she was wearing Stefan's shirt. A small tremor rocked Isabelle as the force of that hatred slammed into her. A low growl sounded from behind her and Jess's eyes instantly darted to Stefan and widened in surprise. His jaw was locked and his eyes blazed with anger as he glowered at Jess. For a moment, the room was filled with a tense fury that shook her, and Isabelle found herself frightened that he would snap.

"We need to call an ambulance!" Kathleen broke the tension as she spun toward the kitchen.

"No!" Stefan snapped, halting Kathleen in mid stride. She turned back to him, her eyes wide in disbelief. "There will be no ambulance. There is absolutely nothing wrong here. You have seen nothing, you know nothing. All of you need to go back upstairs and stay there for the rest of the day. Now!"

Isabelle jumped as he lashed out the last word. A muscle twitched in his cheek, and a vein throbbed in his forehead as he continued to glare at Jess. Isabelle reached instinctively to squeeze his hand in an attempt to soothe some of the anger from him. He turned slowly toward her, his eyes blazing. For a moment he remained rigid, but then his jaw relaxed, and his eyes slowly returned to black. Her hand tightened on his before she released him and turned her attention back to the doorway. Jess, Kathleen, and Delia were already gone.

She turned back around as her mother lifted the towel from Kyle's chest to inspect the wounds. They were healing even faster now. Relief started to claim her, but she was scared that it was too soon to hope that he would be okay. A loud pounding on the back steps jerked her head around as everyone came rushing through the glass doors. Her father's face went white as his eyes landed on Kyle. "No!"

Isabelle stood silently as he rushed toward her mother's side. "What happened?" Ethan demanded.

"The bear trap," Isabelle whispered.

Ethan's eyes widened. "Damn it! We should have taken care of that thing! Why would they go near it?"

Everyone turned to look at Cassidy as she stood huddled behind Stefan. "We just wanted to take a look," she sobbed.

Vicky walked over and wrapped an arm around her shaking shoulders and pulled her against her side. "Is he going to be okay?" David demanded.

"I think so," Stefan said slowly.

Isabelle couldn't stop herself from reaching down to him again. She needed to touch him, needed to feel him, and be reassured by his presence. "Do you want me to do that?" her mother asked anxiously as she waved toward Stefan's wrist.

Stefan looked at her and shook his head. "My blood is stronger, it will help more."

Her mother nodded weakly as her father wrapped his arm tightly around her and pulled her close to him. Stefan stiffened, his hand tightened upon Isabelle's as Kyle bit into his wrist. Relief flowed through him as he drank deeply, and with relish. He relaxed his grip on Isabelle's trembling hand, but she refused to release him.

Eventually Kyle's bite began to lessen as his thirst for blood became less. Stefan pulled the towel back to reveal the wounds. They were still dark, and vicious looking, but they had stopped bleeding, and bone, muscle, and skin had now knitted neatly back together. He pulled his wrist gently away from Kyle's mouth as the boy released him.

"He'll be all right," he said softly. "He'll need more blood, and he probably won't awaken for awhile, but he'll be all right."

He stood slowly, moving away so that Liam and Sera could get closer to their son. "Are you okay?" Isabelle asked worriedly.

He glanced up at her as he nodded. She wrapped her arms around herself as she tried to ease the trembling that remained from her fear for Kyle, and the shock of her realization about Stefan. Isabelle rushed forward and flung her arms around his waist as she buried her head against his chest. Tears of relief slid down her cheeks when he enveloped her.

***

Isabelle sat silently at the kitchen table feeling drained, and completely exhausted. She shifted slightly and leaned back against Stefan. His arms tightened around her waist as she dropped her head to his hard shoulder and nuzzled against his neck. His familiar scent of crisp air, woods, soap, and pure male filled her nostrils. She sighed contentedly as she moved even closer to him. Beneath his familiar scent she could suddenly smell the copper tint of his blood.

She stiffened slightly as the fierce urge to taste his blood surged into her. She had never experienced such an intense urge before, hadn't thought it was possible, but she suddenly wanted it to fill her. She closed her eyes tightly against the yearning, but the smell of it, and the power that radiated from it, caused her mouth to water. She wanted to whimper from the hunger blazing through her, but she forced herself to remain silent, and not let on to the sudden discomfort that consumed her.

She turned her head away from the throbbing pulse in his throat and rested her head against his chest. She forced her attention away from him, and to the people that surrounded them. Ethan, Ian, Mike, Doug, Jack, and David sat silently around the table, their faces as tired and strained looking as she felt. Vicky, Abby, and Julian sat on the island, leaning tiredly against each other. Willow walked in from the living room; her shoulders slumped as she glanced at them through shadowed eyes.

"Is he awake?" Doug asked.

"No." Isabelle sighed and closed her eyes as she snuggled closer to Stefan's warmth, allowing herself to be comforted by the gentle beat of his heart. She stifled a yawn as a wave of exhaustion swept her.

Stefan dropped his head down to rest on hers and inhaled her gentle, reassuring scent. She had taken a shower, her hair was still damp, and the smell of it was clean and refreshing. Beneath the baggy pants and shirt she wore, he knew that she was completely naked. The knowledge of that had caused him to grow hard long ago, and he was desperately fighting against his baser instincts as she snuggled closer to him. The movement caused his erection to jump and throb.

He clenched his teeth against the growing ache in his loins as he shifted the obvious swell away from the gentle curve of her ass. She was completely exhausted, both emotionally and physically, the last thing she needed right now was to know what he was thinking about.

He glanced down at her bandaged foot, knowing that the wound was heeled by now, but the sight of the blood dampened bandage caused anger, and fear, to course through him. He was going to have a talk with her later about putting herself in danger. He knew that she wouldn't like it, but he'd be damned if she got hurt, or something worse. She had to start thinking about herself, about him, if something happened to her...

The thought alone unleashed something wild and primitive in him. It made him want to destroy the world, and everyone in it. His hands instinctively tightened around her, pulling her more firmly against him as he fought back the panic, and fury, that the thought aroused. As long as he was alive nothing was ever going to happen to her, and if she didn't start taking better care of herself, he was going to lock her up somewhere safe. He didn't care if she hated him for it, but he would do it if it meant keeping her protected, and alive. He didn't think he could survive without her.

He stiffened instantly; the realization brought a surge of raging emotions forth. She lifted her head to stare questioningly at him, but he forced his face to remain blank as he met her gaze. He would figure it all out later, talk to her later about it, but not now. She had enough on her mind now. He had enough on *his* mind now.

He kissed her lightly on the tip of her nose and she smiled softly. That smile clenched at his heart and caused him to harden even more. He shifted slightly as he tried to ease the growing pressure in his cock and she dropped her head to his shoulder again. Her long lashes brushed lightly against his neck as her eyes closed.

Liam appeared in the doorway, his face was drawn and tight as he leaned against the frame. "Is he awake?" Abby demanded.

"No, why don't you guys go on up to bed, you look beat."

"But..."

"Go on," he told them, the hard set of his face leaving no room for arguments. "He probably won't be up for awhile."

They exchanged quick glances, but obviously decided that arguing wasn't going to work. They slid off the island and shuffled slowly out of the room. "Good night," they mumbled as they left.

Liam's gaze came back to them. "You guys should head home too, you look like hell."

"You don't look much better," Mike retorted.

"Yeah but I'll look good after some sleep, you look like crap all the time."

"You wish," Mike muttered.

Liam smiled wanly. "Go on, get out of here. You've all done enough, get some rest."

"You sure dad?" Isabelle asked softly.

"Yes."

They exchanged quick looks before climbing to their feet. Isabelle went to get out of Stefan's lap, but he kept his arms firmly around her as he rose swiftly to follow everyone outside. She smiled as she wrapped her arms around his neck and rested her head on his chest. She was immediately comforted by the reassuring beat of his heart, and the warmth of his body. Her eyes drifted closed as he carried her down the stairs and out to the field.

"You really think he'll be all right?" Ethan asked anxiously.

"Yes," Stefan answered.

He glanced down at Isabelle and was astounded to realize she was sound asleep. "Thank you," Ethan told him.

Stefan glanced sharply up at him. "I didn't do anything," he replied, feeling slightly uncomfortable.

"You got there a lot faster than any of us would have, and you knew that they were in trouble."

"I knew that *Isabelle* was in trouble," he corrected.

"Just like in the club."

Stefan shrugged but was careful not to jar Isabelle out of her sleep. "Yeah."

Ethan's smile faded as he glanced down at Isabelle. Stefan pulled her tighter against him, tensing at the thought that Ethan might touch her, but he made no move to. "You were the last thing that she ever wanted you know," he said softly.

Stefan's eyes snapped with fury as they met Ethan's. "Why is that?"

Ethan flashed a bright grin as he met Stefan's furious gaze. "We weren't the anti-social ones for no reason you know."

"What the hell are you talking about?" he growled, his anger growing by the second.

"Calm down," Ethan said gently. "I'm just saying that she stayed hidden up here, never fed from humans, and avoided them at all costs, because this was the last thing that she ever wanted to have happen to her."

It was taking everything that Stefan had not to grab him by the throat and shake some words out of him that made sense. "What do you mean?" he nearly bellowed.

Isabelle shifted slightly; one arm fell limply into her lap. Stefan forced himself to take a deep breath, and calm down before he woke her. "You still haven't figured it out?" David asked incredulously.

Stefan shot him a glowering look. "Figured what out?"

"I thought when you came back here it was because you knew." David shook his head as he closed his eyes and chuckled softly. "Man, you are dense."

"Look..." Stefan hissed, fury building inside of him. Isabelle whimpered softly as she buried her head tighter against his chest, instinctively trying to soothe him in her sleep.

"Isabelle never wanted to find her soul mate," Ethan explained quickly.

The full knowledge of what Ethan had just said slammed into him, knocking the breath from his lungs as he froze instantly. They turned to stare at him, various expressions of amusement on their faces. He didn't find anything at all amusing in the situation.

He shook his head as he glanced down at the woman curled so trustingly within his arms. Even though there were dark shadows under her eyes, and a pinched look around her mouth, she was still the most beautiful thing he had ever seen. Ever touched. Yet it wasn't her beauty that had brought him back here, and it wasn't just his need to possess her body. It had been something else, something more; something that he hadn't understood until that moment. Now, everything was beginning to make sense.

How could he have not known sooner?

He suddenly understood his desperate need for her, her ability to reach him in the club, his inability to be apart from her, and why he still felt the beast clawing at his insides, wanting to break free. He hadn't fully claimed her. He had wanted to feed off of her, to taste her, and have her do the same, but he had held back because of what had happened to her at the club. He had also never allowed anyone to feed from him, until Kyle. With Kyle though it had been necessity, with Isabelle it would be another way of marking her as his. That had been part of what had held him back, he knew that it would have meant there would be no letting go of her, ever. The idea had frightened him then, but now...

His brow furrowed as he looked at her in his shirt. It was ridiculously big on her, the sleeves hung over her elbows and the edge of it ended at mid thigh. A fierce wave of possession swept through him as he realized how delicately fragile she was, how much weaker she was than him. How much she needed his strength, and protection, especially from her own damn recklessness. If she had slipped today, if she had stumbled, than she wouldn't be here with him right now. The demon in him boiled instantly to the front, raging violently against the possibility of losing her. If she had died, it would have destroyed him. He never would have been able to survive without her.

That knowledge frightened the hell out of him.

"Why not?" His voice was strained with the emotions that raced through him as he lifted his head to look at Ethan.

Ethan's eyes were sad and distant as he stared down at his sister. "She never wanted her existence to hinge on someone else's," he answered softly.

Stefan knew exactly how she felt. No wonder she had gone out of her way to avoid him. She had recognized the signs from the beginning. She hadn't been fighting against him, but herself, and the implications of what his arrival had signaled. He understood now why she had fled into the house the first night that he had seen her. Understood why he had been unable to tear his gaze away from her. He now knew why he had been able to feel her panic, and pain that night in the club, why he had been unable to leave her.

He was such an idiot. He should have known what was going on, should have recognized the signs. Hell he was the one that had told David about Liam and Sera, how could he not have known?

He sighed as he closed his eyes and tried to sort through everything. He hadn't recognized it because he had never thought that it could happen to him. He had never given much thought to the soul mate thing. He had heard of it, and he knew what it meant, but he had never thought that it would affect *him*. He had been alive for a long time, and he had never met anyone that he would have even considered changing, or settling down with. After all these years, he hadn't thought that it was possible to find anyone. He knew now that he had been completely, and utterly, wrong.

He closed his eyes and took a deep breath as he tried to absorb, and sort through everything. "Shit," he whispered.

"I'm surprised you didn't recognize it sooner," David said, the amusement in his voice only aggravating Stefan more.

He remembered the way that they had all behaved around him the night that she had gotten hurt, and it suddenly made sense. He opened his eyes and looked down at her. She looked so innocent, and angelic, but he knew how much looks could be deceiving. She was an irritating, infuriating, hellion, and for better or worse, he was stuck with her. He had to admit that no matter how much she may aggravate him, he really didn't mind the idea of being stuck with her for eternity. It was actually a rather appealing concept.

"So am I," he muttered. "How long have you guys known?"

"Since the night at the club," Jack answered.

He glanced up at them. "Why didn't you tell me sooner?"

"You left before we had the chance," Mike reminded him. "And once you came back, we just assumed that you had figured it out."

Stefan frowned as he glanced back at Isabelle. David started to laugh as he turned and walked toward the house. "You look like someone just punched you in the gut!" he called over his shoulder.

He felt like someone had just punched him in the gut. He started walking again, marveling over what he had just learned, what he had just realized. He saw the way that Liam and Sera were together, their constant need to communicate with each other, their need to touch, and the deep love that they shared.

He frowned as he thought about that. He didn't love Isabelle. He liked her, he admired her, he cared for her, but he didn't love her. Did he?

He glanced back down at her as a deep, unknown emotion began to well up inside of him. It was something that he had never felt before, and he didn't understand what it was. He wanted to keep her sheltered, protected, and safe. He wanted to see her laugh, wanted to see her happy. He needed to be with her, and around her. Today, in town, he had felt like he was crawling out of his skin without her. He knew now that it was because he *needed* to be near her, to touch her, to hold her at all times. Was that what love was?

He slipped into the house behind everyone else and carried her swiftly down the basement stairs. He pushed the door open and kicked it closed behind him. Isabelle stirred slightly as he put her on the bed, but she didn't awaken. He undressed her slowly, careful not to rouse her as he pulled off his shirt and the baggy pants.

He stood for a moment, admiring her long, sleek body, and gentle curves. In the moonlight she glistened with a silvery light that highlighted her creamy skin. He tore his gaze from her as he hardened painfully and quickly stripped out of his own clothes. He crawled into bed beside her, gritting his teeth against his carnal urges as he drew her into his arms. She murmured softly, but didn't awaken as she rested her head in his shoulder. It took all he had not to wake her to make love to her, but he knew how badly she needed sleep, how exhausted she was.

It was a long time before he finally fell asleep.

CHAPTER 20

"What are you doing?" Isabelle demanded laughingly as Stefan guided her easily along.

"You'll see," he whispered huskily in her ear.

Chills shuddered down her spine as she moved closer to him, relishing in the feel of his hard, warm body against hers. She didn't think she would ever get used to the way that he made her feel. She cried out suddenly as he bent and swept her up. Her hands instinctively clung to his broad shoulders as he chuckled softly in her ear. "I won't drop you," he promised.

She smiled brightly at him as he carried her swiftly along. She knew that they were going to the new house, but he had insisted on blindfolding her for it. Her heart beat wildly with anticipation as he climbed the porch steps. She was dying to see the house, as they had refused to let her near it the closer it got to being completed, but being this close to Stefan was causing another desire to awaken in her. One that she hadn't been able to satisfy enough over the past few days. She snuggled closer to him, pressing her breasts provocatively against his chest as her hands lightly stroked the back of his neck.

"Unless you want me to take you in front of your brothers, you had better stop," he growled.

Isabelle smiled up at him. "Stop what?" she asked innocently.

"You know what."

She chuckled softly as the door opened and closed. "Can I see yet?" she asked eagerly.

"Not yet."

She sighed impatiently as he climbed the stairs and moved briskly down the hallway. She frowned as she lifted her head from his shoulder. "I think we're missing most of the house." A door banged shut. Isabelle's forehead furrowed, and then cleared as a delicious shiver swept through her. "Where are my brothers?"

"Packing their stuff." Isabelle laughed happily as he set her on her feet and turned her to untie the blindfold. "Keep your eyes closed."

She nearly jumped up and down as the blindfold fell away. "Okay," he whispered in her ear. "Open them."

She gasped in surprise, and delight, as the room was revealed to her. It had been painted in the soft cream color that she had chosen. The wood trim surrounding the room was stained a light oak that gleamed in the sunlight spilling through the windows. Beaming happily, her gaze settled upon the four poster, king size bed, with its beautiful green, white, and yellow quilt. She clearly remembered telling her mother that was the quilt she wanted for her bed, but this bed was definitely not hers. She didn't know where it had come from, but she loved it instantly.

An antique nightstand stood beside the bed, her tiffany lamp, with its multi colored, stained glass shade had been placed on it. At the foot of the bed was the old cedar chest that she'd owned since she was a little girl. Her bureau had been placed against the left wall; beneath two large windows that overlooked the woods. On the right hand side was a large bay window with an emerald green window seat that over looked the sparkling lake. She knew that she would spend many wonderful hours there, curled up on that seat, daydreaming or reading.

"Who did all of this?" she cried as she raced across the room and flung open the doors to the large walk in closet. It was so big that she could easily have put a twin bed in it.

Isabelle laughed with delight as she ran across the room and thrust the door to the bathroom open. She froze for a moment, her breath catching in her throat before she squealed in delight. The walls had been sponge painted a soft rose, and light dove color. A large Jacuzzi tub, that she had never asked to have, had been installed. Her eyes widened in surprise as she rushed over to hop in it. She sprawled out for a moment, amazed that all of her fit with room to spare, before she hopped back out to take in the rest of the room. There was a shower stall next to the tub with a beaded glass door. The counter was the soft marble green that she had ordered, but it enclosed two sinks, instead of just one. Her smile grew even bigger as she realized that Stefan was the one that had made the changes, and seen to the room being finished.

Stefan watched in amusement as she ran back into the room and jumped onto the large bed. "You like it?"

She beamed at him as she swung her arms over her head and jumped up to hit the ceiling. "I love it! Did you do all of it!?"

He smiled as he moved slowly toward her. She stopped jumping on the bed to watch breathlessly as he approached with a predatory gleam in his eyes. "Your mom painted the bathroom. I don't have the patience for that sponging thing."

"And the bed?"

"I couldn't resist it."

He smiled up at her as she moved slowly toward him. Her eyes were bright with happiness and laughter, the smile on her face was breathtaking. She was absolutely beautiful, and at that moment he would have given her the world if she had asked him.

"All I could do was imagine the things that I was going to do to you in this bed," he said hoarsely.

Heat suffused her from head to toe as her body grew taut with anticipation. "And who said you were going to be sharing it with me?" she inquired teasingly.

Although he knew that she was teasing, her words caused something primal to surge forth. He seized hold of her waist, lifted her off the bed, and dropped her on it. She cried out in surprise as he braced his arms beside her head, and leaned over her. "I do," he grated.

She stared breathlessly up at him, momentarily shocked by the fierceness in his gaze. He looked very dark and dangerous as his eyes burned into hers, and his jaw clenched. She hadn't meant to make him upset, but she obviously had, and she didn't understand why. She smiled sweetly as she gently stroked his cheek and tried to soothe the savage look from his face. He softened at her touch, but there was still a predatory gleam in his eyes that she knew well.

"Stefan," she breathed.

He brushed the hair gently off her neck, his eyes latched onto it as they flashed violently. A shiver of fear and desire tore through her as she struggled to breathe. "Do you know what we are Isabelle?" he demanded raggedly.

Her lips parted as she scanned his face anxiously. She knew what they were, and how she felt about him, but she hadn't been sure if he knew yet. She sure as hell didn't know how he felt about her, and she wasn't about to tell him anything if he didn't feel the same way. His eyes were hard and turbulent as they came back to hers. Her hand began to tremble on his cheek as her heart seemed to swell to the point of bursting.

"Do you?" she asked softly.

His mouth quirked in a smile, but it didn't reach his eyes. "Yes, I do." Her breath froze in her lungs as tears sprang to her eyes. "You may have denied it in the beginning, you may even be trying to deny it still, but you will accept it. Now."

She would have laughed over his command, except the look in his eyes, and his words, had left her momentarily speechless. She swallowed heavily as her hand fell away from his face. "Do you realize what you're saying?" she asked quietly.

"Yes, I do," he grated. "Do you understand what I'm telling you? You need to come to terms with this."

Isabelle laughed as emotions so fierce, and stunning, blazed forth. His eyes darkened and flashed dangerously. She realized that he didn't understand that she wasn't laughing at him, but because she was joyously happy. "I have," she assured him quickly.

Slowly the animosity in his body began to ease, and a smile curved his sensual mouth. "Good."

He kissed with a butterfly caress that caused her heart to race, and her body to melt. She wrapped her arms around his neck and kissed him lightly back as she savored in the feel of his hard mouth against hers. When he licked at her lips she parted them willingly to accept his eager, hot invasion.

Isabelle lost herself to the sensation of his mouth, and body, as he moved over her, tasting her, feeling her. Somewhere along the way, their clothes disappeared. She relished in the feel of his warm skin, and hard, taut muscles as he slid over her. The course hair that covered his broad chest amazed her as she lightly ran her fingers through it and marveled in the differences between his body, and hers. She circled his nipples, nipping, and licking at them until they hardened beneath her ministrations.

Stefan slid his hands slowly over satiny skin, mesmerizing every curve, every hollow. He left a trail of kisses down her neck, over her ribcage, before seizing on one of her quivering, hard nipples. Isabelle gasped softly, arching further into him as he drew her into his mouth, nibbling lightly on it as if it were the sweetest berry in the world, which to him, it was. Her hands tightened upon his back as glorious, erotic gasps escaped her.

He slid steadily lower, dropping kisses over her flat stomach before dipping in to taste her tiny navel. She squirmed beneath him, her breath coming faster as her hips instinctively lifted to him, seeking his invasion, his possession. Stefan stood swiftly, Isabelle groaned at the loss of contact, but he seized hold of her hips and pulled her to the edge of the bed. She gasped in surprise as he knelt on the floor before her, using his hands to separate the thighs that she instinctively tried to close.

"Stefan!"

His smile was sly and sensual as he dropped soft kisses along her inner thigh and his tongue left a blazing trail that set her on fire, and melted any resistance she would have made. Hypnotized, she watched in breathless anticipation as his dark head bent between her legs. Her hands curled tightly into the quilt as he parted her soft folds and began to taste her. The wickedness of what he was doing, and the delicious sensations that it arose, drove her nearly mad. She arched wildly against him as he drove his tongue deeper.

Stefan was certain that he had never tasted anything as sweet as her. She was like molten lava, and honey, rolled into one. Her hands released the sheets to curl into his hair, pulling him tighter against her. A feeling of utter triumph came over him as she yielded everything to him. He began to urge her faster, plummeting deeply in and out as her cries became more frantic, and she began to writhe with unbridled abandon upon the bed. He reached up to knead her breasts as he used his thumb to gently stroke the quivering bud between her thighs that was begging for his attention.

She bucked against him, a savage cry escaping her as her hands tightened painfully in his hair. He ignored it as he savored in the taste of her and absorbed the tremors that rocked and seized her.

He pulled away from her, smiling with smug satisfaction as he looked down at her. She was slicked with sweat, and breathless as her passion clouded eyes met his. She managed a tremulous smile as he lifted himself over, seized hold of her luscious mouth and drove himself into her. Isabelle cried out, her fingers dug into his back as another wave of ecstasy crashed over her.

***

Isabelle tossed her sweater into a box and hummed happily under her breath as she danced across the room. She hadn't known that it was possible to be this happy, this complete. She literally felt as if her heart was going to burst with joy. She knew that she was acting like a silly fool, one that was in love. A soft smile curved her mouth as she tossed another sweater into the box. The knowledge didn't frighten her at all anymore.

She knew that she was in love with Stefan, that without him she would wither away and die, but she no longer cared about that consequence. She wanted him, and only him. She hadn't told him that she loved him yet, simply because a part of her was still scared that he didn't feel the same way. She kept trying to tell herself that he did love her; after all he knew they were meant to be together, but that didn't necessarily mean that he loved her.

Well, maybe it did. She wasn't entirely sure, but she thought that if people were destined to be soul mates, than love would have to be a factor, wouldn't it? Her brow furrowed as she tossed another sweater into the box. Her mother and father loved each other dearly, but they had been in love before her mother had known what her father was, before either of them had ever known anything about soul mates. That hadn't happened with her and Stefan, and she wasn't sure if maybe that was the way that it was supposed to work. Maybe they were all supposed to fall in love first, and then find out about it later.

She slid onto her old bed, a sweater clutched tightly in her hand, as she stared at the woods through the window. If she was truly honest with herself, she would admit that a part of her had loved him from the start. She had just been too stubborn to admit it, or acknowledge it. She wished that she hadn't fought against him so hard, against the way that she had felt. She should have run to him with open arms and embraced her future instead of hiding from it, but she had an eternity to make up for her mistake.

Isabelle hopped off the bed, determined to start making it up to him as soon as possible. She was smiling wickedly, and humming again, when she realized that she was no longer alone. She spun quickly to find Jess in the doorway; her eyes were dark and hooded as hatred oozed from every pore of her body. Jess's hair was dripping wet, and her bathing suit clung tightly to her long, lean body. She had made sure that Jess wasn't around when she came in, but obviously she had returned from her swim sometime after Isabelle had left Kyle's side.

"I'll be out in a minute," Isabelle managed to tell her through the lump that suddenly constricted her throat. She didn't want to think about what had once been between Jess and Stefan but she suddenly couldn't get it out of her mind.

Jess snorted as she moved further into the room. "Take your time; it is *your* room after all."

"Not anymore." Isabelle tossed the sweater into the box and turned to grab the remaining sweaters from the drawer.

"Then again, what's mine is yours, right Isabelle?"

Isabelle forced herself to take a deep breath and turn to face her. Jess had every right to hate her, and if it had been the other way around she would have felt the same way, but she had to try and say something, to do something, to ease it. "I am sorry Jess," she whispered.

"Why is it that I don't believe a word you say?"

Isabelle sighed warily, obviously Jess was determined to have it out with her, and there wasn't much she could do to stop her. "You don't have to believe me Jess, but it is the truth. I didn't want for this to happen. It just did. I'm sorry that you got hurt in the process, but there is nothing that I can do about it now."

Isabelle tossed the sweaters into the box and closed the lid. She wanted out of this room in the worst possible way.

Hoisting the box into her arms she hurried around the bed. Jess instantly moved to intercept her. "Jess..."

"You think you're so special? You think you're so great? You're just a little slut, and he'll use you, and toss you aside like the whore that you are!" she hissed.

Isabelle's eyes narrowed as her guilt vanished and anger welled up to replace it. "I told you that I was sorry; there is nothing else that I can say. If you don't accept it, then that's fine. Now get out of my way!"

"I hate you!" Jess screeched.

Isabelle closed her eyes as a tremor seized her body. The malevolence that poured from Jess was enough to knock her blossoming anger away. "Jess..."

She never saw the slap coming, but the force of it staggered her backward as the sound of it resounded throughout the room. Isabelle gaped in surprise as the box fell from her suddenly limp hands and tears of pain instantly sprang to her eyes. Blood filled her mouth, and her cheek stung from the force of the blow. Her hand flew to her cheek, and split lip, as she gazed at Jess in shock. Jess was shaking with fury, her hands clenched in fists at her sides as she took a step forward.

A loud bellow filled the room as Stefan came forward with his eyes blazing. Jess's mouth dropped as she spun toward him. He seized hold of her arms and lifted her easily off the ground as he pulled her forward. Jess cried out in surprise as her feet kicked wildly in the air. Isabelle leapt forward to grasp hold of his arm. "Stefan no!"

The fury that radiated from every inch of him filled the room, and shook her to the marrow of her bones. Jess whimpered as she squirmed wildly in his grasp. "You're hurting me!"

"I'll kill you if you ever lay a hand on her again! If you ever *look* at her again!" he roared. Jess went limp in his grasp as tears filled her eyes. "Do you hear me?" he snapped, shaking her forcefully.

Jess whimpered again. "Stefan, please don't," Isabelle begged, pulling on his arm. She had about as much effect on him as a flea would have.

"Do you hear me?" he bellowed.

Isabelle jumped in surprise, her heart leapt into her throat. "Yes!" Jess cried. "Yes!"

He stood for a moment longer before he finally released her. Jess stumbled back, her knees buckled as she slumped to the floor before staggering quickly back up. Isabelle took a step toward her, meaning to help, but Stefan grabbed hold of her arm and pulled her back. Jess cast them a wild, frantic look, before racing from the room.

"Are you okay?" he demanded.

Isabelle whirled toward him as she ripped her arm free of his grasp. "No!" she yelled. "No, I'm not!"

His face softened as he took a step toward her, but she backed rapidly up, shaking her head as she held up her hands to ward him off. "Isabelle..."

"Stay away from me!"

Stefan's anger blazed back to life as his jaw clenched forcefully. Tears spilled down her cheeks as she wrapped her arms around herself and began to tremble uncontrollably. Her beautiful cheek was reddened, and guaranteed to bruise; blood dotted her split lip, it trickled down her trembling chin. The smell of it, sweet and metallic surged into him and caused something primitive and wild to surge forth. He fisted his hands as he desperately tried to bring it under control, to reign in his wild need to drink from her.

He had been dying to taste her, to have her taste him, to fill her in every way, but he had continued to hold back. He was no longer afraid of what it would mean, but he had seen the fear that filled her eyes whenever he looked at her neck. That fear had kept him at bay, but it was becoming increasingly harder every day not to take her.

Now, smelling her, seeing it on her, he was damn close to losing all control and forcing it upon her. He knew that it was the final step, the one thing that would bind them forever, and that they would have to do it, but he had thought that he had time for it. He knew now that he was wrong. The urge was becoming stronger as their bond grew stronger.

She absently wiped the blood from her mouth. Stefan's eyes fastened on it, blazing with the sudden hunger that rocked him. Isabelle whimpered softly. He looked back at her as she stared at him warily, her eyes bright with tears, and fear. "No," she said softly.

A muscle jumped in his cheek as he fought against the demon inside him. "Let's go."

She shook her head fiercely. Stefan fought against his mounting frustration as he forced himself to take a deep, calming breath. "I need to be alone. I need to think!"

His eyes snapped with fury as they latched onto her. "There is nothing to think about!" he nearly roared.

She jumped in surprise as her eyes darted anxiously toward the doorway. He was terrifying her at the moment. She had seen the fierce hunger in his gaze when he saw her blood, had felt the need that had ripped through him. Isabelle clearly recalled the pain of the last time that someone had drunk from her. It was seared permanently into her nerve endings, into her brain, and she was never going to let it happen again.

His hunger, on top of what had just happened with Jess, was more than she could stand. She was still shaking from Jess's brutal attack, and Stefan's overwhelming fury. She needed to be alone, needed time to think. She was much too rattled for this right now.

"I just need a few minutes," she mumbled, trying to stall for time, trying to get a hold on her shaking body.

"For what?" he hissed.

"She hates me!" He took a step closer to her. Isabelle's eyes widened as she took another one back and her heel connected with the wall. She had effectively trapped herself. He took another step toward her. "Because of you!"

Rage snapped and blazed through him. "There is nothing that I can do about that!"

"Just give me time to think!"

"Think about what?"

"To sort things out!"

He was before her, his arms pinned to the wall beside her head, before she even saw him move. His eyes blazed with a fire so fierce that an involuntary cry of fear ripped from her. "I cannot undo my past Isabelle," he hissed.

"Don't hurt me."

Her whispered plea managed to rip through his fury as her hand fluttered over her mouth. The terror in her gaze and the trembling in her body seized hold of him. Self hatred, and disgust, rolled forth as he slumped toward her. "I'll never hurt you Isabelle," he promised. "I'm sorry about Jess, I truly am, but I can't do anything to change it. She'll be gone soon, and I swear that I won't let her hurt you again."

She bit down on her bottom lip to repress a sob, and instantly regretted the action as a flash of pain shook her. His eyes flashed onto the blood that flowed forth again. Terror, fierce and mind shattering, flared within her. "No!" she screamed as she shoved against him.

For a moment, Stefan was knocked off balance by the strength behind her sudden thrust. Regaining his balance, he seized hold of her arm before she could bolt from the room. She spun wildly and lashed out in panic. He grabbed hold of her hand before she could claw into his face. Isabelle sobbed and jerked at her arm as she frantically tried to break the iron hold on her wrist. He took hold of her other arm and pinned it to her side as he held her firmly.

She tried to struggle free of him, tried desperately to escape, but his hold was like a steel vice upon her. He was ten times stronger than her, fiercer, and more determined. There would be no getting free of him; he would do whatever he wanted to her.

"You said you wouldn't hurt me!" she cried.

Stefan closed his eyes against the tumult of emotions rocking him. Her terror was tangible as it beat against him in pulsating waves. It was the only thing keeping the demon in him at bay, the only thing keeping him somewhat in control. Her words about needing time to think things out, and her attempt to get away from him, had nearly shattered every ounce of restraint he had. It had brought the demon bursting instantly forth.

She was his, and he was growing tired of holding himself back from possessing her in every way. He was growing tired of the fight that she still waged against him, even if she didn't realize that she was doing it. She was afraid of what would happen if he drank from her, but it was something that needed to be done, needed to be completed. Otherwise, he would snap, and force it on her, and she would never forgive him if he did. He would never forgive *himself*. It was going to happen soon though, and whether she was willing, or not.

"I don't want to hurt you Isabelle."

"I can see Stefan! I can see what you want!"

"It's what I *need*!" he hissed. Her eyes, shining with tears, widened. "You are *mine* Isabelle."

"I..." she swallowed heavily as tears slid slowly down her cheeks. "I know that."

He took a deep breath as he clenched his jaw. He knew that she didn't understand what he was trying to tell her. He forced himself to release her arms, she was scared enough without being trapped by him. He walked over and picked up the box, determined to show her that he wasn't going to force anything on her. Not yet anyway. If she kept fighting him he didn't know what would happen. He knew that it would hurt again, if she resisted him, but if she didn't...

He actually didn't know how it would feel if she didn't resist him. All the humans he had fed from had never known because he had blocked it from their minds, and memories. The only person who had ever fed off of him, except Kyle, was the woman that had changed him and it had been the most excruciating experience of his life. He knew why Isabelle feared it, recalled the agony that had seized him, but he also knew that this was something that he wanted, something that he *needed* with every ounce of his heart, and soul.

"Let's talk about this later."

He hefted the box and turned to face her. "Stefan..."

"Later Isabelle."

She wanted to fight with him, wanted to protest his highhanded, commanding manner, but she instinctively knew that he would become enraged again. She had seen the fury that had consumed him, seen the near loss of control that had seized him, and she was scared that it would happen again, and this time he wouldn't come back.

Isabelle shuddered as she wrapped her arms around herself. She knew what he wanted from her, but she also knew that she couldn't give it to him.

CHAPTER 21

"I can't believe that bitch slapped you!"

"Abigail!" her mother said sharply.

Abby sent her a rueful look, but her eyes were full of fire as she turned back to Isabelle. Isabelle shrugged as she added more paint to the roller. "You should have hit her back!"

"She has a right to be mad Abby," Isabelle said softly.

"She does not!" Vicky yelled.

Isabelle closed her eyes and took a deep breath as she prayed for patience. She didn't need her sisters ranting and raving on top of everything else on her mind. All things considered, the day was totaling up to a bad one. It didn't help that Stefan had given her the time that she'd requested, and gone with her father, and David, to feed. Her body longed for his return. It was beginning to become almost intolerable.

She slapped the roller against the wall as she grit her teeth against the clawing ache in her body. "I'm glad she's leaving tomorrow. I don't know how Kathleen has such a miserable bi... witch for a daughter." Abby caught herself just in time as her mother shot her a warning look.

"I don't know what Stefan saw in her in the first place. I mean, how could he be with someone like that?" Isabelle's jaw clenched as a fierce jealousy seized her. For a moment, the room was shaded in a haze of red as her hands tightened in a death grip upon the roller handle. "He could have his choice of women, what..."

"Vicky!" Isabelle threw her roller down and spun to face her sisters.

"What?" she asked in confusion.

"Enough!" Isabelle snapped.

"I was just saying..."

"Why don't you girls go on home," her mother interrupted as she turned to face them. Her eyes focused questioningly on Isabelle. "It's getting late."

They were about to protest, but decided better of it as they looked back at Isabelle. "Okay," Vicky mumbled.

"We'll see you tomorrow," Abby said.

Isabelle sighed as she rubbed tiredly at her eyes. "Care to tell me what's wrong?" her mother asked softly.

"What isn't wrong," she muttered.

"Isabelle..."

She held up a hand, needing a few moments to gather her thoughts. Everything inside of her was a mess. She needed Stefan with her. She had wanted him to go away, to give her time to think; now all she wanted was for him to come back. It hurt when he was gone. She couldn't think, hell she could barely even function, and now jealousy was clawing at her insides again. He had gone to feed. He would be feeding off of women, and she couldn't help but wonder what else he would be doing with them. The thought brought the vampire in her surging to the forefront. She trembled as she struggled to draw it back, to keep it under reign.

Finally, she lifted her head and met her mother's troubled gaze. "I just... I feel... awful," she breathed.

Her mother smiled knowingly and nodded as she dropped her roller down. "He'll be back soon."

"I know it's just that I don't know what he's doing, where he is, or who he's with!"

Her mother's forehead furrowed as the jealousy in her sizzled to fierce life. It clawed at her and ripped her insides apart. "Isabelle, he's not with anyone else."

"How do I know that? You heard Vicky and Abby, he could have his choice of women and I don't know what he's doing with them!"

"He doesn't want anyone but you, Isabelle. You are it, for eternity. I doubted it at first. I thought your father would grow tired of me, or find someone else, or want someone else, but it's impossible Isabelle. As unbelievable as that may sound, it *is* impossible."

Isabelle almost slumped against the wall, but managed to catch herself in time. "Why?"

Her mother smiled softly and shrugged. "I don't know, but if you don't believe me, ask yourself if you would ever want anyone else?"

The answer to that question was instantaneous. "No."

"Trust me when I tell you that it is the same for him." Isabelle nodded wearily as she glanced around the empty living room. She was far from mollified. Her mother and father were different. Isabelle wasn't even sure how Stefan felt about her, besides thinking that she belonged to him, and that they were soul mates, but she wanted more. She wanted his love, and she wasn't sure that she had it. "There's more, isn't there?"

"Does it hurt when dad bites you?"

Her mother frowned as her eyes darkened worriedly. "At first it did, but now it doesn't hurt at all, why?"

Isabelle wrapped her arms around herself as she turned her gaze back to the window. "I was just wondering," she mumbled.

"Isabelle..."

The opening of the door cut off whatever her mother was going to say. Isabelle's heart picked up with anticipation as her arms fell back to her sides. Acute disappointment crashed over her as Ethan came strolling in with Jack, and Ian. Boxes were balanced haphazardly in their arms as they paused in the doorway to take in the half painted living room. "Looking good," Jack commented.

"Us, or the walls?" her mom asked happily.

"Both," Jack replied with a bright grin. "Although, I'm not sure what has more paint on it, you guys, or the walls."

Isabelle smiled as she glanced down at her paint splattered clothing, and arms. She was usually meticulous when she painted, but tonight she had been unable to keep her mind focused on what she was doing. "I'm going to go take a shower," she muttered.

Ignoring the curious stares cast her way, she left the room quickly. She rushed up the stairs, suddenly needing the sanctuary of her room, and the comfort of a shower. She lingered beneath the pounding stream of water, hoping that it would ease some of the torment rolling through her body. When it became obvious that the water wasn't going to ease her pain, she shut it off and climbed tiredly out.

Everything in her hurt. Everything ached. She slid her nightgown over her head, brushed her hair, and moved back into the bedroom. Stefan's scent lingered everywhere, only serving to reinforce the tearing loneliness ripping at her heart and stomach. She sat miserably on the bed, drew her knees up to her chest, and wrapped her arms around them in an attempt to ward off the desolation that was beginning to consume her. Tears slid silently down her cheeks as she watched time slip slowly by.

It was after eleven when the door finally swung open. A cry of delight escaped her as she jumped off the bed and raced over to him. He grunted slightly from the force of her impact as she wrapped her arms around his waist and buried her head in his chest. He kicked the door shut before wrapping his arms around her and pulling her close against him.

The feel of him instantly caused the ache inside of her to ease, but her fear lingered as she tried desperately to get closer to him, to bury herself in him. It wasn't enough, she couldn't get close enough.

He lifted her chin gently with his finger. "What's the matter love?"

She shuddered as the endearment slipped from him and caused her insides to melt. "It hurts," she whispered. "It hurts when you go away." He smiled tenderly as his finger stroked her cheek. "I was scared that you wouldn't come back."

His eyes darkened as his hand stilled on her cheek. "I'm not going anywhere Isabelle, ever." His tone was much harsher than he had intended, but her words had instantly angered him. How could she doubt how he felt about her?

"You left once."

He ground his teeth as frustration seized him. "I'm not going anywhere without you Isabelle. The way that you feel when we're apart, is the way that I feel."

She stared doubtfully up at him; her lower lip trembled as tears coursed down her cheeks. "You can have anyone you want."

Exasperation rolled through him. He was tired of constantly fighting her. She needed to know how he felt, needed to know that she was *his*, and that there would be no separating them. There was only one way that he knew how to do that for sure. Sharing blood would seal their bond; allow her to see into him, and for him to see into her. He couldn't be entirely sure of how she felt until he could open up the pathway of communication between them.

He sighed as he seized hold of her waist, lifted her up, and carried her swiftly over to the bed. He sat on the edge of it, gently settling her onto his lap. Her lashes fell to veil her eyes and shadow her cheeks. He nudged her chin gently, forcing her to look at him. The vulnerability in her gaze tore at his heart. "Isabelle, we're soul mates. You belong to me, you're a part of me, and I *am* a part of you."

She nodded as her eyes searched his face. "But..."

"There are no buts," he said forcefully. "That's the way it is. You may not have wanted it, hell I didn't want it." Her eyes darkened as pain flashed through them. He silently cursed himself. He was supposed to be easing her fears, and doubts, not adding to them. "But I wouldn't change any of it. If I had known that you were here, I would have come for you sooner. I was growing tired of traveling, tired of living alone. When I came here, and saw how happy everyone was, I wanted the same thing. When I first met you, I wanted you with a desire that was so consuming it bordered on obsession. When I left here I had no control over myself, or what I was doing. I have thought of nothing but you since the moment we met."

"What about Jess?"

His hands tightened on her as his eyes flashed with rage. "Shit Isabelle, why can't you ever just listen to what I'm saying to you! Must you always fight me?" he hissed.

Her eyes widened in surprise as she swallowed the sudden lump in her throat. "I don't mean to, I just... I'm jealous," she confessed, her lids lowered to shadow her eyes again as a fierce blush crept into her cheeks.

The confession shot a bolt of pure male satisfaction through him. He was glad that she was jealous, even if it did upset her. It helped to assure him that she truly did care for him, and he was happy to realize that he wasn't the only one in this relationship who became easily jealous. He smiled as he brushed her hair off her cheek and gently pushed it behind her ear. "I can't change my past Isabelle, but the minute that I met you I didn't want anyone else."

He was lying to her, and if he would lie to her about this, he would lie to her about anything. Her eyes flew back to his, narrowed with fury as she stiffened. "Don't lie to me. I smelled her on you!"

His jaw clenched and a vein popped out on his forehead. She glared defiantly back at him, refusing to back down. "I am not lying to you," he grated.

Isabelle struggled to break free of his grasp. He pulled her back; his hands upon her were rigid with anger as he clung to her. She ceased struggling as she turned toward him, her eyes burning a brilliant shade of red. It was the first time he had ever seen her completely lose control of the demon within her, and it shocked the anger out of him.

"If you would lie about this, then what else are you lying about?" she yelled. It took him a moment to realize that it was more fear than anger that had her so riled up, and out of control. He sighed softly as he reached up to brush her cheek. She slapped his hand away as tears filled her eyes. "Don't!"

He took a deep breath and forced himself to remain calm. She was hurt, and angry, and scared that he didn't care for her. Anger was not going to help ease any of that. The only thing he could do to ease it, was to tell her the truth. That was the last thing that he wanted to do. She already wielded enough power over him, without handing her another weapon. "I went to bed that night with Jess, but I didn't finish. Hell, I barely even got started. I couldn't get you out of my head Isabelle. I got no satisfaction that night, or any afterward, until you. That *is* the truth."

She sat silently, her head bowed as she thought over his words. The burning jealousy in her made her want to lash out at him, but she held her tongue. She didn't want to argue with him, but hurt, and fear, were eating away at her. There were so many women in his past, how could he possibly be happy to settle down with just her for the rest of his existence? A tear slid down her cheek, he gently wiped it away as he turned her head to face him.

She lifted her lashes slowly to meet his tender, loving gaze. It melted her to the tips of her toes. "Besides, what about all the men in your past, maybe you'll run off with one of them?"

He tried to keep his tone light and teasing, but the thought damn near drove him over the brink of sanity as a fierce surge of possessiveness tore through him. He would kill anyone that ever thought of taking her from him, of touching her. Her eyes widened as all the color drained from her face. He frowned at her in perplexity as she tore her chin from his grasp.

"There are no men in my past!" she snapped, her eyes flashing violently. "You are it!"

He sighed softly as he realized that she had completely misunderstood. "Isabelle, I know you were a virgin, but you're a beautiful woman I'm sure you had boyfriends in high school," he soothed. "Isabelle..."

"There was no one else," she whispered so softly that he barely heard her. The tips of her lashes were wet against her skin as another tear slid free.

He frowned as he stared at her. "What are you saying?"

Her face flooded with color as she shifted uncomfortably in his lap. She was certain that she had never been this humiliated in her life. This whole situation was so unfair! She fervently wished that she had flung herself at every boy in high school, and every guy she had met since then just so she could be on somewhat of a level playing field with him. Then again, even if she had slept with every guy in high school, his side of the field would still be a lot fuller than hers.

"Isabelle," he prompted gently. He hadn't thought it was possible, but her face turned even redder as she stubbornly refused to meet his gaze.

"You're the first *everything* Stefan."

Again he had to strain to hear what she was saying, but when the words sank in, they knocked the breath out of him. He stared at her in awe, as supreme conquest flooded him. No one, but him, had ever touched her. His satisfaction vanished as another tear slid down her scarlet face. It was then that he truly began to understand what she had been going through, why she was so unsure of herself, and his commitment to her. Where her past was a blank slate, his was a scroll that could cover miles of land. It had to be intimidating and frightening to know that.

He sighed softly as he took her chin again and turned it to him. "Look at me Isabelle." She bit into her bottom lip as she shyly lifted her gaze to his. "There are a lot of people in my past, but I have never felt about anyone the way that I feel about you. Never. You are it Isabelle, the only one that has ever mattered to me. The only one that will *ever* matter."

She stared doubtfully at him before lowering her lashes again. He forced away his anger, and nudged her chin gently. When she looked back at him, he continued speaking. "We are soul mates Isabelle, but the bond isn't complete yet. That's the reason why you have any doubt in me, the reason that it hurts you, and me, when we're not together. Once we forge the bond we'll be able to communicate with each other all the time. It won't hurt when we're apart, and you will never again doubt the way that I feel about you."

She licked her lips nervously, Stefan felt himself harden against her as he watched the delicate tip of her tongue in fascination. "How?" she whispered tremulously.

"We need to exchange blood."

Her face went white as fear blazed in her eyes. "No!"

"Isabelle, listen to me. We have to do this. It makes the bond complete."

"I believe everything you say!" she cried. "I do! I trust you completely."

He sighed softly as he forced himself to remain patient. "It has to be done Isabelle. I need to do it, and soon. I would rather have you be willing, than snap and take it forcefully from you one day."

"You won't," she breathed.

"Yes, I will. I have to; the demon in me has to. I have to mark you as mine, I have to establish that connection, otherwise I will snap. I've been holding back because I know that you're scared, but it's getting harder to control every day, with every moment that goes by. As long as you don't fight me, it will only hurt for a second, and then it won't hurt anymore."

She studied him apprehensively, her eyes dark with dread. "Do you promise?" she whispered tremulously.

"Yes." Isabelle swallowed down the fear that was threatening to choke her. "You can taste me first if you don't believe me."

"I've never bit anyone," she whispered as a little thrill shot through her at the idea. "I'll hurt you."

"No, you won't. You'll know what to do, and I want you to."

She wanted to do this for him, but she wanted it more for herself. She clearly recalled how tempting his blood had seemed the other night. She wanted to taste him, to have him fill her. Something inside of her thrilled at the idea, and craved it. Her hands curled in her lap as she closed her eyes against the fierce bloodlust that ripped through her, and brought the beast surging forth. Stefan pulled her tightly against him as she began to tremble fiercely.

He closed his eyes as he rocked her gently, the need that suddenly radiated from her enflamed his own. He lifted her gently and placed her on the bed before standing swiftly. He had to get away from her so that he could get a hold on himself. She kept her eyes firmly closed as she fisted her hands in her lap. With the soft white nightgown, and her hair flowing freely around her, she looked so vulnerable and innocent that it ripped at his insides and brought a blast of need tearing through him.

He turned away from her, and yanked off his shirt off with fierce, vicious movements. The beast in him was clamoring to get free. He was beginning to fear that he had waited too long, that he wouldn't be able to stop himself from hurting her. If that happened she would never forgive him, and he would never forgive himself. He tore his jeans and underwear off, and took a deep breath before turning back to her. She still sat with her head bowed, and her trembling hands clamped tightly in her lap.

He took a deep breath and forced himself to calm down before moving back and lifting her up. He settled her on his lap and wrapped his arms tightly around her waist. He realized too late that he never should have touched her, never should have put himself this close to her. He should have waited until tomorrow when he had more control over himself. He could see the fierce thumping of her heart pulsing through the vein in her neck; smell the tantalizing, sweet scent of her.

She shook against him, a soft whimper escaped. "Isabelle," he grated hoarsely. "Look at me."

Her shaking increased. She bit into her bottom lip in an attempt to try and stop it, and then cried out as her teeth pierced her skin. She was losing it. Never had she felt this consumed by hunger, by need. She couldn't look at him, he would see it, he would know, and she was certain that the sight of him would cause her to snap.

"Look at me."

Isabelle's eyes were wild and savage when they flew open. Stefan's body clenched as he saw the thin thread of control she possessed. It almost snapped his tenuous hold. He pushed her slightly back, snagged hold of the bottom of her nightgown and tore it off to reveal her magnificent body. His jaw clenched as he took in her full breasts, porcelain skin, narrow waist, and delicate, flaring hips. The triangle of dark hair between her thighs caused lust to surge through him. Her eyes snapped shut as she whimpered softly and buried herself against his chest.

His arms tightened around her as she wrapped her arms around his neck and buried her head in his shoulder. His erection pressed against her thigh, throbbing and warm, as it awakened another hunger. Turning in his lap, she pressed her wet center against him. Pleasure and desire shot so fiercely through her that it ripped away her remaining control. She cried out as her teeth elongated against his shoulder.

"Don't fight it Isabelle." His voice shook from his fierce need as his hands clenched into her velvety skin. "Don't fight *me*."

She shuddered again, but this time it wasn't from fighting against her urges, but the anticipation of what was to come. She moved her mouth to his neck. His breath froze in his lungs, and she knew a moment of satisfaction as she realized that she held him in thrall. That he was as affected by her as she was by him. She lifted her hips and slid onto him at the same time that she bit deep. The pleasure that slammed through her ripped a wild cry free as his blood flowed into her, and his hard shaft filled her.

She felt savage and wild as she clung to him, riding him with abandon. His hands braced her hips as he drove in and out of her, and his mind surged and blended with hers. She could feel his bliss as she rode him; feel his satisfaction as his blood mingled with hers. She could feel his deep and unconditional love for her, along with a need for her that more than matched her own. He tasted so wonderful, felt so wonderful that she could barely stand the delicious torment. For a moment she feared that she would shatter from the exquisite ecstasy that was consuming her entire body. The power that encompassed him shook her as it poured into, and through, her veins. She wanted to cry from the extreme joy and wonder of it all.

Stefan waited until he was sure that all of her fear was gone, sure that she wouldn't fight him. He was trembling with need as he brushed her hair back from her neck. She moaned softly as her fingers dug into his back. Her need blazed into his mind.

He groaned loudly as he bit deeply into her. Pleasure nearly devoured him in its intensity as her sweetness filled him, and a feeling of utter contentment tore through his veins. She tasted just as sweet as he had known she would, just as wonderful. Her mind poured into his, her fierce love nearly shattered him. He trembled as he clung to her and his hands entwined in her thick hair.

Isabelle pulled away from him, a savage cry escaped her as she trembled and shook from the extreme bliss threatening to consume her. She clasped the back of his head tightly to her as his mind seared into hers. She desperately tried to convey her love to him, as he had done to her. She leaned back in his arms, riding him with savage abandon as a feeling of completeness engulfed her. She had no control over herself, no control over anything as all of her inhibitions melted away. She screamed wildly as the orgasm ripped through her, shaking her to the very core of her existence.

Stefan plunged into her as she tightened convulsively around him and tore an earth shattering orgasm from him. He poured all of his essence into her as she collapsed against him. He held her sweat slicked body as he breathed in the enticing smell of their lovemaking. Closing his eyes he relished in the feeling of serenity, and belonging, that filled him. It was almost more than he could bear.

"I love you Stefan."

Her words shook his core, and his heart almost burst with joy. For a moment he was unable to speak through the lump in his throat and the emotions consuming him. She tried to pull away from him, but he refused to let her.

"I love you too Isabelle."

She went limp against him as her tears of joy ran down to wet his shoulder.

CHAPTER 22

Isabelle was in the best mood of her life the next day as she helped her mother prepare for Ian's going away party. For this party, instead of being miserable and brooding, she was so unbelievably happy that she was fairly bursting with it. Vicky and Abby were staring at her in disbelief as she slipped a platter of hamburgers onto the kitchen counter and flashed them a blindingly bright smile. Her mother was biting her lip in order to keep from laughing out loud, and Willow had quickly vacated, mumbling something about morons, and love.

The only moment that almost spoiled her happiness was when Jess came downstairs with her suitcase in hand. She cast Isabelle a scathing look, but quickly lowered her head, and hurried out the door. Kathleen and Delia came down behind her with their suitcases in hand. "You're leaving?" Isabelle cried, as a wave of guilt flooded her.

Kathleen smiled brilliantly as she dropped her suitcases on the ground. "Yes, I need to take Delia clothes shopping, and get her ready for school. Delia, go on out and help Jess."

Isabelle waited until Delia was gone before turning back to Kathleen. "It's not because of me is it?" She would simply hate herself if Kathleen was leaving because of her, and her mother lost her friend, again.

"No dear, it's not." Kathleen reached out and patted her hand reassuringly. "If you're even as close to happy as your parents are, than I wish you all the joy in the world. He wasn't happy with Jess." Isabelle felt tears well up in her eyes as she clutched Kathleen's hand tightly. How did she have such unhappy daughters? Isabelle wondered as Kathleen pulled away from her and walked over to hug her mom tightly. "I miss you Sera. This time, let's not lose touch."

Tears streaked down her mother's face as she embraced her friend. Isabelle looked up as Stefan's presence filled her senses. He stood in the doorway, his large frame taking up more than half of it as he surveyed the kitchen before meeting Isabelle's gaze. Is everything all right? The thought blasted into her mind, warming her to her toes as she smiled happily and nodded.

He remained standing in the doorway, not fully believing her. He had felt her distress outside, and with Kathleen present, he wasn't sure if she was just lying to keep him calm. He knew Kathleen, and actually liked her more than her daughters, but a mother would always protect her children first, and he didn't want Isabelle hurt because of that. He turned slightly as Liam appeared beside him; his brow was furrowed as he watched Sera pull away from Kathleen with tears streaming down her face. Liam relaxed and brushed past Stefan to enter the kitchen.

"Ah, here they both are," Kathleen said as she wiped tears from her eyes. "And where's the rest of the clan?"

As if on cue, Jack, David, Mike, and Doug appeared to say their goodbyes. Stefan walked into the kitchen and made his way over to Isabelle. Some of his tension eased as she melded against him. Kathleen quickly said goodbye to the stooges, hugging each of them tightly before she moved onto the twins. When she was done hugging everyone, and saying her goodbyes, she walked back over to grab her suitcases.

"You'd better treat her good Stefan. There's a hell of a crew here that'll kick your ass if you don't!" she said laughingly.

"I will," he vowed.

Kathleen lifted her suitcases and stood staring at them, a lost look on her pretty face. She dropped her suitcases and spun toward Sera. Stefan stiffened slightly, it was glaringly obvious that Kathleen had more to say, and he was scared of what that might be. Instead of speaking, tears poured down her cheeks and she rushed back over to embrace Sera again. They hugged for a long time before Kathleen reluctantly pulled away, grabbed hold of her suitcases, and hurried from the room.

Liam walked over to Sera and pulled her against him. Everyone silently left the room to give them some privacy. They headed down the back steps to the group gathered in the backyard. Some of Ian's old high school friends, and some of his college friends, had come for the party. They were gathered by the volleyball net, leisurely batting the ball back and forth as they waited for more people to join.

"Let's play," Isabelle said eagerly.

Stefan raised a dark brow in amusement as she smiled up at him. He couldn't refuse her anything, and she knew it. She seized hold of his hand and pulled him to the volleyball net. He stiffened as he noticed the lustful stares directed her way, and his eyes narrowed warningly on the overeager men. They stared back at him for a moment before quickly lowering their gazes. She squeezed his hand reassuringly as she stopped next to Ian, and the stooges walked over to join them.

"Do you have chosen teams for volleyball too?" Stefan asked.

"Of course," Jack replied. "Same as football, except I don't think Liam will be back for awhile. You can take his place on David's team, and Kyle can play again."

Isabelle scrunched her face as Stefan dropped a quick kiss on her forehead and moved to the other side of the net. Kyle came eagerly forward, happy to be included in the game again. She watched him for a moment as he bounced eagerly on the balls of his feet. Looking at him now it was hard to believe that he had been at deaths door only days before, and she was extremely grateful that he was still with them now.

Casting Stefan a soft, grateful smile, she moved to the end of the line and took the ball from Ethan as she prepared to serve. The game moved quickly by in a blur of laughter, and pains. Kyle received a bloody nose, Ian sprained his finger, Ethan was mumbling about a groin muscle, and David and Mike got the wind knocked out of them when they charged the net in an attempt to spike the ball.

Stefan enjoyed watching Isabelle as she played. She was fluid and graceful, with an easy smile on her face as she laughed and joked with everyone. He returned the secret, soft smiles she gave him, as his mind continuously sent her wicked, meaningful messages to her. He forced her to mess up more than a few times while serving and she had returned the favor in kind.

However, it wasn't just Isabelle that was causing him to enjoy the day so much, it was the whole atmosphere. He had felt welcomed by them before, but for the first time he felt truly accepted. As if they were actually his family too. Which, he realized, they were now. With Isabelle, came all of her siblings, her parents, and the stooges. With Isabelle came the family that he had lost long ago, and never expected to have again.

He wiped the sweat from his brow as the game ended with David's team, *his* team, winning the best two out of three. Mike's team, including Isabelle, were all scowling unhappily as they moved over to join them on the other side of the net. "We're going to have to redo the teams now that Stefan's here," Jack mumbled as he pulled his T-shirt back on.

"Kyle's old enough to become a permanent member." Kyle's chest puffed out as he straightened his shoulders. "And with Ian and Aiden gone most of the time, we can just put him on David's team," Ethan said.

"Liam and Stefan are not staying on the same team!" Mike protested.

Lighthearted banter broke out as they made their way back to the picnic tables. Stefan wrapped his arm around Isabelle's waist and pulled her against his side. She grinned up at him as she leaned her head against his shoulder. "What if I take Isabelle?" David asked.

"No way!" she cried as her head jerked up. "I've been on Mike's team since I was twelve years old!"

"Don't worry Issy, you're not getting traded," Mike assured her. "Why doesn't Stefan join our team?"

"Are you insane?" Doug cried. "He's the only one that can catch her!"

"And we all know that she can catch him," Jack replied with a grin and a wink.

Isabelle laughed as she rested her head against his shoulder again. His arm around her waist was warm and secure. She could no longer remember what it was that she had been so afraid of with him. "Why don't we argue about this later?" Ian demanded. "It's my party, and I say it's time for a little fun."

Isabelle lifted her head from Stefan's shoulder to grin at him. "Weren't we already having fun?" she asked.

"You know what I mean Issy," he replied with a grin.

She knew exactly what he meant. "You'd better go get your friends," Jack told him.

"They'll follow us. Ready for one of our family traditions Stefan?"

"If someone would tell me what it is," he replied.

They flashed bright grins as they looked quickly at one another. "Who's going first?" Mike asked.

All of their gazes landed on Isabelle. "No way!" she retorted. "I went last year, it's Ian's turn."

"It *is* Ian's turn," Jack said thoughtfully.

Ian took a step back as they all turned toward him. "Hey! Come on, this was my idea!"

"Which is even more reason why you should go first," David retorted.

Ian grinned at them as they took another step forward. "Fine!" he cried throwing his hands up.

He took off running, and they all turned to watch as he darted past his friends, kicking off his shoes as he ran. He dove into the lake, and came up sputtering. "Cold!"

They all began to laugh as he turned onto his back and kicked himself out toward the middle of the lake. With a war like cry Mike, Doug, Jack, David, and Ethan darted past them, shedding their shoes as they ran. "Oh great!" Vicky cried as she appeared at their side with Abby. "Who started it?"

"Ian," Isabelle answered over the loud splashes and yells.

They both sighed wearily as they shook their heads. "Well, we knew it was coming. Let's go Abby."

Stefan watched in amazement as the twins also ran forward, they usually avoided the group activities. "What is going on?" he asked.

Isabelle grinned up at him. "The end of summer swim," she answered. "We do it every year, although we usually do it a little earlier than this. The lake is fed by a natural stream that comes out of the mountains; it has to be really cold now."

To confirm her statement, Vicky and Abby squealed as they jumped back out of the lake. Doug and Mike instantly came after them, grabbed them, and tossed them back in. Their loud, shrill screams pierced the air as they came back to the surface. "Come on Issy!" Willow cried as she raced by them with Julian, Kyle, and Cassidy on her heels.

Isabelle laughed as she shook her head. "Don't want to go?" he asked.

"Nope," she replied happily as she moved closer to him.

Stefan grinned down at her as he grabbed her waist and lifted her up. She smiled at him as she wrapped her hands around his neck and leisurely kicked her feet. "I'd take your shoes off," he whispered.

"What?" She frowned at him, obviously not realizing his intent until he started walking toward the lake. "Stefan no!"

He held tightly to her as she became as squiggly as an eel. "Isabelle, yes."

She glared up at him as her shoes hit the ground. "If you toss me into that lake I'll..."

"You'll what?"

There really wasn't anything she could say to that, and judging by the smug grin on his face, he damn well knew it. Stefan kicked his shoes off before wading into the cold water. "Stefan..."

He was smiling as he released her. Isabelle cried out in shock as the chilly water enclosed her whole body and turned it numb almost instantly. She came back up, spitting and sputtering as she wiped strands of straggly hair off her face. She glowered up at him as he stood over her, a bright grin on his handsome face, and his hands planted firmly on his hips.

"Aren't you coming in?" she demanded.

"It's a little too cold for me."

The fierce shove from behind knocked him off balance. Isabelle grabbed hold of his arms at the same time, and tugged him sharply into the water. He came back up, sputtering in shock from the cold, and the fact that he had been shoved into it. Her laughter rang loudly in his ears as he turned to look at Ethan and David. They proudly slapped each other's hands, as they grinned smugly down at him. "Everyone goes in!" David announced.

Stefan snorted as he shook his wet hair off his forehead. He launched to his feet after them. They met him head on as they all toppled into the water. Isabelle laughed happily as she watched them splash and tumble with each other. He was part of her family now, a part of *her*, and it was quite obvious that they fully accepted him. Ian, Jack, Doug, Willow, Kyle, Cassidy, and Mike joined in the foray as Vicky and Abby swam over to join her.

"We really didn't need another brother," Vicky said happily.

Isabelle laughed as she turned to face them. The moonlight shimmered over their sleek, golden heads, and lit their bright green eyes. "Trust me, I know."

Vicky smiled at her before she turned onto her back and kicked leisurely at the water. Isabelle turned herself over to float beside her. The water wasn't so cold now that she had grown accustomed to it. In fact, it was rather pleasant. She closed her eyes and allowed herself to drift, taking comfort in the light slapping of the water against her skin. Shouts echoed through the night, she smiled happily as Willow screamed and a loud splash filled the air.

"Where do you think you're going?"

Stefan wrapped his arms around her and pulled her against him. She didn't bother to open her eyes as she rested her head in the curve of his shoulder. His skin was cool to the touch, but his inner heat served to warm her. "Nowhere," she mumbled happily.

"That's right."

She laughed as she pulled back to look at him. His eyes were intense as he met her gaze, his dark hair was slicked back to reveal every hard angle of his face. She stroked the soft bristles that lined his solid jaw. The shiver that racked her had nothing to do with the cold, and everything to do with him. "I love you Stefan," she whispered as she dropped a soft kiss on the hard line of his full mouth.

His arms tightened around her as she wrapped her legs around his waist and pressed herself more firmly against him. He glanced over his shoulder at the crowd gathered in the water still splashing and playing loudly. The humans had joined in the foray, and even Liam and Sera had appeared. "Let's go somewhere a little quieter."

"What?" she asked in surprise.

He grinned as he turned over, and leisurely began to kick through the water with her wrapped securely in his arms. He swam swiftly to the dock, and pulled her behind it. "Stefan," she whispered.

He didn't give her time to protest as he seized hold of her mouth and pushed her back against the dock. He lifted her shirt up to skim across her smooth, silken skin. Isabelle gasped as she wiggled closer to him. He lifted her legs from his waist and quickly unbuttoned and slid her shorts down. "Stefan, we can't!" She released his neck and grasped for her shorts.

He pulled them swiftly off and held them away from her before tossing them onto the dock. He seized hold of her waist, halting her as she turned to try and retrieve them. Turning her back around, he pulled her against him. She squiggled against him, only serving to heat his loins more. He quickly unbuttoned his jeans and slipped them down as he lifted her to his waist. "Stefan!" she gasped, half in protest, half in desire.

He grinned as he slipped his hand between her thighs and delved his finger deep into her tight, wet sheath. "I think you're more than ready for me," he whispered.

Her eyes widened as she shook her head fiercely, but her hips began to move with his finger. He smiled victoriously as he continued to stroke her. "We can't!" she gasped.

"We can." He slipped his hand away from her. She moaned her protest as she instinctively sought to get closer to him. He seized hold of her waist and lifted her onto him. "If you really want to stop though," he whispered huskily as he nibbled on her bottom lip.

She lifted herself up in answer and slid slowly onto him. She moaned in pleasure as heat seared through her entire body. Her hands curled into his back as she clung to him. He planted his hands on the dock behind her, using it to keep him up as she slowly rode them both to completion.

Spent and completely sated, Isabelle dropped her head to his shoulder as she struggled to get her breathing under control. The chill of the water slowly began to penetrate her warm haze. She shivered as she clung tighter to him.

"Come on, let's get you warm," he whispered as he reached behind her to grab her shorts.

He slid them quickly back on as she shivered and shook against him. He rubbed her arms and body, trying to put some heat back into her as he kicked through the water. A fire was going now; its flames were bright against the dark night as it illuminated the people gathered around it. Reaching the shore, he found towels and their shoes waiting for them. He grabbed a towel and wrapped it tightly around her, enthusiastically rubbing it against her skin.

"They're all going to know," she whispered, her voice thick with embarrassment.

He chuckled softly as he dropped a quick kiss on the top of her head. "Trust me, they already know."

She pulled back to look at him, her face a dark shade of red. "I know that, but, I uh... oh forget it."

He kissed the tip of her nose as he gently eased her to the ground and wrapped the towel tightly around her trembling shoulders. "I understand love."

She offered a tremulous smile as she clung to the towel. He grabbed the other towel and wrapped it around her as he grabbed their shoes. "You need this." She handed the other towel out to him but he wrapped it back around her as he pulled her against his side.

"Not as much as you. That fire looks inviting."

She shivered as she buried herself against him and followed him toward the large, leaping flames. Laughter floated through the night, beckoning them almost as much as the giant flames did. Isabelle felt her embarrassment rise as they moved steadily closer. "You guys must be popsicles!" Vicky cried as she rushed over to hand Stefan a blanket.

He pulled the towels away from Isabelle and pulled her against his chest. Wrapping the blanket around them both, he used his hands to rub some heat back into her. She shivered as she wrapped her arms around his waist and buried her head in his chest; the heat in her face was hot against his cool skin. Stifling a laugh over her foolishness, he lifted her gently up and sat on the ground with her in his lap.

They sat for a long time, absorbing the heat of the fire as drinks and stories were passed around. Ian left with his friends to go to a club, Liam and Sera slipped silently away, and the younger children went off to bed. Stefan was content to stay by the flames, holding Isabelle tightly within his arms, and warming them both. He had never thought to experience such peaceful bliss in his life, and he was reluctant to leave it.

David, Doug, Mike, Jack, and Ethan sat silently by, watching the flames as they slowly died down. Isabelle yawned softly as her fingers curled into his still damp shirt. "Tired?" he asked softly.

She nodded as she stifled another yawn. He brushed the damp hair off of her face as he lifted her easily up. "Good night guys."

"Hold on, I'll go back with you," Ethan said.

Jack and David climbed to their feet behind him, and tucked their blankets under their arms before heading over to them. Mike and Doug stood and walked over to the buckets of water sitting on the other side of the fire. Stefan waited for the three of them before turning and heading into the shadows of the house. He was halfway across the field, when he felt it. Freezing instantly, his hands tightened protectively upon Isabelle. She lifted her head to stare at him questioningly as Ethan, David, and Jack stopped walking.

"Stefan?" Isabelle inquired.

He shook his head slowly as his gaze quickly scanned the open field and woods. His nostrils flared as his eyes narrowed, and a fierce, defensive urge surged through him. He shifted Isabelle in his arms, and lowered her to the ground as the disturbance in the air grew closer. She released him slowly; her eyes were wide and questioning as she searched his gaze. His eyes snapped to the left as a shimmer in the air caught his attention, a shimmer he knew that the others wouldn't be able to see.

He pushed Isabelle behind him as he turned to face it. "Hello Stefan."

Isabelle tried to peer around Stefan's shoulder to see the man that had spoken, but he shoved her roughly back again. "Brian!" David cried in surprise.

Isabelle poked her head around Stefan's side, determined to see him. He was tall and muscular, nearly as big as Stefan, and nearly as gorgeous. His hair was the lightest platinum blond that she had ever seen, so light that it was nearly white. His eyes were a piercing ice blue as they drifted down to look at her. There was a coldness in his gaze that was unnerving as his mouth curved into a small smile. She knew instantly that he was one of *them*, but there was something off about him, something not quite right. It reminded her of the men from the club, only it wasn't as strong as it had been with them. Still, she knew that he was dangerous.

"What are you doing here?" Stefan growled, pushing Isabelle back again.

She didn't protest his high handed manner; she didn't want to look at him anymore. His oddness frightened her. "I just came to see an old friend."

"We stopped being friends awhile ago Brian."

"Stefan, in our life span, two years is not a long time. Who's the girl?"

Stefan stiffened as a low growl issued from him. Isabelle couldn't stop herself from looking at the stranger again. Brian's gaze darted back to her and a sly smile curled his full, hard mouth. Stefan's hand curled painfully into her upper arm as he held her forcefully behind him. She couldn't suppress a whimper of pain. His grip instantly lessened, but he didn't relinquish her.

"What do you want?" he snapped.

Brian's eyes came back to him, cold and brutal. They were no longer the eyes of the man that had been his friend for well over a century, but those of the man that he had become. "I need a place to stay."

Stefan shook his head in firm denial. "You are *not* staying here."

Brian's eyes narrowed as they snapped with fury. "I helped you out when you needed it."

"Yes you did, but you're not staying here."

Brian folded his arms over his chest as he rocked back on his heels. "Can we talk privately?" he inquired coldly.

It had been awhile since they had parted ways, and Stefan hadn't expected to ever see Brian again. He didn't know what had brought him here now, nor did he think that it could be good. However he did owe Brian his life, and he owed it to him to listen to what he had to say.

"David, take Isabelle back to the house."

"What?" she demanded as she grabbed Stefan's shirt. He pulled her from behind his back and held onto her arm as he waited for David to come forward. "Stefan..."

"Go with them Isabelle."

"But..."

"Go!" he commanded more sharply than he had intended.

Isabelle's eyes spit violet fury at him as David took hold of her arm. "I can walk on my own!" she snapped as she jerked her arm free.

'Please be careful,' she whispered into his head. His gaze flicked toward her, but he made no other indication that he had hear her.

She turned away from him as Ethan and Jack moved to stand behind her with their gazes locked warily on Brian. Stefan waited until they were safely in the house before he turned his attention back to his old friend. A small smile of amusement curved Brian's mouth as he met Stefan's glower. "Who's the girl?"

"That's none of your concern," Stefan grated. Brian's eyebrows rose but he simply nodded as he rocked back on his heels again. "What do you want?"

"I told you, I need a place to say," he replied.

"And I told you that you can't stay here."

Brian tilted his head as he quickly scanned the field and houses. "There is a lot of our kind here."

Stefan shrugged negligently; he didn't want Brian to know anymore about this place than he had to. "What kind of trouble have you gotten yourself into?"

Brian's eyes were dark and distant as they slowly came back to him. "Do they know about you?"

Stefan stiffened as his eyes narrowed angrily. "Of course."

"*All* about you?" he drawled.

Stefan took an angry step forward. "You're not staying here!" he snarled.

"I take that as a no, which means that the girl doesn't know either."

Stefan took another step toward him; his rage was reaching a boiling point. Brian's careless demeanor instantly vanished as he stiffened. "You'll stay away from her, or I'll kill you!" Stefan hissed.

Amusement flashed over Brian's features as he studied Stefan questioningly. "I'm merely suggesting that maybe she would like to know a little bit more about you. It would probably be in her best interest, don't you think? Maybe they would all like to know a little more about you. They might not be as willing to let you stay then. I have nowhere else to go, and I need help. You *will* give it to me Stefan, or I will have a long chat with this family."

"I'll kill you," he growled.

"You could try, but I've still been killing Stefan, have you? She is a pretty girl."

Red filled his vision as he seized Brian by the throat. Brian's claws ripped across Stefan's chest and spilled blood. Stefan's hold on his throat tightened as he slammed a fist into Brian's stomach, causing his breath to whoosh loudly out of him. Brian lunged forward, hissing and spitting as his fist connected with the side of Stefan's head. The blow left him momentarily startled, but he recovered in time to block Brian's next swing.

Brian blurred suddenly, and disappeared from Stefan's hold. He swung around as Brian reappeared behind him. He crouched low as a fierce growl escaped him. "I'm not here to fight you Stefan!" Brian hissed.

"You're not welcome here!"

"You either help me, or when the others arrive, you'll be on your own."

Trepidation clutched his chest as Brian's words sank in. "The others?"

Brian nodded briskly as he rubbed his abused throat, and warily eyed Stefan. "I'm in trouble, and they're tracking me. They'll follow me here, and when they do, they aren't going to leave peacefully."

"What the hell have you done?" he bellowed.

Brian shrugged negligently. It took every ounce of control Stefan had not to lunge at him again. Not to kill him where he stood. "I pissed off a few people."

"Who?" he growled.

"Some of our kind, some *older* ones of our kind. The ones here are young Stefan, they'll be no match for them, and you know it."

Running his hand tiredly through his hair Stefan closed his eyes against the fear that was squeezing his chest. If they came here, if Brian had led them here... Shit, they would kill everyone. His mind instantly sought out Isabelle. Her fear beat at him, but he didn't open his mind to her. He didn't want her to see, or hear, what was going on.

"So you want my help?" he demanded.

"You're one of the strongest ones I know Stefan. I didn't know where else to go."

Stefan snorted tiredly. It had taken him a long time, and a lot of death, to become one of the strongest. He had always suspected that he would pay for it in the long run, now he knew that he had been right. His gaze darted to the house as a crushing feeling of impending doom descended upon him. He'd intended to keep Isabelle sheltered from his past, from the darkness that lurked within his soul. Now he knew that it wasn't going to be possible.

"That was a long time ago Brian," he said softly. "Things are different now."

"Not that long ago, I can still feel it in you. You may fool them, but I know what you are Stefan. We were together for a long time."

"Things are different!" he spat.

Brian quirked a dark eyebrow at him, as his eyes narrowed questioningly. "Why, because of the girl?"

Stefan's hands clenched as fury shook his body. "You shouldn't have come here," he growled.

"Well I did, now you have to decide what you're going to do."

He already knew what he was going to do, what he would *have* to do. "If I help you, you'll leave here and never come back."

Brian nodded briskly. "Fair enough."

"If any of them get hurt, I will kill you."

"Fine."

"How long do you think it will be before they find you?"

He shrugged again. Stefan's eyes flared as he took a threatening step toward him. "A day, maybe two," Brian answered quickly.

"Do you care to tell me what you did?"

"I killed one of them."

Stefan snorted as he shook his head and his gaze darted back to the house. Shit, what the hell was he going to do?

He didn't want Brian anywhere near any of them, but he was right, even if they *both* left the others would track Brian here, and they would destroy everyone that lived here. His time here was done; no one would forgive him for bringing this down upon them. For the first time, he regretted stepping foot on this land and meeting Isabelle. He wished like hell that he had never come here.

He didn't know what he had been thinking, there was no way for him to escape his past, and it was about to come barreling down on all of them. He would be lucky if none of them got killed. He would gladly have sacrificed his life, but he knew that Isabelle would waste away and die without him. He couldn't allow that to happen. For better or worse, she was stuck with him, and he was going to do everything in his power to make sure that she remained safe. He wished that he could take it all back, wished that there was some way to set her free, but there was nothing that he could do.

"How many are coming?" he asked quietly.

"Four, maybe five."

Stefan whirled back to him. "How strong are they?" he hissed.

"They have me on the run," Brian said with a casual shrug.

"You son of a bitch! I should kill you now!"

"You need me, and you know it. We can do this together. It will be just like old times."

"The old times are over with."

Brian shrugged again. "So you say, but you're still a killer Stefan."

"I know what I am!" he snapped furiously. "Let's go."

He turned on his heel and headed toward the house. "Are you going to tell them?"

"I'm going to have too."

"The girl..."

Stefan's hands fisted as fury suffused his entire body once more. "I swear I will rip your throat out if you go anywhere near her."

Brian chuckled softly and Stefan desperately fought the urge to hit him again. "I don't want her, but she reeks of you Stefan. They'll go for her too."

"I know that Brian. That's why she's getting the hell out of here, with everyone else."

He pounded up the porch steps and hesitated at the doorway. "I can still destroy you, don't forget that."

"I know."

"Stay away from all of them, I mean it."

Brian nodded quickly. Stefan eyed him warily for a moment more before opening the door. Isabelle, Ethan, Jack, and David were sitting on the countertops in the kitchen. Their eyes locked on Brian as he followed Stefan into the house. Isabelle's gaze instantly darted back to him, and widened in surprise as she leapt off the counter. "You're bleeding!" She cast Brian a scathing glance as she hurried toward Stefan.

Brian grinned at her as he closed the door behind him. "I'm fine," Stefan assured her as he grabbed hold of her hands before she could touch the wounds on his chest. Her gaze was worried and troubled; her delicate eyebrows were drawn together as she studied him questioningly.

"What's going on?" Jack demanded.

Stefan lifted his head to look at them as Brian leaned casually against the door with his long legs crossed before him and his arms folded over his chest. "Brian seems to have gotten himself into a little bit of trouble," Stefan replied coldly.

"What kind of trouble?" David asked.

"Hey, I know you." Brian straightened away from the door as he stared questioningly at David.

"Philadelphia," Stefan reminded him sharply.

Brian nodded slowly; a sly smile curved his mouth as he studied David. "That's right; you were the one whose friends were in trouble. How did that work out?"

"You're at one of their houses," David replied.

"Well, that's good. Stefan and I never did believe in that soul mate crap, but I guess there must be some truth to it."

Isabelle's eyebrows furrowed, her mouth pursed tightly as she glanced sharply at Brian. The uneasiness in her stomach was beginning to grow by the second. Her gaze darted back to Stefan, but his face was cold and impassive as he studied David, Jack, and Ethan. His hands on her arms were just as impersonal as the rest of him. She swallowed heavily, as her gaze scanned the jagged wounds in his chest. They had already healed tightly; the only evidence of their existence was the dry blood on his shirt, and the jagged rips in it. He still wouldn't look at her, and he had effectively shut her out of his mind. Something was going on with him; something that she didn't understand, but instinctively knew wasn't good.

"What kind of trouble?" she asked tremulously, hoping to draw his attention back to her.

"The kind that's going to follow me here, and soon." Brian drew her attention again as his gaze, curious and troubled, focused upon her.

David, Ethan, and Jack slid off the counter; their bodies were tense as their eyes narrowed. "Then you should probably leave," Ethan said coldly.

"It's not that simple. They'll track me here no matter what. I either leave, and Stefan faces them by himself, or I stay, and Stefan helps me."

"We're here, we can help," Jack said.

"You're like pitting a lamb against a lion," Brian snorted disdainfully.

"Brian!" Stefan hissed in warning.

"It's true," he retorted.

"And you're that much stronger?" Ethan demanded.

Brian's eyes narrowed as he met Ethan's hostile gaze. "I could snap your neck before you could even blink."

Ethan's eyes sparked red. "Enough," Stefan said coldly, as he stepped forward to ward off a fight that would not end well.

"And you? Are you that much stronger Stefan?"

He finally turned his gaze back to Isabelle; he couldn't keep putting it off. Her gaze was dark and turbulent as she stared questioningly up at him. There was an aura of hurt surrounding her that would have shredded him, if he hadn't already steeled himself for the fact that she was going to be hurt, and he was going to be the one to do it.

He remained silent as he stared at her, his jaw locked, and his eyes as cold as black ice. She didn't know the man that stood before her, and she was beginning to realize that she never had. The feeling turned her heart to a cold lump, and caused her stomach to twist into tight knots. She refused to acknowledge it though. If she did, she knew that she would completely break down, that she would lose all control and never stop crying.

"Well Stefan," she prompted.

"Yes."

Isabelle refused to acknowledge the agonizing pain that ripped through her as she lifted her chin slightly. She knew where that kind of power came from, what it meant. She could smell it on Brian, feel it radiating off of him. She had smelled it on the others, but she had never smelled it on Stefan. Not once had she sensed anything wrong with him. She didn't understand any of this, and her sense of betrayal was threatening to choke her.

"Why don't you smell like him, or like the others at the club?"

Stefan's eyes narrowed as Brian straightened away from the door. Jack and David cast her questioning looks. "What are you talking about, what smell?" Jack demanded.

She turned to stare at them in confusion. "Don't you smell it?" she asked.

The confusion in their eyes was her answer. She turned back to Stefan and Brian, her forehead furrowed as she frowned at them. "Well I do," she said forcefully. "Brian's nowhere near as bad as the ones at the club, but he still smells off. But you," she stared angrily up at Stefan as loathing began to burn through her body. "You don't smell like that. Did you cover it up somehow?"

Stefan shook his head as he stared at her in confusion. The fact that she could even tell that something was off with Brian was amazing. Someone of her young age, who had never fed from a human, shouldn't be able to sense it at all. For a moment he thought that it was his blood in her, but if she had known about the ones at the club than that wasn't the cause. His gaze darted to Ethan. "Do you smell it?" he demanded.

Ethan's jaw locked as his eyes, and nostrils, flared. "Yes."

"What the hell are you talking about?" Jack exploded impatiently.

"He's a killer, he smells of death," Isabelle said coldly. "And so is Stefan."

"Was," Stefan replied, just as coldly.

"Till when?" she demanded.

Stefan's jaw locked, his eyes flared, and a muscle in his jaw began to jump. His hands clenched on her arms as she stared defiantly up at him. "That doesn't matter."

"Till when?" she hissed.

"About two years ago Stefan suddenly got a conscience." Brian's lip curled as if the words disgusted him.

Isabelle's eyes widened in surprise, she turned to stare at him in disbelief. "You weren't when I knew you," David said in shock.

Brian snorted as he straightened away from the door. "Of course we were."

"Brian," Stefan growled in warning.

"Were you ever going to tell me?" Isabelle asked softly.

"No."

She forced herself not to wince at his harsh admission. The fact that she truly didn't know the man she had given everything to nearly shattered her. It took every ounce of strength and pride she had to remain standing, to remain looking at him, and not to flee the room like a coward.

"What made you change?" She was immensely proud that her voice didn't shake.

"*I* did."

"Why?" Isabelle asked softly.

Stefan shifted his stance, his hands on her arms tightened. "There are some of us that are like the men that you met at the club," he told her. "Brian and I used to kill them in order to stop them."

"Plus we got all of their power, and when a vampire kills a human they get stronger. When we kill one of our own, we get a *lot* stronger."

Stefan ground his teeth as he forced himself not to lash out at Brian. He was deliberately trying to bait them, deliberately being a jackass, and he was pissing Stefan off. Now, however, was not the time to beat his old friend into a bloody pulp. There was much more behind the story than Brian was letting on, but he seemed determined to try and paint everything in the worst possible light. It was because Stefan had left Brian when he changed his ways, but he was not in the mood to tolerate his insolence.

"You ever kill a human?" Isabelle asked softly.

"One."

The color drained from her face, as for the first time she showed some kind of emotion. "Why?" she whispered.

"It was a hunter Isabelle; it was him, or me."

Isabelle's gaze darted to Brian, he smiled slyly at her. "That's when Stefan got a conscience."

"Now is not the time to talk about this," Stefan bit out sharply. "You need to start packing."

"What?" she demanded angrily.

"You're not staying here."

"I'm not leaving!" She ripped her arms free of his grasp as she tilted her chin defiantly.

"You're all leaving."

"No we're not!" Jack declared.

Stefan was trying very hard to keep a hold on his temper. Isabelle was still staring at him as if he was a monstrosity, and Jack, David, and Ethan looked about ready to explode. "This is our home," Isabelle declared.

"I know that Isabelle," he hissed. "But you are going to have to leave until this is over."

Her eyes flashed a violent shade of red as she glared furiously up at him. "I think you should leave, and take *him* with you!"

He sighed impatiently as he fought the urge to drag her from the house now. "They're coming here no matter what Isabelle, and when they find everyone here, they won't leave until you're all destroyed. You cannot be here for that."

Isabelle's jaw clenched furiously as she folded her arms over her chest. David, Ethan, and Jack remained silent but their bodies were tense and anxious. "I am not leaving my home!" Isabelle spat.

"None of us are," Ethan growled.

"If you want to stay, that's fine. Isabelle *is* leaving," Stefan said firmly.

"The hell I am!" she snarled as her nostrils flared, and her eyes blazed red.

Stefan took a step closer to her. "I will drag you out of here kicking and screaming if that's what it takes," he hissed.

Isabelle glowered at him. "If you drag me out of here, I will hate you for the rest of my life Stefan."

He refused to acknowledge the pain that her words aroused. It didn't matter if she hated him or not, as long as she was safe. He could live with her hatred; he couldn't live with her death. "Then you will hate me."

Isabelle's eyes widened in surprise as pain and anger filled their violet depths. "How could you do this?" she whispered.

"Go pack." Her jaw clenched as her hands fisted at her sides, but she made no move to leave. "Now!" he roared.

Isabelle jumped in surprise as his command whipped over her. She looked at David, Jack, and Ethan for help but their gazes were wary as they met hers. "Go Isabelle," Ethan said softly.

"You're taking *his* side?" she nearly shrieked.

"If it means keeping you safe, yes," Jack answered.

Tears of frustration filled her eyes, but she refused to shed them. "And what about you?" she asked more calmly.

"We're staying," Ethan said.

"Tying the lambs up for the lions?" she taunted. "You're not much stronger than me Ethan."

Anger flashed through Ethan's eyes as he met her defiant gaze. "Go pack Isabelle."

She fought the urge to scream with rage and frustration. It took all she had not to fly off the handle and turn into a raving lunatic. She couldn't believe that they were taking his side and that he was going to force her to leave. She couldn't believe that Stefan had kept so much of his past from her. She pushed down the hurt that realization caused, and clung desperately to her anger. It was the only thing that was going to get her through this.

"Go Isabelle," Stefan ordered.

"Go to hell!" she snapped. "You don't have a say in this, and neither do you guys! I am not leaving!"

"I have a big say in this." Stefan spat as he took another step toward her. He towered imposingly over her as she continued to glare up at him, refusing to back down, refusing to concede defeat. "You'll either go willingly, or you'll go forcefully, but you *are* going."

"Let's get two things straight Stefan, no matter what, I am not going willingly. I make my own decisions about *my* life, whether you like it or not!"

He grasped hold of her elbows, his fingers dug painfully into her flesh as his face twisted into a brutal snarl. Isabelle stifled a cry of fear in the face of his fury as she continued to glare at him defiantly. "I do have a say, when your life directly affects mine!" he hissed. "Just as mine directly affects yours!"

"Let go of me," she responded icily.

His hands tightened on her elbows as his eyes blazed a furious shade of red. "You will go pack, and you will do it now!"

Isabelle refused to struggle, it would be useless anyway, and she didn't want to give him the satisfaction of overwhelming her. "I hate you."

His eyes flickered for a moment and hurt blazed through them before the fury quickly returned. Isabelle wanted to find satisfaction in the fact that she had hurt him, as much as he was hurting her, but she found none. Spitefulness was not something that she took joy in, nor was the obvious pain that had flared through his eyes. Besides, she didn't hate him, she could never hate him. She wanted to take the words back, but she couldn't. It was too late now.

"That's fine," he replied coldly. "You can hate me for the rest of our days Isabelle, but you *are* leaving."

He released her and took a step back. His face was as cold as granite, and just as hard. His eyes were shards of black ice that revealed no emotion at all. She took a deep breath in order to fight back the tears that threatened to overflow. They were no longer tears of frustration, but of hurt, and regret. "Go," he ordered hoarsely.

She didn't even bother to look at Jack, David, and Ethan as she lifted her chin and left the room. "Now what?" David asked.

Stefan fought back the turmoil of emotions clawing to break free as he turned back to them. Anger was evident in every inch of their taut bodies as they fiercely met his gaze. "Now I'm going to talk to Liam and Sera. I would suggest that you rethink staying here, and leave with Isabelle."

"We're not going," Jack replied coldly.

He nodded briskly as he turned away from them. Brian moved quickly away from the door. "Stefan." He turned back to meet Ethan's steady stare. "When this is over, you're leaving."

He showed no sign of the hurt those words caused as he kept his face completely impassive. "Isabelle will have to come with me."

Ethan's eyes flashed as his jaw clenched. "You son of a bitch," he hissed. "Why didn't you stay the hell away from her?"

Stefan flung the door open, it slammed so hard against the wall that the glass shattered from the window, and the plaster cracked and broke. He didn't bother to close it as he strode down the steps and into the field.

CHAPTER 23

The door swung open, but Isabelle didn't bother to look at him as she threw the last of her clothes into a backpack. He hadn't come back to the room last night, a fact she was extremely grateful for. She didn't want to talk to him now; she didn't want to see him now. Most of her anger had faded and all she had left was a sense of loss, hurt, and betrayal. If he had just told her about his past maybe she could understand. All she knew now was that he had been a killer, and judging by the amount of power that he possessed, he must have enjoyed it, and done a lot of it.

She couldn't forgive herself, or him, for the fact that she had given everything to a man that she didn't even know. The worst part was there was nothing she could do about it. They were bound together now, without him she would die. She couldn't even leave, couldn't go anywhere without him. Her life was irrevocably tied to his.

"You're mother has rented hotel rooms for you, and your younger siblings," he informed her bluntly.

She didn't answer him as she moved into the bathroom to finish packing the rest of her things. She didn't know how to fight against the hopelessness that she felt. Didn't know how to change what had become her future. She still loved him, she truly did, but she could never trust him again. She didn't want to live the rest of her life like that. It was far too long of a time to be with someone that she didn't trust, and that had hurt her this badly. It was so very unfair.

She had never wanted this to begin with, and now, when she had surrendered everything to him, she was acutely reminded of all the reasons she had been so terrified of it. She cursed fate, and the world, for throwing her together with someone like him. Why couldn't she have been stuck with someone who was honest, and good, and caring, instead of a liar and a killer?

Tears filled her eyes as she threw her toothbrush and hairbrush into a plastic zip case before heading into the bedroom. He had closed the door, and was now leaning against it. His eyes were hooded as he watched her. She threw the travel case into the bottom pocket of her bag and closed it tight. She lifted it up and finally turned to face him.

"Why didn't you tell me?" she demanded.

"You didn't need to know." She snorted as she shook her head and turned to gaze out the window. No, he wouldn't think that she would need to know. "It would have made no difference anyway. You are *mine* Isabelle, for better or worse. We will always be together. I tried to leave you, but I couldn't, and we will die without each other. Would it have made a difference if I had told you?"

She turned back to him. "Yes. At least you would have been honest with me, now..."

"Now nothing," he interrupted harshly.

"You hurt me!" Isabelle closed her eyes as she wrapped her arms around herself. She hadn't wanted him to know how badly he had hurt her. "That is the difference," she whispered in a strangled voice.

Stefan closed his eyes against the pain that flooded him. He had stayed away from her last night because he didn't want to see her hatred, but the hatred seemed to be gone now, and in its place was something even more painful to him. However, there was nothing that he could do to stop it, or change it. He had tried to distance himself from his past; he should have known that it would be impossible, that it would catch up with him.

"I cannot change anything."

"No you can't, and unfortunately neither can I." She struggled to keep herself under control. "I wish that you had never come here and yet..."

Her voice trailed off as she lowered her head. "So do I Isabelle, so do I."

She rapidly fought back the tears that wanted to fall, but she couldn't allow them. His words wounded her more than she had ever thought they would. She had found such happiness with him, had known a moment of true contentment, and now it was all gone. She wasn't entirely sure that she would change him coming here. Until he had arrived, she hadn't known just how lonely she was, but never had she been this hurt before.

"I will do everything I can to keep you safe. I never thought that this would happen, but there is nothing that I can do about it now, and for that I am truly sorry. You will never know how sorry."

She snorted slightly as she shook her head. "No, I suppose I won't."

"After this is over we're leaving Isabelle."

"What?" Her head shot up as her mouth dropped open. "I'm not leaving my home!"

"I'm no longer welcome here."

"But..." Tears spilled down her cheeks as her words trailed off. It didn't matter, if he didn't stay than she couldn't. The overwhelming sense of loss that descended upon her nearly threatened to swallow her whole. She'd lost everything that she cared about in less than a day, and she couldn't help but blame him for everything that he had robbed her of.

He couldn't stay away from her any longer; the pain that she radiated was more than he could bear. He reached out to grab her, but she instantly backed away as she shook her head violently. "Don't touch me!" she cried. "Don't ever touch me again!"

His hands fell limply back to his sides as he took a step back. "You'll have to forgive me eventually Isabelle."

"I'll never forgive you!" she spat. "You've taken everything away from me! If you think that I'll ever forgive you, you're insane! I wish I had never met you! I wish..."

Her voice trailed off as sobs racked her body. He reached for her again, but she quickly avoided his grasp. "You *will* forgive me," he commanded as if that would work. "Now let's go."

She shook her head in denial. Stefan's patience snapped as he seized hold of her arm. She cried out angrily and tried to rip free of him, but he refused to relinquish his hold upon her as he pulled her angrily behind him. "Let go of me!"

He spun around and grasped hold of her chin as he jerked her head up. "I will never let go of you!" he hissed. "You had better get used to that fact, and realize that nothing is ever going to separate us!"

The fury and anger that radiated from him shook her, but she refused to back down, refused to cower like she wished to. He was a killer, and they had invited him into their homes, into their hearts. Her family had accepted him, had considered him one of them, but they had all been betrayed. "It's not by choice!" she shouted at him.

"Maybe not now, but it was."

"That was before I knew you were a monster!"

Stefan grit his jaw and refused to respond to her. Let her think what she would, he knew the truth, and he would be damned if he took the time to explain it to her. She had made her decision about him, and if she wasn't going to give him the benefit of the doubt than he wasn't going to lower himself by telling her the truth about everything. Or Ethan either. Liam, Sera, and the others had been a little more understanding, had actually listened to him, but not those two.

"Let's go," he pulled her roughly forward.

Her eyes spit violet sparks of fury at him as she tilted her chin, ripped her arm free, and hurried down the hall.

***

Isabelle tossed her backpack onto the bed, and slumped down. The hotel was cold and dreary compared to the warm comfort of her room. *She* was cold and dreary. Every part of her felt deflated, and beat. She felt completely hollow, and alone. Vicky and Abby placed their bags down and plopped onto the large bed across from hers.

"Isabelle..." Abby started.

"I don't want to talk about it."

She kicked her shoes off and slumped back on the bed. The sun was just beginning to set, but she took no joy in the brilliant colors that it cast across the darkening sky. She was hurt and lonely, she instinctively wanted to reach out for Stefan, but she refused to let herself do it. He had been keeping her shut out since last night; she didn't want to meet with the cold wall that he had erected around his mind again. The possibility that he could be hurt, that she may never see him again, had taken firm root. Her fear for him only added to the utter misery she was in.

"Isabelle." She turned slightly. Her mother was standing in front of the door, Vicky and Abby were gone. She had been so absorbed in her own unhappiness that she had never even heard them leave. "We need to talk."

She braced herself as she pushed herself up. She had been waiting for her mother to confront her about Stefan, waiting to hear her censure of him, and to tell her that he was no longer welcome at their home. "I'm sorry about all of this," she mumbled.

"Why? You have no need to be."

Isabelle shrugged as she played with a lose thread on the tattered bedspread. "I know you must be angry."

"No Isabelle, you're angry, not me."

Isabelle's head shot up in surprise. "What?"

Her mother sighed as she walked over to sit across from Isabelle on the other bed. "I love you sweetie, but you are very judgmental sometimes..."

"I am not!" she protested.

"Yes, you are. You've never fed from a human, you don't believe in it, but you censure those around you that do..."

"I do not!"

"Will you let me finish," her mother said impatiently. Isabelle locked her jaw and nodded briskly. "I know you disapprove of everyone else doing it; you've said it more than a few times. You believe they shouldn't have to, but they've never hurt anyone, and yet you still disapprove of it..."

"They can use bags, like me."

"Isabelle, let me speak!" her mother snapped. Isabelle's eyes widened in surprise, her mother hadn't yelled at her since she was a child. "As I was saying, you are judgmental. It is *their* lives Isabelle, they aren't hurting anyone, and it is in our nature. It's the way that we survive. I've never fed off of anyone simply because your father has supplied me, but I would have if I needed to, or wanted to," she added quickly when Isabelle opened her mouth to protest.

"They want to," she continued. "Because they prefer it. It is their right to do what makes them happy, as long as they don't hurt anyone..."

"But Stefan did!" she cried, unable to stop herself.

Her mother clenched her jaw as she took a deep breath. "He killed our kind Isabelle, not ones like us, but the *wrong* ones, the ones that you met at the club. Didn't he tell you this?" Isabelle wasn't going to admit that he had told her, but that she hadn't seen the difference. "I'm going to take your silence to mean that he did tell you, and you didn't want to hear it, or that you never gave him a chance to tell you."

"He said something like that," she admitted reluctantly.

Her mother sniffed softly and shook her head. "Your father and the stooges have killed our kind, and they did it for me. Were they wrong?"

"Did they do it just for power?" Isabelle retorted.

"No, they didn't. Are you so sure that is the only reason that Stefan did it?"

Isabelle's jaw clenched as she met her mother's cloudy eyes. "That's what Brian said."

"Yeah, and I'm sure that he always tells the truth. Brian isn't like Stefan, and you know it."

She raised an eyebrow as she stared at her mother. "And how would you know that?" she demanded.

"Stefan told me that you and Ethan can sense that there is something wrong with Brian, just like you could sense it about the ones outside the club. I can't do that; neither can your father, or the stooges. The only thing we can figure is that because the two of you were born vampires, your inherent abilities are stronger than ours. You can detect them somehow, yet you sensed nothing about Stefan."

"How do you know that?" she snapped.

Her mother frowned at her. "Because you would have said something to one of us, or Ethan would have, or one of the others would have told us. *Every* one of your siblings can sense something wrong with Brian. None of them felt it about Stefan, did you know that?"

Isabelle was beginning to feel like a chastised child, and she wasn't relishing the feeling. "No," she mumbled petulantly.

"You judged him to quickly Isabelle."

"He killed a man!" she yelled.

Her mother sighed softly as she clasped her hands tiredly before her. "Your father killed a man; does that make you dislike him?"

"He did it to protect you!"

"Stefan killed a hunter Isabelle. It was either him, or that man. Who would you rather was alive?"

Isabelle closed her eyes as tears of self disgust and anguish welled up in her eyes. Was her mother right, had she judged Stefan too harshly? "Why would he kill our own kind if it wasn't for power?" she asked in a strangled voice.

"You'll have to ask him."

"Did you?"

"Yes."

She knew that her mother wasn't going to tell her anymore than that. She opened her eyes and wiped the tears from them. "If you were satisfied with his answer, why did you tell him that he had to leave?"

"I didn't, and neither did your father, or the stooges."

"Then why does he want to leave?" she demanded.

Her mother smiled softly as she shook her head. "I have two sets of twins Isabelle, but neither of them is as alike as you and Ethan. Both of you are very set in your ways, your judgments of people, and you will do anything to make sure that the other isn't hurt. Your anger also gets the best of you both on many occasions."

"Oh," Isabelle said softly. "But he brought these people to our home!" she cried, unwilling to be so completely wrong. "He has driven us out of our homes and placed all of us in danger!"

"Brian did that."

"Brian is his friend!"

"*Was* his friend Isabelle, they haven't been friends in awhile, but you probably didn't take the time to learn that either."

Isabelle hung her head as shame and despair rushed through her. She recalled the things she had said, the things that she had done, and she truly hated herself. She was beginning to realize that she may have completely misjudged the entire situation. She had said that she would never forgive Stefan, now she was beginning to wonder if he would ever forgive *her*. However, he had lied to her and deliberately kept his past from her. She clung to that fact as a last, desperate line, for her rapidly fading anger.

"You trust him?" she asked in a choked voice.

"I do."

Tears flowed down her face. If her mother trusted him, and Stefan had told her everything, then she *was* completely wrong. Oh God, he must hate her! She hated herself. "Why didn't he tell me whatever it was that he told you?"

"Did you give him a chance?"

Isabelle shook her head as tears streaked down her face and she began to sob. "He must hate me!" she almost wailed.

"He could never hate you Isabelle."

"I told him I hated him!"

Her mother sighed loudly and came to sit beside her; she rested her hand gently on her shoulder. "You were angry at him, confused, and blindsided. He'll understand."

"And if he doesn't?"

"He will. He loves you Isabelle, he knows all your faults, and all of your good points already. He knows that you anger quickly, and that you just as quickly get over it. He *will* understand Isabelle."

"I don't understand," she whispered. "I love him with everything that I have. Yet I was so quick to throw that all aside when I thought that he had lied to me, and in a way he *did* lie to me. He kept a lot hidden from me."

"Isabelle, you need to talk to him. Sometimes the past is just something that people only want to forget. You need to put your judgments aside, and realize that everyone has faults, even you."

"I know I do," she whispered miserably.

"And you have many wonderful qualities too, don't ever forget that. Stefan loves you for all of them. Just like you love him for all of his faults and qualities, and I'm sure that he has many too."

"He is bossy, arrogant, highhanded, and commanding," she mumbled. "He didn't even consider letting me stay at home."

"Of course not," her mother replied with a laugh. "Your father had my bag packed before I could count to ten. In this situation Isabelle, it's not even worth putting up a fight. Their main concern is our safety. You would have better luck talking to a wall than you would of changing their minds. You have to pick your battles, this is not one you will win, trust me on that fact."

"And apparently neither was my last one," she whispered.

Her mother sighed as she brushed Isabelle's hair off her forehead. "No, but we all make mistakes. Everything will be all right, you'll see."

"I have to go talk to him. I need to see him." She suddenly needed him with an intensity that shook her.

"You can't go tonight Isabelle, but you can go tomorrow, ok?" her mom said gently.

Isabelle glanced out at the dark sky. "What if they come tonight though?"

"Then we can all return home tomorrow."

"What if something happens to him?" she whispered. "What if I lose him and one of the last things I ever told him was that I hated him?"

"Nothing will happen to him Isabelle, he's stronger than most."

"What about the others?"

Her mom's hand tightened on Isabelle's shoulder. "They won't interfere, not unless they have to. They know their limits, besides your father knows I'll kill him if he gets himself hurt." Isabelle laughed softly as she dropped her head to her mother's shoulder. "It will be all right," she promised gently.

Isabelle prayed that she was right. She closed her eyes and allowed her mind to reach out to Stefan. If she couldn't see him, than she could at least connect with him and let him know that she was sorry. She felt the brush of his presence, but that was all. He still had her shut out. Tears streaked down her face as she tried to figure out why he wouldn't let her back in. She feared that her mother was wrong, that he would never forgive her.

CHAPTER 24

Stefan stood silently on the porch, his arms crossed firmly over his chest as he rapidly scanned the horizon. They were coming, he could feel it, and they were near. He turned to the people gathered behind him. "They're strong," Liam said softly.

"Yes," he replied. "Don't forget that they can't get in the house unless invited. If anything goes wrong, that is where you go."

Liam nodded briskly, but his eyes were dark and turbulent as they met Stefan's. "That goes for you too. Don't do anything stupid Stefan. I won't lose my daughter because you do," he growled.

"I won't," he assured him.

"They're here," Brian said softly.

Stefan turned as three men materialized in the middle of the yard. He could sense their power, but it wasn't as strong as he had thought it would be. He glanced sharply at Brian. "You couldn't have handled this?" he snarled.

"There's more."

Stefan turned back around. He shut out the presences of the men before him in order to search the night. He could sense them out there, waiting in the shadows. "Fools," he muttered.

"How many more are there?" Mike asked.

"Four," Brian answered.

"Two in the woods, two more behind the house," Stefan supplied.

"How do you want to do this?" Brian asked.

Stefan was silent as he watched the three men on the lawn move slowly forward. He didn't want the others getting off the porch. These vampires weren't as strong as he had thought they would be, but they were stronger than them. If they got off the porch they would be putting themselves in danger. Isabelle truly would hate him forever if something happened to anyone in her family.

"Wait for them to get closer," Stefan instructed. "I don't want you guys leaving this porch unless you have to."

"We can handle ourselves," Ethan said coldly.

"You can, but we're going to need you at our backs, and if you split up you'll be shredded. Stay on the porch," Stefan growled.

The men in the field stopped twenty feet away, and stood waiting. Stefan glanced back over at Brian. "After this..."

"I'm gone," he assured him.

"If you find me again Brian, I'll kill you myself."

"So you've told me."

"So I mean!" he snapped.

Brian turned to look at him and nodded briskly. "I know."

"Let's go."

Stefan stepped off the porch, and strolled out to the center of the field with Brian at his heels. The men were foolish enough to rush at them. The fight was swift, brutal, and vicious. Between the two of them, the three men never stood a chance. By the time that Stefan had dispatched the first one and turned toward the second, Brian was done with the other. The two from the woods came rushing out as the last of the first three went down.

"Idiots," Brian muttered as they spun to face the new threat. Stefan tore out the throat of one as Brian slammed a hole through the chest and ripped out the heart of the other.

Stefan was slightly breathless as he spun toward the porch. They were all still standing there, watching them in wide eyed amazement. Stefan focused his attention on the two that had been behind the house, but they were gone. "What the hell?" he muttered.

Brian took a step closer to him as he dropped the heart and stomped on it. He wiped the blood absently on his jeans as he quickly scanned the night. "I guess we scared them off," he said.

Stefan frowned as he shook his head and looked at the five scattered behind them. "They should have attacked when we came out here."

"Come on Stefan, you have the two of us, plus seven vampires standing on the porch. They realized it would have been suicide. Thanks for the help," Brian said with a bright grin.

"You didn't need it," he growled.

"I would have if they had all attacked at once, and you know it."

"I still don't understand why they didn't. They were stronger than the others."

"They couldn't defeat us."

"No, but still..." Stefan's voice trailed off as he nudged one of the dead ones over. "Where did you run into these guys?"

"Portland."

"Well, that was quick." Awe was evident in Ian's voice as they all approached.

"Of course it was," Brian said.

Stefan turned toward them, wiping the blood from his mouth and hands as they stopped a few feet away. "Where did the other two go?" David asked.

"Ran for the hills like the cowards they were," Brian replied.

Stefan was amazed at the amusement that crossed all of their faces, even Ethan's. "Well, guess we know not to piss you off," Jack said.

"Hey!" Ian cried as he moved forward. "That's one of the guys from the club!" He pointed toward the brunette that Stefan had dispatched of first.

Stefan turned back around, his frown deepening as he stared down at the unseeing man. He felt a moment of triumph as he realized that he had taken care of one of Isabelle's attackers, something he had wanted to do since that night. "So is that one," Jack said as he pointed to the last man, another brunette.

A growing feeling of unease began to settle in his stomach. He kicked the other men over, but none of them had light blond or bright red hair. "Way to go!" Ian cried as he slapped him on the back.

"Was there a redhead and a blond with these men?" he asked Brian.

Brian frowned thoughtfully and nodded. "Yeah, come to think of it, there was. The one I killed had brown hair though."

Stefan's eyes narrowed as he searched the night for a hint of their presence. "The blond is the one that bit Isabelle," Jack said.

The bottom of Stefan's stomach plummeted as he suddenly realized why they had left. They may have come here with every intention of killing Brian, but once here, they had scented something else, something even better that had been denied to them. "Brian lets go!" he hissed.

"What?" he asked in surprise.

"Now!"

Stefan's panic was growing by the second. They had a head start, a fairly good head start. He blurred into the night as he raced across the field. "I hate it when he does that," Jack mumbled. "We're going to have to put a bell on him."

"Where the hell is he going?" Mike demanded.

Brian stood silently for a moment more. "They attacked this girl Isabelle?"

"Yeah," David replied.

Brian's eyes narrowed. "That's where they're going."

"What!?" they all yelled.

Brian didn't wait to answer them, he took off, following Stefan's scent as he blurred into the night.

"Let's go!" Liam hissed. "Now!"

***

Isabelle rolled over and punched her pillow again. It didn't matter what she did, she was never going to get comfortable, never going to go to sleep without Stefan beside her. She contemplated going over to the next room to see her mom, she was certain that she wasn't asleep either, but she knew that if she woke up Willow, and Cassidy, she would never hear the end of it. She sighed as she flipped onto her back to stare at the ceiling. It didn't help that Vicky was snoring softly, and Abby had just finished mumbling something about cookies.

She tried to reach out for Stefan again, but he was still shut out from her. She rolled back over and curled into a ball as she tried not to think about what that meant. He hated her now, she was sure of it. She didn't know why he hadn't told her of his past, why he had deliberately lied to her, but she was certain there was a good reason. Her mother wouldn't trust him if there wasn't, and the others wouldn't trust him either. Ethan had told him to leave, not the others. They didn't hate him. She didn't think Ethan hated him either, but he had done the same thing that she would have if their roles were reversed. They *were* too much alike, arrogant, judgmental, and quick to anger, but also highly protective of each other. She didn't blame Ethan, and she was certain that once she got everything straightened out, Ethan would come around.

She just had to get everything straightened out first, and she truly hoped that Stefan would give her a chance. That he would be able to forgive her, and that he hadn't believed her when she said that she hated him. She wished that she could take those words back, but she couldn't, and he wouldn't let her into his mind to tell him that she really did love him. If something happened to him, she would never forgive herself. She wasn't even sure that she could forgive herself now. She had been so cruel to him, so hurtful.

She shut the thoughts out; they did her no good now. She would talk to him tomorrow. He would be all right. He would be fine. She would beg for his forgiveness if she had to. The idea of doing that didn't exactly sit well with her, but for the first time in her life, she was willing to put her pride aside, if that was what it came to. She hoped that it wouldn't, but she would do it if she had to. She owed him that much, and more, much more.

She sighed and flopped back over again. "Would you stop doing that," Abby muttered irritably.

"You were the one talking about cookies just a minute ago," Isabelle whispered back.

"Cookies?"

"Yeah."

"I could go for some cookies," Vicky mumbled. "At least I'd have something good to eat while listening to Isabelle sigh and moan."

"How could you hear me over your snoring?" Isabelle retorted.

"I don't snore!"

"You snore louder than a chainsaw!"

"Yeah you do," Abby agreed.

"Whatever," Vicky mumbled.

Isabelle rolled over to look at them. Abby had propped her head up on her hand and was staring at her from over Vicky's back. Vicky was scowling at her from half lowered lids. Isabelle managed a tremulous smile as she lifted herself onto her elbow. "I didn't mean to wake you," she apologized.

"This bed sucks anyway," Vicky mumbled.

'Isabelle!'

Stefan's voice slammed into her mind so fiercely that she almost fell out of bed from the shock of it. 'Stefan?'

'They're coming Isabelle, get to safety now!'

'What?'

'It's the men from the club, they'll find you! Go now!'

Isabelle jumped up and threw the blankets aside as his panic surged into her and flared her own to near epic levels. Her eyes instantly fell on Vicky and Abby. "Get up!" she yelled.

"What?" they demanded as they bolted up in bed.

"Get up! Now! Hurry!"

"Isabelle..."

"They're coming here. The men from the club, they're coming here!"

"Oh no!" They bounded out of the bed simultaneously.

"Get in the bathroom," she commanded.

"What?"

"Isabelle..."

She grabbed hold of Abby's arm and propelled her toward the bathroom. "Vicky move," she urged frantically.

Vicky rushed over to the bathroom and flicked on the bright, florescent light. It flashed for a moment before blazing to life. Isabelle blinked against the flare as she shoved Abby into the ugly little green room. "Stay in here!" she hissed.

"Isabelle, wait! What about you?"

Isabelle ignored her as she raced across the room to grab the tiny wooden chair in the corner. She ran back to the bathroom and thrust it inside. "Use this to block the door, and don't you dare come out, no matter what!" she ordered.

"Isabelle..."

"Do it!" she snapped and slammed the door shut.

She waited until she heard the chair being placed against the door before she ran over to the other door. Her hands were shaking as she fumbled to get the chain into place. 'My mother!' she screamed to Stefan.

'It's you they want Isabelle! *You* they're tracking. Your mother has been warned.'

Isabelle bit back a sob as she turned back around. Vicky and Abby were stuck in here with her. 'I have to get out of this room!'

'No!'

'Vicky and Abby are in here!'

'Don't you dare leave that room!'

Isabelle glanced wildly around. They could come in here, she knew that. People stayed in this room, but they didn't *live* here. It was no one's home. She left the room, and took them away from her sisters, or she stayed and led them right to them. It wasn't a hard decision to make. She spun back around, trembling as she reached to slip the chain free of its lock. Her hand froze midway there.

'Stefan...'

'Stay in that room!' he commanded.

'Stefan, they're here.'

His roar of fury was so loud that she swore it echoed through the room. It took her a moment to realize that it wasn't his bellow that filled the room, but the shattering of the large plate glass window beside her. Isabelle screamed as air filled the room, and a darkness that had nothing to do with the night, rushed in to meet her. She recognized the putrid smell instantly as it swamped into her mind, and nearly drowned her with its memories of pain and fear.

She ripped the chain free, and unlocked the deadbolt as hands seized hold of her. Isabelle swung wildly as she lashed out with her claws. She sliced his face open and blood sprayed his blond hair with blood. She lashed out again, fear for her sisters serving to make her more savage as she caught him in his chest. She would do everything in her power to make sure that this monstrosity didn't get anywhere near them.

The door burst open behind her; it slammed into her back, and knocked her to the floor. She cried out as her shoulder slammed into the wall and pain pierced down her side. Splintered wood, and shattered plaster rained down around her as the ruined door crashed to the floor. She scrambled back up as the other one came at her. "Kill her!" the blond hissed.

The redhead came eagerly toward her as his eyes gleamed with bloodlust. Isabelle jumped to her feet as the blond turned toward the bathroom door. "No!" she screamed.

She launched herself at the redhead at the same moment that her mother raced through the door and flung herself at his back. He hissed in fury as he stumbled backward, and her mother's claws tore down his back. Isabelle lunged at him and tore his chest open with her nails. The blond, distracted by her mother's presence, came back toward them as Willow and Cassidy flew into the room.

"Get out of here!" Isabelle screamed at them.

They skidded to a halt, their eyes wide as the blond turned toward them. Fear tore through her as they turned to run back out of the room. He disappeared before her eyes, coming to a halt in front of them to block their exit. "Veal!" he hissed.

"Mom!" Willow screamed.

The door to the bathroom burst open as Abby and Vicky raced out. Isabelle felt as if her heart stopped beating for a full moment. She was so focused on everyone else that she had completely forgotten about the man before her. He flung her mother off, knocking her to the floor as he reached out and seized hold of Isabelle's arm. She swung out instantly, but he grabbed hold of her other arm and twisted it painfully to the side as he forced her to her knees. She bit back a whimper of pain as she lifted her chin to glare defiantly back at him.

"I've been dying to see you on your knees," he said with a cruel smile.

"Fuck you!" she spat.

"Isabelle!" Vicky screamed.

Isabelle swung up, ignoring the tortuous pain in her arm, as she caught him across his stomach. Blood spurted over both of them as he twisted her arm all the way over and knocked her to the floor. Agony tore through her and she almost screamed, but managed to stop herself in time. Fear flowed through her as he knelt over her, and pinned her shoulder against the wall. He was so strong, so much stronger than she was. There was no way that she could fight him. Thoughts of her family rushed over her as the sounds of a battle filled the room, but there was nothing that she could do to help them, she was completely trapped, and he was going to kill her.

The roar that filled the room was so loud that it drowned out every other sound instantly.

Relief flowed through her. The redhead released her arm and spun away from her, but it was already too late. Stefan seized hold of him, ripped his head back, snapped his neck and ripped out his heart. Isabelle stared in amazed surprise as the man fell lifelessly to the ground. She couldn't believe how quickly Stefan had managed to kill him. The man had been much stronger than her, much stronger than anyone she had ever known. Except Stefan, she realized.

Swallowing heavily, Isabelle struggled back to her knees. She cradled her wounded arm as she lifted her head to meet his red filled, furious gaze. The ferocious snarl on his face vanished instantly, and his eyes turned back to black as he knelt before her.

"Where's the other one?" she gasped out.

"Dead. Are you okay?" he demanded.

"Yes."

He brushed the hair back from her face, his eyes intent as he studied her worriedly. She flung herself forward, and wrapped her good arm around his neck as she clung to him. Tears of relief and joy flowed down her face. "I'm sorry!" she sobbed. "I'm so sorry."

"Shh," he whispered gently as he enveloped her in his strong embrace. "Don't cry Issy. It's okay."

"No it's not."

He held her tightly in his arms as he savored in her sweet scent and comforting warmth. She lifted her head from his shoulder, her eyes bright with tears as she glanced behind him. "Is everyone ok?" she asked.

"We're all fine," her mom said as Brian burst through the door.

"They're dead already?" he asked, sounding highly disappointed.

"Yes," Stefan replied. He stood slowly, pulling Isabelle up with him. Brian's eyes landed on her and a soft smile curved his mouth. Stefan stiffened as he drew her tighter against his side, and his eyes narrowed dangerously on Brian. "Don't you have somewhere else to be?"

Brian shrugged negligently as he turned to survey the destruction of the room. Isabelle pulled away from Stefan; she scowled at Brian as she ran over to hug her family. Stefan watched her, his tension, fear and anger still simmered just beneath the surface. She had been placed in too much danger for his liking, way too much. He couldn't seem to shake the beast in him as his emotions swung wildly out of control. He shot Brian a glaring look as he strode past him, and grabbed Isabelle as she turned away from hugging Vicky and Abby.

He tucked her back against his side, ignoring the confused glance she shot him as he allowed himself to be comforted by her presence. He closed his eyes as he let her heat envelope him, and soothe the raging tension that lingered within.

"Sera!" Liam burst into the room; his eyes were wild and frenzied as he raced past Stefan to his family. The others came slowly forward as they picked through the rubble, and bodies, that littered the room.

"I'll take care of this," Brian volunteered. "You guys should get out of here. I'm sure someone's called the police by now."

Stefan nodded briskly. "I'll get Kyle and Julian," Doug said.

"They're in the room next to mine!" Sera called out.

"Damn kids sleep like the dead," Mike muttered as he turned to follow Doug.

"You sure you can handle this?" Stefan asked Brian.

Brian snorted as he raised an eyebrow. "Are you kidding me?"

"Remember what I said."

"I know you'll kill me if I come back. Trust me I've had enough of Oregon. Now, get out of here."

Stefan nodded as he led Isabelle forward. She was still cradling her arm, but he didn't have the time to look at it now. They needed to get out of here as soon as possible; he could already hear the distant wail of sirens. "Take care of him," Brian said softly.

Isabelle stopped before Brain, her head tilted slightly as she studied him. He smelled off, but it wasn't like the others, not like she had first thought anyway. There was a lingering odor of death around him, but it was different, it wasn't as strong. There was also a lingering loneliness and despair in him that reminded her of what had existed in Stefan when she had first met him. For some reason, she didn't think that Brian was a truly bad guy. Although, she wouldn't mind punching him in the face for all of the trouble he had caused.

"You're not as far gone as you think or as you like to pretend you are. You can come back," she told him.

His mouth quirked in wry amusement as he studied her. "And how would you know?"

Stefan's arms tightened around her, but she ignored the subtle hint as she met Brian's gaze. "I just know," she answered.

The smile slipped from his mouth as he turned toward Stefan. "Never thought I'd see you like this, guess that soul mate thing is true after all," he said softly. "Take care of her."

"I intend to," Stefan replied. "Take care of yourself."

The amusement was instantly back in Brian's eyes. "Of course."

Stefan tried to lead her away, but she remained where she was for a moment more. She wanted to help Brian, to assure him that he wasn't the bad guy that he obviously thought himself to be. "Remember what I said," she whispered softly.

Brian glanced back at her, his face hard, and his eyes cold again. Isabelle sighed softly and turned away from him. There was nothing more that she could say, or do. He would make his own decisions; she could only hope that they would be the right ones. Mike suddenly appeared in the doorway with Kyle slumped over his shoulder.

"There's a crowd gathering, Doug's taking care of the ones that have come outside but we have to go."

"I'll take care of everything," Brian assured them. "They'll never know what happened."

"Does he have the power to do that?" Isabelle asked Stefan as he led her out to the idling cars.

"Yes," he answered as he opened the backdoor of Jack's car for her.

She waited for him to slide in beside her and close the door. "Do you?"

"Yes."

She leaned against his side. "Will you tell me everything?"

"Yes."

CHAPTER 25

Isabelle woke slowly the next morning and instinctively snuggled closer to Stefan as she drifted awake. She didn't remember being placed in the bed, or losing her clothes, but both had occurred. She almost purred as Stefan ran a hand lightly down her back, causing shivers of delight to course through her. She moved closer to him, savoring in the warmth of his body as his hand dipped between her legs.

She gasped and jerked as pleasure coursed through her. His mouth seared into her neck and back as he left a trail of hot, lingering kisses across her skin. Trembling with need, Isabelle was swept away by his touch as he continued to make slow love to her with his hand. Isabelle moaned her displeasure when his hand slid away from her. She was about to roll over, when he slid on top of her and his hard body pressed against her back.

"Stefan," she gasped in surprise as his strong thigh parted her legs.

"Shh," he soothed as he lightly nibbled on her ear.

Isabelle forgot all about her fear as he slid slowly into her, enfolding her as he moved over her. Isabelle was whimpering with pleasure when he seized hold of her waist and pulled her to her knees. She was swept away by the feel of him, and the delicious sensations that flooded her body as his movements became more demanding. His hands encircled her, fondling and caressing her breasts as he lightly teased her nipples.

Isabelle cried out with the force of the orgasm that ripped through her, shaking her legs, and causing her entire body to convulse with pleasure. His arms held her up as he drove fiercely into her, groaning loudly as his trembling arms tightened around her and he spilled into her.

She collapsed onto the bed, panting for air, and trembling from the shivers of delectation that still wracked her. Stefan fell beside her, pulling her on top of his chest and entrapping her against him. She sighed happily as she nuzzled his chest and relished in the feel of him against her. Her hands curled tightly around his neck, and lightly played with the soft hair that curled at the base of it.

He gently smoothed back her hair as he lightly stroked her back. Isabelle didn't want to move, didn't want to think about anything, but she knew that she had to. She had to know the truth, and she couldn't put it off forever, no matter how much she wished to.

"Stefan..."

"When I was eleven my family and I were coming back from the theater when we were attacked." He knew what she was going to say before she even spoke. The time for the truth had arrived, and he wanted to get it over and done with as soon as possible. His hold tightened on her as he opened himself up to memories that he had been trying to forget for a long time.

"There were three of them, two men, and one woman. Vampires. They trapped us in an alley, and killed my mother and father instantly. My brother was sixteen at the time, and my sister had just turned fifteen. My brother tried to stop them, he went after them, but he was useless against them. My sister grabbed me and started running toward the street. I tried to go back, but she wouldn't let go of me. My brother's dying screams followed us out of that alley."

Isabelle shuddered against him; tears welled in her eyes as she continued to stroke the back of his neck. His voice was hard and cold as he spoke, and it revealed no emotion. If it weren't for his hands tightening upon her waist, and the increase of his heartbeat, she would have thought that the death of his family had had no effect on him.

"We were sent to live with my aunt and uncle in Wales. Neither my sister, nor I, ever spoke of what had happened again, not even to each other. I think we were both scared that we would end up in Bedlam; at least I knew I was. She married three years later and moved back to London. I didn't see her again until I was eighteen, and by that time, she had a son. That was the only time I tried to talk to her about what had happened. She screamed at me and told me that they were just thieves, and that I was crazy. When I pressed the issue, she told me to get out of her house, and to never come back. I never did.

"After that, I searched London. I knew what I had seen, what they were, and I was determined to seek vengeance for my family. When I couldn't find them there, I went to the continent. I spent a long time searching France, Spain, and Germany before moving onto Italy. That was when I met up with a group of vampire hunters, and joined them. I was twenty one at the time."

Stefan paused to take a deep breath. Isabelle remained silent, her hands curled tightly into his neck as she fought back the tears that wanted to flow. Tears she instinctively knew would cause him to stop speaking. He didn't want her tears, but her heart was breaking for the boy that he had been, for the cruel twist of fate that had ripped his family away from him, and caused him to grow up in an instant.

She couldn't even begin to imagine what it would be like to lose any of her family, it was like a knife in the chest just thinking about it. She couldn't imagine what it had been like for him to see them murdered, and so viciously. She wanted to cry for the man that had gone to his sister, only to be turned away by the only family he had left. If the woman had still been alive, Isabelle would have ripped her to shreds for being so cruel to him.

"For the next five years I searched the continent, destroying any vampires I came across. I found the two men in that time, both in Greece. With the help of my newfound friends, I was able to overtake, and destroy them, but the woman still evaded me."

"I ran into her again two years later, in Dublin. Her name was Brenda." His voice was strained, and his hands dug painfully into her soft skin. She knew that he wasn't aware of it, and she made no sound, no protest to let him know. "She recognized me, remembered me. I was alone against her, consumed with vengeance and hatred, but it wasn't enough. She won the fight, but thought that it would be more fun, more *amusing* to turn me into the one thing that I had hated for the last sixteen years.

"She changed me, instead of killing me. I fought like hell against it, but as you know, the harder you fight, the more it hurts and the harder it becomes to fight. She forced her blood into me, and disappeared. After that, I had nowhere to go, no idea of what to do. I couldn't return to my friends, they would have killed me instantly, so I left Europe and went to Canada."

Isabelle could no longer hold back her tears; they slid down her cheeks to wet his shoulder. Pain engulfed her for the man that he had been, for the man that he could have been if things had been different. She bit back a sob as his hands eased on her waist and he began to stroke her back again. She was the one that should have been offering comfort, not the other way around. She snuggled closer as she stroked his neck. She sought to ease some of the anguish that radiated from his body. He sighed softly, nuzzling her neck for a moment before speaking again in a softer, less cold voice.

"I spent the next fifty years traveling between Canada and the states. A lot of our kind had come here. It was a wonderful place for them to feed. People could just disappear into the wilderness with no questions asked.

"I hunted the killers amongst our kind, feeding off of them, and growing stronger. I couldn't go for the most powerful ones; they would have destroyed me. So I bided my time, destroying the newer ones until I grew stronger. I met Brian in Boston when I was seventy eight. He had been changed twenty years earlier, his wife, and children were murdered at the same time."

Isabelle shuddered as she bit back a fierce sob. "He was just as determined as I was to avenge their deaths. He had been doing his own hunting, destroying any vampires that he came across. We fought, I could have killed him, but I didn't. I could sense that he wasn't evil, wasn't like the others. Brian's powers hadn't matured enough for him to sense the same thing about me. When I explained to him that not all of us were evil, that we aren't all cold blooded monsters, we joined together to hunt the ones that were.

"With Brian's help I was able to kill even more, to go after ones that were even stronger. After a hundred years, we found the two that had killed Brian's family. They were the strongest we had ever come up against, but we were able to destroy them. Both of us left the battle severely wounded, but much stronger from their blood.

"That was when we decided to go back to Europe. Most of the older ones had remained on the continent. Our strength steadily grew as we moved through the continent, hunting and destroying everyone that we could find.

"I never found Brenda, and after thirty years we decided to return to the states. By this time, I was beginning to fear that I was never going to find her, and that she may already dead. It was twenty years later that I ran into her in New Orleans. By that time, I was stronger than she was. I had been feeding off of some of the most powerful of our kind, absorbing their strength and powers. Brenda lived off of humans and took pleasure in destroying families, but their blood wasn't as strong as the blood that I had been thriving on.

"The battle was short and brutal, and when it was over, I was left with nothing. For the last two hundred years I had been consumed with a need for revenge. It was the only thing that had driven me, the only thing that had kept me alive. After Brenda was dead, there was nothing left to fuel me.

"Brian and I continued our mission, but it wasn't the same. I was just going through the motions, just surviving. I began to realize that all my existence had ever been, and ever would be, was nothing but death and destruction. There was nothing left to drive me, except for survival, and the need to try and make sure that no other families were destroyed, but it wasn't the same.

"I wasn't much better than the monsters that I had been killing. I had also thrived on it, for the same reasons that they did, for the power. Granted, I didn't destroy families, I didn't take innocent lives, but I was a brutal killer all the same."

Isabelle shuddered; never had she thought that this side of Stefan could exist. Never had she dreamed that it could be possible. It frightened the hell out of her.

"Two years ago, we ran into a group of human hunters. I killed one of them, Brian killed two. Neither of us had ever killed a human before, and it rattled us both. I vowed that I was done, that I would never kill anyone, or anything, again. Brian was more determined than ever to destroy everything in his path. He hasn't been killing humans, but he has taken everything to a darker place than he ever had before. It gives him a purpose, something to live for.

"I lost everything that day when Brian and I went our separate ways, the idea of killing anything again made me sick. I had done the one thing that I had vowed never to do, the one thing that made me exactly like the monsters that I had been killing for centuries and I hated myself for it.

"I just wanted to live in some semblance of peace, but I never found it. Everywhere I went, I was alone. That's when I started settling down with just one girl at a time, for a couple of months at a time. It was at least someone to have around for a little bit so that I wasn't completely alone, but it wasn't enough. I was still alone, no matter what I tried to do. Until I came here, until I met you, and felt alive again for the first time since I was a little boy. Felt as if I had found a place where I belonged, and had a purpose other than death."

Isabelle sobbed softly into his shoulder as she clung to him. She couldn't imagine such loneliness, such pain. She ached everywhere for what he had gone through, for what he had lived through. She hated herself for the words that she had uttered the other night, the hurt that she had inflicted upon him. There was no way that she could take the words back, no way to erase his past, but she vowed that his future would be better. She would make sure of it.

"I'm so sorry," she whispered. "I'm so sorry for everything. I didn't mean it. I love you Stefan. I love you more than anything. Please forgive me."

"There's nothing to forgive," he assured her.

"There is!" she sobbed. "What I said to you the other night, the way that I reacted was completely unforgivable. I should have listened to you; I shouldn't have jumped to conclusions. I should have known."

"Isabelle, you were angry and upset, I understand that."

His forgiveness, and caring words, didn't help to ease the anguish that she felt. They only made her feel worse. She wouldn't have forgiven him so easily if it had been the other way around, but he readily did. It made her hate herself even more.

"How can you be so understanding?" she demanded.

"Easily," he said with a laugh. "I know you Isabelle, you're quick to anger, quick to judge, and very quick to lose your temper. But you're also strong, proud, determined, loving, and one of the most loyal people that I have ever met. I love you for all of those reasons, the good, as well as the bad. I wouldn't change a thing."

He really wasn't making her feel any better; he was just making her feel worse as she wept into his shoulder. "I'm sorry that you lost your family," she whispered. "I wish that it had never happened."

"It was a long time ago Isabelle. It may have taken me awhile to come to terms with it, but I have. It is the past, and the two of us are going to have a wonderful future."

"Yes we are," she vowed fervently. "I promise we will."

He laughed as he dropped a soft kiss on her neck. "Stop crying Isabelle. I hate it when you cry."

She tried to stifle her sobs, but she couldn't stop the tears that continued to flow. "Why didn't you tell me?"

He sighed as his hands stopped stroking her back. He reached around and gently pulled her head out of his shoulder. He turned her toward him as he tenderly wiped the tears from her cheeks. Her eyes were filled with misery, and sadness, as she hesitantly met his gaze. Her lower lip trembled slightly as she valiantly tried to hold back her sobs.

"When Brian and I first met David, I was surprised about the way that he talked about his friends. For the last hundred and fifty years all I'd had was Brian, and death. David had an air of freshness and innocence that shocked me. When he talked about how none of his friends had ever killed, and how amazingly close they all were, I wondered what it was like to be that innocent, and naive. He knew what our kind could be capable of, but he didn't let it corrupt him.

"When I came here, you were so naive, and so beautifully innocent that the last thing I wanted was for anything dark to touch you. Until that night at the club, you had no idea how cruel and vicious the world could be. I didn't want you tainted by it, and by what I was. I wanted to keep you protected from it, and I had mistakenly thought that the past was over with. You gave me a reason to live, to feel, and I never wanted to take anything away from you. I wasn't about to let darkness into your world Isabelle."

Tears slipped free as she stared into his dark, warm eyes. There was so much tenderness, so much love radiating from him that it shook her soul. She stroked his cheek lightly, extremely grateful that somehow fate had managed to throw them together. That it had managed to give her someone as wonderful as he was. She truly realized just how lucky she was to have him in her life.

"You told my mom all of this."

He frowned. "I didn't tell your mom any of this. You and Brian are the only two that know."

Isabelle stared at him in confusion. "She said that she had asked you why you killed our kind, and that you told her."

"She asked me if I had a good reason for killing our kind, I told her yes, and that was all."

Isabelle closed her eyes, dropped her head to his shoulder, and moaned softly as she realized the full extent of her stupidity, and foolishness. It made her feel even worse that her mother had put such blind faith in him, when she hadn't been able to. "I'm such an idiot," she mumbled.

He laughed as he rolled her over and pinned her to the mattress with his hard body. "You are anything but an idiot Isabelle, you're just stubborn. Your mother knows that."

Isabelle opened her eyes to look up at his twinkling black ones. "We don't have to leave," she whispered softly. "Ethan and I are a lot alike, he didn't mean what he said, and he'll come around."

He grinned down at her as he brushed a light kiss across her mouth. "I know that, trust me, I know."

Isabelle frowned at him as he smiled happily down at her. "What is Europe like?" she asked softly.

"It's beautiful."

"Do you want to go?"

His smile faded away as he stroked her cheek. "We can stay here Isabelle. I like it here, your family is here, and I know that this is where you're happy."

"Yes, but I've decided that I want to see the world, and I want you to show it to me. We'll always be welcome here, always be able to come back, but I would like to go if you want to."

He smiled softly as he bent and placed a feather light kiss against her lips. "I would love to show you everything Isabelle," he whispered.

She smiled brightly as he brushed her drying tears away. Seizing hold of his hand, she brought it slowly to her mouth. Drawing one of his fingers inside, she began to suck and lick on it as she savored in the taste of him. His eyes clouded with passion as he watched her with fascination. She released his finger and wrapped her hands around the back of his head

"First things first though," she whispered.

"What's that?" His voice was deep and husky as she felt him harden and lengthen against her thigh.

Her smile turned sly and seductive as she brought his head down. "I need to show you just how sorry I am, and how much I do love you."

He grinned down at her, as his eyebrows quirked in amusement. "That might take a lot of persuasion."

By the end of the day, she had completely managed to convince him.

Made in the USA
San Bernardino, CA
23 January 2014